Celebrate the joys of Christmas in Regency England, where five master storytellers ring in the season with warmth, cheer—and love. . . .

Sandra Heath's "Merry Magpie"—a bird as noisy as he is nosy—has a bad habit of screeching secrets, turning his masters against each other. But the Yuletide has a way of warming hearts, even those of the feathered persuasion.

The memory of one kiss from an elfin girl is enough to warm an Irish sailor for many chilly nights. Home for the holidays, he'll do whatever it takes to get his love—now prim and staid—under the mistletoe, in **Emma Jensen's "Following Yonder Star."**

A confirmed bachelor cannot forgive himself for a long-ago sin—that is, until his niece's educator teaches him a thing or two about Christmas in **Carla Kelly's "Let Nothing You Dismay."**

In **Edith Layton's "Best Wishes,"** a pair of newlyweds discovers—during their first quarrel over holiday plans—that making up is indeed the best gift they can share.

A down-at-the-heels benefactor finds that a single penny—his last—is worth more than riches when it brings him face-to-face with a breathtakingly beautiful Christmas angel in **"The Lucky Coin"** by **Barbara Metzger.**

Regency Christmas Wishes

Five Stories by

Sandra Heath

Emma Jensen

Carla Kelly

Edith Layton

Barbara Metzger

A SIGNET BOOK

SIGNET
Published by New American Library, a division of
Penguin Group (USA) Inc., 375 Hudson Street,
New York, New York 10014, USA
Penguin Group (Canada), 90 Eglinton Avenue East, Suite 700, Toronto,
Ontario M4P 2Y3, Canada (a division of Pearson Penguin Canada Inc.)
Penguin Books Ltd., 80 Strand, London WC2R 0RL, England
Penguin Ireland, 25 St. Stephen's Green, Dublin 2,
Ireland (a division of Penguin Books Ltd.)
Penguin Group (Australia), 250 Camberwell Road, Camberwell, Victoria 3124,
Australia (a division of Pearson Australia Group Pty. Ltd.)
Penguin Books India Pvt. Ltd., 11 Community Centre, Panchsheel Park,
New Delhi - 110 017, India
Penguin Group (NZ), 67 Apollo Drive, Rosedale, North Shore 0632,
New Zealand (a division of Pearson New Zealand Ltd.)
Penguin Books (South Africa) (Pty.) Ltd., 24 Sturdee Avenue,
Rosebank, Johannesburg 2196, South Africa

Penguin Books Ltd., Registered Offices:
80 Strand, London WC2R 0RL, England

First published by Signet, an imprint of New American Library,
a division of Penguin Group (USA) Inc.

First Printing, October 2003
First Printing ($4.99 Edition), November 2007
10 9 8 7 6 5 4 3 2 1

Copyright © New American Library, a division of Penguin Group (USA) Inc., 2003
"The Lucky Coin" copyright © Barbara Metzger, 2003
"Following Yonder Star" copyright © Melissa Jensen, 2003
"The Merry Magic" copyright © Sandra Heath, 2003
"Best Wishes" copyright © Edith Felber, 2003
"Let Nothing You Dismay" copyright © Carla Kelly, 2003
All rights reserved

Ⓟ REGISTERED TRADEMARK—MARCA REGISTRADA

Printed in the United States of America

PUBLISHER'S NOTE
These are works of fiction. Names, characters, places, and incidents either
are the product of the authors' imagination or are used fictitiously, and any
resemblance to actual persons, living or dead, business establishments, events,
or locales is entirely coincidental.

   The publisher does not have any control over and does not assume any
responsibility for author or third-party Web sites or their content.

Contents

The Lucky Coin

by Barbara Metzger

1

"A penny for your thoughts, young sir."

At his fellow passenger's words, Sir Adam Standish dragged his eyes from the view outside the coach window, where the desolate winter scenery was as bleak as his prospects.

"I fear my thoughts are not worth even that much," Adam told the wizened, whiskered old man in the seat opposite him.

"Nonsense," the ancient replied. "All thoughts are worth at least a pence, be they good thoughts or bad, happy or sad. Why, ofttimes the telling alone is of value, and good conversation is priceless on such a journey as ours."

The trip to London was tedious indeed, yet Adam was not one to confide in others, nor speak of his personal woes to friends, much less to chance-met strangers. He shrugged and turned back to the window.

"A woman?" the graybeard persisted.

Now Adam had to laugh, although there was no humor in the sound. "If I could afford a woman, wife or mistress, I would not be making this desperate, and likely futile, visit to my bankers."

"Ah, money, then. I should have guessed a well-favored young gentleman like yourself would have no trouble with the ladies."

No, Adam thought, the old man should have known he

was below hatches by the worn boots on his feet and the
frayed cuffs on his sleeves, unless the fellow's seemingly
knowing gray eyes were failing. In that case, the granfer
should have realized his fellow passenger was badly dipped
by the absence of a valet to rectify those same faults. For
that matter, a baronet with brass in his pockets hired his own
coach and team, instead of riding the common stage.

None of which, of course, was the curious old man's
business, but Adam was nothing if not polite, especially to
his elders, so he nodded. "Yes, money is at the root of my
problems, or the dearth of it, at any rate."

"A spot of bad luck, is it?"

Now Adam made a rude snort. "A spot? More like a spill,
a storm, a veritable swamp of bad luck." And without meaning to, he began to tell the old man opposite him about his
beloved estate Standings, about the debts he had inherited
along with the title and acreage, about the flood and the fire,
the blight and the bugs, the drought and the drop in prices
for what little the fields could produce. Something about his
companion's interest, the compassion, perhaps, in that gray
gaze, made Sir Adam go on to express his hitherto unspoken
frustrations that no matter how hard he worked, he never
found himself gaining on his deceased father's debts. For
every step forward he took, Fate seemed to send him two
steps backward. Now, when he was close to his goal of making a profit at last, he could lose everything instead, if the
bank would not extend his credit until the spring. He could
make his quarterly payments now, but then he would have
no funds left for seeds, for stud fees, for keeping up the
wages of his few loyal servants. He would not mind going
cold and hungry, but he could not ask the same of his poor
tenants and their children.

Instead, he was going to ask the bank to let him delay his
mortgage payments, on the promise of spring lambs and
cows in calf, well-turned fields and the latest techniques
from the farming journals. Surely begging mercy from the
money changers was a forlorn hope, like trying to wring

water from a stone, but one he had to attempt. Adam hated having to beg, but he hated worse the idea of having no gifts for his dependents on the quickly approaching Boxing Day after Christmas, not even an apple.

"So you see," he concluded, "my thoughts are as dismal as the state of my purse. You must be sorry you asked, now that I have rambled on about my difficulties through the last changes." Indeed, somehow the time had sped by in his telling, for they were close to London now, with its increased traffic and noise.

"Nay, I do not regret prying into your affairs, young sir, only that I am unable to be of assistance."

"I never meant to imply—"

"Of course you did not." The old man reached into his pocket for a coin. "I would like to offer more, but at least I can give you the penny I promised."

Adam held up his hand. "No, I cannot take your money." In his shabby coat and battered hat, the withered relic appeared to be in poorer straits than Adam.

Gnarled fingers tossed the coin in Adam's direction just as the coach came to a stop at their destination. "Take it. It might change your luck." With more liveliness than Adam would have thought possible—surely with more enthusiasm than Adam felt for their arrival—the old man jumped down from the carriage, doffed his hat toward Adam, and disappeared into the busy courtyard.

Adam tucked the coin into his fob pocket. Lud knew there was room, for he'd had to sell his timepiece a year ago. Then he took it out again to toss. Heads he would go to his banker first; tails he would hire a room for the night, to brush the dust off his apparel and make a better appearance, as if he were not at point non plus. Heads won, which was not at all what he wanted. In fact, if he never had to see Mr. Ezekiel Beasdale again, he would be far happier.

Being a man of duty and conscience, however, despite being a man of meager funds, Adam tucked the coin away, hefted his satchel, and took himself off to visit his banker.

He should have saved the walk. In fact, he should have saved the entire trip to London. Then he might at least have the price of a fine Christmas goose.

Mr. Beasdale was not receptive to Adam's elucidation as to the future profitability of Standings. In fact, the heavyset, ruddy-faced banker was not receptive to the baronet at all. He kept Adam waiting in the bank's central office, with clerks and customers alike taking note of the poor country turnip come to plead his case, or so Adam felt, standing with a battered satchel between his scuffed boots. His welcome was even colder in Mr. Beasdale's private office.

"What's that? An extension until spring? Impossible, I say. This is a bank, sir, not a philanthropic foundation. We are a lending institution, which means we need our money returned, in order to lend it out again." The man's fleshy jowls shook with indignation over Adam's apparent incomprehension of elementary finances. "Why, I have to answer to my partners."

And Mr. Beasdale would have to answer to his Maker, Adam thought, for the lack of Christian charity at this of all seasons. He did not say his thoughts out loud, of course. He stood and bowed slightly, ready to leave.

"It's nothing personal, mind," the portly banker said, holding him in the richly carpeted room. "By all accounts you are a hardworking young man with no apparent vices. You do not gamble, like so many of your peers, or throw good money after bad, like your parent before you."

How could he, with no funds to stake?

Beasdale lowered his thick eyebrows to study Adam's appearance. "Nor do you seem to be a slave to fashion, spending your fortune in tailors' bills."

Adam had no reply to that obvious comment. "Whatever money I earn goes back into the land."

The banker nodded, sausage-shaped fingers straightening the papers in front of him. "Not enough, though, is it? Mayhaps you'd best consider another avenue."

Adam smiled, but it was more of a grimace. "I suppose

you are going to advise me to find a wealthy female to marry. That is what my servants and tenants recommend. Even the vicar suggested I use my time in town to find a well-dowered lady to pull Standings out of River Tick. Of course we both know that no noble family is going to give its daughter's hand to a down-at-heels baronet. What is your counsel, then, that I find a rich merchant who wants to raise his daughter's standing in society?" Adam had no intention of taking such advice, but he did go on, not trying to hide the scorn in his voice: "I suppose you have an unwed daughter, a niece, godchild, or, heaven forfend, a spinster sister, an ambitious female who cannot find a husband on her own."

Now the banker lumbered to his feet. His jowls flapped and his cheeks turned red. He pounded a meaty fist onto his desk. "I, sir, am a merchant. A Cit, a tradesman, and a rich one, with my sister's only child in my care. And I would sooner see my niece, nay, any girl of mine, wed to the Fiend himself than a feckless fortune hunter. Raise her social standing? Why, you could not afford to pay your wife's subscription fees at Almack's, if you could guarantee her vouchers, which I doubt. You have no entrée to the polite world, no lofty peerage, no vast ancestral holdings. You have nothing but an empty stable, a rundown farmstead, and a ha'penny baronetcy. And even if you had something to offer—not that I put great value on titles and society tripe—I would not want any female under my protection to be bartered off to pay your puny way."

Spent, Mr. Beasdale sank back in his seat, mopping at his damp brow. "What I was going to suggest, you arrogant, impertinent pup, was that you find yourself a job. The world of commerce could use diligent, honest workers. But I see that, like so many others of your useless ilk, you would rather wed your fortune than earn it. So good day."

What could Adam say? That he had no intention of spending the rest of his life with a woman he did not love, not even to save his ramshackle estate? That Mr. Beasdale would be fortunate to find a coal-heaver to wed his niece, if

she resembled the puff-guts in looks or temperament? That
he had thought of taking a position, or taking up arms for the
king, but too many people were relying on him at home? No,
he could not say any of that, deuce take it, because Mr.
Beasdale had only spoken the truth. He wished he could
make the beef-faced banker eat his words, but Adam was,
when all was said and done, worth less than that penny in his
pocket.

2

*L*ucky coin? Hah! Sir Adam took the pence out of his coat. The only thing it might be good for was to purchase a peppermint to get the bad taste of Beasdale's conversation out of his mouth. He had promised to send the payment on the due date, and Beasdale had not looked up again from his papers, saying merely, "See that you do."

Adam rubbed the coin, wishing he had ten of them. Ten might buy enough spirits to keep him company in the taproom of the posting inn until the first coach left for Suffolk in the morning, saving him the cost of a bedchamber. Oblivion in a bottle, that's what he needed, not a bit of superstitious folderol. Then he might forget that the next mortgage payment would take every shilling he possessed, leaving nothing for wages or winter forage. Damn and blast the banker! And damn Adam's feckless father for taking out such loans to fund his failing stables. And damn the old gnome who'd handed him a penny for his thoughts, giving him hope when there was none.

As he rubbed the coin, though, its color brightened. Gold? No, it was the wrong size for any gold coin he knew. For that matter, the smiling face was no king or queen he recognized. He rubbed harder, removing the tarnish to reveal a scrolled tree on the obverse side, with no words or dates of identification. Botheration, the thing wasn't even a real coin. Well, it might be real, but not in this country, not in this century, which was precisely in keeping with how Adam's luck had been running.

Bah! Hard work had won him nothing. Careful planning and parsimony had not advanced his cause. Now luck had proved just as worthless.

He was about to toss the useless thing away when he walked past a shop with a jumble of merchandise in the small bowed window. SCHOTT'S ANTIQUITIES, the sign above the door read. RARE COINS AND JEWELS BOUGHT AND SOLD.

"Why not?" Adam murmured to himself. He could see only one customer in the shop, a woman in a red velvet cape whose back was to Adam. Her dark-clad maid waited just inside the door, holding a thick, paper-wrapped parcel. Behind the counter was a small, elderly man with thick spectacles and a fringe of gray hair around his head. Most likely the proprietor, Adam thought, deciding that the fellow looked knowledgeable, at any rate. And what did Adam have to lose anyway? A good luck coin that was neither good luck nor coin of the realm. Perhaps it might have some value to a collector. Ten pence would be enough.

As he went in, the maid stepped aside, shifting the weight of her package. A bell over the door chimed and Mr. Schott looked up to greet and assess his newest client.

"I will be with you shortly, sir. Please feel free to look around meanwhile."

"Take your time. I am in no hurry." After all, Adam had nothing but time until tomorrow morning. He started forward, thinking he might as well examine a case of pretty baubles instead of the watches that would make him regret his own missing timepiece. But as he moved, the red-caped female turned, too, and he was turned to stone, it seemed, right there in a cluttered curiosity shop. His satchel fell to his feet from lifeless fingers, and he did not even notice. How could he when all he saw was the most beautiful woman in London, no, in all of England? A young lady, she could not be much above two and twenty, with dark curls and sparkling green eyes and cheeks bright from the cold.

Her face was framed by the white fur of her hood, making her appear more like an angel than a real woman. A Christmas angel, he thought, except that her mouth was made for kisses, all soft and rosy.

He thought he could stand there until Doomsday, or until the shop closed for the night, or she left, memorizing everything about this exquisite vision. Then he would not be going home to Suffolk poorer than when he came after all, not with a perfect, precious masterpiece indelible in his mind. Lud, how he wished to . . . No, that was even more foolish than standing like a marble statue, staring at a lovely stranger.

Then she smiled at him. Foolish or not, Sir Adam Standish wished with all his heart that she were his.

Jenna had to smile at the large gentleman standing in Mr. Schott's establishment. He looked so out of place in the crowded little shop with its delicate treasures, so bewildered and so . . . endearing. Yes, that was it, endearing, with his windblown brown curls and loosely tied neckcloth. The tilt to his lips and his soft brown eyes made him appear comfortable, friendly, trustworthy, and vastly appealing, unlike the starched and suave London gentlemen of her acquaintance. If they were chill politeness, he was warm familiarity, without ever saying a word. Something about him just seemed solid and sun-touched, while the bucks and beaux of town were paper-thin creatures of the night or shadowed drawing rooms. Miss Relaford did not know how she had come to have such a high opinion of the gentleman's character in so short a time, but she did. She had known him forever, it seemed, this perfect stranger. Why, she almost felt tempted to straighten his cravat and brush a curl off his forehead, while touching his smooth cheek and that cleft in his chin and the laugh lines around his firm mouth and—

Jenna blushed at her own thoughts. Heavens, when did she get so forward? Besides, the gentleman was most likely here to buy his sweetheart a special Christmas present, a ring or a brooch, she guessed from where he was headed.

That was what everyone seemed to be doing so close to the holidays, even Jenna. Not that Miss Relaford was purchasing a treasure for her beloved, for she had none despite her advanced age of one and twenty, although she had suitors aplenty. After buying small gifts, handkerchiefs, perfumes and such, to go with the coins she would give to the servants, Jenna was shopping for the perfect offering for her uncle, her only remaining family.

She had settled on the beautifully carved wood bookends, a lion on one side, a unicorn on the other, that her maid was already carrying, for Uncle did love his library. Since Jenna did not wish to use her allowance—which was Uncle's own money—to purchase his present, she was also going to ask the reputable Mr. Schott to appraise some of the curios her late father had collected on his seagoing travels. The sooner she concluded her business, the sooner the antiques dealer could assist the large gentleman, so she turned her back on his too-tempting smile and started to untie the strings of her reticule.

Once her back was turned again, Adam found his wits, or what was left of them after being knocked to flinders by the lady's smile. Pretending to inspect the contents of the glass cases, he edged closer. Oh, how he wished his circumstances were different, that he could make her acquaintance, if she were not already wed or promised, of course. Undoubtedly she was, being such a beauty. Her garb bespoke wealth, besides elegant taste, and the combination had to be irresistible to any red-blooded—or blue-blooded—man. London chaps could not be such slowtops as to let this prize slip through their fingers. Adam's own fingers were itching just to touch her cheek, to see if it could possibly be as satin-soft as it looked.

He would have to settle for another glimpse of her profile under the hooded cape, perhaps a whiff of her perfume. He stepped closer still, but only detected the ribbon-tied sprig of evergreen she had pinned to her cape. Gads, his angel even smelled like Christmas! He chuckled softly at his foolish notion. What a gift she would be for some fortunate fellow to unwrap.

Jenna turned at the pleasing sound, wondering at its cause. She looked over, to find the other customer closer than she thought, more handsome than she thought, with a smile on his lips. She might have been bold enough to ask what the gentleman had found amusing among the knick-knacks—after all, both Mr. Schott and her maid were there to see to the proprieties, and it was the season of good cheer—but the bell on the door rang again.

This time a roughly dressed man entered the shop. He was unwashed and unshaven, and pushed rudely past Jenna's maid, who grumbled about his manners. Bad manners were the least of the problem, for the man pulled a knife from out of his brown frieze coat, and not one of the other occupants of the store thought for an instant that he had come to have the weapon appraised.

"Right, then," he said with a snarl, waving the knife and looking furtively toward the door. "I'll be havin' the gold an' the gems an' the cash in the till." He picked up Adam's satchel, dumped the contents on the floor, and threw it toward Mr. Schott. "Fill it, an' be quick about it."

Damnation, Adam thought, that was his only clean shirt and his shaving gear. He took a step toward the would-be thief, but felt a small hand on his arm, pulling him back. He patted the hand reassuringly. Nothing would happen to his angel, not while he had breath in his body. While the robber was watching Adam, waiting to see if he would take action, the maid dashed for the door, shrieking.

"Blast it! Move your stumps, old man."

But instead of moving, Mr. Schott groaned once, clutched at his chest, and fell to the floor.

Jenna gasped. The thief cursed again and grabbed up the nearest valuables he could find, brandishing the knife while he shoved a collection of snuffboxes off the counter into Adam's satchel. Then he waved the blade in the woman's direction, his glittering, shifting eyes focused on her reticule.

That was too much for Adam. His shirt was one thing, but his Christmas lady was another. He pushed her out of harm's way just as the thief snatched at her purse, and swung his fist at the knife-wielder's arm.

The blade went spinning and the satchel went sailing, snuffboxes—and one last stocking of Adam's—scattering across the floor. But the thief had the lady's reticule and he was making a run for the door. Adam chased after him, then slipped on a snuffbox. He caught his balance and raced onto the walkway to see the robber getting away. He made a flying leap and almost caught the blackguard, but missed. He lost his footing, landing chin-first on the pavement, catching the reticule by its dangling strings as he fell. The thief would have stayed to wrestle over the purse, but the maid was calling for the Watch, people were coming out of doorways to see about the commotion, and carriages were halting in the street. Instead the felon let go, gave Adam a kick to the ribs, and started to turn for the nearby alley. Despite the agony, Adam reached out and grabbed the man's leg, sending him, also, tumbling to the ground. The cutpurse lay still, his head against a lamppost.

Winded, his chest afire where the heavy boot had connected, and certain his teeth were loose from the jar to his chin, to say nothing of the blood, Adam could only blink at the contents of the lady's reticule, spilled from the torn fabric. Ten small gold coins, just like the one in his pocket, were inches from his nose. Not nine, not eleven, but ten. He counted them, rather than count his broken ribs. Hadn't he wished his own penny was increased tenfold? He shook his head to clear it from the absurd notion.

Which was when the maid, panicked into thinking Adam was a partner in crime to the fleeing felon because he still grasped the reticule, hit him on the back of his skull with Miss Relaford's gift to her uncle, the carved wood bookends.

3

*W*ell, at least he would not have to worry about paying for a room that night, not while he had free accommodations. Of course there were bars on the window, no candles left burning, and nothing but a straw pallet under Sir Adam's aching bones, but someone had strapped together his ribs and put a sticking plaster on his chin. Now if only the prisoner in the next cell would stop the banging, he might be able to figure a way out of this latest catastrophe. The banging, unfortunately, was coming from inside his own head, so he closed his eyes again and tried to shut out the pain. His thoughts would not let him. What a disaster this whole London trip had turned out to be. He would wish the entire thing undone, except for the image of the fur-trimmed female. She was almost worth hanging for, although Adam did suppose Mr. Beasdale would vouch for him. Then again, the blasted banker might tell the authorities how desperate Adam was for money, heaping motive upon happenstance. If he was going to hang, though, he would love to get his hands on the miserable old gull-catcher who had handed him the blasted coin. He might as well swing for murder as thievery.

Adam sighed and tried to rub the pain away. Nothing could be done until morning anyway, but, Lord, how he wished the lady did not think he was a scoundrel.

* * *

"Here now, get up. You've taken enough space as is." A tall man with stiff, pointed mustachios and a red waistcoat was standing in the narrow doorway, gesturing for Sir Adam to leave.

The baronet rubbed his eyes, looking at the tiny cell where he had spent the night. "You mean I am not under arrest?"

"No, we just had nowhere to put you, unconscious as you were. Found your card in your pocket, Sir Adam Standish, correct?"

Adam nodded, then thought better of the movement when his head started to pound again.

"Of Suffolk, but it didn't say where you were staying here in London, naturally, so we brought you to Bow Street after the surgeon did his job, after seeing to Mr. Schott. The lady insisted."

Adam sighed in relief. "So she didn't think I was partners with the thief."

"She swore you tried to help, and that you recovered her reticule." The Runner peered at Adam, who was sure he was looking as disreputable as any street beggar. "That's correct, isn't it?"

"Yes, on my word."

"Well, it was her maid who did you in, anyway. Harum-scarum female. Wept in my office for hours, even though the surgeon said you'd live. Old man Schott, too."

"He wept?"

"No, he'll live."

"I am glad. He seemed a decent sort. But you say she cared?" Adam did not mean the maid, of course.

The Runner knew it, of course. He'd seen the lady, too. "Aye. She came herself, as soon as she made sure the old shopkeeper was settled, in case we had any doubts as to the circumstances. Gave a complete deposition, too. Cooperative, not like that maid what did nothing but caterwaul."

"What is her name?"

"The maid? Hessie or Henny or something. Oh, you

mean the lady?" he asked with a grin, smoothing the point on his waxed mustachio. Then he handed Adam a card.

Miss Jenna Relaford was inscribed on the card, with an address in Half Moon Street.

"Miss," Adam murmured, not quite to himself. He could not keep from smiling, either. "Miss Jenna." Just right. "Miss Relaford." It rolled off his tongue and left a sweetness behind, and an undoubtedly foolish grin on his face, for the Bow Street man laughed.

"A rare treat, she is. Best not keep her waiting."

"What, Miss Jenna—Miss Relaford—she is here?"

"Aye, wanted to thank you in person, she said. She brought you your satchel, she did, and the maid cleaned your other shirt. They brought you a new neckcloth, too, seeing as how yours was used to mop up the blood on your chin." The Runner handed over the carpetbag and another parcel. "The necessary's out back, and there's a mirror by the rear door."

Adam was already trying to comb his curly hair with his fingers, in the places that did not hurt too much to touch. "A minute. Tell her I will only be a minute. Two, maybe, to tie the neckcloth. There is nothing I can do about the bloodstains on my coat, I suppose, or the scuffs on my boots or—"

"I don't suppose that's what she came to see."

Adam gathered his wits and returned to terra firma. "No, she simply wishes to thank me, as you said. A courtesy from a polite lady."

If the Runner had any opinions, he kept them to himself, pointing Adam to the rear door, and to his office, where Miss Relaford and her maid were waiting. "Oh, and you'll have to sign for this when you get there," he said, handing over a small leather purse.

Adam raised his brow in inquiry.

"It's the reward, a'course. No, I forgot you slept through the hearing last night. There was a bounty out for Fred the Flick, one of the nastiest customers we've come across. You're the one what apprehended the gallows bait, knocked him straight out, you did, so he was quiet as a lamb for us to get the shackles on. None of my men had to face him and his knives, for what we're all grateful, asides getting him off the streets. So you get the reward. Enough to buy you a new coat."

To the devil with a new coat. The hogs would not care if his had bloodstains. The purse felt hefty enough for small Christmas gifts for his servants and the tenants' children, and for a fine feast for everyone in the Standings tradition. Perhaps there might even be a bit left to live on, once Mr. Beasdale had his money. The reward would not extend to seeds and stud fees, of course, but it was something, by George, something more than he had before. And he had Miss Relaford waiting. Hadn't he been wishing for an introduction, some way to see her again? Why, it was almost worth the broken ribs, the battered chin, and the bashed-in skull.

He hurried out the rear door, painfully shrugging out of his coat as he ran. The Runner called out after him; "Good luck, sir. Good luck to you."

She was even more beautiful today. Her fur-lined hood was down so he could see the dark brown hair piled atop her head, with tiny wisps of curls trailing across her forehead, onto her cheeks, and down her neck. She still looked like an angel to him, a wealthy angel whose father would laugh at the notion of Sir Adam Standish paying his addresses, if the man did not have him horsewhipped for the presumption. But if a cat could look at a queen, Adam could look at Miss Relaford. And so he did, instead of speaking.

Her maid, waiting by the door again, coughed. Jenna worried that perhaps the poor man had been more injured than the surgeon had declared. Perhaps his mind was disordered, or his jaw was cracked, not just his chin.

She had been her uncle's hostess for years now, and an accredited beauty before that, so she was used to men: men of rank and fortune and authority, as well as their aides and assistants. One stolid young baronet with sticking plaster on his chin and his tongue stuck to his teeth was not going to faze her. Well, not much, she told herself, feeling an odd weakness in her knees.

"Please forgive my presuming an acquaintance when we have not been formally introduced," she said when he had still not uttered a word, "but I saw your card. I am Miss Jenna Relaford, Sir Adam, and I am in your debt." She made a curtsy, then held her gloved hand out for him to take.

Instead of the polite salute she expected, a handshake or a sham kiss inches above her fingers, Sir Adam took her hand—and held it. "The debt is mine, ma'am, for not acting sooner, for allowing that muckworm to upset you."

"Gammon, it is not your duty to protect every woman you encounter."

He still held her hand warmly in his bigger one, looking into her eyes. "I would make it my duty. That is, a gentleman always looks after those weaker than he is."

"How chivalrous, but what could you have done? Attack the miscreant in the store while he still held a knife? Then you might have been injured worse, and all for a silly reticule."

"It is yours. He had no right to take it."

"Of course not. But no one should die for my paltry possessions. Bad enough you were hurt in my defense."

"I do not feel the pain." That was not a total lie. All he was feeling right now was the slight pressure of her hand in his—and a loathing for ladies' gloves. Even through the leather, her hand was soft and small, yet strong enough to get a grip on his heartstrings.

"No matter," she said. "I do wish to thank you for your efforts. I would not like to have lost the coins my late father sent back from his travels. I might have sold them if they proved to have any value, but I did not wish to see them stolen."

"I have one, you know."

Jenna took her hand back, needing more self-discipline

than force to retrieve it. "No, I counted. I had ten to show to Mr. Schott and I had ten when I picked them up from the ground."

Adam reached into his pocket, where the peculiar penny still remained, despite his tripping and travails. He held it out.

"Why, it is exactly like my coins! Where did you get it, and what is its history and its worth?"

"As to its original denomination or its present value, I have no idea. That is why I was going to consult with the antiquarian." Adam did not wish to admit he was going to sell the coin for whatever he could get, even if he had to melt it down for its metals. He had no reason to advertise his poverty beyond the condition of his clothes.

"But where did it come from?"

So he told her about the little old man in the coach, and his claim that the penny might bring Adam good luck. He laughed at the nonsense, but there he was, inches away from the loveliest woman in his experience. He took the coin back with far more respect than he had shown it before.

"Do you think he was Irish? They are a superstitious lot, I understand. Or perhaps a mystic from the East? A well-traveled Gypsy?"

Adam shook his head. "He might have been a leprechaun himself, for all I know, or a heathen witch doctor. He did appear to be a proper Englishman, although an ancient one. Perhaps he was Merlin, come back from his cave to grant a boon."

Jenna smiled at that. "But isn't it amazing, do you not think, that we each possess the same oddity?"

"Amazing," he agreed, staring into the dancing brilliance of her green eyes.

Jenna blushed, and her maid coughed again.

Brought back to the matter at hand—and how did Sir Adam come to possess her hand again?—Jenna said, "Yes, well, I am afraid we shall have to wait to ask Mr. Schott. The physician recommended bed rest for at least a week. Oh, and that reminds me. He bade me offer you this." She claimed her hand again and reached across a scarred desk for an ermine muff that matched her mantle's lining. From the inside she pulled another leather pouch, which jingled pleasantly, to Adam's ears.

More money! Adam felt almost rich, but he did not want Miss Relaford to think that the coins might make the least difference in his life. Certainly not that it affected how many meals he ate a day! Why, her bonnet likely cost more than his new funds added together. So he told her, "I cannot accept Mr. Schott's largesse. I did nothing, truly."

"You definitely kept the scoundrel from making off with a fortune in snuffboxes, and who knows what he might have done without your presence, with just an old man and two women in the shop? You deserve the reward. Furthermore, you must accept it or Mr. Schott's feelings will be hurt. You can always give it to charity."

Adam gave a rueful laugh. "Oh, I think I can find a worthy use for his coins, never fear."

Despite not understanding the joke, Jenna smiled back. "Yes, well, then I had better be going, and let you proceed about your business."

"You had not ought to have come to such a place at all. But thank you." There was nothing more he could say, no reason to keep her here, the devil take it. Adam tucked the money away while Miss Relaford pulled up the hood of her cape. She would be leaving, out of his life as quickly as she'd entered it, but not out of his thoughts, he feared, forever. "I wish . . ."

"Yes?"

No. It was impossible. How could he see her again when he was due back in Suffolk or when he was as out of place in her world as she would be milking his dairy cows? But how could he stop himself from wishing?

He might have said it aloud if she had not spoken first: "Perhaps, if your business is not too pressing, you would come to tea this afternoon? I am certain my uncle would also like to thank you for your efforts on my behalf. Three of the clock, at Half Moon Street?"

Adam decided he would walk to the full moon itself for the chance to spend more time in the company of Miss Jenna Relaford. He nodded. The pounding in his head turned to chimes of joy.

4

*H*ow peculiar, Adam thought, once he had left Bow Street. Ever since he had been given the odd little coin, strange things had occurred, illogical, improbable, and incomprehensible things. Like now, when he had wished for another opportunity to see Miss Relaford, and an opportunity instantly arose. Adam had never truly believed in the efficacy of prayer, although he never mentioned such to the vicar, attending services nearly every Sunday. He had never believed in the magic of wishes come true, either, whether wishes on stars, in wishing wells, or in Christmas puddings. For that matter, he had never believed much in luck, although he had cursed the Fates for his misfortunes often enough. Was that the same?

Adam pondered as he walked, not paying much attention to his surroundings. He was an ordinary chap, with his feet firmly on the ground, he told himself, not any mystical, poetical, portent-seeking fellow. All of the recent events must simply have been coincidences, having nothing whatsoever to do with his wants or wishes. On the other hand, the one clutching Miss Relaford's card as though it were his ticket to Paradise, he had never believed in love at first sight before, either.

What else could this feeling be? His innards were tied in knots, his tongue was as thick as a sheep hide, and the thought of taking tea with the young woman almost made him drool. He was thirsty and hungry, that was all, he told himself. And did not believe himself for an instant.

Could it be mere infatuation with her looks? No, for Miss Relaford was as charming as she was beautiful, sweet and intelligent, too.

Lust? Adam shook his head and muttered a denial to himself. A woman with a small child in hand anxiously crossed to the other side of the street.

Oh, at the thought of Miss Relaford's soft hand, soft lips, soft skin, he grew hard enough, but the feelings Adam felt for her after such a brief acquaintance went much further. He had never had so burning a need to make a woman happy before, to cherish her and protect her. Why, he'd just made a fool of himself again, insisting he see her to her waiting carriage as if a whole building full of Bow Street officers could not keep Miss Relaford safe. And he was counting the hours, multiplying out the minutes, until he could see her again. If that was not love, what was? Perhaps he'd ought to consult one of those poets after all. They were always going on about the tender emotion.

Tender, hell. His head was tender, his ribs were tender. His heart was a maelstrom of confusion, and the whole mess was too much for his aching head to contemplate. He needed a meal and a room and a bath. Then, maybe, he could begin to understand what was happening to him.

Just in case, though, Adam tucked Miss Relaford's card in his fob pocket, next to the lucky coin, closed his eyes, and made a wish. "I wish I were worthy of her love," he said. Nothing was different when he opened his eyes, of course, and nothing happened except that a woman with rouged cheeks passed him on the walkway, winked, and said, "You're worthy of mine any day, dearie."

Adam took a room for one night at the coaching inn, intending to catch the next day's stage to Suffolk. He paid extra to have the inn's staff do the best they could with his stained coat and scuffed boots, while he did the best he could with his injured ribs. After a hearty breakfast and a long hot soak, Adam tied his new neckcloth—of finer linen than any he owned—higher than usual, to try to hide his discolored chin. He brushed his damp curls back, over the gash in his head, and brushed his teeth, twice.

Then he went shopping for a bouquet of flowers to bring to Miss Relaford.

Roses, of course, pink like the blush on her cheek. Or sweet-smelling violets. A rare orchid, perhaps. A bouquet of wildflowers would be more in keeping with his country-man's taste, and purse, but this was London, not the country. And it was December, not June. The street-corner flower sellers offered red-berried holly, mistletoe, and ribbon-tied boughs of fragrant evergreens for decorating, dried lavender and clove-studded apples, not posies for a lady.

The shop he found had ferns and ivies and orange trees, and a small selection of flowers from forcing houses—at prices that would have forced him to part with far too much of his recent windfall. He might give his soul to the lady, but not food out of his dependents' mouths.

"I still have a bouquet of roses what weren't fetched yesterday," the florist told him when the man saw Adam turning away. "You can have 'em cheap. They ain't too droopy yet, and the red's so dark, your gal won't notice the brown edges on the petals."

A few petals fell off when Adam carried the roses out, so he held them close to protect the bouquet from the blustery winter wind as he walked to Half Moon Street.

He checked Miss Relaford's card again, as if the thing were not etched in his brain, and then stood outside the house in despair. It was worse than he'd thought; she was wealthier than he suspected. The place was immense and immaculate, with nary a speck of soot on any of the myriad windows. Why, some of his windows at Standings did not even have glass!

Lud, what was he doing here? He might have turned and gone back to the inn, but he was no quitter, else he'd have given up on Standings ages ago. What he was doing here, Adam told himself as he tried to straighten his hair that the wind had disarranged, was taking tea with a lovely lady, so he might have another pleasant memory to take home with him, nothing more. Still, he could not help wishing he made a better, more dashing appearance. Miss Relaford was so beautiful while he was so blasted ordinary, if one ignored the garish colors of his chin. Brown hair, brown eyes, brown coat, and brown breeches—how boring. He sighed and raised his hand to the gleaming door knocker.

Just as he let the knocker fall, a gust of wind, stronger than before, blew up. It would have carried a hat away, if he'd been wearing one, but it played havoc with his hair instead—and with the roses. Adam did not have time to smooth his hair again for the door immediately opened to reveal a butler so niffy-naffy he could have served in a duke's residence. Hell, Adam thought, the fellow could have been a duke. At his side was Miss Relaford herself, her mouth open in an *O* of astonishment. Even the superior servant seemed taken aback.

Adam bowed, and handfuls of rose petals fluttered off his head and his shoulders, swept by the wind onto the tiled hall. A few were lodged in his neckcloth and lapels and the top of his waistcoat.

Dashing? He felt like dashing for a hackney to carry him away! Well, that tiled floor was not going to swallow him up, and a fellow seldom died of mortification, unfortunately, so Adam did the only thing possible: he held his collection of now bare stems out to Miss Relaford and said, "For you."

Her lips twitched. The butler's lips twitched. Adam's lips twitched, and then they all burst out laughing. The butler recovered first, recalling his position and his dignity, even if his mistress and her unconventional guest had forgotten theirs. He cleared his throat, announced that he would see about a broom, and made a decorous exit, although they could hear one last chuckle as he headed down the hall.

"That's what comes of a poor country clodpole trying to impress a princess, I suppose," Adam said, still grinning.

"Are you?"

He laughed again. "Poor? Countrified? A clumsy fool? All of them, my lady, I assure you."

Jenna brushed a rose petal off his shoulder. "Trying to impress me?" It was little more than a whisper.

Adam could only sigh, take up her hand, and bring it to his lips. "With all my heart, if only I could."

The butler returned and cleared his throat again.

"Are you coming down with something, Hobart? You would not wish to be ill at yuletide," Jenna said. She did, however, take her hand out of Sir Adam's and invite him to follow her to the library where some of her father's other curios were displayed, until her uncle returned for tea.

They admired carved jade horses and purple beads made of clamshells, examined a case of dead butterflies and another of oddly shaped pearls of different colors, for her maid's sake.

The maid was mending in the corner, for propriety's sake.

What they were actually doing was admiring each other, examining their startling new feelings. They let their hands touch over each ebony figurine and their shoulders brush in front of the paintings. They compared their tastes, learning about each other in the process and liking what they learned, very much indeed.

As they went from object to object, Jenna told Adam about her merry papa, the second son of an earl, who had fallen in love with a merchant's daughter and eloped with her aboard one of her father's ships. She died in childbirth, but James Relaford stayed at sea, becoming wealthy in his own right, ignoring the scandal, ignoring his family, ignoring everything but the baby daughter left with his wife's brother and sister-in-law. Now he was gone, as was Jenna's dearest aunt, and the grandfather earl who had never acknowledged her birth.

Adam in turn told her about his beloved Standings and his horse-mad father whose schemes had sent them into penury, if not yet bankruptcy.

"We have both had great losses in our lives," Jenna said. "And yet you have your lands and I have an uncle who cares for me as if I were his own daughter, so we are more fortunate than many others."

Adam agreed just as they heard the front door opening, then steps heading down the tiled hall in their direction.

"Uncle," Miss Relaford said, "may I present Sir Adam Standish. Sir Adam, my uncle, Mr. Ezekiel—"

"Beasdale!"

"Standish?"

"This is your uncle?"

"This is your hero?"

"This is your niece?"

"This is preposterous!" Beasdale looked about to suffer an apoplexy, his face was so red. "How dare you, you villain, dangle after my niece when I particularly warned you against such a course? Here I was thinking of relenting on that payment date, but now? Extend further credit to an encroaching, unethical parasite? You might consider yourself clever to scrape up an acquaintance with my niece on such short notice, but I consider you no better than a worm, a slime-slithering—"

"I take it you two have met?" Jenna asked in a quavering voice.

But Adam was not daunted, not at all. He raised his chin, bruises and all. "I do not consider myself the least clever, else I would have asked the name of Miss Relaford's uncle before I leaped to her assistance. As it is, you impugn my honor, sir. If circumstances were otherwise, I would ask you to name your seconds. Instead, for Miss Relaford's sake, I shall bid you good day."

"Wait!" Jenna called as Adam turned for the door. "Uncle, I do not know what you are concerned about, but I swear Sir Adam and I met by chance. He was bringing a coin to Mr. Schott's to be appraised. The same type of coin I showed you at breakfast yesterday. Let him see, Sir Adam," she added, with a silent plea for him to understand a loving uncle's obsession.

Adam took the coin out of his pocket. Then, for Miss Relaford's sake, he relented. "I had no other reason for entering that shop yesterday, Mr. Beasdale. I swear it."

Beasdale examined the coin. "Harumph. I suppose I owe you an apology, then. And my gratitude for keeping my poppet safe." He mopped at his forehead with a monogrammed handkerchief. "And I guess I shall have to extend that deadline after all."

Adam had more pride than to take crumbs from a begrudging hand, especially in front of Miss Relaford. "No, sir. That is unnecessary. I have come into a bit of the ready, enough to tide me over until spring. I shall make do."

Beasdale harumphed again, but was pleased, they could see, pleased enough to sit to tea with his unwanted guest.

"But do not mistake my gratitude or my hospitality," he told Adam while Jenna was busy filling cups and plates. "I will not have a titled fortune hunter paying suit to my niece."

Adam almost wished the banker to the devil, but he was Miss Relaford's uncle, and she seemed fond of the old curmudgeon. The tea could have been ditchwater and the cakes might have had bits of macadam instead of poppyseed in them, for Adam's appetite, and his pleasure in the day, had fled. He made his farewells as quickly as politeness allowed.

Miss Relaford walked him to the entryway. As the stiff-backed butler held the door open, she pressed a card of invitation into Adam's hand. "I am having a small party on Friday evening in honor of a friend who is recently wed. I would be pleased if you could attend."

"I am sorry, ma'am, but I must be returning to the country. And your uncle . . ."

"This is my party. And if you are concerned about the company, not everyone will be as disapproving of your cir-

cumstances as my uncle. My school friend married Lord
Iverson, and some of his friends will be coming, as well as
Uncle's business associates and their families."

"Ivy? Why, I went to university with him. You say he is
married?"

"To Uncle's best friend's daughter, who was my bosom
bow, Miss Sophia Applegate. Then you will come?"

He had no formal evening wear. He had no hope of winning over Mr. Beasdale. He wished it could be otherwise,
but why torture himself further by spending more time in
Miss Relaford's company? "I shall think about it," was all
he could say, knowing he would think of nothing else.

"Please," she said, and only went inside when the butler,
who was not ill at all, but would be soon with the door open,
coughed again.

5

"*H*ow could you, Uncle?"

Mr. Beasdale merely harumphed into his second serving of tea.

"Not only were you discourteous to a guest in your house," Jenna went on, "but you insulted a gentleman who might have saved my life. The officer at Bow Street said that thief was a dangerous criminal."

"He's poor," said the banker, reaching for another macaroon.

"Of course he is. Wealthy men do not steal ladies' purses."

"Not the thief. Standish."

"So what?" Jenna asked, moving the plate farther from her uncle's reach, for the sake of his waistline. "You and my mother were poor once. You always told me how your father started life as a free trader."

"He's a nob."

"Pooh. A mere baronet. My grandfather was an earl."

Beasdale's snort said what he thought about that, and about all titled gentlemen in general. "Like half of the swells, this one is in debt. He owes the bank more than he's worth."

A frown formed on Jenna's forehead. "Was he the one who took out the loans?"

"No."

"Has he defaulted on his payments?"

"No, dash it. Am I to be interrogated in my own home, besides starved?"

Jenna placed one slice of lemon cake on his plate, a small slice. "I have one more question. Although Sir Adam seems to be a brave, kind, honorable gentleman, you will still refuse him permission to call?"

Put like that, Beasdale had no good answer. He set his plate aside, his stomach roiling. "I only want the best for you, my dear."

"What if I consider him the best, the finest gentleman I have ever met? What if he is what *I* want?"

"Faugh. It is too soon for you to know. He'll be leaving soon, anyway, back to his goats and hens."

"Sheep and cows, Uncle, and a few hogs. And perhaps he will not leave town so shortly. I invited him to the dinner for Lord and Lady Iverson Friday."

"Where he'll fit right in with those other useless swells, all puffed up with their own consequence."

"Sir Adam is not like that, and you are sounding like a French revolutionary. Besides, he might not attend. He did not exactly accept my invitation."

"Good. I think I will have that piece of cake after all."

"Will you be polite to him if he does come?"

Whatever Beasdale muttered was lost in the sounds of swallowing. Jenna persisted: "You would not be so selfish, would you, to deny me the opportunity to get to know such a pleasant gentleman simply because he does not suit your notions of an eligible *parti*?"

"Since you have invited him already, what would be the use? Perhaps it's for the best. Once you get to know the chap you'll see that you two won't suit at all."

She smiled, a soft, private smile that quite ruined Beasdale's digestion for good. He groaned. "Devil take it, poppet, I only want your happiness. You would not be content in the country, minding those ducks and geese."

"Sheep and cows, Uncle. But are you saying that if, by

some chance, which is far too early to consider"—although she had, of course; her blushes gave her away—"I did marry Sir Adam, you would not invite me to visit here?"

"Do not be foolish, girl. I am not like that idiot earl who disowned your father. You will always be welcome in my home, no matter whom you marry."

Jenna stood up and bent to kiss her uncle's cheek. She drew back when he added, "Of course, I'd be more welcoming if you were to wed Leonard Frye, the new junior partner. He comes from a powerful investment family. He is prudent and polished and knows what is proper."

"Mr. Frye is also a prig." Jenna called for Hobart to take the tea cart away. "I'd sooner wed one of Sir Adam's hogs."

"Harumph."

Adam, meanwhile, was walking back to his inn, thinking of the visit. Beasdale was as stiff-rumped as ever, but his niece was even more of a delight than Adam had thought possible. Her conversation, her wit, her humor, all entranced him deeper than her physical beauty ever could. The only thing he did not like about Miss Relaford, in fact, was that she was so far above him. Granddaughter to an earl, by George. Niece to a nabob, botheration. No amount of wishing was going to make him worthy of such a prize. Blast it.

What made Adam feel worse was that he'd never really considered marriage before. He always knew he could not afford a wife, and he was too practical a fellow to hunger for what he could not have—or at least he had been before this trip to London.

Thinking of hunger made him stop to buy a hot meat pie, since the few bites he'd taken at Beasdale's house were not nearly enough to satisfy his appetite. Neither, now, was the mere glimpse of heaven enough to satisfy his yearning.

He wanted a life companion, someone to share his thoughts, share his woes, and share his successes, besides sharing his bed. He wanted a friend, but one who would give him unquestioned, unconditional love. He wished he could find someone who believed he was worthy of being loved in return, despite all his faults and failings.

He did. A small dog followed him and his dripping meat pie back to the inn.

"'Ere now, I don't allow no dogs in my inn."

Adam looked down, surprised to see the dirty brown mongrel was still at his side. "He's not my dog. He just followed me for a taste of my meal."

The innkeeper frowned at the small dog in disgust. "And next 'e'll be beggin' from the customers. 'Arry," he called to one of the ostlers, "come get another cur for drownin'."

"Drowning?" Adam echoed, looking at the animal, which was shivering with the cold, but which wagged his tail.

"Right. Else the blighter'll be gettin' in the way of the horses, or stealin' food from the kitchens, or chasin' the chickens m'wife keeps out back. For sure 'e'll bring fleas in with 'im, was I to let you take 'im to your room."

He'd drown the dog because the creature was hungry and lonely and cold? Hell, Adam was hungry, lonely, and cold, too. No one was going to drown him, or his new dog. "I'll be leaving then, and taking him with me."

The innkeeper shrugged. He already had Adam's money for the room. Now he could rent it out again.

And now Adam had no place to sleep, with darkness falling. He had a ragged dog, too, which meant the hotels he knew would not accept his custom either, had he wished to spend another part of his purse on a room. He also had his lucky coin, though, for all the good it had done him. He might as well wish for a featherbed and silk sheets!

As he left the courtyard of the inn, picking his way between carriages and horses and hurrying grooms, he picked up the dog. The innkeeper was right, the poor little fellow might have been trampled. What were a few more mud stains on his coat anyway? No one would care, back at Standings. And there were worse things than flea bites, although Adam could not think of many offhand.

He could feel bones through the matted fur and promised the dog another meal soon, and a bath. The pup licked his cheek as Adam negotiated the inn yard, satchel in one hand, dog in the other. "I just wish I had somewhere to take you."

Then a handsome phaeton raced into the yard, splashing more mud on Adam and the dog. A scarlet-coated officer leaped down and tossed the reins to one of the grooms who came running. The driver shouted "Sorry" toward Adam and strode for the taproom. He turned back. "Standish? Is that you, man?"

"Johnny Cresswell? Good grief, how long has it been? And you are still as cow-handed as ever!"

"But a lieutenant now, I'll have you know!"

With bear hugs and back slaps, the two old schoolmates exchanged welcomes, while the dog danced at their feet, barking. Adam led his two companions to a quieter corner. "Are you on leave? How long will you be in town? How are your parents?"

"Not precisely on leave," the lieutenant answered, "for I took a ball in the shoulder." Seeing Adam's look of concern, he added, "I am fully recovered, but the War Office is keeping me here until I am needed for courier duty. The parents are well, the last I heard, but the roads to Yorkshire are already near impassable, more's the pity, so I will not be going home for the holidays. And you, what brings you away from your country fastness?"

"Business," was all Adam said. "I leave tomorrow."

"Well, you'll stay with me at Cresswell House tonight, of course."

"I could not . . ."

"What, you'd leave me to rattle around the mausoleum of a town house by myself with nothing but servants for company? Don't be a nodcock. Besides, there's to be a party for Iverson on Friday. You'll have to stay for that. He'll be pleased as punch to see you there. Did you hear old Ivy put on leg shackles?"

"Yes, I was actually invited to the party." Adam bent, pretending to brush dirt off the dog. "I did not bring my formal clothes." He did not say he did not own anything fitting for Miss Relaford's gathering, nor that he could not spend the money on useless fripperies. "No time to have something made up."

Cresswell waved that aside. "We're of a size, and all my formal wear is stowed in the attic. If something needs altering, my batman is a wizard with a needle. I, of course, shall wear my dress uniform. Impresses the ladies, don't you know."

Johnny was already handsome, with blond hair and blue eyes and a raffish, dimpled smile. The tavern girls had always looked at him first, until they heard Ivy's title. They barely noticed Adam, even then. Now, with Ivy taken and Johnny in his dress uniform, dripping gilt and ribbons . . . Adam's heart sank to his shabby boots. "Miss Relaford?"

Cresswell nodded. "Met her at the wedding. A regular Incomparable."

"Yes, I thought so, too."

The lieutenant looked more closely at his friend, hearing the plaintive note. "Ah, sits the wind in that quarter, then?"

"The wind does not sit at all. It blew straight past me, on Beasdale's breath."

"Well, if it is any consolation to you, he'd never let the fair maid go off to follow the drum with a mere lieutenant either. But cheer up, old man, who knows what other well-dowered daughters will be at the party? Ivy found a pretty one, with no trace of her father's coal mines in her manners."

"You don't mean to tell me Iverson wed an heiress simply for her father's money, do you? I knew he was punting on Tick, but . . ."

"Hell, no. Miss Applegate's a beauty, too, and likes horses as much as Ivy does. He fell arsy-varsy over the girl." Cresswell shook his head. "I never would have believed it possible myself."

Adam believed it.

"Well, come on then," the lieutenant said, "let's be off. I am sharp-set, and Cook will be thrilled to have another mouth to feed."

Adam looked down. "What about the dog? He seems to be mine now."

"Bring him along, of course. He looks like he could use a decent meal even more than we can. Have you given him a name?"

"Lucky," Adam decided on the instant. What else?

6

*F*iend seize it, there was a feather mattress! Adam sank down upon it and, with a hesitant hand, pulled back the cover. The sheets at Cresswell House were fine, but they were not silk, thank goodness. Otherwise he would have to doubt both his sanity and all the laws of nature as he knew them. As it was, he was having trouble believing the amazing coincidence of finding Johnny Cresswell just when he wished for a place to stay the night.

He could not have found more comfortable accommodations at the Pulteney or the Grand Hotel, if they had found his person and his purse acceptable, which he doubted. Here the servants were more than anxious to please. With none of the family in residence except the young officer, and no other guests, Adam was their best hope of earning extra money for Christmas.

The lieutenant's man was altering a coat to fit Adam's more muscular frame. The cook was fixing a special dinner. The stable lads were giving the dog a bath, while the head groom was making Lucky a leather collar and lead. The housekeeper was even arranging a bed for the dog in Adam's room, out of an old yellowed petticoat from the rag bag . . . a silk petticoat.

Adam shook his head. No, what he was thinking was impossible. On the other hand, he decided to stay on for Miss Relaford's party. He would send funds back to Standings in the morning, so there was no need for him to race home to-morrow, not when he had such luxurious digs in town, and not when he could see the woman of his dreams once more without having to be asleep. Just a few hours ago he had decided not to stay, not to torment himself further with what he could never have, but now . . . Well, now the impossible seemed not quite so improbable, and never was not so far away.

After the best dinner Adam had had in years, and after they had caught up on all the news of other schoolmates, the progress of the war, the price of corn, Lieutenant Cresswell suggested they go for a hand or two of cards to one of the gambling parlors, far more entertaining than the sedate gentlemen's clubs.

"You must know," Johnny told him, "that I am feeling particularly lucky tonight, having found an old friend to share my meal. I hate eating by myself."

Adam had never thought about it, but now that he did, he realized that he ate all his meals with an agricultural journal or a newspaper propped in front of him. Conversation would be nice, and a pretty face to look at. Not that Johnny was not good company, just not the company he'd rather have. He said, "I am glad to be of service to stave off your solitude, but, as for the cards, you'll have to excuse me. My funds are limited enough without chancing the loss of a single groat."

"You never were much of a gambler, now that I recall. Still, come along, won't you? There is always free wine and pretty girls, and you are growing as somber as a Sunday sermon. Besides, one never knows. If I win enough, I might even be able to repay that blunt you lent me."

"I never lent you—oh, you mean the hundred pounds? Lud, I never meant that as a loan. It was a gift, so you could buy your colors when your father would not advance you the ready. I could not go off to fight for king and country, not with my own father ailing, so I provided the funds for you to go."

"Yes, but with brass you could ill afford to give, that inheritance from your mother. I never forgot, although I must admit the money has been in and out of my hands any number of times. Still, I have every intention of repaying you."

Granted, when Adam gave over the money, he had not known quite how bad things were at Standings, but he did not regret helping his friend. "Gammon. If I had not given you the blunt, my father would have used it to buy more horses, or to wager on the ones he already owned."

"Yes, well, my own pater still keeps me on a tight rein or I would have repaid you ages ago. It always seemed I had a pressing need when the dibs were in tune. Now I am beforehand with the world, thank heaven, and living at Cresswell House at no expense, so perhaps tonight we will both be lucky."

"I have to admit that sum would be more than welcome to meet my own commitments so, yes, let us go to your gambling den for wine, women, and wagering. Lud knows I wish that you end the night a wealthy man!"

There he was in his borrowed finery, looking fine as five pence, with more than five pence in his pocket for once, yet Adam was not truly enjoying himself. The ladybirds held no interest for him, and he had barely recovered from the day's headache, so saw no reason to give himself another pounding skull by overindulging in wine. He did find some old friends to greet, but they were more interested in losing their blunt than making conversation. Some of the others present were not men Adam wished to know, not with their glittering, feral eyes and nervous, darting hands.

For the most part, he watched Lieutenant Cresswell play. Johnny was not any Captain Sharp, but neither was he a gullible flat. He won some, then lost it back, then won a bit more. He went from faro to piquet to the dice to vingt-et-un. Adam could not see what pleasure anyone got in watching their stacks of counters disappear, but he supposed the mere thought of winning was enough for the serious players with their intense stares and sweating brows.

"Here," Cresswell said, holding out his heavy Bath blue superfine, having decided to leave off his uniform for the decidedly off-duty night. "Be a good fellow and hold my coat, won't you? It's deuce hot in the place." He looked around. One of the men at the roulette wheel had his coat on inside out, to bring him luck. "Perhaps the cards will go my way without it."

They did not, and in a way Adam was relieved, as if somehow his own wishes might have weighted the dice or marked the cards in his friend's favor. He wanted Johnny to win, naturally, but naturally, not by any havey-cavey happenstance.

The wagering went on, and Adam was starting to yawn, wondering when his friend would have enough of this empty enterprise, when a commotion arose by the door. A liveried servant was trying to gain entry that the doorman wished to deny. Adam could hear shouts about disturbing the gentlemen at play, about a message, about life and death.

"Let him in, man, if his news is so important," Lord Symington, one of the men at Johnny's table, called across the smoke-filled room as he put down his cards. The others followed suit, the dealers held the decks, the croupier stopped the wheel, and the ladybirds ceased their twittering. All eyes followed the footman as he headed straight for the table where Johnny sat.

Oh, no, Adam thought, frantically trying to recall his earlier words. Had he wished Johnny won his fortune at the tables? Or had he, as he feared, simply wished that Johnny become wealthy tonight? The surest way for Lieutenant Cresswell to come into an instant fortune was to inherit it, on the demise of his father. Racing through Adam's thoughts were feather mattresses and gold coins and reward monies and invitations to parties he was never meant to receive and women he was never meant to meet . . . and a dog. Lud, what if his wishes were coming true? He'd be murdering Johnny's father!

He liked the man. Lord Cresswell had always tried to be

strict with his devil-may-care son, curbing his wilder starts, but only out of affection, Adam knew, not out of meanness. He'd been kind to the other boys at school, earning their respect. Zeus, he could not die just so Adam could pay off his mortgage!

Adam grabbed the lucky coin out of his pocket, staring at it as if the penny piece could tell him its intentions, its essence, its magic. "No," he whispered. "I take it back. I'd like the hundred pounds, but I do not wish any harm to befall Johnny's father. I do not wish it, do you hear?"

Johnny heard, and looked at Adam quizzically. He would have asked for an explanation but then the footman neared their table. Adam held his breath. The messenger reached them and beamed at Lord Symington. "A boy, my lord. Your lady wife has been delivered of a healthy son!"

The cheers and congratulations and champagne toasts rang out. None were more sincere than Adam's.

"We might as well go home," Lieutenant Cresswell said after the noise had abated and the new father had rushed off to see his wife and infant, breaking up that game. "The cards are cold tonight anyway."

The weather was cold, too, that bitter December night, so Adam held out Johnny's coat for him. A bit unsteady on his feet after a night of imbibing and then all those recent toasts, the lieutenant dropped the coat, then bent to pick it up. In his fumbling, a paper fell out of the pocket.

"Zeus only knows what it is. Haven't worn this old coat in ages. Too hot in Spain, don't you know. If we hadn't been up in the attics finding you clothes, I never would have unearthed it."

The light in the gaming parlor's hall was too dim to read by, so they stepped outside, toward a streetlamp.

Johnny unfolded the paper and read it. "Why, it's a draft on my father's bank, for a monkey!"

"You have five hundred pounds, and you've let it sit in a coat pocket for months or years? Deuce take it, Johnny, not even you could be so careless with your blunt."

The lieutenant staggered back against the lamppost. "I swear I never knew it was there. Here, see if it bears a date."

He held the check out, and Adam saw Lord Cresswell's signature, and a date some four years earlier, one month after Adam's mother's death, one month before Johnny left for the Peninsula.

"He must have put it in my pocket when I went to say farewell," Johnny calculated, "after ranting and raving over my enlisting, how I was breaking my mother's heart and endangering the succession." The lieutenant blew his nose, pretending that it was the cold night air making his eyes water and his nose run.

Adam brushed a bit of dampness from his own cheek. "He truly cares for you."

"Yes, although the old rip would be hanged before he admitted it. Damn, how I wish I could go home for Christmas—after we go to the bank tomorrow morning!"

"We?"

"Of course. That hundred pounds is yours, my friend, with interest if not a reward for helping me find the check." He put his arm around Adam's shoulder as they waited for a hackney cab, and laughed out loud. "By Jupiter, did I not say you brought me luck?"

7

*T*hey went to Lieutenant Cresswell's father's bank first, then Adam went on to his own financial institution.

"What, back again, are you?" Mr. Beasdale scowled across his paper-covered desk, his face growing red at Adam's effrontery. "You are deuced persistent, I'll say that for you. My niece thinks I ought to grant you that extension, since you have convinced her what a hardworking chap you are. In a matter of minutes. Bah! That is why females do not have authority over their own assets. They would give the whole away to the first silver-tongued devil they meet."

Adam knew he was anything but a smooth talker, but he was not here to defend his character—or offend his angel's uncle. "No, sir," he said. "I am here to tell you that I no longer need to delay my payment. I wish to pay part of it in advance, in fact, while I am still in London."

Mr. Beasdale eyed him from under bushy eyebrows, knowing full well Adam had nothing of value left to sell to make the sum mentioned. "What, have you taken to capturing wanted criminals for the reward money? Or have you become a highwayman yourself? No, I suppose that like others of your sort you quickly turned to the baize table and hit a streak of luck."

"I was lucky, yes, lucky in my friends. Lieutenant Cresswell repaid a loan I made to him some years ago."

"I know of that young wastrel. Anyone who would lend

good money to such a here-and-thereian is a bigger fool than Cresswell himself. He would only lose it betting on a curricle race or the color of the next horse to pass by."

"He used my mother's bequest to me to purchase his colors," Adam answered in a quiet tone that refuted contradiction, "to go fight the French. I was happy to lend him the blunt, and he has proved to be an exemplary officer, earning mention in the dispatches. He was wounded in the service of his country. Just recently he came into funds to pay me back."

"So you say. His father is no squeeze crab, from all I hear. Why did he not pay the lad's way?"

"Because he thought as you did, that Johnny was a reckless daredevil, taking any challenge or chance."

"So you helped young Cresswell thwart his father's authority? If you think that recommends you to me, you are mistaken."

"I helped my friend follow his dreams. Sometimes a parent does not truly know what is best for a child, and sometimes a father has to let his grown son make his own mistakes, to become his own man. Nestlings will grow up and fly away, despite all the love of a mother or father . . . or uncle."

"Harumph," was Beasdale's only reply to the not-so-subtle gibe. "I suppose the only way he could pay you back was with gambling winnings."

"No, he had the money from his father, who must have reconsidered. And before you blacken poor Lieutenant Cresswell's name further, he carefully invested most of the money in the Funds, after giving me my share."

"Well, perhaps he does have a modicum of sense after all," Beasdale conceded. "I am sure his father will be relieved that his heir is not a total want-wit." He straightened a stack of papers on his desk as if to conclude the meeting.

"There is one other thing, sir: Miss Relaford's invitation to the party for Lord and Lady Iverson."

"Yes? What about it?"

"I wish to accept, with your permission."

"You are asking me?"

Adam brushed at the sleeve of his—of Johnny Cresswell's—coat. "The invitation came from Miss Relaford but the gathering is being held in your home. I would not want to offend you if my presence is unwelcome."

He was not asking about any silly party, and they both knew it. He was asking permission to address the banker's niece. A lesser man, a conniving fortune hunter, for instance, would have accepted the invitation without a scruple for Beasdale's wishes, using the occasion to further his own cause. Beasdale had to respect Sir Adam for the courtesy.

"Harumph. I suppose you'd better come along to tea this afternoon, then, to tell Jenna herself that you are going to be accepting. I am liable to forget." Right after he forgot the combination on the bank's vault.

Adam brought the dog with him. One could tell a great deal about a person, he had always believed, by how he or she treated an animal. Not that he had any doubt that Miss Relaford was the kindest, sweetest, most gentle female in all of creation, but she was a Londoner, unused to being around anything but horses or the occasional kitchen cat. What if she were afraid of dogs, or thought them vermin, as the innkeeper had, or thought that all four-legged creatures were beneath her notice? That would not bode well for Adam's future. He was a farmer and needed a farmer's wife, not a mere decorative beauty.

Jenna did not disappoint him, instantly bending to scratch Lucky's ear, without regard for getting brown dog hairs on her jonquil gown. She sent Hobart the butler back to the kitchens to fetch the dog a bowl of water.

Beasdale, however, was a surprise.

"Why, I had a pup just like this one when I was a lad," he said, patting his ample lap in invitation for Lucky to join him on the damask-covered chaise. He called after Hobart to fetch some of the kidneys from breakfast for the dog, too.

When he heard about the near drowning and how Adam came to own the dog, he smiled at the baronet for the first time.

He said, "You can always tell a lot about a man, I always believed, by how he treats a dog."

Jenna smiled at Adam, too, relieved as much as he was by her uncle's approval.

They were both hopeful until Jenna's uncle added, "Of course, a dog is all devotion and no deliberation. A pup will love a poor man as easily as a rich one. Foolish creatures cannot think ahead to their next meal, or worry that their owner will not be able to provide one."

Adam's hopes lasted as long as the dish of kidneys. Mr. Beasdale approved of Adam's dog, not his courtship of the banker's niece.

Beasdale was discussing Lucky's aptitudes and possible antecedents with Hobart, who felt the mongrel's best point was that he belonged to Sir Adam and not the Beasdale household.

Meanwhile, Jenna spoke for Adam's ears only, next to him on the love seat. "Don't worry. He likes you."

"I know. He follows me everywhere."

"Silly, I mean my uncle."

"He does? He did not seem at all pleased that I am accepting your kind invitation for Friday's gathering."

Jenna was pleased enough for all of them. She decided to have dancing, after all. How better to have Sir Adam at her side? "Oh, I am certain my uncle is coming to admire you. He invited you for tea this afternoon, didn't he?"

"That's true. He did not have to."

"So you will have your extension soon."

Adam set his tea aside to look into the loveliest green eyes he had ever seen. The color of Christmas pine boughs lighted with golden candles, they were, and he was mesmerized by their glow. An extension was not what he wanted from Mr. Beasdale. "I no longer need extra time to make my payments. I came into a bit of cash last night. Actually, a friend who owed me money came into it, so I am solvent again. With excellent prospects for the spring," he added, lest she think he led a hand-to-mouth existence, which had not been far from the truth. He could not lie to her, so he explained, "I would be doing fine, except for a run of bad luck. My luck has definitely changed." He did not have to say that meeting her was the proof. His smile said it for him.

Jenna returned his smile, thinking that, although his business was concluded, Sir Adam had stayed on in town. She would have the orchestra play nothing but waltzes, to match the lilt in her heart.

Beasdale frowned in their direction until Lucky reached up and licked his chin, drawing the banker's attention away from the two grinning mooncalves.

"My uncle is merely protective of me," Jenna explained away the glare. "He does not mean anything by it."

"Of course." Adam, however, knew Beasdale's scowl meant no trespassing. He sighed, wondering what it would take to change the banker's opinion of him. A miracle, most likely.

"And I have been singing your praises to Uncle Ezekiel, too."

Was that miracle enough? Adam had to be encouraged by his lady's championing his cause, and had to be amused also. "How do you know I will not run away with your uncle's money, never to repay his bank what I owe?"

"I know because I have heard you speak of the land and the people. You would never abandon them, no more than you would a poor dog."

"You know all that after so short a time?"

Suddenly shy, Jenna looked down. "I think I knew it from the first time you smiled at me."

Adam held her hand under cover of her jonquil skirts. "I, too. I thought you were a Christmas angel, and I wished I could be worthy of you. I fear your uncle will never consider me to be."

"He is not as close-minded as he appears, but I am his only chick."

"No, he is right to be wary of impoverished gentlemen, with you his heiress. We could all be fortune hunters. I am glad he would not give your hand to the first needy man who offered, but, deuce take it, I wish your uncle were not so wealthy!"

Adam could have bitten his tongue off. He had no more made his impulsive wish than Hobart reentered the room and whispered in Beasdale's ear. The banker's high complexion faded to the white of his neckcloth, and he half rose, sending Lucky to the floor.

"What is it, Uncle?"

"Ruined. We are ruined."

Jenna and Adam were both standing now, ready to go to his aid if necessary. He waved them away and sank back onto his seat. "The *Majestic Star* went down with all hands, with all its cargo. We are ruined."

"Did you not have insurance on the ship?" Adam asked.

"Leonard Frye, the bank's junior partner, was supposed to pay it. He ran off as soon as he heard about the ship, and no one knows where. There is suspicion he embezzled the insurance money and fled when the loss became known. We are ruined."

Jenna was weeping. "All those men. Dear Captain Ingersoll."

Adam naturally put his arms around her in comfort.

Beasdale was shaking his head. "Good thing you did not marry that dastard, poppet."

"Captain Ingersoll?" Adam asked.

"No, Frye," Beasdale answered. "And take your hands off my niece, Standish. I cannot let her wed a poor man now. How would you keep her? In a pigsty? No, she has to marry money, so I know she and her children are cared for, now that I cannot see to their welfare. I owe my sister's memory nothing less."

"Uncle!" Jenna protested while Adam was frantically trying to remember the words of his latest wish, that Beasdale not be so wealthy. He desperately unwished it.

And Hobart came back, with a handsome, well-dressed man of about Adam's age, who was out of breath.

"Frye?" Beasdale stared at the man. So did Adam, whose hopes of winning Miss Relaford's hand were again as dashed on the rocks as the *Majestic Star.*

"Yes, sir. I am sorry I took so long to get here, but I raced to the harbor myself to verify the ill tidings, and I have excellent news! It was the *Majestic Tzar* that went down, not our ship!"

"Not . . . ?"

"No, sir. The *Star* is reported on course and on time."

"And the insurance? It is paid?"

"Of course, not that we will need it, I trust. Why do you ask?"

"No reason, none at all. Good job, Frye. You'll stay to tea, won't you? Jenna, my dear, fix Mr. Frye a cup. You know how he likes it."

Frye did not like the dog, which did not sit well with Mr. Beasdale. Frye did sit next to Miss Relaford, in the choice seat Adam had so recently occupied.

Adam refrained from wishing the well-favored young man to perdition, although he was sorely tempted.

And Jenna suggested that, since Adam was staying on in town until her party on Friday night, perhaps he might care to see the sights, the galleries and exhibits. Adam would go look at a pig dancing on a dung hill if it meant another minute in Miss Relaford's company, so he accepted.

Frye spilled his tea, and Mr. Beasdale went "Harumph." Jenna offered Lucky, not Mr. Frye, the last biscuit, and Adam went back to Cresswell House whistling.

8

$\mathcal{T}$he rest of the week passed too quickly, and too slowly. For Jenna, the days passed too slowly. She was waiting for the dancing and the mistletoe and a chance to slip away for a private moment or two, away from the careful chaperonage her uncle insisted upon for the sightseeing excursions. She knew her own heart and thought she knew Adam's, but he was too much the gentleman to speak without her guardian's approval. When Uncle saw Sir Adam among their friends and acquaintances, surely he would relent. When he saw that the baronet was the only man of all she had ever known whose very presence delighted Jenna, surely he would put her happiness above Adam's finances. If not, surely the mistletoe and wassail and her low-cut red velvet gown would encourage Adam to set his scruples aside for the evening. Who knew where that could lead? To the altar, Jenna wished with all her heart.

For Adam, the days rushed by too quickly. He feared these were his last hours of contentment: the bliss he found in seeing Miss Relaford's smiles, the joy in feeling her touch as he helped her up stairs, the warmth of her thigh next to his on the carriage seat, the elation of knowing—hoping—that she was coming to care for him as much as he cared for her. What if there was not time enough to win her affections, to convince her that his love could provide what was important, what his income could not? He would have to return to

Standings to a cold, empty, barren life, for Adam doubted he could ever love another woman.

He was careful to refrain from making wishes, except to wish that he would prove worthy of Jenna's love. Nothing happened to convince him—or Mr. Beasdale.

Fast or slow, the night of the party for Lord and Lady Iverson arrived.

For all the masterpieces and works of art Adam had seen this week, none compared to Miss Relaford in her red velvet gown. He might never be able to afford such a gown for her, or the pearl and diamond pendant at her neck, and he might never get to touch the milky skin the low bodice revealed, but just the sight of her greeting the guests in the drawing room before dinner took his breath away.

No, that was the hearty slap on the back from his old friend, Lord Iverson, jarring Adam's still-sore ribs.

"Move along, man," Ivy teased. "No ogling the hostess, pretty as she is. I want to make you known to my wife. Darling, here is my friend Standish, the one to whom I owe that hundred pounds."

Ivy's wife was a petite redhead with freckles and a radiant grin. She was dressed in the height of fashion in ecru satin, with a strand of pearls so large and heavy that she might have fallen over on her elegant little nose, but for her arm tucked comfortably, lovingly, possessively in the crook of Ivy's elbow. Adam could instantly see that his friend was smitten, and wished them every joy of— "What hundred pounds?"

"Why, the wager we had about which one of us gudgeons would marry first. Don't you recall?"

Adam remembered something about a Benedict's bet while they were just out of university, in London, on the town. They were foxed, and if he had the right occasion, Ivy had a buxom blond barmaid on his lap, swearing he would never step into parson's mousetrap, that bachelorhood was simply too much fun. Of course he would marry, Adam had countered. Ivy needed to ensure the succession to his title.

He, on the other hand, would never take a wife to live in genteel poverty. Ivy had laughed that Adam was too tender-hearted a chap to live his days alone—and the bet was on, with the first to wed having to pay the forfeit.

"I forgot that silly schoolboy twaddle entirely until now," Adam confessed. "So must you. Consider it a belated wedding gift."

"Nonsense, man. It's a debt of honor, and one I am eager to pay, seeing how I am reveling in my wedded state. Lud, what fools we were."

Adam's eyes followed Miss Relaford around the room as she greeted this guest or that, making certain everyone's needs were seen to. "No, we were just young."

Ivy watched him watching her. He smiled. "I was right, though, was I not? You do not wish to live your life as a lonely old bachelor, with a cat for company."

"A dog," Adam murmured without looking at his old friend. "I have a dog now. Lucky."

"Yes, you are," Ivy said. "She is a fine girl. Not to compare with my own bride, of course, but a perfect choice." Lady Iverson was speaking with an older couple a few feet away, but not far from her husband's side.

"What? Oh, no, you misunderstand. There is no . . . That is, I have not . . . Mr. Beasdale . . ."

Ivy was still smiling. "I understand, all right. You always were the slow, deliberate one of us. It was Johnny Cresswell who fell in love every other week."

They both picked the lieutenant out of the small crowd, an easy enough task to do with the laughing officer in his dress uniform and a handful of young ladies in their pastel gowns surrounding him. "He has not changed, has he?" Lord Iverson asked. "But you, Adam, do not wait too long. You've selected the prime blossom, but others will be buzzing around the nectar if you don't pick it soon."

Sure enough, Leonard Frye was hovering at Jenna's shoulder, casting surreptitious glances down her décolletage. "Excuse me, will you, Ivy? Tell Lady Iverson . . . a pleasure. I need to go strangle someone. That is, I need to straighten my neckcloth."

Ivy took his arm. "Not in Beasdale's parlor, you don't. That will not win his favor, you know." Then, to distract his old friend from the sight of that mushroom Frye holding a glass to Miss Relaford's lips, Lord Iverson went on: "I say, you are looking quite the thing for a turnip-grower. Mind telling me the name of your tailor?"

"Johnny's attic, and Johnny's batman. I do not even have the wherewithal for a valet of my own," Adam despaired.

Ivy slipped a folded note from his pocket into Adam's. "Now you do. Our debt is paid."

Another hundred pounds! What he could do with that! For a start, he could tip Hobart the butler to rearrange the dinner seating.

Hobart might like the coins and he might like the young man, but he liked his job better. Mr. Beasdale himself had altered the seating chart from Miss Relaford's original plan, and so it would have to stay, so that Hobart might stay in his comfortable post.

Lord Iverson, as guest of honor, sat to Miss Relaford's right. Mr. Frye, as Mr. Beasdale's choice for nephew-in-law, sat at her left. Jenna scowled down the entire length of the flower-decked table at her uncle.

Adam was seated between the new Lady Iverson's hard-of-hearing aunt and her younger sister, who was barely out of the schoolroom. The chit not only had Ivy's wife's red hair and freckles, but she also possessed spots and a stammer. Adam scowled sideways at Frye, causing Miss Applegate to stutter into speechlessness.

Neither the baronet nor the banker's niece enjoyed the meal. Everyone else seemed to, savoring course after course and glass after glass. The younger sister grew giddy and the elderly aunt dropped her hearing trumpet in the syllabub. At Miss Relaford's end, Lord Iverson was everything polite, speaking of his honeymoon trip and his horses. For the first time Jenna found his lordship's polished manners tedious, except when he spoke of his schooldays with Sir Adam. Mr. Frye was simply tedious.

At last it was time for her to lead the ladies from the room, with a last frown in her uncle's direction and a whisper to Hobart to see that the gentlemen did not tarry long over their port and cigars. She wanted to dance. Soon. With the partner of her own choice.

Adam took Jenna's chair at the end of the table near Ivy, and Lieutenant Cresswell took Frye's seat when the young financier left to visit the necessary. Ivy's new father-in-law joined them and, to Adam's regret, so did Mr. Beasdale.

Five gentlemen of such disparate ages, backgrounds, and interests could have little common ground for conversation except the weather, which topic was quickly exhausted. It was December. It was cold. It was going to grow colder.

Then Ivy, somewhat in his cups, asked about Standings, trying to promote Adam's courtship by recalling the mellow brick country home, the charming village and scenic vistas, the nearness to Newmarket. If Adam could have kicked his old friend under the table he would have, but Ivy had pushed his chair back. The last thing Adam wanted to speak of was his dilapidated estate, the fields left fallow for lack of funds to seed them, the boarded-up windows, the races that had taken all of his father's money, or the needy townsfolk who went hungry because Standings could not provide employment. He could do more now, with his friends' contributions to his coffers, but not enough. He wished Ivy would change the subject.

Ivy did. "I say, Adam, do you still have those magnificent Thoroughbreds of your father's?"

That was worse. The horses were the first thing to be sold at the previous baronet's demise. Beasdale already knew it, of course, since he held Adam's father's notes. Still, Adam hated having to admit that the horses were gone these past years.

"What about that vast stable block?"

That was the only thing about the estate that his father

had maintained. "It is in good condition, empty except for a few hens and the plow horses."

"And the training oval?"

Adam kicked at Lieutenant Cresswell's leg, to get him to get Ivy to put a sock in it. Instead, Johnny yelped.

"Sorry," Adam said. "And yes, the track is still there, so overgrown I have been letting the cows pasture there. I hope to plow it under, perhaps next spring. Why?"

Ivy nodded toward his father-in-law. "I promised Mr. Applegate that I would find work. I am of a mind to raise horses."

Mr. Beasdale made a rude noise. "Can't make any money off the hay-burners. Standish here ought to know. Ruined his father, didn't they?"

"He was betting on the horses," Ivy replied before Adam could respond. "I intend to sell them. And making a fortune is not the point. I married one, along with my beloved wife. But my esteemed father-in-law is correct: a man needs some direction in life, a goal, a purpose. I bear a useless honorary title, with no seat in the Lords, if I were inclined toward politics, which I am not. I have no profession and few skills beyond the dance floor and the card room—but I do know good horseflesh."

"Always did," the lieutenant agreed, lifting his glass in tribute to Lord Iverson's equine expertise.

"And my wife shares my interest in horses."

"Always did," Mr. Applegate echoed.

"So what are you getting at?" Adam asked.

Mr. Beasdale seconded that: "Standings is entailed, so you cannot buy it."

"Lud, I don't want to purchase the place, I already have a country seat. I merely want to rent the stables and the training fields."

"You have been drinking too much," Adam told him, not daring to hope his friend was sober enough to make sense.

"What, a paltry few glasses of wine? I can hold my liquor better than that."

"Always could," Lieutenant Cresswell chimed in, which earned him frowns from Ivy and Mr. Applegate both.

"Seriously, Adam, I would like to take a long-term lease on those portions of Standings that were always given to the horses. And perhaps the dower house for when my wife and I come to supervise the efforts. You have not rented out the cottage, have you?"

At Adam's stupefied head shake, Ivy went on: "You would not be bothered, for I truly do not mind hard work, and can hire your extra laborers to help get the place in shape this winter. You won't need them until spring, correct? After that, I'll bring in my own grooms and trainers, unless you can recommend local men."

Adam thought of the head stableman who had stayed on, simply because Adam could not pay him a pension. He thought of the villagers, and he thought of beautiful horses again running on his land. He thought of a steady income, and he thought of Miss Relaford. He thought he might stand on Mr. Beasdale's dining-room table and crow like a rooster, if only his friend were not too castaway to remember in the morning.

"Sounds reasonable to me," Mr. Applegate said. "My gal won't be happy unless she has horses."

Mr. Beasdale was doing mental calculations, coming up with numbers that made Adam's head spin, but Applegate just nodded.

Ivy tried to convince Adam by saying, "You won't have to do a thing except collect the rent."

Not do a thing? Adam could do everything he had wanted to for years! He could fix his tenants' houses, invest in modern equipment, refurbish his own home. He could make Standings a profitable, self-supporting establishment fit for a lady, even a wealthy one. He . . . could not take advantage of his friend's state of mind. Newly married, recently made wealthy, buoyed by love and afloat in alcohol, Ivy might regret the whole scheme in the morning, if he remembered it at all. "I have a suggestion. Why don't you and your lady wife come to Standings for Christmas to look over the situation for yourselves, to see just how much work will need to be done before you can bring a horse there? You are invited also, Mr. Applegate, and your family, to help your daughter decide if she could live, even part of the year, in the dower house. Standings is no elegant country mansion, and I can only offer plain country fare, but I will have a fortnight to decorate and make it festive for you for Christmas."

Then he turned toward Lieutenant Cresswell. "And you, Johnny. You know you do not wish to spend the holiday here in town without your own family, so please come. There is good shooting, parties at the neighbors, and Squire has three pretty daughters."

The lieutenant was delighted. "I can bring my father's London staff, too, to help get the place ready for company. They'll like the time in the country—and the raises I will see they get. And the chef likes nothing better than to show off for guests. Thank you. I accept."

Adam looked at Mr. Beasdale. He cleared his throat. "I would be honored if you and your niece would come to my home, humble though it might be, for Christmas. We will have carols and skating and a Yule log, all the traditions of a country Christmas I think Miss Relaford will enjoy. And . . . and I would greatly enjoy having her there."

What could Mr. Beasdale say, when his old friend Applegate was waiting on his answer, when Iverson was so eager to go, when they all knew Sir Adam for an honorable man—and when the baronet's future was so suddenly turned rosy? If he said no, his niece would never forgive him and he'd lose her anyway.

"I do wish you would come," Adam quietly urged.

"Well, then, ask the girl. It's up to her. If she wants to go, I suppose the bank can get along without me for a few days. Frye can take my place. Looks like he won't be taking anything else, deuce take it."

9

*B*easdale might have agreed to visit the rundown rural holding. He might have given his unspoken, begrudging approval of Sir Adam's suit, but he had not given up. He insisted on leading off the first dance with his niece. Then he claimed she ought to dance with Lord Iverson, while he had a set with the redheaded bride.

Having done his duty by his goose-cap dinner partner and by an arrogant Iverson cousin who complained about the low company after eating at the banker's table, Adam was free to seek out the partner he wanted.

Frye was there ahead of him. He wished . . . he wished . . . Before Adam could think of anything dire enough that would not set the house on fire or cause panic among the ladies, Jenna put her hand on his arm.

"I am sorry, Mr. Frye, but I did promise this set to Sir Adam."

Lud, Adam wondered, why had he not thought of that, merely wishing that she would choose him?

She had, and the small orchestra started to play a waltz.

"Do you think we might sit this dance out? That is, not sit, but stroll a bit, perhaps to the library?" Adam asked.

What, after she had been waiting all week for this dance? Jenna refused, saying it would not be proper for the hostess to disappear on her own.

It would be proper enough if she returned as an engaged

woman. Adam could not ask for a private conversation of that nature here, though, not with so many eyes on them. "But I am not a very good dancer."

"Gammon, I saw you with Lord Iverson's cousin." Jenna was careful to keep her jealousy of the elegant, well-bred female out of her voice. "You did very well."

Adam made a last try. "But that was not a waltz. The dance is slow to catch on in the country, you know, so I am woefully inept." He was clumsy at wooing, too, it seemed, if he could not get her to go off with him.

"The waltz is quite simple, and I really would like to dance."

"Well, then, I can only hope I do not disappoint you."

He did not. With Jenna in his arms, even as loosely held as society dictated, his feet found the rhythm on their own, while his mind's attention was on how glorious she felt, how her perfume teased his senses, how the velvet gown made soft swishing sounds as she moved in the turns of the dance. He twirled more, just to bring their bodies closer together.

As for Jenna, she felt as if her feet barely touched the ground, as if she were dancing on clouds. She forgot the party and the guests, and forgot to step out of Adam's embrace when the music ended. Luckily, the orchestra struck up another waltz.

Frye came toward them, noted their matching starry-eyed expressions, shrugged his shoulders, turned, and asked another heiress for a dance.

Without asking, Adam swept Jenna into their second waltz, but this time he turned and twirled, dancing right out the drawing-room door, down the hall, and into the softly lighted library.

They could still hear the music, and danced on until it ended, but close enough to shock any would-be witnesses. The only one to see, though, was the dog Lucky, which was curled up by the fireplace, waiting for the scraps after supper. Adam and Jenna ended the dance with a kiss that would have sent Beasdale into apoplexy for certain. Lucky wagged his tail once and went back to sleep.

"I should not have done that," Adam said in apology, although he did not regret the kiss one whit.

"I am sure there must be a bit of mistletoe around, so it is perfectly acceptable. A Christmas kiss, you know."

Was that all she thought it was? Lud, Adam was going about this all wrong. He took a step away from her, so he could think better. "I, ah, brought you here to ask a question."

Jenna's smile could have lit a hundred libraries. "Yes?"

"Would you come to Standings for Christmas? Your uncle says he will, if you will. A few others are coming, a small gathering only, nothing formal, you see, for I cannot provide . . . That is, Ivy is thinking of renting my stables to set up a racing stud, and so I can . . ." He took a breath and started again. "Well, he is coming to see if he likes it, with his wife, of course, and her family, so then I invited Johnny Cresswell, who would be alone in town otherwise, and he will bring his chef so we don't have to eat mutton every day which is about all . . . Um, I was hoping—"

"Yes, I would be pleased to come visit at your home."

"—That you might come to see if you like it, and might want to stay. Did you say yes?"

"Yes."

So he kissed her again, mistletoe or not, and soon had her seated in a big leather armchair that was not really designed for two people, but was more than comfortable, with Jenna sitting in his lap.

"You do know," he said, "that if you come, I do not think I can ever bear to let you go again?"

"Where would I go, when I only wish to be by your side?"

That called for more kisses, until Adam recalled the rest of his mission. "You do know how much I love you, don't you?"

"Tell me."

He showed her instead, whispering soft, tender words between kisses. "And we can be married there? You will make me the happiest of men, if I am not already?"

"Uncle can procure us a special license. We can be married anywhere you wish."

"Lud, I never thought so many wishes could come true. Do you know that almost the first time I saw you I wished I could take you home with me as a present, a perfect Christmas angel to keep for myself."

"What, to unwrap and put on a shelf?" she said with a laugh.

"No, to keep by my side, to cherish forever. Although the unwrapping part does sound lovely." His fingers gently touched the edge of her gown's neckline, skimming the creamy flesh that rose above.

Jenna's hands were on his neck, his shoulders, his well-muscled chest. "And I wished to get to know you better the first time you smiled at me."

"Do you believe in love at first sight, then?"

"I do now."

"What about wishes? Do you believe that if you wish for something, perhaps on a lucky coin, it can come true?"

"Why not? There must be magic in the world, or I never would have found you."

"I am beginning to believe that, too. So much that I wished for has happened. You love me, and your uncle will give us his blessings, Standings is saved, and we will have friends surrounding us, as well as my grateful tenants. And you love me," he repeated. "Surely I am the luckiest man who ever lived."

Hearing his name, the dog wagged his tail again, thumping it on the hearth.

"I even have a good dog, although your uncle hinted he might like to take Lucky back to town with him, so he does not miss you too much. The dog certainly seems content and well fed here, and Beasdale would be lonely."

"That is one of the reasons I love you so, because you are always thinking of others, even my uncle."

"How can I not be generous, when all my wishes have come true, except for one?"

"Which one is that? I'll speak to my uncle. My dowry . . ."

He touched a finger to her lips that were rosy from his kisses. "No, there is nothing money can purchase. What I really wanted, what I kept wishing, was that I were worthy of your love." He gave a rueful chuckle. "Nothing ever happened."

"Of course not, my foolish love. For you always were worthy. You always will be, good luck or bad, for the rest of our lives. I only wish we live long enough to see our children's children grow up."

And they did, and gave each one a lucky coin at Christmas.

Following Yonder Star

———◆———

by Emma Jensen

Portsmouth, 10 December, 1807

Dear Alice,

Forgive my tardiness in replying to your most recent letter. I have little excuse other than to say I had not imagined the preparations that would be necessary for my ship's departure. My mind and time have been wholly occupied with a beckoning sea.

No, Alice, that is not entirely true, and we have always been so open, so honest, you and I. Near ten years of acquaintance and affection has made lying to you an unpleasant, perhaps impossible act. I shall not begin now. I have a greater excuse for not writing. I have been for these weeks debating how to reply. Your letters have been so cheerful, so informative of the happenings in our little corner of Kildare. You succeed so well at bringing me right into Mrs. Logan's parlor, full of lace doilies and invasive cat hair, into your grandfather's study and its smell of gunpowder. Such news as the safe delivery of a fine colt to David Doon's prize mare and a finer boy to his wife on the very same day made me smile, and I do agree that David's celebrating was probably equally divided between the two new lives.

I digress here. I could happily recount all the news you've written to me, anything to keep from having to say what needs to be said. I sail out within the sennight for the Mediterranean and points beyond. I will serve in His Majesty's navy until such time as I am no longer needed. After that, only God knows. With luck, I will see the world. There is no need at all for me in Kilcullen. Arthur will *succeed our father someday; he will marry and have a son and I will be one more fortunate step from the title and its responsibilities.*

I wish my departure could have been different. No doubt I should wish that I could be different. I cannot. Our characters are formed long before we have the will or ability to forge them. Forgive me, Alice. I will not be returning to Kilcannon for the holidays. I do not know when or if I will return at all.

Yours ever,
Gareth

1

*A*lice Ashe, like the tree from which some diminutive and distant ancestor had taken his surname, had grown up to be flexible. At the moment, she was crouched atop a ladder in the corner of the drawing room, one hand gripping the plaster ivy garland that ringed the molding, the other a garland of very real, very prickly holly.

She had suggested that perhaps this was a task for one of the house's very able footmen. The suggestion, sensible as it was, had not been well received.

"Honestly, Alice," Lady Kilcullen had scolded from her spot on the overstuffed sofa, "there are simply some matters one cannot leave to the servants."

Decorating massive Kilcullen House for the coming holidays was apparently one of those matters. And Alice did not mind, or wouldn't have, if she'd had the time to spare. But there were a great many matters that Lady Kilcullen did see fit to leave to the servants, including some she quite probably should not. Alice was now responsible for the bookkeeping, the stores, and the staff itself. She had joined the household on the assumption that she would be seeing to the needs of its lady. Half a year later, she was running the house.

She tried not to think of the dozen or so duties yet to be

done that day as she fumbled with the holly. "Higher," Lady Kilcullen commanded from below. Alice sighed, ignored yet another holly prickle in her thumb, and raised the garland.

She was doing her very best to regard her companion with peace and goodwill. After all, the Dowager Countess of Kilcullen had been widowed a mere six months. Always pampered, accustomed to a great deal of attention and little exertion, Clarissa Kilcullen was oppressed by mourning, depressed by solitude. This would be her first Christmas not only without her husband, but without the heady round of festivities that rang out the Irish year.

She was also expecting her first child by Twelfth Night. The very social, very vain Lady Kilcullen would be spending the jolliest days of the year confined to her sofa, balancing her cups of tea and eggnog on her very round belly.

Alice secured the last spray of berries to the garland and climbed down from her perch. She'd spent the better part of the day up and down ladders, in and out of various niches and alcoves. Preparations for an Irish Christmas began early, could easily fill every day in December, and really didn't end until January. As much as Alice loved the season, she found herself mentally ticking off each day until this one would be over. She was tired. She needed tea, a long, luxurious bath, and several days on an overstuffed sofa with a good book.

She would settle for the tea. Between the holidays and the impending birth, there was too much left to be done for her to grow lazy now. And besides, Lady Kilcullen had taken up residence on the best seat in the house at the beginning of the month. She showed no signs of vacating it in the immediate future. Alice chose a hard-backed chair nearby.

"You look terrible, dearest," Lady Kilcullen commented. With neither relish nor malice, Alice knew, but it wasn't a pleasant sentiment, for all its honesty.

Garbed all in dull black, heavy with child, the countess was still easily the loveliest creature in Kildare. She always had been. Tiny, slender, flaxen-haired, ivory-skinned. A fey fairy in a land where fairies were revered. True, she wasn't precisely slender at the moment, but pregnancy had brought a glow to her skin, a brightness to her already startlingly blue eyes. And there was little doubt that she would be back to form within weeks of the birth. She'd decreed as much. And what Clarissa Kilcullen wanted, she got. Always. Had Alice not loved her completely, she might have loathed her utterly.

But no, that wasn't in Alice's character. From the moment she had first seen Clarissa, mere hours old in their mother's arms, she'd loved her in the way only sisters can. Despite the immediate bossiness, the tantrums, the sometimes comical refusal to use what was a perfectly good head. From infancy, Clarissa had needed only to rely on her beautiful face.

"Rouge," she went on wistfully. Clarissa needed such cosmetics as rouge like a duck needed a rudder, but she'd always loved playing with the little pots and bottles. "You need color."

"The window trim could use a coat of paint," Alice said mildly. "I'll see about slapping a bit of it on myself."

Her sister sniffed. "You needn't be *quite* so plain, Alice. If you would but put a bit of effort into the matter, you would be entirely passable. For heaven's sake, just look in a mirror occasionally! You will see how very right I am."

Alice knew precisely how she looked. Small, like all the Kildare Ashes, like her sister. But the resemblance ended there. Alice's hair was an earth brown, with a tendency to curl wildly when left to its own devices, her eyes more the gray of a stormy sky than celestial blue. She had an unremarkable, straight Ashe nose, a wide mouth at its best when smiling, and skin prone to brown in the sun and mottle with emotion.

Alice knew she had been pretty . . . once. But in the shadow of her sister's glory it hadn't really caused much notice. And in the last eight years had faded enough to be more or less forgotten.

She used the looking glass to make sure her clothing was neat and her hair wasn't too wild. Even if she'd had the inclination to gaze longer at her reflection, she really didn't have the time.

The mantel clock chimed four times. "How the days do drag," Clarissa sighed. Alice sympathized. Between mourning and her advanced state of pregnancy, Clarissa was forced to endure long days without either paying visits or receiving them. True, their cousins paid the occasional call, as did the vicar's wife. But both were endlessly dour, both invariably were looking for money in one form or another, which annoyed Alice to no end. And despite the toadying and flattery that went with such visits, Clarissa was always happy to see the end of them, too.

The cousins, she commented, came to gloat over her rotund form. Mrs. DeVere came to gulp the expensive tea and devour the fine cakes, neither of which were to be found at the vicarage. Then she would launch into the need for new stained glass, new altar cloths. *New prayer books, for heaven's sake! Can you countenance it, Alice. Why on earth should I fund new prayer books when I have never read the old ones!*

At the moment Clarissa was staring glumly at the copy of the novel *Emma*. It had been a present from Alice the year before. Sheer desperation had made Clarissa take it from the shelf in the last weeks. Perhaps in another year, Alice thought, she might actually open the cover.

Clarissa brightened. "I know. We'll have a game of cassino! Fetch the cards and play with me, Alice."

Play with me, Alice. Help me dress my doll. Push me in the swing, Alice. Alice had been dressing dolls and pushing swings for the last twenty-three years. The most recent demand for a push had been the week before, despite a thin sheen of frost on the wooden seat. Clarissa's advanced state of pregnancy had ultimately put an end to the request, but not without a few sighs and pouts. And there would be a new little creature to dress soon enough. Alice smiled with that thought. Then shook her head sternly.

"I cannot. The linen should be sorted today for laundering." Kilcullen House, with its fourteen bedrooms and countless cupboards, had a rather impressive collection of linens. "There are gift baskets to be filled for the tenants. And Cook needs to discuss the menus for the holidays. I've more than a full plate." Alice gave her sister an even stare. "Unless, of course, you'd care to take on one of the tasks."

"Don't be silly!" Clarissa waved a delicate hand over her belly. "How could I possibly?"

"Of course." Alice smiled wryly as she rose to her feet. True, the day-to-day managing of a house would be difficult for a woman in her sister's present state. Which did not explain the previous twenty-three years of helplessness, but was a tidy excuse now. "Here." She lifted a half-completed chair cover from the floor where Clarissa had tossed it. "If you're diligent, you might have the set complete by the time the child departs for a grand tour . . . or sets up her own household."

Alice nearly dropped the frame when Clarissa seized her wrist. "Oh, Alice, it must be a girl! It must. I could not bear . . . I cannot stay . . ."

It was a familiar refrain, becoming more so as the birth approached. "Clarie." Alice gently pulled her arm free, clasped her sister's hand in hers. "Of course a girl would be lovely. Just like you, all gold and cream. But just think: a little boy, a solid little fellow with a rolling bear on a string behind him. A boy like Arthur—"

"To tie me to this place! I could not bear it, Alice. I cannot bear another year. If I'd known—"

"Hush, dearest. You'll only upset yourself."

Alice squeezed Clarissa's hand in understanding. Losing Arthur at Waterloo had been hard for her sister, but not perhaps for the expected reasons. Not that the marriage had been a bad one. The earl had been kind, if a bit dull and distant. Certainly distant. During the three years of his marriage he'd never been home for more than a fortnight or maybe two, at the most. He'd been compelled by his duty to his country and joined His Majesty's army. He'd done his duty to his title and estate, marrying the beautiful, well-born neighbor and getting her with child on one of his leaves from his regiment. Then he'd made her a widow—a widow who'd done her best, really, to mourn a man she hadn't quite known.

The Ashe girls had been acquainted with Arthur and his family since arriving in the neighborhood nearly twenty years earlier. No one had expected Clarissa to marry the young earl, no matter how beautiful she was, no matter how wealthy and eligible he was. Their characters had been so very different; their paths had so rarely crossed once he'd gone off to school. But eventually Arthur had come home to Kilcullen, Clarissa had decided that his title and fortune—and posh London town house—would suit her perfectly.

Perhaps had Arthur lived, there would have been travel, seasons in London, life away from calm, provincial Kildare. But life had a way of dealing the hand least expected. Alice, who had grown up to be flexible and who had been dealt one particularly dream-shattering hand herself, was philosophical on the matter. Clarissa, accustomed to getting precisely what she desired, was not. A boy child, she alternately sighed and ranted, would tie her to Kilcullen. A girl would not.

Alice refrained from commenting that this was a blessed event in a joyous time of year and perhaps should be approached with a tad less self-interest. And she would never, ever be so small as to retort that at least Clarissa would *have* a child, whatever the sex.

"There's nothing we can do about the matter now," she announced, as usual half soothing, half matter-of-fact. "Worries are for later. I believe . . . yes, a pot of chocolate is for now. And a game of cassino. When," she added sternly at her sister's happier squeak, "I have seen to the linens."

She rang the bell, requesting chocolate and a sweet from the maid who answered. A visibly cheered Clarissa even poked her needle a few times into the chair cover. But as Alice reached for the door, she announced, "You mustn't stop me every time I speak on it, you know. I do wish everything had been different. And I'm allowed to make any wish I like, Alice."

"Of course you are, love. Of course."

Alice closed the door behind her and, just for a moment, leaned her back against it. She, too, had spent so many joyless hours wishing everything to change, to go back to the way it had been. But such wishes were futile and eight years was a long time. Ample time to forget—and adapt.

She never would have imagined herself at nearly seven and twenty to be living, as she was, in this house. Not as she was: a reluctant housekeeper to the house's reluctant mistress. But when Arthur had died, leaving his helpless young wife to wait out her pregnancy in the huge, empty house, it had seemed the most natural thing in the world for the elder sister to move into Kilcullen House and take command. *Well, of course Alice will go,* friends and neighbors declared, never so much as considering otherwise. *Unmarried, almost certainly never to be so. Alice is such an adaptable girl. She'll bend to the task. Besides, what else has she to do?*

What else, indeed? She had nowhere else to be, no one else to answer to. Just Clarissa, and their grandfather. She had been running their little household as long as she could remember. It had seemed the most natural thing in the world—or so she reminded herself in such moments as these—to pack a few dresses into a valise and travel the half mile to the great house.

Their grandfather had been happy enough with the situation; he'd been great friends with Arthur's father and had spent countless happy hours on the estate. Now he had the vast acreage, well-stocked library, and even better-stocked wine cellars essentially to himself. "A bit of a holiday," he'd chortled when Alice suggested the temporary rearrangement. "Now, where did I put my gun case?"

And so they'd come, satchels in hand, to await the coming of Clarissa's baby. Such a joyous event, new life in the dead of winter, the late Earl of Kilcullen's lasting mark on the world. Alice was busy. She was needed. Perhaps a bit too much so. But after all, what else had she to do?

She had sheets to count.

Sighing, she levered herself away from the door. She had far better things to do than feel sorry for herself. It occurred to her that she ought to find her grandfather. He'd been distracted at luncheon and she hadn't seen him since. But then, it had been raining steadily for the last several hours. Chances were he was tucked up happily somewhere with a book. She would send a maid to find him.

It was an hour later when Sorcha, the youngest among the house's downstairs staff, appeared. Alice, kneeling amid several towering piles of table linen, promptly lost count of the napkins when the girl announced, "I'm sorry, miss, but I can't find Sir Reginald anywhere."

Alice felt a familiar sinking sensation in her belly. "And the study case?"

"Opened, miss."

Apparently she hadn't hidden the key quite well enough. "Don't fret, Sorcha. Someone will bring him home. Someone always does." True enough. And she would worry when she had to, not before.

"There is good news, though, miss. There's a caravan coming up the drive. The travelers are here."

"Early this year." Alice got to her feet. "Go tell Lady Kilcullen, then alert the staff."

The maid hurried out. When Alice entered the foyer a few minutes later, most of the servants were already spilling onto the drive, eyes bright and coins jingling in their pockets. Clarissa waddled into view, cheeks pink above a pink Kashmir wrap. "Well, hurry and put something on, Alice! It won't do to keep them waiting!"

Alice found her own serviceable wool cloak and followed the crowd out the door. The household, Clarissa included, was gathered around a battered wagon that was tented with colorful panels of canvas. Just visible among the throng was the Gypsy family: father with a bright kerchief on his head and a gold hoop glinting in one ear; stunning, black-eyed mother in a crimson shawl; several children in worn wool. It was a hard life the travelers led, Alice knew. Never resting for long, driven out of fields and towns far more often than they were welcomed. But at Christmas it was different. In Ireland at Christmas, one opened one's kitchens and pockets for the Gypsy families.

She watched the transactions. There were amulets and charms: horseshoes and Bridget's crosses woven from rushes, little velvet bags filled with herbs and mysterious stones. She watched as one maid bartered over an ointment meant to remove freckles. Another purchased a poppet filled with clove and sage, meant to bring love. Nearby, the groom on whom she had her heart set was having a hushed discussion with the father. Alice rather suspected there was something naughty in the pouch that changed hands.

She waited until the staff had made their choices before stepping forward. Clarissa was sorting among a collection of fragrant sachets, prettily sewn with lace and ribbon. Alice eyed the holiday wreaths. She could have made any of them herself, but buying from the travelers was a tradition she intended to keep. She was just reaching for a wide circlet of holly berries when a hand closed tightly around her wrist.

The woman it belonged to was even tinier than Clarissa, with silver-white hair and a face like a walnut. In the midst of the wrinkles was a pair of the sharpest, blackest eyes Alice had even seen.

"'Tis the time of year for charity," she informed Alice tartly, her voice an odd if appealing combination of country Irish and distant Continent. Alice promptly reached into her pocket for her money pouch. The old woman cackled cheerfully. "Nay, nay, I'm not meaning that, though you'll make a good choice with the wreath."

She tugged at Alice's arm, pulling her closer. "Heed me well, *cailín*. Search your heart for kindness. 'Twill be needed as the holy days come."

"Oh, Alice, is she telling your fortune?" Clarissa shoved an armload of pretty fripperies into Alice's arms. "I haven't so much as a penny with me. How careless. But you'll take care of it, won't you?" To the old woman, she announced, "You'll tell my fortune, too. Alice will pay you."

The woman gave Clarissa a quick glance. "You want me to tell you whether 'tis a boy or girl you carry."

"There! Isn't she clever, Alice! She knew precisely what I wished to hear. Oh, I do so love magic!"

Alice had every respect for the traveling fortune tellers. They were clever, indeed. One had to be to understand precisely what each listener should hear. She did not, however, think there was any magic whatsoever involved.

"Well?" Clarissa demanded. "Which is it to be?"

The old woman closed her eyes for a moment, then replied, "As much as you wish for one outcome, another wishes the opposite. Who has the most to lose will be the one to gain." She smiled beatifically and folded her hands at her waist.

Clarissa blinked. "*That* is all you have to say? That cannot be right. You meant to say *girl*. Just that."

"I see what I see. I can't be doing more just to please you."

Clarissa blew out a dismissive breath. Alice, however, was impressed. Of course there was no trick to the prophecy. There was always divided opinion over a baby's sex, after all. But the rest really was clever. If Clarissa bothered to think on the matter, she would certainly decide that she had the most to lose by producing a boy. Hence, she would get her girl, and would pass the remaining weeks of her pregnancy contented and pleased with the prediction.

To Alice's surprise, the Gypsy waved away the coins she

offered. "I'll take nothing for my words." The younger traveler, however, was happy to accept payment for Clarissa's
baubles and Alice's wreath. As soon as the last transactions
were complete, the family would drive their caravan 'round
back and the staff would welcome them into the kitchens. As
the sisters turned to go, the older woman called, "Remember, find charity in your heart, *cailín*. You're the bending
sort, but you've wild winds blowing your way!"

Alice smiled. Wild winds, indeed. Heaven only knew
what the house would be like once Clarissa's child chose to
arrive.

"Fate sets us on our paths, *cailín*, before we've the way
of guiding our feet. Change what you can; accept the rest!"

Alice stopped in her tracks. But when she turned, the old
woman had disappeared into the wagon. Clarissa prodded
her in the arm. "Do move *your* feet, Alice! I'm cold and ever
so hungry. Do you suppose Cook has made an apple tart? I
do so want my daughter to have rosy cheeks . . ." Apparently, she had already found her message in the gypsy's
words.

Alice carried the woman's message to her through the
rest of the evening, through dinner where Clarissa prattled
away about dolls and dresses and their grandfather made no
appearance, through an hour of cassino and another hour of
reading *Emma* aloud, waiting for Clarissa to go to bed.

Fate sets us on our paths, cailín, *before we've the way of
guiding our feet.*

*Our characters are formed long before we have the will
or ability to forge them.*

But no, it was mere coincidence that the words were so
similar. And only the time of year making her think of that
letter. She hadn't thought of it in ages and ages. Since last
Christmas, surely . . .

The pounding of the front door knocker made her jump
in her seat. She set aside the menus she hadn't quite been pe-
rusing and hurried into the hall. *About time, Grandfather,*
she scolded silently. He would grumble at his escort, who-

ever it might be this time, scowl at her, and demand something to eat. It would be the end of just another day in Kilcullen.

But it wasn't her diminutive grandfather standing framed in the stone doorway. And Alice knew, as she stumbled to a halt a dozen steps from the tall figure in the dark, caped coat, that there would be no more predictable days at Kilcullen. More than that, her deepest, most fervent wish had been answered. Eight years too late.

"Alice." The voice was the same: deep, rough, created by some mischievous angel to set women's hearts thumping. And thump went Alice's heart.

The face was the same, too, if harder. The same broad forehead and sea green eyes beneath a sleek sweep of night-dark hair, the same Roman nose and wide mouth. Unsmiling. He'd smiled so often, so easily in his youth.

"Gareth," she whispered. Then, lifting her chin to meet his eyes, "I beg your pardon. Mr. Blackwell."

They stood facing each other for a long moment. Then he smiled, finally. And it chilled her.

"I suppose that's all the welcome I can expect." He shrugged and stepped into the hall. "Well, here I am, Alice, home to await the blessed event." He glanced around the foyer that had heard the patter of his first steps, the eager skipping of childhood, the impatient ring of a young man's boot heels. "I trust there is plenty of whiskey around to get me through the anticipation."

2

*G*areth Blackwell had managed to stay away from home for eight years. At that moment—for every moment, actually, since hearing of his brother's demise—he would gladly have given everything he possessed to make it nine.

Alice.

Perhaps he should have been surprised to find her there, but very little surprised him anymore. *Alice.* She had changed. Of course she had. This was a woman of twenty-six rather than a girl of eighteen. It was the same little form, the same little face: heart-shaped and so very pretty, surrounded by the same wild brown curls. But utterly different, somehow. It was, he decided, as if the girl he remembered in sunlight had stepped into the shade.

That was it. In the past, her face had lit each time she had seen him. It had, he realized now, made him feel ten feet tall. This Alice was regarding him with no expression whatsoever.

He waited for her to speak. Alice, his Alice, had never been one for silence. She'd been inclined toward strong opinions, fond teasing, the occasional blast of temper. Which, no doubt, was what he was in for now. She would think he deserved it. And while he might have mixed feelings on the matter, he was prepared to let her rant. It was the quickest way into the house and toward the whiskey. He waited. She blinked. Then, "I'll go see to having a room prepared for you, sir. We did not anticipate your arrival." With that, she turned her narrow little back on him and walked away.

She was nearly at the door to the back hall when he found his voice. "Alice!"

She stopped, faced him. "Yes?"

"I am not . . . I am . . . Well, hell." He couldn't be sure what he was. It was a new sensation, and not a pleasant one.

Whatever else he might have found to say to her was stalled by a cry from the stairs.

"Gareth!"

He blinked at the vision trundling toward him across the floor. The last time he had seen Clarissa Ashe, she'd been fifteen, unusually beautiful, and so slight that a goat sneeze would have blown her over. Now, at twenty-three, she was just as lovely, but she looked as if she'd swallowed the goat.

"Gareth," she said again, hands extended. "You've come. I'm so glad."

"Clarissa. I'm so sorry, you know. I would have come sooner—"

"Yes, yes, of course. I did so hope you would be at my wedding, but Arthur didn't mind overmuch, so I forgave you."

Before he could reply, she rushed on, "We have missed you. At your dear father's funeral . . ."

He'd been in the Indies then, recently sold out of the navy, wealthy and comfortable with the sun and spiced rum. By the time news of his father's demise had reached him, it was winter and traveling had seemed an unnecessary exertion. He'd sent a letter to Arthur.

"And now, with Arthur gone . . ."

Greece. A little island full of olive trees and cool taverns. Ouzo and lush, black-eyed barmaids. He almost hadn't come home. He'd mourned the brother he'd never really known with dry eyes and several bottles of wine. He'd tossed a handful of coins into a fountain, promising the stone Dionysus there half of his fortune if he would put in a good word with the rest of the gods about Arthur's unborn child. Then he'd booked passage. To Turkey.

He had taken four months to return to Ireland.

"Well, now you're here, and won't we be a merry party this Christmas!" He realized Clarissa had been prattling the whole time. "Counting the days, of course." She tugged on his hands, drawing him nearer. "And we must remember, you and I, to make the same wish on Christmas Eve."

"And that is . . . ?"

"Why, for a girl, silly! That would quite settle things for both of us, would it not? You shall have the title, I shall be free to do as I please. Quite settled. Now, I've been trying to persuade Alice to play with me all day, but she simply will insist on doing the dullest chores. Backgammon, Gareth? Or perhaps piquet? I would be more than happy to wager."

From the corner of his eye, he could see Alice quietly talking to a maid. Completely ignoring him.

"A wager!" he announced loudly and saw her jump. "But not on a game."

"No?" Clarissa clapped her hands eagerly. "On . . . ?"

"On the outcome of your blessed event. If it is a girl, I forfeit; if a boy, you do. Now, my dear, what do you wish for?"

Without a second's hesitation, Clarissa announced, "I should like a strand of pink pearls. Not to speak ill of your mother, Gareth, but she was rather selfish when it came to her jewels. She took the very best pieces with her and the Kilcullen pearls are not at all to my taste."

Yes, he agreed, his mother had been rather selfish. Always. And especially with her time. She'd had very little to spare for her sons. As for the jewels, she'd purchased a great many during his father's lifetime. She'd had every right to take them with her when she remarried, a year almost to the day after the earl's death. Her new husband was an age-old friend of her first, without a title, but with a fortune and estate in the neighboring county. Gareth had a very good idea that the attachment had predated the wedding by more than a few years. His mother, after all, had been a great one for seeing to her own pleasures.

"Pearls it is," he agreed.

"And should I lose?"

"Should you lose, I claim Arthur's gun collection as your forfeit."

Clarissa blinked at him. "But you have always loathed hunting."

"True." Being forced by one's sire to shoot small furry creatures at the age of seven could do that to a boy. "As a matter of fact, I should like to have a selection should I ever choose to dispatch myself."

"Oh, Gareth, how you jest!"

Perhaps, he thought, but one never knew what the prospect of a lifetime tied to the estate would do to his sanity. He forced a smile. "Just look at it this way, madam. You win either way. Arthur's guns are no loss to you."

She laughed, but then sobered quickly. "Oh, no! You must ask for something more dear than that. You must!"

"Why?"

"Because," she said earnestly, "I must be the one with the most to lose. The old Gypsy said so!"

Before he could begin to make sense of that pronouncement, there was a clatter of hooves on the stones outside. Even through the heavy wooden door, Gareth could hear the lurid stream of curses. He knew that voice.

A footman hurried to open the door. The scene there was enough to raise Gareth's brows. Two young men, farmers by their clothing, both with the height and girth of the average ox, were carrying a much smaller man up the stairs. Each had a meaty fist around one of his upper arms and were supporting him effortlessly, his feet dangling a good foot above the floor. He was cursing with enough force and creativity to put a seasoned sailor to shame.

"Grandfather!" Alice had slipped forward and was facing her muttering grandsire, hands planted on her hips. "You promised!"

Unlike his granddaughters, Sir Reginald Ashe hadn't changed at all. He was just as elfin, just as hale and hoary as he'd been the day Gareth left. Garbed, much as always, in ancient leather jerkin and buckled knee breeches, he had one hand wrapped tightly around a wooden box, the other waving an ineffectual fist at his escorts.

"I did nothing of the sort, girl! And I'll say again, let go of me, you hairy behemoths!"

"Just helping you in, sir," the young man holding his right arm replied jovially. He and his companion lowered their burden to the floor and let go. Sir Reginald stomped into the foyer with a huff. He stopped in front of Alice and glared at her from beneath shrubby brows.

"You're breaking my heart, you are," he muttered.

Alice sighed. "That is hardly my intention, Grandfather."

"Hmph." He turned his glare to Clarissa. "Get off your feet," he commanded.

"Yes, Grandfather." She kissed his cheek and chided, "You did promise." Then, "Look who's come home."

The old man looked at Gareth for the first time. "About time," he grumbled. "Your grandda would have taken a birch stick to you right sharpish, you know."

Gareth nodded. "Very likely, sir."

Sir Reginald huffed. "Should probably do it myself." He appeared to be gauging the six inches and four stone Gareth had on him. Not to mention the fifty years. "Can't be bothered tonight. Remind me tomorrow." With that, he stalked creakily toward the stairs, box still gripped tightly to his chest.

"Grandfather," Alice called after him. "Your dinner—"

"Send up a tray! And none of that warm milk rubbish. I'll have a bottle of claret."

When he'd disappeared into the gallery, Alice turned to the right-hand ox. "Where did you find him?"

"My west field. Knee deep in mud."

"And Mr. O'Neill?"

"Danny Leary's seeing him home. No harm done."

Alice nodded. "Well, thank you, Mr. Sullivan. I . . . we are so very grateful. Will you come in for a glass of something?"

The ox shook his head. "Best not. The missus will be waiting up for me." The grin he'd clearly been working hard to suppress spread across his face. "He's determined, he is, Miss Ashe. Nearly curled my ears, cursing at me."

"Yes, I am sorry—"

"Ah, now, don't you be apologizing. No blood shed and 'twas as lively a night as I've seen this fortnight and more. Eh, Finn?" His companion grinned and nodded. Sullivan bowed awkwardly. "We'll be off then. M'lady. Miss Ashe." And, belatedly, to Gareth. "Sir. 'Tis a grand thing to see you've come home." Then, still chuckling faintly, he left.

Gareth had no idea what had just transpired, but he was weary enough from travel and homecoming not to care. Besides, the man's parting had been as pleasant as Clarissa's welcome. The number of people glad to see him home had just equaled the contrary, even if one was a stranger . . .

"Was *that* Tommy Sullivan? That behemoth? But he can't be more than sixteen . . ."

"More like twenty-four," Alice said coolly.

"Good God. Amazing what happens when a fellow leaves home."

"Isn't it? Years pass, families alter, boys grow to men . . ."

He searched her face for anger. All he saw was cool calm. "Alice . . ." He wasn't certain what he was meant to say, but decided best to get it out of the way. He had a whiskey decanter nearly in his sights. "Perhaps we—"

"If you will excuse me, sir. I leave you in the lady of the house's capable hands." Alice kissed her sister, kissed one of her own fingertips and brushed it over Clarissa's bump, then headed for the stairs. She paused at the first step. "If you are hungry, I will arrange to have a tray sent up to your room."

"No," he replied, a bit sullenly even to his own ears. "Thank you."

"As you wish. Good night, then. Breakfast is at eight. We don't keep town hours here." With that, she turned her back and disappeared up the stairs.

Well, he mused, what had he expected? A feast featuring a fatted calf? Open arms and starry smiles. Perhaps he had, he conceded. Or perhaps he'd known better all along.

He turned to find Clarissa studying him. Or, rather, surveying his attire, her pert nose wrinkled in obvious distaste. Perhaps his coat and breeches were a bit the worse for wear, but it had been a long day in the saddle, after several interminable weeks of travel. Seeing her in stark black, with that disconcerting bulge at her middle tugged at his conscience, though damned if he knew why. He'd come, hadn't he?

"Perhaps you ought to take your grandfather's advice and . . . er . . . sit down."

She smiled. "I think I will retire, actually. I haven't my usual liveliness of late. You will be here in the morning, won't you?"

"Of course." For the moment, at least, he had nowhere to go.

"Good. Sleep well, Gareth. I *am* glad you've come home." She dimpled at him and he smiled back. "Alice is wonderful, to be sure, but she is not the most diverting creature. You are certain to amuse me endlessly." Then she, too, was gone, leaving Gareth standing alone in the middle of the cold foyer.

"*Welcome,* and be damned," he muttered aloud, startling the maid who had appeared from the back hall.

He promptly sent her off to find him a bottle of whiskey, then followed her upstairs. She led him to the room he had occupied until he'd left home. It was just as elegant as he remembered, reasonably comfortable, and completely devoid of anything personal. He wondered what had happened to his possessions: his models of ships, his books, the special globe that opened to show a map of the heavens painted inside.

Weary, but knowing he wouldn't sleep, he crossed the

room and drew back the curtains. The sky was still heavy, opaque from the day's rain. But he knew what he would see had it been clear. The constellations: Draco, Perseus, Cassiopeia, the two Bears. And their stars, the names as mysterious and exotic as the lands he had eventually followed them to: Arcturus, Miram, Betelgeuse, Alula Borealis. And of course Polaris, the North Star. The star of sailors and explorers and long-departed wanderers. He had followed Polaris, in a way, as he'd come from Greece. Westward leading Polaris, guiding him back to a place where he had never really belonged and had no desire to be now.

Bottle in hand, careful not to spill any of its precious contents, he dropped back onto the bed and stared at the canopy. God help him if Clarissa's child was a girl. If it was, the best case scenario was that he would forget thirty years of stargazing and take to howling at the moon.

Down the hall, Alice turned away from her own window. She drew her dressing gown more tightly around her. She was cold, despite the fire still burning merrily in the grate. She'd been standing by the icy window for too long, looking at the blank sky. *Perseus, Cassiopeia, Andromeda.* How many nights had she and Gareth stood under the stars, naming them, trying to outdo each other at recounting the myths connected to the constellations—the more dramatic and bloody and lovelorn the better. She had cherished every minute.

Alice had adored Gareth Blackwell from the first time she saw him, striding into his mother's drawing room with all the brash confidence of his twelve years, whistling and trailing mud in his wake. He'd been so beautiful, so totally unconcerned with his mother's pinch-lipped annoyance. Alice, eight years old, newly orphaned and handed into her grandfather's loving if inept care, had been dazzled.

Perhaps it was that he was the younger son, second in everyone's attention to his brother. Left behind when Arthur went to Eton, left in general to the care of indifferent tutors and fond but unchallenging servants. Perhaps he had genuinely liked her. Either way, he had cheerfully accepted her adoration, allowed her to tag after him whenever they met, eventually become her dearest friend. She had adored him from the first time they met. She had fallen head over heels in love with him six years later.

It had taken a further two years, two years of her wishing upon daisies and dandelions and stars. Two years of walks in Kilcullen woods and nights watching the skies, of the neighborhood winking and smiling and whispering *young love*. But at last he'd kissed her. Once. Days before he left. Her last view of Gareth until tonight had been of him racing toward Dublin and beyond on his father's best horse, his laughter trailing in his wake.

Alice had had eight years to plan for this. Eight Christmases from the first, the first he didn't come home. It had taken her two to accept he wasn't coming back to her, three more to stop longing. But she *had* stopped longing. She'd had to. The alternative, that of years spent yearning for him, heartsick, had been too much for her practical head. So she had tried to forget how sweet her dreams had been, and when she couldn't forget, tried to remember with the fond detachment of adulthood.

And how very successful she had been. When sporadic news came of him, she listened attentively but without emotion. She expressed her pleasure at his success in the navy, was relieved when he sold out without having been wounded, followed his sporadic missives to his family as he wandered the world.

And eventually, no one looked at her with pity when his name was mentioned. People stopped commenting on the irony of the elder Blackwell boy marrying the younger Ashe girl, when their siblings had been the ones expected to wed someday.

No promises, she'd reminded herself again and again, until her heart stopped aching. They had made no promises to each other. They had spent one heady month, hand in hand as they walked. Kissed once, tentatively, under the ash boughs. Or rather, Alice amended now, *she* had been shy and tentative. Gareth had been much as he ever was: strong, assertive, that current of impatience roiling just beneath his surface.

Now Alice stopped halfway between the window and her bed. She tilted the dressing-table mirror until she could see herself, a bit shadowed in the firelight, but clear enough. She reached out one hand, traced the reflection of her cheek with a fingertip. She wondered if he thought her very changed. Of course he did. She was changed. *My lovely elf,* he'd called her as he'd kissed her cheeks, her eyelids, her lips. Then, more gruffly, *Run home now, elf. This is no place for the likes of you.* Or, Alice thought might have been unspoken, for the likes of him.

Perhaps while he was holding her he'd already really been gone, his insatiable mind out in the world. Perhaps there had been no future in his kiss after all, only a goodbye.

And now it didn't matter. Tipping the mirror away again, Alice slipped out of her dressing gown and into bed. She needed to sleep. There was so much to do to prepare for Christmas, for the baby. Gareth would stay until the birth, until he knew whether he would be the Earl of Kilcullen or remain the Honorable Gareth Blackwell. Either way, he would probably be gone again within a sennight.

Remember, find charity in your heart, cailín.

Forgive me, Alice.

Our characters are formed long before we have the will or ability to forge them.

Well, that was it, then. She was the pliant, reliable Alice Ashe; he was the wild, roving Gareth Blackwell. He had come home and she was going to be as welcoming as she could be. Even if she went mad in the process.

3

*I*t was past ten when Gareth wandered downstairs the following morning. He remembered Alice's stern announcement regarding breakfast, but was hopeful nonetheless. Damned if he knew why, but Ireland made him hungry. He wanted something to eat. Then he intended to find Alice.

The sunny east parlor where his mother had always breakfasted was empty. So was the small family dining room. As he wandered through the downstairs rooms, Gareth tried to conjure up happy memories. He must have run through the portrait hall, clattering a stick along the panels, ridden a hobby-horse through the drawing room's sliding doors and into the music room. Odd. All he could recall was *leaving* the house: skidding along the marble foyer floor before launching himself down the front stairs, rattling the glass panes in the library's French door in his impatience to get to the lawns that sloped away from the house. Climbing the ivy outside his window. Up to the roof to see the stars. Down to the gardens to meet Alice.

The sun had been shining the day he left, a summer sun in the middle of autumn, sparking quartz lights in the drive's gravel. He'd spurred his horse into a canter, a full gallop as they passed under the canopy of ancient elms lining the exit from the estate. He'd had London in mind. He hadn't looked back.

From the drawing room, Gareth stalked into the foyer. The front door was open; a stream of servants bustled in and out, carrying holly and pine boughs. Gareth breathed in the scent of Christmas and crisp December air. Footmen bowed and swept out of his way as he approached the door. He stopped on the stone steps. He had arrived in the dark. Now, in the morning, the gravel drive stretched out before him, a wide, bright ribbon arcing away toward Kilcullen village. Dublin would be beyond that, London beyond that. One step would take him out the door, a few more to turn east . . .

He took another deep breath, then returned to the house. Maybe he would find something to eat in the formal dining room. Arthur had always been a formal creature, had taken absurd pleasure in sitting in their father's massive carved chair at the table. It would have been just like him to have all his meals served on the twenty-foot expanse. Even as a boy, Arthur had taken his future as lord of the manor very seriously. Gareth found himself smiling at the memory of the two of them seated at opposite ends, only their eyes showing above the snowy cloth. It was one of his few child-hood memories where he'd been sitting still. He had even fewer memories of playing with his brother.

Arthur, as the heir, had rarely been home. Ironic, really. It had been Gareth, the spare, not considered important enough to send away to school, who had known the estate best. He'd certainly covered every inch of it on foot or on horseback. He had been desperate for adventure. Ultimately he'd created it: imaginary pirates in the waters of the big pond, highwaymen on the dirt roads, dragons among the old stone circle in the meadow.

He had left home as soon as he possibly could. Or, rather, when he'd come into a small inheritance left to him by his maternal grandmother. It had been just enough to buy him a military commission. His father had had more than enough money, but little interest. He'd brushed off Gareth's requests with vague promises or curt dismissals. *Go shoot something* had been a frequent one.

Gareth was reminded of this as he reached the dining room. One of the earl's favorite trophies was mounted above the fireplace just opposite the door: a massive buck with spreading antlers. The sight of the thing had always made Gareth rather sad. Now, it made him blink. Someone had looped a glittery strand of beads around the buck's neck, draped a garland of holiday greenery over the antlers. The creature looked far more cheerful than it ever had.

Then Gareth stepped fully into the room and found both Alice and an abundance of food. He stopped in his tracks, amazed by the sight. She was in his father's chair, only a pale forehead and halo of curls visible. Covering the table, end to end, was what looked to be the supplies for a crusade. There were several towering stacks of rush baskets, countless piles of rosy apples, endless wrapped hams, mounds of walnuts. As well as what appeared to be every fruitcake in Kildare.

"Good morning," he said.

Startled, Alice bobbled an apple. It bumped to the floor, where it rolled slowly in Gareth's direction. He bent to pick it up, rubbed it on his sleeve, and took a large bite. "Tasty."

She had two rosy spots of color on her cheeks. "Good morning." She ducked her head, hiding the appealing flush as she shuffled several papers. "I hope your rest was comfortable."

So very polite. "It was, thank you." He could do polite, too. "I fear I am interrupting your work." Whatever the hell it was she was doing.

"Mmm." Apparently politeness didn't quite extend to false demurrals. "I am hoping to have the Christmas baskets delivered by next week."

Gareth surveyed the mess as he polished off the rest of the apple. "A new tradition?"

"A very old one, actually, gift baskets at the holidays from the great house. One would almost think you weren't Irish."

"I daresay Ireland herself would have forgotten," he said dryly, then, "I don't recall my mother going to this effort."

"Your mother," Alice replied mildly, "was not an advocate of Irish tradition. The new lady is."

"Bosh. Clarissa couldn't care less. You, on the other hand, have green in your veins." He leaned in, snared another apple. "Tell me, Alice. How long have you been shouldering your sister's duties?"

"I have been *helping* since your brother's death. Clarissa is unable—"

"Clarissa is unwilling. No, no, don't scowl at me. She and I are of a kind. It was Arthur who was the dutiful one. To his king, to his land." To himself, he murmured. "Even if I were so inclined, I wouldn't know where to begin."

"You might begin by not taking food from the mouths of babes."

Gareth paused with the apple halfway to his mouth. "You are jesting."

"Am I?" Alice raised a brow, then waved a sheet of paper. "Let's see. That apple might have been intended for the Perrys. They have three little girls. Or Mary Sullivan had twins in February. Boys. The MacNeils have six children, the Haggertys nine."

"Who on earth are all these people?"

"Kilcullen's tenants, as it happens. *Your* tenants."

He grunted and set the apple down, intact. "Don't start with that, Alice. There will be ample time to prod me into due diligence should the worst come to pass."

"Was I prodding you? Goodness, how uncomfortable that sounds. I shall endeavor not to prod."

Gareth propped one hip against the table. "You know, you are not making this any easier."

She regarded him calmly over a large ham. "I have no idea what you mean."

"Rot. Perhaps I deserve it. No doubt I do. But we were little more than children." He closed his eyes wearily. "God,

Alice. What is it that you want from me? It's been eight years. I am sorry I hurt you—"

"You broke my heart."

Alice watched his mouth open and close soundlessly. Well, if he was startled by her candor, she was even more so. If she had ever been so blunt, she'd lost the habit over the years. Compromise and diplomacy left little room for frankness.

He had broken her heart. It was the only time she'd said the words aloud. And the only time she would.

Our characters are formed long before we have the will or ability to forge them.

He was still staring at her, silent. She could see regret in his eyes, but she knew it wasn't the regret of a man who felt he'd made the wrong choice. He quite probably was sorry he'd hurt her, maybe even more so now that she'd let him know how much. Gareth had never been cruel, merely careless.

"I shouldn't have come home," he muttered finally. "Not like this, anyway. If I'd known—"

"Gareth." Alice leaned forward and, carefully clearing a space, folded her arms on the table. "Of course you came home. It *is* your home. And there is no reason we can't manage to share it, at least for the time being, until matters are settled. Yes, it hurt when you left. But you made me no promises then, and as it happens, I want nothing at all from you. You are not responsible for me; you never were."

He studied her for a moment through narrowed eyes. "When did you take up serenity? You used to be such a feisty little thing."

"I used to be a great many things, I expect, but I don't think feisty was ever one of them." She found herself wondering if he really remembered her as she did him—or whether time and carelessness had wiped memory away. "We *were* young. And cannot be expected to see everything as it was."

"Mmm. You threw a rock at my head once."

"Well, yes, I did that, but only after you'd tipped me into the pond." She'd been eight, he twelve.

"You filled my best boots with water."

"I did, didn't I?" She remembered his face when he'd thrust a foot in. Then he had poured the contents of the second boot over her feet. She knew he had wanted to dump the water over her head, but had refrained. He'd been fifteen, on his way to manhood. "You promised to take me fishing, but went without me."

"You tried to set my horse free."

"I didn't—"

"In the dead of winter."

Yes, she'd done that, too, thinking he was going to join his father's hunting party. She'd been fourteen, he eighteen. He'd yelled for a minute or two, then lifted her easily, plunked her down into a pair of boots several sizes too large for her, and made her come with him to retrieve the horse. Then he had, for the first time, talked to her as adults would, as equals. They had discussed the hunt, how they both abhorred it. She'd told him about her parents, how she still missed them so much it ached. He'd told her of his desire to see the world beyond Ireland. He had talked about stars.

It had taken an hour of plodding through cold, muddy fields side by side for her to fall in love. The horse, of course, had been waiting for them in the warm stable. Gareth, she'd decided, had known it would be.

She smiled now with the bittersweetness of her memories. "I half expected you to climb onto the horse the minute we returned and ride away toward the sea."

Perhaps, she thought, it would be better for all if he got on his horse now and took himself back to wherever he'd been. Gareth was so much more Irish than he thought. The rover, the rambler, with his feet itching for the road, his eyes on the distant horizon. It was, she knew, part of what she'd once loved so about him. How easy it would be to condemn him for it now. How easy and how uncharitable.

"Had you not been with me, I might have."

She hadn't forgotten for a minute how very green his eyes were. She had forgotten how soft they could be.

"Oh. Gareth."

"Well." His gaze dropped to the apple core he still held, then to the crowded table. Alice watched as he strode over to the mantel and dropped the thing into a china vase resting there. Then he pointed upward. "Your handiwork?"

She glanced at the buck. "Yes. I thought he needed . . . some holiday cheer." She thought Gareth might need some, too. He was looking so grim again. Heaven only knew why she was taking it upon herself to cheer him. Or prod him. 'Twas the season . . . "Here." When he turned, she polished an apple on her sleeve and tossed it to him. "Come with me."

"Where?"

"Outside," was all she said as she rose gracefully from her seat.

The ribbon binding her bodice beneath her breasts was emerald green, Gareth noticed as he followed her from the room. The cloak she collected herself was a cheerful red. The combination, with her winter white dress, was charming. And very Alice. She'd always dressed well, with little touches of whimsy. Like the sprig of holly he could now see tucked into her hair as he helped her with her cloak. The top of her head didn't even reach his shoulder and he was tempted, just for a fleeting second, to brush his lips over the glossy curls.

He couldn't remember not feeling protective of Alice. As little as she'd ever needed protection, tiny as she was, he had still wanted to shelter her from the pains of childhood, of adolescence. The very first time he had seen her, a forlorn little figure in his mother's parlor—her first visit, not a month after she'd lost her parents—he'd felt the urge to take care of her. And he'd continued to feel that way, long after she had proven her strength and resilience, through the rocks and the freeing of Cinn the horse and the bossy scoldings.

Then it had changed. So slowly that he hadn't realized it

was happening. He had gone from enjoying their meetings to craving them. He had wanted to hold her hand, not just have it tucked companionably through his arm on occasion. He'd wanted to kiss her. He had wanted to kiss her rather desperately.

But he had held himself in check, hard as it was. Until one night when he was twenty, she sixteen, and he could take it no longer. October. On a brilliantly clear night with stars filling the skies. He had meant to tell her that he was leaving Ireland, if only briefly. Instead he had kissed her. How sweet it had been. Sweet and deep and blood-stirring enough to shock him to the core.

He'd left a week later.

"Gareth?"

"Hmm?" He blinked. Alice, crimson hood up to frame her face becomingly, was waiting in the open doorway.

"Are you coming?"

For an instant he debated refusing. There were so many other things he could do. He could go back upstairs. He could find a good book. He could find a calendar on which to tick off the days before he could leave again . . .

He grabbed his coat and followed her.

She didn't speak as she led him through the west gardens and toward the Kilcullen woods, merely smiling slightly when he demanded again to know where they were going. After a few minutes, Gareth realized he didn't care. He had wanted to walk away from the house from the moment he'd entered it, and here he was—walking away from the house.

"Ah, good morning, Mr. Hennessey!" Alice called.

They had reached the privet hedge. A stooped figure straightened and waved a cheery greeting. "Good morning, Miss Alice!" The man lifted his tweed cap, revealing a bald pate and craggy face that broke into a wide grin. Gareth stopped in his tracks. He had seen that smile a hundred times. Usually shining up at him from the base of a tree he had climbed. And more than once, in his childhood, from the top of a ladder when he'd needed rescuing from a tree far easier to get up than down.

"Hennessey." Suddenly he was grinning, too.

"And I thought ye'd be sure to have forgotten me," the old gardener beamed. "Welcome home, Master Gareth. 'Tis grand and no doubt to see you home again."

"I . . ." He couldn't do it, couldn't say it was grand and no doubt to be home. "Thank you. You are well?"

"Oh, fine, fine. The rheumatism acts up a bit, old bones . . . But you don't want to be hearing about that." The fellow turned his smile to Alice. "A fine morning to be out and about, miss."

"It is indeed. I thought to take Mr. Blackwell with me to find a bit of Christmas."

"Did you now? Well, may you find it. 'Tis out there." He lifted his hoe. "I'd best be getting back to work. Welcome home, sir."

Gareth caught himself whistling as he and Alice descended the slope leading to the woods. It was Hennessey who had taught him how to whistle. Macatee the head groom had taught him the best bawdy tunes. He would have to go in search of Macatee, assuming the man hadn't retired. The navy was the world's best repository for bawdy songs and Gareth thought he might have a few that hadn't reached Kildare.

The path grew slippery suddenly and Gareth saw Alice struggle to keep her footing. He reached out, grasped her arm, and, as if he'd been doing it every day, tucked her hand through the crook of his elbow.

"Thank you," she murmured. Her cheeks, when he glanced down, were pink in the crisp air, her eyes bright. Winter suited her. It always had.

They walked in companionable silence until they entered the woods. In an instant, eight years—more—dropped away. Gareth recognized a spreading oak where he had played Robin Hood as a boy. He heard the quiet flow of the brook where he'd floated leaves, bark, and little boats made for

him by the estate's blacksmith. His own naval fleet. He and
Alice had sat on the mossy bank more than once, having the
sort of discussion only youth can appreciate: too serious for
their age, too earnest for adulthood. He glanced down at her,
wondering if she remembered.

She must have. "Youth is its own excuse."

"As good as any, I suppose. But thank you." He had a
feeling she'd just excused more than adolescent intellectual
blathering. "Now, would you care to tell me why we're
here? To reminisce?"

"No, actually. I thought I would come look for the *bloc
na nollag*."

She hadn't planned on choosing a Christmas log so soon.
Something in his face, however, as he'd faced her over the
dining table, had put the idea in her head. Gareth needed to
be out of the house. That hadn't changed. Beyond that, he
needed to see the estate again. Altogether too soon, it might
be his. Best to start with the good memories, and the woods
were the best place to start.

"There." She pointed to a fallen branch. "How about that
one?"

He guided her over, snorted at her choice. "Too small. It
needs to fill the hall hearth."

"Very well, then. That one."

Too thin, too lumpy, too rotted. They tromped over the
mossy earth, surveying log after log. Any number would
have done, but they had slipped back into the amicable bick-
ering of years past. As Gareth rolled his eyes at yet one more
of her choices, Alice smiled to herself. Then laughed scorn-
fully at his.

Perhaps, she thought, perhaps he would stay. Perhaps.
And perhaps they would be friends again.

"There! *That* is our log." Gareth removed her hand from
his arm, lifted her by both elbows, and swung her to face a
massive, craggy beast of a log. It was nearly as tall as the
fireplace and easily twice as wide. Alice told him so. "We'll
cut it to fit," he announced. "Now tell me it's perfect."

"It's perfect."

Nodding in satisfaction, Gareth drew a handkerchief from his pocket and, with a flourish, spread it over the top of the log. Then he lifted her again and settled her on the makeshift seat. Alice regarded her feet, dangling a good foot from the ground, and laughed.

"I must look like a little girl!"

He stepped back, stared at her. "You look," he said eventually, voice low, "like a wood elf among the greenery."

Her pulse skittered. "Gareth—"

"Yes, yes, I know. You dislike being called an elf."

True, she always had. Until now. And he so obviously hadn't meant anything by it. Certainly hadn't meant to . . . unsettle her. She slid down from her perch and handed him his handkerchief.

"I'll send some boys out to fetch this." She patted the log, then dusted her hands briskly on her skirts. "I should be getting back. There's so much to do. The gift baskets, menus, gifts . . ."

Gareth stared at her for a long moment, then shrugged and tucked the handkerchief back into his pocket. "You've taken on too much, you know."

"It's Christmas. Someone has to manage things."

She hadn't meant to sound as sharp as she did. He'd rattled her. And she, apparently, had just needled him.

"It isn't me, Alice," he said shortly.

"Not yet, perhaps. But the estate, the title—"

"Arthur's. Arthur's baby's. I don't want it. Any of it. I never did."

"I know," she said softly. "But you might not have a choice."

For a moment he looked ready to yell. Then, slowly, his lip uncurled, his shoulders relaxed. "Don't prod me, Alice. And don't try to bolster me into some noble resignation. You'll only be wasting your time and your breath."

"Fine." For a moment *she* wanted to yell. "Fine." She sighed instead and managed a smile. "Shall we go home?"

She thought she heard him mutter something about *home,* but took his advice and neither prodded nor commiserated. She took his arm, warm and corded with muscle beneath her hand, and started back toward the house. In the distance, she could see a farm wagon wending its way toward Kilcullen village.

"Tell me something," Gareth commanded as they went.

"If I can."

"Why was your grandfather in Tommy Sullivan's field last night?"

She had expected him to ask sooner or later. She debated lying, but couldn't see why.

"He was dueling."

"What?"

"Dueling. Or at least pretending. He and Thaddeus O'Neill try to blast at each other at every opportunity."

"Good Lord, why?"

Alice shrugged. "I've never been entirely clear on the matter, but it has something to do with an argument they had. Forty-three years ago. Or was it forty-four?" She smiled at his incredulous expression. "Yes, well, they both consider it an enduring matter of honor." And pleasure, she thought. Both entertaining and serious enough to have them sneaking about like brigands on their illegal ventures.

"For forty-odd years? Good Lord, that seems rather a lot of hatred to carry with you."

"Hatred? Oh, they're very fond of each other. They're also proud, determined, and endlessly foolish."

"Why did I never hear of this?" Gareth demanded.

"You haven't been here. As it happens, for decades, Mr. O'Neill was either in Dublin or Tullamore, so it was just a matter of keeping an eye on them on the several days a year when he passed through. But Mr. O'Neill's grandniece married the Earl of Clane several years ago, and they spend the holidays at Clane. It's close enough that Grandfather and Mr. O'Neill are able to meet nearly as often as they like."

Gareth stopped and stared down at her. "Let me see if I

understand this. Nearly half a century ago, they had a spat and have been dueling at every opportunity since. Correct me if I am wrong, but the purpose of a duel is to settle the matter in one shot, so to speak."

"You are absolutely correct. But neither has *been* shot, so they feel they must keep at it."

"Good Lord, Alice. You seem almost amused."

"Resigned, perhaps. Never amused." She shrugged again, certainly not about to explain to this man how each time her grandfather went missing, she feared the worst. Went cold with the thought of losing yet another man she loved. "With each passing year, the chances of them actually striking each other has diminished. My grandfather is seventy-nine, Mr. O'Neill a few years older. And someone always brings them home."

"Brings them home. Not as yet stretched out on a board. Honestly, Alice."

Exasperated, she faced him squarely. "Do you believe adventurous spirits belong only to the young? You probably do." She blew out a breath. "What would you have me do, Gareth? We cannot prevent people from doing foolish things just because we wish it. Life doesn't work that way."

"Now, elf—"

"Don't," she said sharply, then carefully softened her tone. "I haven't the energy or desire to argue with you, Gareth. May we declare an entente and simply be pleasant to one another?"

"Of course." He offered his arm again, the picture of politeness.

As they went, Alice couldn't help but notice that the trees above them were full of mistletoe. Gareth didn't look up at all.

4

Gareth arrived back at the house just in time to change his clothes and join the Ashes in the drawing room. He'd escorted Alice home, then headed straight for the stables. He found his old horse, Cinn, contentedly munching oats in a box stall. And he found Macatee: still head groom, still ginger-haired and ruddy-faced, still shouting at his underlings, so glad to see Gareth that he lifted his cap with enough enthusiasm to send it flying. Then he barked at his minions, sending them scattering, and ushered Gareth into the warm tack room.

They shared a bottle of nutty local ale, something they had done so many times before, quietly, the earl's son and the earl's servant. And Gareth, lounging in a battered chair, legs up on a saddle rest, basked in the welcome. More fatherly than his father, Macatee had been the one to teach him to ride, to drink, to sing bawdy tunes. And to care for the four-legged denizens of the estate. Even now, several dogs of indeterminate breed snored on beds of horse blankets. A little ginger cat leaped into Gareth's lap. He stroked it absently as he recounted his travels to Macatee.

He had ridden wild horses in Andalusia, swum with dolphins among the Cyclades. He hadn't been quite so keen on Egyptian camels; they smelled. But he'd made a peace of sorts with the one that carried him along the banks of the Nile. And had been reluctantly reminded of Alice each time the stubborn creature batted its impossibly long eyelashes just before head-butting him.

After his time with Macatee, he saddled Cinn himself and did a slow tour of the estate. Nothing really had changed. He supposed it was new grass greening the hollows, new moss blanketing the trees and the standing stones. But it looked just like the old moss, and the standing stones hadn't changed in thousands of years.

As a youth, Gareth had been able to embellish Kilcullen land with his fantasies. Now it just stretched before him out of sight. Rather like the years, he couldn't help but muse, should he inherit.

He took a late luncheon in a small pub, served by the owner himself, who said little but beamed all the while. Then he rode back toward the house, into the forest, and climbed an ancient oak tree, where he passed the end of the afternoon wondering when he would see the sea again. He had never seen stars like those he'd found while sailing the Mediterranean. As the months passed, he found every constellation he had ever known. And he thought every December to write to Alice, to tell her. But each time he abandoned the idea. He hadn't known what he could possibly say, as it would never be that he was coming home.

In the end, as he made his way north from Greece, he ended up following the stars.

Now, in fresh clothing, pleasantly tired and hungry, he wandered downstairs to join the Ashes for the requisite predinner gathering. He hadn't noticed before, but the house looked slightly different than it had when he'd left. The paint looked fresh, the wood paler and glossier. A few notable pieces of the heavy Gothic furniture his parents had favored had disappeared from the hallways. In their places were smaller, lighter tables and chests he recalled from his early childhood when his grandmother had still been in residence.

There was a massive, full-length portrait of his brother on the stairway landing. It was an Arthur Gareth had never known: a bit portly, uniformed, whiskers coming to a point nearly halfway to his nose. And next to that picture was one of Gareth himself. It was the last one painted, the year before he left. God, how young he looked. It was a good picture, he mused now. The painter had been talented, and astute. The window behind the boy he'd once been was open, with green fields stretching to the horizon; his hand rested on his heavens-and-earth globe. His eyes didn't meet the viewer's, but looked toward something beyond.

He wondered who had hung the pair there. Their old portraits had been in the gallery when he left: Arthur front and center, he well off to one side. His parents wouldn't have bothered moving them. It was their images that had adorned this space. Perhaps Clarissa . . .

"I hope you don't mind."

He glanced down to find Alice at the bottom of the sweeping stairs. She had changed into a pale yellow dress that glowed slightly in the waning light. "Mind?"

"That we moved your parents. It seemed right at the time." Her lips curved. "And, with all due respect to the departed, it grew a bit wearing to be frowned upon each time one went up or down the stairs."

He knew exactly what she meant. "A nice landscape might have been a better choice." But he smiled back. "The house is different."

"Oh, not so very," she insisted quickly. "We've only moved a few things, changed some upholstery—"

"Alice." He walked down to join her. "You don't have to explain. I don't particularly care. And it is Clarissa's right to do as she pleases. Although"—he stared intently into the little upturned face, so pretty and so easy to read—"I daresay Clarissa has done little, unless she got it into her head to redo the countess's chambers in pink and gilt, with rampaging cherubs and red-cheeked china spaniels."

Alice laughed. "Shepherdesses, actually. She doesn't much care for dogs." She gestured toward the drawing room. "I was just going in. Clarissa and my grandfather will be glad to see you."

Clarissa, certainly. Gareth wasn't so certain of Sir Reginald. Their only meeting thus far had involved vague threats of violence.

Alice watched the emotions play across his face: amusement, resignation. Clearly he wasn't looking forward to the evening. She wondered if he was looking forward to anything, save leaving. As they headed to the drawing room, she darted a quick glance up at the portrait, then at the man beside her. Still so handsome, but grown so hard. She regretted snapping at him earlier. It served no purpose and only made her feel small. And tired, as if she were going head-on into a stiff wind.

"Gareth!" Clarissa brightened at the sight of him. "At last. I am so terribly bored and no one seems to care. Alice will keep flitting in and out of the room and Grandfather has not yet come down. Do come tell me what you did today!"

He crossed the room to take a seat beside the sofa. "I toured the estate, actually."

"How dismal. And what else?"

"Well, I helped your sister find a Christmas log in the woods."

Clarissa rolled her eyes. "Oh, Gareth, how dull that must have been."

Perhaps for him, Alice thought, but not for her. For her, it had been illuminating. And rather lovely while it lasted.

"It wasn't a day in London," Gareth replied with a smile. Clarissa's eyes lit, as they always did, at the mention of London. "But it wasn't a bad day at all. Would you care to hear more? I wandered through the village, saw a few members of the neighborhood, and a great many sheep."

That, Alice decided, must not have been particularly interesting. In fact, it was probably enough to send him running back to the Continent. "You must have seen how Kilcullen has grown," she offered. "The Ingrams have opened a bookshop and there is even a haberdashery of sorts." As if an extra shop or two might make a provincial little backwater more appealing to a man who'd seen most of the capitals of Europe. "Lord Clane has been known to purchase gloves there when passing through. And Arthur was even able to have his uniforms made at Doolan's."

Gareth turned toward her. He looked mildly amused, as if he knew precisely what she was doing. Which he very probably did. "I've found I prefer Italian leather and French tailors, but should I find myself in need of anything, I shall know precisely where to go."

Alice sighed to herself. Years ago she would have bantered back, taking him to task for wearing coats worn through at the elbows or boots so battered that they sagged. As a boy he'd been untidy, as an adolescent carelessly disheveled. Now, even had she still felt easy enough to tease, it would have been forced. In his dark blue superfine coat and fawn breeches, he appeared precisely what he was: a well-heeled gentleman far better suited to Rome and Paris than rural Ireland.

"I suppose you'll have to give some custom to the local merchants," Clarissa announced breezily. "Support the tenants, and all that. But of course you'll be in London during the season. Arthur did so love to tell me about the session in Lords. Goodness, I wish he hadn't. There is no conversation quite so dreadful as politics."

Gareth's mouth had thinned at the mention of Parliament. Yet one more duty that went with the title. He'd always declared himself a Whig, supporting Irish independence from England and sending his arch-conservative father into sputtering fits. Alice knew the Earls of Kilcullen had been Tories since time immemorial. She also knew that much as the young Gareth had believed in his ideologies, he had never once considered fighting for them on the benches of Parliament. If nothing else, the Honorable Gareth Blackwell loathed sitting still.

"Perhaps," he said after a moment, tone deceptively bland, "I will merely be accompanying a nephew to Astley's."

"Escorting a sister-in-law and niece to Gunther's!" Clarissa shot back and in that moment Alice had a very clear idea of how bumpy the ride ahead was going to be. *Who has the most to lose will be the one to gain.* Someone was going to be made very unhappy by the birth of this child. And that was very, very sad. Her eyes strayed to the holly garlands and pine boughs decorating the room.

Happy Christmas, she wished herself, and sighed.

Fortunately, her grandfather chose that moment to totter into the room. He'd glared at her over breakfast, grunted at her at luncheon, and patted her absently on the head now. He never held a sulk for long. Alice would have been delighted, had not his returned cheer usually meant he was plotting his next escape.

"What's for dinner?" he demanded of Clarissa who, as usual, had no idea.

"Roast pheasant," Alice informed him.

"Splendid, splendid." He made his way to the drinks table and poured himself a large sherry. "Drink, boy?" he asked Gareth.

"I, ah . . . thank you."

Alice had a very good idea that Gareth had expected a scolding, or to be threatened again with a good caning. He might still get it, but for the moment Sir Reginald seemed content with merely pouring him a considerably smaller draught of sherry than his own. Not that Gareth would mind that much. He had always been more of an ale sort. He accepted the sherry with only the smallest grimace.

Sir Reginald settled himself creakily into the chair beside Alice. "You look peaky, girl. Not getting ill, are you?"

"No, Grandfather. I am quite well."

"You do look rather colorless," Clarissa added her opinion, albeit fondly, "though I suppose not much more so than usual. Has she not altered greatly since you saw her last, Gareth? I am forever encouraging her to put a bit of color in her cheeks, but she will not heed me."

He dutifully gave her a careful perusal and Alice wondered if her immediate flush would satisfy her sister's demand for color. She wondered, too, how Gareth could possibly answer. As much as he had always teased her privately, he would never be so callous as to do so in public. Yes, she had changed and, for the first time, felt a sharp tug of sadness for her lost bloom.

"I think," he said slowly after a moment, "that Alice looks very much as she always did. One of a very lovely pair." He turned back to Clarissa, who graced him with a smile that had stupefied a great many lesser men.

"How very gallant," she murmured.

Alice felt something softening around her heart.

Their grandfather snorted. "Didn't teach you such pretty speech in the navy."

Gareth actually laughed. "There was nothing pretty about what I learned in the navy. In fact, had I stayed a week longer, I should have been wholly unfit company for these ladies, indeed."

"Sold out, did you?" Sir Reginald demanded.

"I did. Several years ago."

"Don't suppose you made much money."

"Actually, sir, I did quite well."

"Did you, now? Well, that's something. How'd you spend it?"

He hadn't. Or at least very little. Not that he hadn't tried, but he had been just responsible and sober enough during his first months back on land to make a series of investments that had done far better, even, than expected. He was a wealthy man. Somehow, that didn't seem important to share. Instead, he announced, "I traveled."

"Traveled. Hmph. To where?"

Gareth wasn't quite sure where to begin. "Spain, Gibraltar, Morocco, Egypt." He'd seen the great pyramids, stood in the shadow of the Sphinx. He'd shooed asps from his rooms. And thought of Alice with her sharp tongue. He'd dined with princes, discussed astronomy with learned men whose forefathers had been studying the stars while his were still living in stone huts and pounding each other with clubs. And thought of Alice, with her eyes shining in the night.

"Egypt," Sir Reginald muttered. "Morocco. Running among the heathens and infidels. Enough to send your father spinning in his grave."

That had only been part of the appeal, Gareth thought humorlessly. "Yes, I'm sure it would be." He jumped when Sir Reginald slapped a bony knee.

"Daresay your grandfather would've been dashed proud of you," he chortled. "A toast to adventure, boy!"

Bewildered, inexplicably gratified, Gareth lifted his glass.

One very satisfying meal and several glasses of port later, he found himself back in the drawing room. Dinner had been an unexpected pleasure. They had eaten in the small family dining room. Whether out of habit or necessity due to the piles of foodstuffs on the formal table, he didn't know. And didn't care in the least. There had been a cheerful fire crackling in the hearth, glinting off his grandmother's crystal. Clarissa had prattled to the extent that Gareth could give most of his attention to the wonderful food. Alice had been quiet, thoughts clearly elsewhere, but she had responded when addressed, and smiled whenever their eyes met.

She and Clarissa had left as soon as the pudding was finished. Gareth had wanted to follow, but had instead passed the next hour with Sir Reginald plying him with port and questions about his travels. Only when the old man had eased back in his seat and commenced to snore, glass still dangling from his fist, could Gareth leave. He was more than a little disappointed to find the drawing room empty, only a discarded and, he decided, rather ugly square of half-embroidered linen to show that the ladies had sat there at all.

Well, they'd no doubt gone off to bed. Gareth supposed he could do the same. Nights in this house had always dragged endlessly. Except for those when he'd gone out one window or another. He was too old now to go climbing out a window. Beyond that, when he left again, it would be through the front door in broad daylight. He started up the stairs.

Alice was waiting for him on the landing. "Come with

me," she said and, not waiting to see if he followed, walked quickly down the hallway.

"Where—"

"Shh. You'll see."

Intrigued, a little drunk, he followed her, through a doorway, up another flight of stairs, and into a windowless chamber. Now he knew where they were headed. The ladder was in place, the trapdoor open to the night. Alice went first. Gareth managed not to look up her skirts. Within moments, they were on the roof.

His telescope was waiting for him.

"I found it in the attics last month," Alice said as he circled the thing, running his hands reverently over the shiny brass. "I had it cleaned and brought up here while you and Grandfather were having your port."

Gareth could only nod his thanks. This collection of metal and glass had been his first unshakable dream, his first love. When his father had refused to purchase it for him, he had saved the money himself. His pitiful allowance, the odd gift from his grandmother. It had taken him a year. The day before his fifteenth birthday, he'd commandeered the coach to take him to Dublin to collect his prize. His father had walloped him soundly on his return, but he'd had his telescope. As an adult, he had often thought that the hours he'd spent here on the roof, looking at the heavens, had saved him somehow.

His father had loathed the telescope, scorned the time Gareth spent with it, calling his son a *stargazer* as if it were a shameful thing to be. Had the earl been fit enough to climb to the roof, he would certainly have pitched the thing over the side. He'd ordered it destroyed more than once, but the staff had protected the telescope, protected Gareth.

He bent now, pressed his eye to the eyepiece. Tightened one knob, loosened another. And there, suddenly, was Ursa Minor, Polaris shining brilliantly. He heard himself laugh aloud and felt a small, quick squeeze at his shoulder, gone in an instant.

He had forgotten Alice was there. He stepped away from

the telescope, grinning like an idiot, giddy. "Go on," he urged. "Have a look. Tell me what you see."

"Heaven," he heard her whisper, almost before peering through the lens. When she straightened, smiling, eyes luminous, Gareth couldn't help himself. He swept her off her feet and into a tight circle. She was soft, pliant in his arms, her laughter musical.

Gareth stopped. But he didn't put her down. She braced her hands against his chest. But she didn't push. Her face was nearly level with his, elfin and lovely in the starlight.

"Alice . . ."

There was the distinct thump of a door below them, followed by the crunch of gravel beneath hurrying feet. Suddenly Alice was pushing against him. With nothing to do but set her down, Gareth did. She promptly rushed to the edge of the roof and peered over.

"Oh, dear."

He could hear her sigh from ten feet away. He joined her and looked down. He had a very clear view of Sir Reginald Ashe scurrying away from the house, gun case clasped tightly to his chest.

"Grandfather!"

Sir Reginald stopped as if he'd been shot. Then he turned slowly, glanced up. "Alice? What on earth are you doing up there?"

"Coming down, as it happens. I'll let you back in the front door."

"Now, Alice—"

"I'm on my way."

Grumbling audibly, shoulders slumped, Sir Reginald turned and trudged back toward the house. Alice sighed again, briefly met Gareth's eyes. "Well, that was perhaps a disaster averted," she said quietly. Then she slipped past him and disappeared down the ladder.

He wasn't quite quick enough to quash the fervent wish that she'd been speaking only of the thwarted duel.

5

*A*sennight later, Alice glanced over the last of the gift baskets and wondered if she had the energy left to deliver them. She had been determined to make this Christmas as traditional and merry as possible. With the baby arriving, she wanted everything to be just right. Side by side with Kilcullen's staff, she had polished, washed, and scrubbed. She'd spent the morning on hands and knees, cleaning every claw foot on the dining room's claw-footed chairs with sand. Ordinarily that would have been a maid's duty, but as the entire staff was already stretched to its limits and it was a task Alice's mother had performed herself, Alice had hunkered down and gotten to it.

Seated now, with a steaming cup of tea in front of her, she was stiff, exhausted, and very slightly overwhelmed. Tomorrow was Christmas Eve. The rest of the baskets had to be delivered today, and there was a join tonight. Most of the neighborhood would be gathered in the one inn's banquet and ballroom for a night of drinking, singing, and storytelling. As much as Alice loved Kilcullen, land and town and people, she would have preferred to go to bed. Now. But someone from the great house had to attend. Clarissa was unable. Their grandfather had been secretive for several days; Alice was determined to keep an eye on him. And she wouldn't ask it of Gareth. Even if she had any idea where he was.

Gareth had been scarce every afternoon all week. Scarce

all day, to be honest. He slept late, breakfasted in his room, then disappeared in the direction of the stables. Occasionally Alice would look up from her work or a game of cards with Clarissa to see him riding past the house, coat flapping behind him. He appeared for several luncheons, was always home for dinner, and was invariably charming to Clarissa. He teased her, amused her, read Byron aloud to her with goodwill and appropriate flourish. He took his port with their grandfather. He rearranged Christmas decorations when asked, and met Alice's polite conversation with equally polite responses.

He was pleasant, charming even, and the uncertainty of it all was driving her to distraction.

In those few minutes on the roof, Alice had felt the years fall away. She hadn't seen so much as a flash of joy in Gareth since he'd come home. But she'd seen the joy then, a flash bright enough to warm her. To make her want to set him free—and hold him very, very close. In fact, she'd been on the verge of throwing her arms around his neck and kissing him until they were both breathless.

If she closed her eyes and concentrated very hard, she could actually feel the pressure of his lips on hers all those years ago. She could feel the heat emanating from him, smell the faint aroma of soap and leather that clung to his skin and clothes.

She had been closing her eyes altogether too much lately.

It wouldn't work. It would never have worked. She was content, happy even, with her quiet life in Kildare. Her childhood, even before her parents were gone, had been too full of travel and upheaval. She'd had to adapt one too many times. Gareth craved change and adventure. *Needed* it. Even if, as she'd wished so fervently after he left . . . Even if, and it didn't really merit a fleeting thought, they had somehow found a way to come together, it wouldn't have worked. One of them would have been miserable.

No, she thought, much better this way. Whatever happened with the title, Gareth wouldn't be home much, perhaps not at all. He'd been half gone as soon as he walked through the door. The morning after their time on the roof, Alice had walked by his chamber while the maids were tidying. She hadn't meant to snoop, but it had been impossible to miss the leather valise propped beneath the window. It was empty, but it was there, rather than being stored away with the rest of his things. Ready to be packed at a moment's notice. Whether in a day or fortnight or six months, Gareth would leave.

It was so much easier, safer this way. Calmer. The problem, of course, was that try as she might to deny it, she was on the edge of the storm. One more hour—one more minute, even—with Gareth as he'd been that night and she was in danger of falling every bit as much in love with him as she'd been eight years before.

Gareth leaned companionably on the fence next to Tommy Sullivan. He had been riding past when he spied the young farmer walking through his pasture among his sheep. Sullivan waved and Gareth had decided to stop. Within minutes, they were discussing sheep, Tommy with enthusiasm, Gareth with a combination of horror and amazement that he had anything at all to contribute. But he'd spent enough time in Greece among their never-ending sheep, enough time in tavernas with the friendly locals, to have learned more than he'd ever wanted to know. Language, it seemed, had not been an impediment. He found himself thoroughly conversant in ewe.

Without being aware of it, he had apparently become knowledgeable on the subjects of drainage, stone walls, and orchard maintenance as well. Over the past week, he'd discussed those subjects at length with several of the estate's other tenants. He had even made a handful of suggestions that were met with consideration and approval. Of course no one had wanted to talk about camels, but he was forced to admit to himself that he could have conversed about them, too.

"You've a grand stretch of land far side of the forest," Tommy was saying now. "Good for a large flock. And sheep are good for the land."

Gareth wanted to disagree, out of sheer perversity. He couldn't. Sheep were good for the land, controlling the vegetation and fertilizing the earth. Their wool was a profitable commodity, the shearing and spinning and weaving employment for the people. And while Gareth was not a lover of either mutton or lamb, a good part of Ireland was.

"Sheep," he muttered, and Sullivan, as if reading his mind, chuckled.

"Think, sir. You might have been born to land that favors pigs. Now, will you come in for a drink?"

Sullivan's pretty wife served them a pitcher of ale with plates of hearty brown bread and sharp cheese. Nearby, the couple's twin boys sat sturdily on a brightly colored quilt, tugging at the ears of an old hound. The dog's tail thumped rhythmically against the floor; its tongue darted out occasionally to lick a plump fist.

Sullivan followed Gareth's indulgent gaze. "'Tis a good life I have here."

Yes, Gareth thought it might be. The work was hard and unending, but there was a reward at the end of the day, support and assistance when it was needed. Kilcullen's tenants looked out for each other. They always had. The earls had more or less looked out for the tenants. That was their duty, one that no doubt could have been performed better. Schooling for the children, Gareth thought. Surplus grains stored away on the earl's grounds, at the earl's expense, should a harvest be poor or a winter unusually hard. Funds for young men to marry, to study a trade when there were already enough brothers working the land, to join the army. If these were his decisions to make . . .

He halted that train of thought, drained his mug. "Thank you both for the hospitality. I have enjoyed myself."

"I'm glad." Sullivan rose with him. "You're welcome anytime. Will you thank Lady Kilcullen, sir, for the basket. Miss Ashe delivered it yesterday and 'twas a treat to see. Mary's already opened the cheese and the boys are halfway through the pudding."

"I'll be sure to tell . . . her ladyship." He didn't think he would be mentioning it to Clarissa. She would only yawn and roll her eyes. Alice would be glad to hear that her gift was appreciated.

Alice. As he swung onto Cinn and rode from Sullivan's yard, Gareth tried to decide, for the thousandth time in only seven days, what he was going to do about Alice. It might have been all the damned mistletoe about, or how she looked in the moonlight. Or the fact that it had been a long time since he'd held a woman. Whatever it was, he was spending far too much time thinking about kissing her. Thinking about how soft and warm and *right* she'd felt in his arms.

But women like Alice weren't for kissing and leaving. Bad enough that he'd already done that once. He wouldn't do it again. Women like Alice were for marrying, for coming home to and cuddling in front of the fire.

Gareth supposed he would have to marry eventually. Certainly if he ended up with the title. But he knew he needed a woman who wouldn't tug on his conscience too much. Alice did. She poked at his calm and his conviction when they were together and haunted him when they were apart.

He had stayed away from her as much as possible, out of the house during the day and trying to keep a stretch of carpet or expanse of table between them when in the house. Some vague sense of duty—and Cook's marvelous food— had him coming home for meals. Then, he often felt compelled to spend the odd hour with Clarissa. She was confined to bed and sofa now, clearly uncomfortable and, wholly unlike her, taking pains to hide it. Perhaps, he thought, motherhood would be the thing to coax her out of her very extended childhood.

He was on his way back now. He would stay until late afternoon. Then he would head out again, to Kilcullen village and the pub. He had discovered, more or less by accident, that the place filled as the day waned. Men would arrive: farmers, bakers, even the local solicitor and physician, lifting pints and spinning tales. On the first late afternoon Gareth had been there, he had stayed at his table in the corner, not wanting to intrude on their familiar camaraderie. But first one man, then another and another, had toasted him. It had seemed rude not to buy a round. And soon he'd been in the middle of the throng, chatting with men he'd known as a boy and with their sons, who had been boys themselves then.

Now he looked forward to his hour in the warm, smoky room. If he did receive more deference than he probably deserved, it was balanced with humor and the odd piece of advice. And as gratefully as the gathering accepted his rounds of drinks, there was always someone purchasing the next pint and pressing it into his hand. As it happened, he was drinking far less than he was used to, sipping each pint slowly so his companions would have less to pay for.

Several days ago old Manus Phelan had brought in his fiddle. Since then, he'd been joined by his son Padraig on the flute and Donal Clancy on the bodhran drum. The music was lively, provincial, and Gareth was very much hoping to have more of it today.

Whistling a lilting reel, he guided Cinn down a rocky hillock toward the stream. He'd been riding the horse long, if not hard lately, covering miles each day. Cinn wasn't so young anymore and seemed to appreciate a few minutes with his feet and muzzle in the cold water.

Apparently someone else had the same idea. Several children, shabbily if warmly dressed, were watering a pony in the stream. Across the way, Gareth could see the brightly colored caravan of a traveler family. The children glanced up as Cinn waded into the stream, eyed Gareth with wary but not unfriendly eyes.

"Good day," he greeted them.

"G'day, sir." The youngest, a girl, reached out a hesitant hand to touch Cinn's muzzle. She laughed as the horse gave her fingers an affectionate nibble. "'E's pretty. What's 'is name?"

"*Cinniúint,*" Gareth replied, and was startled by a cackling laugh from behind him.

An old woman walked toward them, arms full of kindling. She was tiny, weathered, but gave an impression of surprising vitality. "*Cinniúint* is it? And what would you be knowing about Fate, young man?"

"Probably not nearly enough, madam," he replied, and dismounted.

She approached him until her nose was a mere six inches from his coat buttons. To Gareth's surprise, she reached out a bony finger and prodded him in the chest. "You're after denying yours," she snapped. "Always have done."

"Madam—"

"*Tost!*" she shushed him. "Do you know what a second chance looks like?"

Amused, deciding this fortune teller was far more diverting than most, Gareth shook his head. "I fear I do not, madam. Perhaps you will tell me."

She snorted. "As if I'd be knowing that. I've never needed one, m'self. But you'd best have a care. Fighting what's meant to be is more dangerous than trying for the stars. The door's closing, young man. Best decide which side you're to be on."

Gareth waited. When she said nothing further, he demanded, "That's it?"

"Aye."

"You're not going to tell me that I'm to have my heart's desire by the New Year—or tumble into a well on Twelfth Night? Come now, madam."

She poked him again, but chuckled. "Saucy boy. Well, as to the first, 'tis possible, I suppose, though I've no faith in the quickness of your head. As for the other, watch how much ale you swill. Or stay away from wells. *Sin é. That* is all."

Gareth reached into his pocket and pulled out some coins. She waved them away. "'Tis the season for charity, so have my words and welcome." Then she gathered up her wood and trundled off.

He handed a half crown to each child. "Happy Christmas, sir," they chorused.

"Happy Christmas," he said absently and, remounting Cinn, continued on his way.

Well, he mused as he crested the hill, advice and fortunes alike were worth precisely what one paid for them. He thought Alice would have been most diverted by the encounter. Perhaps he would tell her about it.

Then again, he thought, perhaps not.

No sooner had he decided *not* to speak to Alice than she drove into view. Bundled in copious wool head to toe, scarcely visible among the piles of baskets filling the dog cart, she was unmistakable. And if the pace with which she was driving her pony was any indication, she was in something of a hurry.

Alice almost lost her grip on the reins when Gareth loomed up nearly in her path. She pulled the pony to an ungainly halt and pushed several feet of wool muffler off her face. "It isn't wise to leap onto the road like that. Someone might mistake you for An Cú and shoot you."

Oh, he was handsome when he laughed. The corners of his eyes crinkled; his wonderful mouth curved like a harp. "The Hound, if I am not mistaken, rides only at night. And I daresay you're doing his job for him, taking from the rich and delivering to the common folk."

"Yes, well, perhaps then he will take his job back."

Alice hadn't meant to sound so sharp, but she was tired, rushed, and having Gareth dash up like, yes, a romantic and fabled highwayman was wreaking havoc on her calm. He leaned in; she skittered away from him and got a raised brow for it.

"Would you like some help, Alice?"

"Help?"

"Mmm. You know: assistance, aid, a strong back and ready hands."

She liked his hands. "I know what it means, Gareth."

"Yes, you're a clever elf. You know what it means, but seldom ask. It's not a sin to need help on occasion."

Not a sin, of course, but if she didn't fill her time, if she weren't the one to be relied upon . . . what would she have left?

Alice let out her breath in a soft sigh, took a tiny leap of faith. "Thank you. I would be glad of your assistance."

"Splendid. Lead on."

They carried on, Gareth keeping pace with the cart. "What time shall we leave tonight?"

"Tonight . . . ?"

"For the Christmas join. I've received no end of invitations and assumed you would be attending."

"I . . . yes, of course. And you intend to go?"

"Certainly. Food, drink, singing carols and Donal Clancy on the bodhran. Who would want to miss it?"

Who indeed, Alice thought, stunned that he was even considering joining the join. Who indeed. It was just the sort of entertainment she would have expected him to shun: rustic, traditional, and tied so thoroughly to Kilcullen. "Gareth, are you teasing me?"

"Teasing you?"

"About tonight. You are not truly going—"

"I've said I was. For heaven's sake, Alice, what are you going on about . . . ? Ah. I think I understand. Whether I wish to go is less important than whether others wish me to stay away. Fine."

"No!" she nearly shouted. Then again, more gently, "No. That isn't it at all. You'll be welcome and no question. In fact, I think it marvelous that you wish to attend. I am merely surprised."

He actually looked hurt, an emotion Alice didn't think she'd ever seen in him before. "Is it as laughable as I suspect? The thought of me finding a moment's peace of mind in Kildare? Finding that there is an essence of *home* for me?"

"Not at all. Don't be silly. There isn't a door here that isn't open to you."

"What did you say?" he demanded sharply.

"There isn't a door . . . Oh, you don't believe me. I'm sorry for that, sorry for questioning you. But I'll show you."

And she did. In each house they entered, they were welcomed warmly. There was deference in people's attitude toward Gareth, of course there was. He was the son of the old lord. He was perhaps the next one. But there was friendly interest, too, and an acceptance past earls had never received.

Gareth, for his part, lost a little more of his reserve with each basket they delivered. At the Nolans', he stood stiffly inside the door while she delivered the basket and chatted with the family. At the Whites', he graciously accepted the offer of a cup of cider and seat at the scarred table. And in the midst of the chaos that was the MacNeils', he crouched in the dirt yard for a few minutes to play mumblety-peg with three of the couple's sons, then joined the adults inside for eggnog and a plate of Mrs. MacNeil's gingerbread.

Alice wasn't in a hurry anymore. In fact, she wished she hadn't delivered most of the baskets during the past two days. She was savoring every minute, and the minutes flew by.

Too soon, they were home again. Gareth handed cart and Cinn over to Macatee and followed Alice to the back door. "Thank you," she said softly, "for the help."

"It was my pleasure."

She believed him. Enough to press, "None of it is so bad as you feared, is it? The people *like* you, Gareth. They were deferent to your father, respectful of Arthur, but they *welcome* you. I cannot speak for your peace of mind, but Kilcullen *is* your home."

He stared at her for a long moment. Then he gave a humorless laugh. "I suppose it might once have been. If things had been different. But not now."

"Gareth—"

"I'm not what Kilcullen needs, Alice," he muttered. "I am not Kilcullen."

What a terrible shame he thought so, she mused sadly as he stalked away. Because, as far as she was concerned, he was *precisely* what and where he should be.

6

The last ball Gareth had attended had been in the Welsh castle belonging to the Duke of Llans. He'd served with the duke's brother in the navy, and it hadn't taken much coaxing on his friend's part to get him to go. The guests had come from as far afield as Russia. For Gareth, whose ship was moored at Port Enyon, it had been a short trip and an extremely decadent one. For more than a sennight, he had reveled among the highest aristocracy of the land, not to mention two deposed sovereigns of foreign lands and one current one. The clothing had all been in the first fashion and frequently jewel-encrusted, the food prepared by chefs who'd fled Versailles, the music composed for the occasion by the German composer Beethoven. Gareth had been paired at whist with a Russian princess, had discussed the war with an exiled French marquis. He'd eaten tiny quail eggs stuffed with caviar and drunk wine smuggled from the Spanish royal cellars. He had fallen a little bit in love with his hostess, Susan, the Duchess of Llans.

None of it compared to the spectacle before him now.

The upstairs room of Kilcullen's little inn was filled to bursting, without so much as a baron in sight. Instead, potato farmers rubbed elbows with clerks. The vicar was forehead to forehead in conversation with the knacker. All were garbed in Sunday best, scrubbed and brushed and polished.

It didn't matter in the least that copious amounts of soap and water hadn't quite erased the aroma of the farmyard.

And there was more. A motley collection of foodstuffs filled the tables: pots of colcannon, roasted beets, mutton, and plum puddings. Gareth had himself peered into a pot containing something that smelled delectable, but looked like worms. The ale flowed freely; one's glass never reached the half-empty point without someone hurrying to fill it.

His musical comrades from the pub were there, joined by more fiddles, *uillean* pipes, goatskin bodhran drums. A tiny space had been cleared off to the side for dancing. It had expanded to cover half the floor and even now a little man with a solemn face and elbows like knives was doing a high-stepping jig that bounced him repeatedly off Gareth's side. Children darted in and out among the revelers, sneaking biscuits, gingerbread, and the occasional sip of ale from the tables.

Gareth wondered if first his parents and later Arthur had been invited to these Christmas celebrations. Perhaps, but they certainly wouldn't have come. They might have sent a keg of something, or a side of beef, but the Earls of Kilcullen had never mingled among their tenants. The idea of breaking bread with a farmer would have been laughable.

"Ah, you've no plate, Mr. Blackwell!" Clucking her tongue, Mary Sullivan disappeared for a moment, only to return bearing a plate so laden with meat and potato and onion that she was using two hands to carry it. "There you go, then." She beamed and shoved it into his grasp.

"Silly woman!" her husband chided, grinning. "Are you after making him sick? There's enough there to feed the lot of us." He deftly removed the plate, replacing it with an overflowing tankard of cider so potent that Gareth could smell it coming. "This'll see you right."

This, Gareth decided, would see him flat on his back within the hour. He took a few sips, then found himself empty-handed, but only momentarily, as old Mrs. White replaced the tankard with a massive slab of Christmas fruitcake. "'Twill make you sweet," she informed him, eyes twinkling, "and the girls will follow you like bees to honey."

Heeding no message his brain was sending, Gareth's eyes slewed to Alice. She was dancing, had been dancing almost from the moment they'd arrived. She had scarcely put a foot inside the door when Mr. Halloran, the prim, black-clad solicitor, had swept her out onto the floor and into a merry reel. From there she'd gone into the hands of the vicar and a country dance, through another several sets with young men too hale and hopeful for Gareth's taste. And now she was hand in hand with three other women, doing a series of graceful, quick-stepping moves that spoke of centuries of Irish *céilís* and boundless hearts. Gareth had no idea where Alice had learned traditional Irish dance. He had a very good idea that he could watch her for a very long time.

Pink-cheeked, eyes bright, her hair slowly freeing itself from its pins, she looked like a wild Irish girl, the sort that bards and poets and distant sailors sang of. She looked very much like she belonged in the midst of these cheerful, simple people. But then, Gareth mused, one of Alice's great strengths had always been her ability to bend with the wind. She would no doubt seem just as much at home wherever she was, whomever she was with. That was Alice.

The song ended. Alice and her companions skipped to a laughing halt. Gareth saw several young men approach and thought he might have to interfere. But Alice shook her head and slipped from the floor. Gareth lost sight of her in the crowd. He wasn't much of a dancer, had never been given instruction or had a great inclination to learn. He thought he could manage a country dance, however, and would coax Alice into dancing it with him.

He was distracted for several minutes as people thrust more food and drink in his direction. Tommy Sullivan bent his ear on the subject of building a paddock; Finn O'Toole wanted to hear again how in Africa, goat was a staple food. When Gareth looked for Alice again, it was to see her sitting with her grandfather and a brilliantly white-haired gentleman who was dressed to the nines in fashions of the last century: green brocade coat, yellow satin knee breeches, ruffles at his throat. He ought to have looked out of place in the gathering, but he had a plate of mutton stew on one knee, a tankard balanced on the other. He was nodding along to the music, completely off the rhythm, and appeared happy as a stoat. Curious, Gareth made his way over.

Alice's heart gave a cheery little thump at the sight of him. She couldn't help it. His cravat was loose, a lock of midnight-dark hair had fallen onto his brow, and he had a spot of what might have been apple tart on the lapel of his coat.

"You appear to be enjoying yourself," she commented.

He grinned. "I am being fed into submission."

"Yes, well, that's an Irish party. Ah, you haven't met Mr. O'Neill." She gestured to the man beside her grandfather. "Mr. O'Neill?" Then louder, "Mr. O'Neill?"

The man jumped. Alice suspected her grandfather had just prodded him in the ribs. "Eh? Ah, the prodigal son. Reggie's been telling me about you. Home to stay, I trust. Man can't gad about all his life. Bad for the heart."

Gareth darted Alice a look, but bowed politely as she made the introductions. "Mr. O'Neill is the music critic for the *Freeman's Journal* in Dublin."

"Is that so? Are you enjoying the music tonight, sir?"

"Nay, nay, not at all, young man. I'm here for the music!" To her grandfather, O'Neill muttered, "Shove over, Reggie. Let the boy sit."

Gareth did. Alice could have taken pity on him, but she decided to let him attempt conversation with the rather deaf O'Neill. And he tried, gallantly, for several minutes. Only after his query as to the man's journey from Clane had been met with the reply, "Fish? Only on Friday, boy," did he give up.

The musicians struck up a familiar tune. Treasa Clancy took a seat beside her husband and began to sing in a sweet, strong voice that carried above the chatter and laughter. One by one, people fell silent. Then, one after another, new voices joined in.

"On the second day of Christmas, my true love gave to me two turtle doves . . ."

Alice would have loved to sing along, but she knew better. She had a voice like a wet cat in a tin drum. Instead, she let the more able do the singing and mouthed the words to herself.

Gareth leaned closer. "This is a rather English tune for an Irish gathering," he commented dryly.

She smiled. "Not at all, actually. Where were you through all the caroling of your childhood?"

"Knowing my parents, you need to ask? They'd send a servant out with a few coins to pay the wassailers *not* to continue."

"What a pity." Yet again, Alice's heart ached for the lovely, lively little boy who'd been forced to grow to manhood in such a cold home. "Well, the 'Twelve Days' is an Irish song to the core, written when Catholicism was a crime. Each gift stood for a teaching of the Church. The song could be sung right beneath the noses of the Protestant interlopers without them having any idea how they were being fooled. Very clever and rather wonderful."

"You seem to forget that our ancestors *were* the Protestant interlopers."

She shrugged. "Times change. And I love the song."

"Four calling birds, three French hens, two turtle doves, and a partridge in a pear tree . . ."

"Tell me," he coaxed and she wondered if she would remember it all.

"The partridge in the pear tree is Christ in the manger— or on the Cross. The turtle doves are the Old and New Testaments. The three hens are Faith, Hope, and Charity; the four birds the four Gospels."

"Five golden rings . . ."

She ticked the rest off on her fingers. "The first five books of the Old Testament, the six days of creation, the seven sacraments, eight beatitudes, nine orders of angels. Ten commandments, eleven faithful apostles, and the twelve articles of the Apostles' Creed."

"Well, I'm impressed, Miss Ashe. You would have made a good Catholic."

"No," she shot back tartly, "I should probably have made a very poor one, but I like a good story as much as anyone."

Once upon a time, there was an elf who lived in the ash tree woods near a great castle. She fell in love with the prince who lived there, but he left to go out into the world to seek his fortune . . .

Alice shook her head, annoyed with herself. It had been a great many years since she had thought to live a fairy tale. Since she'd lost her father, certainly. He had been the one for fairy tales. She had tried to carry on, to spin magical stories for Clarissa, who had expected her life to go happily ever after. Alice had grown pragmatic. Clarissa, she thought fondly, still believed.

"On the twelfth day of Christmas, my true love gave to me . . ."

If all went as expected, Clarissa would have her baby by Twelfth Night. By that twelfth day of Christmas, so much would be decided. Boy or girl, Kilcullen or London. Whether Gareth would stay a bit longer or leave as soon as the christening was done.

"Alice."

She had grown so accustomed to having him about. Accustomed to the sight of him, tousled and not quite awake at breakfast, to the sound of his boot heels ringing in the hall as he hurried into the drawing room at night. Accustomed to him saying her name.

"Alice."

"Hmm?" She blinked, then turned to find his face close enough to hers that she could see the faint lines that fanned from his eyes. Time in the sun, she thought, on board a ship or traversing a golden desert. Oh, yes, they were the eyes of a roving lad: sun-touched and bright and just a little wicked.

"Dance with me, elf," he said softly, and Alice's pulse thrummed.

"I . . . I don't think—"

"No, don't. If you do, you'll recall that I have two left feet and no sense of timing. Just come along. Excuse us, sirs," he said to their companions, both of whom were otherwise occupied with draining their tankards, and pulled Alice to her feet.

He danced very well indeed. Guiding her through the lilting country dance, he was graceful, confident, and a pleasure to behold. As Alice wove in and out of the set, returning again and again to the warmth of his grasp, she silently corrected half of his assertion. He had two perfectly good feet, suited for dancing—and for wandering the world. His sense of timing, however, was poor indeed. He had come back into her life after eight years out of it, come back when she was calm and content. He had swept out of her past like a mischievous wind and blown her serenity to pieces.

How could she ever have thought she wouldn't fall in love with Gareth Blackwell a second time? She'd never stopped loving him in the first place.

Stunned, heart pounding in her chest, she missed a step, then another. Gareth grinned at her and clasped her hand more firmly in his. "Tired, elf?" he teased, and it was all she could do to stay in the set. She wanted to run. Instead, she concentrated on the movement of her feet—*step, turn, slide, step, turn, slide*—until the music ended.

She tugged her hand free. "Thank you," she murmured, eyes on the floor. "I should . . . I must . . ." Then she fled.

Gareth watched her go, bemused. He hadn't stepped on her toes. He hadn't teased or even made a dull comment on the weather. One moment she'd been beside him, little hand warm and nearly lost in his, and then . . . "Well," he muttered, and started off after her.

He didn't get more than ten feet before the vicar's wife appeared in his path. He'd met the woman twice. She prattled and, he suspected, used her impressively long nose to poke into everyone else's affairs. Now she was nattering away and gesturing to a figure cowering behind her. ". . . Miss Powers . . . without partner. Surely, sir, you would not shirk a gentleman's duty . . ."

The very young Miss Powers looked both mortified and hopeful. Gareth sighed and forced a smile. "It would be my honor."

By the time he had partnered Miss Powers, a Miss Skeffington, two Miss MacLeishes, and several giggling girls whose names he missed, an hour had passed. Alice, he saw, was seated in a far corner, flanked by two old ladies, a sleeping infant on her lap. He started briskly toward her, and nearly flattened little Mr. Dunleavy, the postmaster.

"A moment of your time, Mr. Blackwell?" the man squeaked. "I'm thinking of putting a sty back of my house—bit of bacon now and again, you know, nothing too adventuresome—and was wondering if you had any words you might care to impart on swine . . ."

Midnight had long since come and gone before Gareth found himself near Alice again—in the carriage on the way home. She sat, still and silent, beside her grandfather, who was snoring gently into his jabot before they'd left the inn's yard. Gareth's head was reeling from both the endless stream of farm talk and never-empty glass. It wasn't a time for chatting. It was a time to mind his stomach and hope it didn't betray him on the bumpy road. He was tired, nauseated, and convinced he hadn't had a better night in a very long time. He had left the party with a steady stream of slaps on the back, wishes for a happy Christmas, and a slew of gifts from Kilcullen's tenants. They were piled on the seat next to him, mainly things for Clarissa's baby that kind souls had brought to the join: soft wool blankets, carved wooden animals, and tiny knitted caps. Gareth hadn't even found it in himself to care that some of them were pink.

Alice disappeared as soon as they reached the house, bidding him a soft good night and mumbling something about

Clarissa waiting up for a report and gossip. Gareth helped her weaving grandfather up the stairs and to his chamber.

"Thank you, young man," Sir Reginald said with solemn dignity. Then he went facedown onto the bed and proceeded to snore again. Gareth removed his shoes, wrapped the counterpane around his diminutive form, then left him alone.

He made his way to his own chamber and promptly decided that he wasn't ready for bed. He dismissed his valet for the night, found his warmest coat, and headed for the roof. The air was crystal clear and cold enough to make his face tingle. It was a perfect night for stargazing.

A footman had located a battered wooden armchair for Gareth earlier in the week and he settled himself in it now. The rim of the telescope's eyepiece was icy cold. He rubbed it with his gloved fingers until it was warm enough to tolerate against his skin. Then he looked for Polaris.

Sailor, sage, astronomer—through the ages, all knew to locate the North Star first. The rest would follow. And there it was, twinkling merrily down at him. *Star light, star bright, first star I spy tonight.* The nursery rhyme drifted into his head. *How I wish with all my might to have this wish I wish tonight.*

And on Christmas Eve, too. Little Mrs. Nolan had stopped him on his way out the door, twinkled up at him. "Remember to make yourself a fine wish," she had instructed him firmly. "No wish made on an Irish Christmas Eve goes unanswered."

What to wish for, then? There were enough possibilities to keep him busy until Christmas morning. For Clarissa to have a boy child, of course. Hadn't that been his most fervent hope since learning of his brother's death and her pregnancy? For passage back to Mikonos, olives and ouzo on a whitewashed terrace overlooking the Aegean. For the coming year to bring spring rains and summer sun to Kilcullen's crops . . .

Gareth pushed the telescope to the side. He leaned back

in his chair and gazed up at the sky. The lens was a wonderful thing, but when one's view was so narrow, one missed the entire picture. He found Polaris again. The North Star that guided wise men and shepherds to Bethlehem. Guided sailors home.

Draco, Orion, Cassiopeia. Andromeda, who had been chained to a rock as a sacrifice to a sea monster. It suddenly occurred to Gareth that Alice was chained, too, in her own way. To Kilcullen, a home not her own, as a sacrifice to Kilcullen's mistress, to a child that wasn't born and wasn't hers, either.

Star light, star bright . . . A wish. For Alice . . .

Gareth woke up with a start. He blinked, oriented himself, and discovered that it was early morning. He was chilled, stiff, and couldn't feel his posterior at all. Grimacing, he levered himself from the hard chair and stomped some feeling back into his feet. Absurd, falling asleep sitting up, and outside, too. He had had plenty of these mornings during his time in the navy, a few more during his travels when too much drink had drowned out comfort and common sense. He tossed the canvas cover over the telescope. He would crawl into bed and grab a few hours of sleep.

He wandered to the edge of the roof to stretch and take a quick look at Kilcullen in the early morning light. It was a beautiful sight, the hills and fields dusted with frost, a lone figure treading over the faintly glittering earth . . . Gareth looked again then, cursing, hurried back across the roof and swung down the ladder.

By the time he reached the spot where he had spied Sir Reginald, the man was nowhere to be seen. But Gareth knew the direction he had been heading and he followed, muttering under his breath all the while. Ridiculous. Inexcusable. Two grown—no, *old*—men waving guns at each other, making Alice tense with worry, no matter how hard she tried to hide it. Gareth was damned if he was going to let her grandfather ruin this day for her. He was going to get the old coot home, over his shoulder if he had to, and back into bed before anyone knew he was missing.

Gareth crossed briskly through the shadowy stone circle, broke into the light of the bordering field. There they were, the old fools, pacing dramatically away from each other. Thaddeus O'Neill was wearing an emerald green, ermine-trimmed velvet cape. Sir Reginald was shrouded in hairy wool from head to toe, ancient dueling pistol grasped in a gloved hand. Both were weaving slightly, whether from effects of the night's revelry, age, or the uneven ground.

"Oh, for heaven's sake," Gareth muttered, and struck out across the field. "Sir Reginald!" he bellowed.

He saw the man flinch, watched as he turned, nearly bobbled the gun, and caught it in both hands. Gareth heard the boom, saw the flash. He didn't feel the impact. He did feel himself flying backward, felt the thump of his head against the earth. "Well, I'll be damned," he thought, perfectly clearly.

Then everything went black.

7

Alice had risen with the rooster's crowing and knelt now on the nursery floor among the gifts from the night before. How very generous the people of Kilcullen were. Clarissa had spoken to no more than a handful during her time as the Countess of Kilcullen, but dozens had given gifts to her unborn child.

Colm Nolan had carved a set of little wooden sheep, no mean feat considering that his hands were gnarled from arthritis and half a century of hard work. His wife had knitted a cloud-soft wool blanket in an intricate pattern of traditional Celtic knots. There were more of these blankets, and tiny buntings, knitted with designs as old as the standing stones. And there were more wooden animals: sheep, cows, ducks, some painted, some on wheels with cords so they could be pulled along. Kilcullen itself was in the gifts: the trees and the animals, the rushes woven into St. Brigid's crosses.

Alice smoothed a little blue cap against her skirts. It was Nora Bergin's work, and no surprise. The Bergins had five boys; there hadn't been a pink object in that house in twenty years. Alice traced a finger along the soft edge. She couldn't remember when she had given up the hope of having her own children. Some years ago, certainly. If she were honest, and this was one area where she'd been remarkably successful at lying to herself, she had put away her dreams the moment she'd realized Gareth wasn't coming home. She had wrapped up her heart and her hopes and gone on with her day. Alice the Reliable. Alice the Adaptable. She had adapted to a life without Gareth; she'd kept her family from fraying at the loss of her parents, the loss of Arthur.

She would hold herself together now.

The blue cap joined the pile of boy's clothes. She lifted a pink blanket to her cheek. So soft. Like the little person it would swaddle.

"Isn't that pretty."

Alice turned to see her sister in the doorway. "Mary Sullivan sent it. You're up early."

"I've been sleeping so poorly." Clarissa moved slowly into the room, one hand pressed to her back, and lowered herself into the rocking chair that sat beside the Kilcullen family cradle. "My back has been paining me all night." She touched a hand to the cradle's side, setting it to rocking slowly. "What a monstrosity."

It was a bit excessive, all frills and flounces and carved family crest. Alice smiled. "Ours wasn't much better. I remember how very tiny you looked among all the lacy cushions. Mama was forever pretending she couldn't find you so I could be the one to lift you out."

Clarissa stretched out her free hand and brushed it over Alice's shoulder. "I know I'm a troublesome creature, Alice, and I want you to know that I do appreciate all you've done. All you've always done for me."

Alice felt tears welling in her eyes. These moments were rare for Clarissa, but all the more precious for their rarity. "You are a joy, darling. You always have been."

Clarissa rocked for a moment. "So much blue," she sighed. "They all want me to produce the next earl."

"Oh, I don't know. I think it's more a matter of what people think *you* want."

"But I *never* said I wished for a boy!"

"Not to us, dearest, but the Nolans hardly know that."

Alice moved the pile of blue blankets to the side. "Anyway, it was never in your hands, nor theirs."

"No." Clarissa rubbed a hand absently over her belly. "I shall take what I am given, I suppose. Ah, and don't you be kicking me like that," she murmured, "or I'll be forced to believe you are a boy."

Alice walked over to rest her hand where her sister's had been. "I have a difficult time believing there's any room at all in which to kick."

"Tell that to the baby." Clarissa linked her fingers with Alice's. "I'm frightened, Ally."

"I know, darling. But you'll be fine."

"Promise?"

"Promise."

Clarissa relaxed her grip and they sat in companionable silence for several minutes. The sun had risen to the level of the window by now and lit the honey wood of the floor, the samplers of letters and animals and fairies that decorated the walls, the work of generations of Blackwell girls.

"I have a promise of my own," Clarissa finally said.

"And that is?"

"I will *never* teach my daughter to embroider chair cushions!"

Alice laughed. "A good thing, too!" She glanced up as Sorcha appeared in the doorway, red-faced and breathless. "What is it?"

"Oh, miss," the maid gasped, "something terrible has happened!"

Alice was already on her feet. "Grandfather."

"Nay, nay. 'Tis the master . . . er, Mr. Blackwell."

Fear like an icy fist clutched in Alice's stomach. "Sorcha . . ."

"They've just carried him in, Miss Alice. He's been shot."

Gareth opened his eyes to muted light and shadows. His shoulder burned like fire; he felt as if someone had taken a mace to his head. He blinked to clear his slightly hazy vision. The canopy above his head was familiar; he was in his own bed. A noise to his right caught his attention. He turned his head slowly, carefully toward the window.

Alice was there. She was quietly setting a candlestick on the window ledge.

"Not starting the wake yet, I hope," he grunted.

She spun, dropping the unlit candle to the floor. She ignored it and hurried over to the bed. "Oh, thank heavens. Oh, Gareth!"

She grasped his hand. He wanted very much to wipe away the single tear that slid down her cheek, but his free arm was attached to his injured shoulder. Instead, he squeezed her hand gently. "I'm all right, elf." He tried rotating his shoulder and decided it wasn't a wise move. "Your grandfather *shot* me."

"Yes, I know. He feels absolutely wretched about it."

Gareth grunted. "I suppose I'll have to forgive him. He should have done it eight years ago when I abandoned you."

"Hush. Don't be silly—"

"No, Alice, I need to say . . ." He grimaced. "Christ, my head hurts!"

"You hit it on a rock."

"Of course I did. I couldn't have merely been shot. I suppose there's as reasonable an explanation as to why my mouth feels as if someone swabbed it with a sheep."

Alice released his hand and poured him a glass of water from a carafe beside the bed. "Mr. Gladbury was a bit liberal with the laudanum, I imagine." She gently helped him sit up and held the glass while he sipped. "He's a great believer in it." She plumped several pillows behind Gareth's back and he leaned back with a muffled groan.

"I always thought he was aptly named. Glad to bury his patients. Giving a man laudanum after he whacked his head. God help us."

Gareth remembered now: a lot of shouting, a lot of blood. And, to add insult to injury, he'd suffered through an intensely uncomfortable carriage ride into the village, the local physician with very cold hands and a large draught of something wretched-tasting. He didn't recall anything after that.

Alice's hand was cool on his forehead. "You should rest now. I'll just light the candles and leave you."

He wasn't about to let her leave, but she was already back at the window, collecting the candle and setting it carefully in the brass holder. There was one already sitting on the second windowsill. "I thought we'd decided to postpone the wake."

She smiled at him over her shoulder. "Candles in the window on Christmas Eve. To guide the spirits of those who've died in the last year home."

"Arthur."

"Mmm. And to guide anyone in need of shelter and hope."

That, Gareth decided, was him. He needed hope, needed it desperately. "Alice—"

"Be sure to make your Christmas Eve wish before you go to sleep again."

He watched as she struck a flint and lit the candles. The soft light brought a glow to her skin, burnished the loose curls around her face. He knew he had never seen a lovelier sight. "I already made my wish, as it happens."

"Did you? Good. I hope it comes true."

"Oh, so do I." Gareth saw another tear slip down her cheek even as she turned her face to hide it. "Alice. Come back here."

"You should rest . . ."

"Please." He patted the mattress beside his hip. She came back, perched herself tensely right on the edge, and stared down at her hands. "Don't you want to know what I wished for?"

"Oh, no. That's for you—"

"I wished for you."

She looked up then, eyes wide and shadowed in her elfin face. "For me?"

"Well, for a second chance, anyway. I . . ." Years of loneliness and regret squeezed at his heart and he felt the prick of tears at the back of his eyes. "I know I don't deserve it, but I'll beg nonetheless. Please, Alice, let me love you. As I did . . . better than I did. Perhaps if I'm very good at it, in a few years you'll come to love me again."

Hope and joy swelled so fiercely within her that Alice thought she might burst on the spot. Suddenly she was laughing and crying at the same time. "Oh, Gareth, I never stopped!"

She was ready to tell him about her own wish: that he might, just once, kiss her as he once had. She didn't have the chance. His hand snaked out to wrap around the back of her neck. In an instant, she was flat against him and he was kissing her in a way he never had. As if his very breath depended on it. When he finally released her, her lips were tingling, her heart was going like thunder, and she was seeing stars.

"Well," she managed after a moment, "you're *very* good at that."

His smile was quick and wicked. "I can be better." Then he sobered. "You'll marry me, Alice. As soon as possible."

Heart bursting, she could only nod. Then, after a moment, "I've one request to make of you."

"Anything."

"I will go anywhere with you, Gareth, gladly. But I would very much like to come home for Christmas every year. Could you stand that?"

"*That* is your request?" He smiled again, but this time with a hint of sadness. "You could ask me for the moon and stars, sweetheart."

"I know. But I'll settle for a piece of Ireland. I understand your need to travel. Even if Clarissa's baby is a girl, you needn't be here all the time—"

"*We* will be here. At Christmas, at the harvest, whenever

possible. If the baby is a girl, I'll have to be in London for the parliamentary sessions, but other than that, we will be here in Kilcullen."

"But, Gareth, you don't want the title, the responsibility. And you shouldn't have to shoulder it."

He shrugged his uninjured shoulder. "I've found that my feelings have changed on a few matters. If the title comes to me, so be it. Kilcullen is well worth whatever work comes with it."

"And if the baby is a boy?" she asked, a new hope rising.

"Then we'll build our own home nearby. Raise children and sheep and throw massive joins at Christmas. I know a duke who would greatly enjoy an evening in the company of the Sullivans."

This time it was Alice who kissed him, with enough joy and enthusiasm to leave them both breathless. And she might have gone on kissing him until Christmas morning had not a voice interrupted from the doorway.

"Alice!"

They both jumped and Alice nearly tipped herself off the mattress. "Clarissa? I . . . oh, dear. Well, you see . . ."

"Your sister has graciously consented to marry me," Gareth announced smoothly and, Alice thought, a bit smugly.

"Yes, yes, splendid," Clarissa replied. "And I do say it's about time. But we've more pressing matters at the moment."

"Clarie?" Alice was off the bed in an instant. "What is it?"

"This baby isn't going to wait until Twelfth Night, apparently." Clarissa clutched the door frame, face pale. "Oh, heavens. It's time!"

The Merry Magpie

by Sandra Heath

1

"*B*eggin' your pardon, my lord, but it *is* Marchwell Park you want, isn't it?" The postilion leaned into the hired chaise to awaken his young gentleman passenger. Christmas Eve was bitterly cold, and a flurry of fine snow whisked past the lantern that swung on an adjacent cottage.

"What in God's own name—?" Startled into shivering wakefulness, Sir Charles Neville struggled to get his bearings as he heard the storm soughing through bare-branched trees. For a moment he thought he was back in Madras, where Bay of Bengal breakers thundered constantly upon the exposed shore; but then the raw cold and stray snowflakes reminded him he was in England again, his long journey from India almost at an end.

It wasn't easy to collect his thoughts because he was exhausted and the blustering December air seemed to hail from the Arctic itself. The heavy greatcoat he'd managed to purchase on disembarking in Portsmouth wasn't as warm and protective as he'd hoped, with the result that the penetrating cold seemed to lie upon his skin like a layer of frost. By all the saints, he'd never thought he'd miss the Madras heat as much as this.

The tired postilion, no longer in the first flush of youth, stamped his feet and rubbed his gloved hands in an effort to restore some feeling to his extremities. He was swathed in capes and scarves, a jockey hat tugged low over his forehead, and his rather weasely face looked demonic in the moving light of the lantern as he addressed his passenger again, more exasperatedly this time. "Is it Marchwell Park you want or not, Lord Melville?"

"Don't shout, damn it, I'm not deaf!" Charles sat up properly and tipped his top hat back on his sun-bleached blond hair. He had long since given up trying to educate the numskull about his correct name and rank; besides, right now it was probably an advantage for the gatekeeper *not* to know who the new arrival really was.

The postilion wisely moderated his tone. "Begging your pardon again, my lord, but I asked you three times and you didn't awaken."

"Even so, as you know perfectly well that Marchwell Park is where I'm going, I hardly see why you suddenly need to confirm it again. Perchance it is your memory that is defective, not my ears." It was Christmas Eve and a hefty sum had already been demanded before setting out on this drive from the coast to Lady Marchwell's estate near Windsor, so if this was some eleventh-hour ruse to extract more money . . .

Well versed in the uncertain temper of the aristocracy, the postilion was at pains to be reassuring. "I remembered, sir, but then the gatekeeper said that as all Lady Marchwell's Christmas guests had now arrived maybe I'd come to the wrong address. He thinks it's probably Marshgrove House you want, farther toward Windsor, so it seemed best I should check with you . . . just in case."

Charles's pulse quickened and he looked again at the cottage, belatedly recognizing it as one of the twin lodges that flanked the impressive armorial gates on the road from Maidenhead to Windsor. "Kindly tell the gatekeeper to stop asking damn-fool questions and just let us through. Lady Marchwell has no idea I'm coming, but will receive me." Charles crossed his fingers as he spoke, for he was by no means sure how his wife's doting aunt would react to his sudden return. The last time he'd passed through these gates was when he'd been thrown out and told never to come back. Yet here he was, chancing his dubious luck again. He was twenty-eight now, older and hopefully wiser, and had come back from the other side of the world to tackle the past.

"Very well, sir." The postilion closed the chaise door and went to speak to the gatekeeper, who seemed most reluctant to admit a newcomer, no matter how titled.

Charles watched the two men arguing, then his attention returned to the cottage, where an uncurtained window allowed him to see a plump woman and two little redheaded girls laughing as they sorted through some freshly gathered greenery for decorating their home. Festive joy would be their lot over the coming days, he mused enviously, conscious that happiness, Christmas or otherwise, had eluded him for six wretched years now. No doubt this one would not prove any different, for in his heart of hearts he expected Lady Marchwell to send him away again without even deigning to see him. And why should she not? After all, he had been a faithless husband to her beloved niece, whose tender heart he'd broken most cruelly.

He repented his sins, oh, how he repented them, but wishing the past could be undone would not bring about the reconciliation he yearned for. He had to face Juliet's only relative, and throw himself on her mercy. Maybe after all this time she would relent at last, and tell him where his wife now lived. Would it be too much to hope that Juliet was here at Marchwell Park for Christmas? Too much to hope that the wedding ring he now wore on a purple ribbon around his neck would soon grace her finger again?

That had been his wish ever since separation. It was a fragile longing, a prayer that was whispered only in his soul, where his true self now hid away behind the false smiles and air of confidence he presented to the rest of the world. He had learned a very hard lesson, but learned it well, and if he had the chance of speaking to Juliet, he would . . . what? Convince her? Win her forgiveness? Sweep her into his arms once more? He doubted it. More likely he'd be obliged to creep away again with a monstrous flea in his presumptuous ear.

At last the postilion persuaded the gatekeeper to relent, and quickly hauled himself back onto the nearside of the two horses before the fellow changed his mind. His whistle pierced the racket of the storm and the chaise jolted forward again. Charles heard the groan and clang of the opening gates, and glimpsed the gatekeeper's startled face on realizing that Lord Melville was in fact Sir Charles Neville. The black sheep had returned, ensuring the resurrection of a scandal that had dominated society's gossip at the end of 1813.

That winter's abominable weather had paled to insignificance beside the shocking and very public failure of the Neville marriage. A terrible scene had been conducted in full view of Lady M's multitudinous Christmas guests, and soon the entire *monde* had gossiped about it. Before long society's servants had the juicy tale as well, and for all he knew Lady M's odious one-eyed pet magpie, Jack, being the most impudent, inquisitive, iniquitous, invariably inebriated member of the feathered tribe he'd ever come across, had also broadcast the story over the treetops. The whole of creation had condemned Sir Charles Neville, not his lovely spouse. "And with good reason, you fool, with good reason," he chided himself sadly.

To this day he didn't really know why he had strayed from the wife who meant the world to him. There was no excuse, no mitigating factor to grant him even a morsel of justification. It wasn't that he had fallen out of love with Juliet, quite the opposite in fact, for he adored her more each day. Simply because his friends were still enjoying their wild, unattached youth, he had begun to resent a marriage that had hitherto brought him happiness. He became convinced that because he and Juliet had married so very young—at their 1811 wedding they had been eighteen and twenty respectively—he had been unjustly denied the wild oats that was every young man's right. Taking it into his puerile head to sow those oats anyway, he had not merely indulged in some fleeting meaningless amours, but had taken a mistress.

The first infidelity with the actress Sally Monckton might possibly have been pardoned, for it had been the result of too much champagne, and too much greenroom revelry with his old comrades from Oxford days. With her flirtatious smiles, comely charms, and saucy brown eyes, she made it very plain that she was his for the asking. His resistance had been abysmally conspicuous by its absence. He recalled feeling deeply ashamed when next he faced Juliet, but she sensed nothing and their life continued as before.

Then, quite by accident, he met Sally again. He'd been in a sulk because he and Juliet had a stupid quarrel over nothing. His male vanity being a little bruised, he petulantly chose to be unfaithful again. His arrogant, immature reasoning had been simple; he'd done it once without discovery, so he could do it again. And he did, for almost the whole of 1813.

He made excuse after excuse to explain his absences from his and Juliet's Grosvenor Square home, and like so many husbands before him he had been so sure of his wife, so certain that she would always be there for him, so convinced that she would never find out anyway, that he deemed himself above suspicion.

How wrong could he have been? Due to that thrice-cursed magpie—aptly named after Jack Sheppard, the infamous thief hanged at Tyburn in 1724—his sins had been uncovered. Juliet had not been able to accept such deliberately prolonged unfaithfulness, and in the six years since she rejected him he had yearned over and over to repair the damage to his marriage. Also during that time he had devised many a novel way of disposing of the diminutive plumed Cyclops responsible for his downfall.

He lowered his glance, knowing full well that it was wrong to blame the magpie. Juliet had not been as unaware of her husband's misdeeds as he imagined, for his inner guilt had been displayed in his outward manner. Increasingly Juliet had known that something was wrong, and her suspicions could not help but center upon the likelihood of another woman in his life. To then discover that he had gone to the length of actually keeping a mistress was too much betrayal by far. So he'd lost the only thing that really mattered to him. And it served him right.

Charles sighed as the chaise rattled along the wide gravel drive toward the brilliantly illuminated Thames-side mansion. Overhead there was a barely discernible lacework of naked branches that in summer provided a cool bower of leaves; he and Juliet had driven here through sun-dappled shadows on their June wedding day. They had laughed and held hands, and the air had been sweet with the fragrance of the rose garlands on the open landau and the lilies-of-the-valley in Juliet's bridal posy. The memory stung tears to his dark blue eyes. Just to be here at Marchwell Park again was sufficient to unman him. Suddenly he was assailed with doubts. He should have stayed away and begun a new life in some remote corner of the realm . . . yet even in India the yearning for Juliet had remained fresh and poignant. There wasn't a place in the entire universe that was far enough away to free him from her spell.

He drew himself up sharply. It was Christmas, the season of goodwill and hope, and he would never forgive himself if he didn't strive to mend his marriage. Maybe it would never be possible, maybe Juliet had given her heart to someone else now; maybe so many things . . . But they were still wed, and he desperately wanted to be her husband again. In every way.

Lady Marchwell's sixteenth-century mansion drew nearer by the second. It was a modest but beautiful imitation of Hampton Court, with the same red Tudor brickwork, courtyards, towers and cupolas, but it was only a third the size of its palatial forerunner. All of a sudden he felt that the hopes he'd nursed for so long were about to be dashed. He looked away from the mansion, and in doing so turned his attention in the direction of the Thames. There weren't any lights glimmering between the great willows that grew along the riverbank. Wasn't anyone staying at the Retreat? A shadow fell softly over his hopes, for a light would definitely have signified Juliet's presence.

Other memories now rushed back. During the four years he and Juliet had been together as a married couple they had always spent Christmas at Lady Marchwell's delightful fishing lodge, which stood on a four-acre island that divided the river into two channels. The Retreat was a thatched cottage orné that had been built in 1790, and the island was called Magpie Eyot because of the flocks of the handsome birds that were always to be found in its tall trees.

"Oh, Charles, it is pronounced 'eight.' Eeyots are Bedlamites!" he murmured, remembering Juliet's infectious laughter as she teased him for mispronouncing the old Anglo-Saxon word for island. Her deliberate corruption of idiot into eeyot had become one of their silly sayings after that. Anyone whose common sense was called into question was always an eeyot. "As I was an eeyot for destroying my marriage," he said to himself.

The postilion's shout wrenched him from his reverie as the chaise drew to a halt beneath the porte cochere at the front of the house. Sprays of festive conifer shuddered on the porch pillars, and a woven circle of ivy shook against an arched door that would not have looked out of place on a church. The stone griffins guarding the steps had red ribbon necklets, but the bright splashes of color looked forlorn as the wind moaned and whined past the chaise.

Through the windows of the nearby great parlor, which blazed with candlelight, Charles could see Lady Marchwell's many guests dancing Christmas Eve away beneath festoons of holly, mistletoe, bay, myrtle, and ivy. Gold and silver apples shone amid evergreen arrangements on walls and mantels, and ribbons moved gently in the heat from the roaring fire in the immense stone fireplace. Everyone wore

Tudor costume, and he could just hear that the tune they danced to was "Greensleeves." Hopefully he raked the scene for Juliet, but she wasn't there.

Another beam of bright light struck suddenly into the darkness as two of Lady Marchwell's footmen hastened out to attend the new arrival. "Now to face up to things," Charles breathed, steeling himself for the coming minutes.

The footmen descended the shallow flight of steps, and the senior of the two opened the chaise door and lowered the iron rung. Only when he straightened and saw the gentleman who climbed down did his manner change to one of dismayed uncertainty. Would her ladyship wish Sir Charles Neville to be readmitted after all this time?

Charles gave a wry smile. "Don't fret, James. Should there be a problem I will assume full responsibility."

The man was taken aback. "You remember me, sir?"

"As you remember me, for as I recall you were among those who bundled me unceremoniously into my carriage when I last departed these hallowed walls."

The man went red. "Er, yes, sir, I fear so. I also fear that her ladyship may not wish you to—"

"Indeed she may not, but there is only one way to find out, is there not?" Charles interrupted. Shivering in the cold, he flexed his hands in his gloves as he began to ascend the shallow flight of steps toward the open door.

James stood there indecisively, then ran after the awkward arrival, which prompted the postilion to quickly shout, "Hey! What about the rest of my fare?"

Charles halted and turned, shoving a fat purse into James's hand. "I agreed to pay the fellow half the fare on leaving Portsmouth and the remainder on arrival, but I may yet need the chaise if Lady Marchwell sends me packing. Take this and inform the fellow that he will be paid when my fate is known, otherwise he will be obliged to take me on to Windsor before he sees another farthing. Do not unload so much as a single valise in the meantime."

Again James hesitated, feeling uncomfortably sure that

Lady Marchwell would indeed send Sir Charles packing. Maybe, in the interest of staying in employment at Marchwell Park, the wisest thing for any footman to do would be to send him off without her ladyship even knowing he'd been here . . .

Charles guessed the man's thoughts. "Don't even entertain the thought of manhandling me, James, for this time I'd have the better of you in seconds. I learned a trick or two in the East which would leave you turned inside out, and no mistake."

Turned inside out? James's eyes widened, and without a murmur he took the purse and returned to the chaise to speak to the indignant postilion.

"A wise decision," Charles observed, then continued into the red-and-white tiled entrance hall, where the same family portraits were arrayed in the same places on the oak-paneled walls, and the grand staircase was as seasonally garlanded as always. A Yule log crackled in the hearth of the handsome carved-stone fireplace, and the sounds of merriment and music from the adjacent great parlor were loud. Every December the house bulged at the very seams with family and friends, and an excellent time was had by all. Evergreens were everywhere, confirming Charles in the long-held belief that every year Lady Marchwell denuded the woodland on the boundary of her land. No hostess decorated her home more lavishly for Christmas, or celebrated more generously; and no invitation here was ever willingly declined.

Another footman, who did not know him, requested his name and then took Charles's top hat and gloves and laid them carefully by the copper bowl of holly on the carved oak table in the center of the hall. As he was divested of his coat, Charles detected the delicious smell of hot spiced wine and mince pies coming from the kitchens. The same Christmas fare had been in preparation during the agonizing moments when his deceit had been laid bare to Juliet. He had been standing in this very spot, having just returned from Sally in London, when Juliet came downstairs to greet him.

Then Jack the magpie's mischief had intervened, and suddenly a marriage had lain in ruins.

The footman interrupted Charles's thoughts. "If you will wait in the library, sir, I will go to her ladyship."

The library, directly across the hall from the great parlor, was a suitably private place where raised voices and harsh recriminations could not be overheard. As the footman hurried away into the grand parlor to find Lady Marchwell, Charles paused for a moment, toying with the shirt frill protruding from the cuff of his tight-fitting dark blue coat. After the more casual attire he'd adopted in Madras, these fashionable English togs were damned uncomfortable. What with a starched neckcloth, close-cut waistcoat, and pantaloons that might have been painted on his person, he felt like a Christmas capon trussed, stuffed, and glazed in readiness for roasting.

His glance moved to the heavily carved door of the library. "And there, if I'm not mistaken, is the oven," he said as he crossed toward it.

2

As Charles proceeded in trepidation to the library at Marchwell Park, his estranged wife Juliet lay on a cushioned wickerwork sofa in front of a roaring fire where fresh pinecones hissed and spat among the leaping flames. Her handsome green eyes reflected the flames, her pale complexion was blushed to pink, and she was sipping hot chocolate from a bone china Wedgwood cup painted with a river scene. She was twenty-five years old and attractive, with even features, a slightly retroussé nose, and a generous mouth. Her sparkling character, neat figure, and natural grace had once made her the belle of many a ball, but she did not sparkle much now, and much preferred a quiet life at home.

Light brown curls tumbled loosely around the shoulders of her fern-colored merino robe, beneath which she wore a nightgown, because Christmas Eve or not, she had decided to retire early. There was no reason not to, for she had dismissed the servants to their families and celebrations, and was alone in the house without any plans to do anything except perhaps read a little in bed before putting out the candle.

The cozy room she was in was called the drawing room, but did not really warrant such a grand description, being intimate, quaintly rural, and brightly furnished. It had blue wickerwork chairs and sofas with white convolvulus embroidered on the sky blue cushions, and latticed paper twined with painted creepers that covered not only the walls but the ceiling as well. Alternating with the wallpaper were mirrored panels set in rough elm frames, and the Axminster carpet, woven especially for the room, suggested a bluebell wood in spring. Diamond-paned windows, arched and elegant, reached down to the floor and were adorned with borders of stained glass. In summer they were flung open to the grounds, the notion being that nature was invited into the house, making it difficult to tell where the one ended and the other began. It was meant to conjure the picturesque country home of a gamekeeper or farm laborer, but was far too luxurious and fashionable to be convincingly rustic.

Summer was far away now, however, and the winter wind drew down the chimney, making the pinecones twinkle and the red-ribbon decorations on the mantel lift gently. The scent of conifer drifted from the sprays Juliet had gathered that day, and like everything else associated with Christmas—mulled wine, mince pies, chestnuts, roast goose—it brought thoughts of Charles. From time to time the memories were so keen that her finger still seemed enclosed by the wedding ring she had discarded on discovering the extent of his unfaithfulness. She was aware of weakly permitting the past to still dominate her life, but at this time of the year her resistance seemed to fade away completely, exposing pain that was as fresh and hurtful as if those events of 1813 had only happened recently.

Sometimes she was glad that Jack the magpie had finally forced things to a head; sometimes she wished with all her heart that the truth had remained buried. She paused. Did she *really* mean that? Could she honestly wish to have remained in that dreadful half world of unproven suspicions, fretful for answers, afraid of those same answers, and feeling sick with misery that happiness seemed to have slipped away behind her back? She had been aware for some time that Charles was keeping something from her, for she had glimpsed it in his eyes, sensed it in his odd reticence about his visits to London, and felt it in the hesitance of his love-making. Something was wrong, but whenever she asked he denied it. Slowly but surely a rift had appeared between them, but he had pretended not to notice, which only added resentment to her burden of hurt bewilderment. From there it had been but a short step to wondering if there was some-one else in his life.

Looking back she wished she'd been difficult with him, or had screamed and made scenes, but she hadn't. What an eeyot he must have thought her. The old pet word brought a lump to her throat, and she clenched a fist and dug her fin-gernails into her palm, a ploy that always seemed to keep tears at bay, although she did not know exactly why. It had certainly worked during those dreadful moments when Jack's instinctive thievery had forced Charles's shabby secret into the open.

The denouement took place in the entrance hall at March-well Park. She and Charles were actually staying in the Re-treat for Christmas as always, but she had been with her aunt in the main house when he returned from yet another of his unexplained visits to London. The house was full of guests, mostly in their rooms at that moment dressing for the Christ-mas Eve ball, which that year had a fairy-tale theme. It was evening and she was already in her costume as she ran down the staircase to greet him. She was dressed as Titania, in a gauzy sea green gown and tiny sequined wings. Her hair flowed loose, and her smile was bright, for she had resolved to do all she could to close the chasm that marred her mar-riage. The delicious fragrance of mulled wine and baking mince pies permeated the house from the kitchens, but it was only afterward that she'd become aware of it; only af-terward she'd come to hate it.

Now, as her thoughts wandered back to those final mo-ments, time seemed to peel away and suddenly it was Christmas Eve 1813 again, and the bitterest winter in living memory had just begun . . .

*   *   *

"By all the saints, it's cold outside!" Charles declared, his spurs jingling on the Tudor-tiled floor as he crossed the hall to the table, where a footman waited to take his heavy olive green greatcoat, top hat, and gloves. In the seconds before the outer door was closed Juliet heard the crunch of hooves on frozen gravel as a groom led his horse away.

Her nerve faltered suddenly, and she hesitated at the foot of the staircase with a hand on the dark wooden rail. Outside icicles hung from eaves and hedgerows, a freezing mist had settled over the land, and chimney smoke was kept close to the ground; but inside all was bright, warm, and welcoming. The customary copper bowl of holly stood on the carved oak table in the center of the hall, its berries bright and cheerful in the light from the wheel-rim chandeliers and roaring fire. The servants had not long finished adorning every sill, cornice, jamb, rail, and alcove with the greenery that was essential for the festive season, and now she was aware of the fresh scent of conifers.

She studied her husband anxiously. Charles was twenty-two, tall and striking, with blond hair and bluer-than-blue eyes, and there was a rugged strength about him that in spite of her unhappiness still drew her like a moth to a flame. His taste was impeccable, from the cut and quality of his greatcoat, to the superb lines of the damson coat and gray breeches he wore beneath it. The ride from London had not disturbed the excellent knot his valet had earlier achieved in his starched muslin neckcloth, nor had exertion wrinkled the fine striped marcella of his waistcoat.

He appeared the epitome of all that was handsome and admired in a gentleman, but in the depth of her heart his unhappy wife had begun to question his faithfulness. There was something going on that he wished to keep from her, and every instinct told her discovering what it was would break not only her heart but their marriage. Was there a more handsome man in all England? she wondered. With his complexion still tanned from the late summer he gave the impression of spending most of his days outdoors, yet of late he had become a denizen of London's drawing rooms. What did he do when he was away from her? Who was he with?

Conscious that she had remained at the foot of the stairs, Charles waited until the footman had helped him out of the greatcoat before turning. His glance swept over her fairy-queen gown. "How now, proud Titania," he murmured.

"How late, tardy Oberon," she replied.

"True, and for that I beg forgiveness. But you have my word that I will be dressed in time for the ball." His easy tone was forced, she decided, increased doubt sweeping her resolution aside. Pride would not allow her to debase herself by playing the sweet trusting wife.

Her silence made him uneasy. "Are you angry with me?"

"Should I be?" she asked, countering question with question.

Their eyes met again for a moment before she looked away. He hesitated, then nodded at the footman. "You may go now, but please leave my coat," he added.

Surprised that such an undeniably damp garment was not to be spirited away to the kitchens to be dried and aired, the man did as he was bade, resting it neatly over the back of a tapestry-upholstered Tudor chair by the hearth.

When he had gone, Charles held out his hand to his wife. "I confess to being chilled to the very marrow, so let us go closer to the fire," he said.

Slowly Juliet left the staircase, but she ignored his out-stretched hand and went to the fireplace, where the customary Yule log winked amid the flames. From the corner of her eye she saw Charles's hand fall away again, and knew that he looked at her for a moment before joining her. They stood side by side, their faces glowing with flamelight, but there was a chill in their silence.

"Is something wrong, Juliet?" he asked at last. "Are you unwell?"

"I am in excellent health," she answered.

"Juliet, I—"

What he had been about to say would never be known because Jack's loud, staccato chatter interrupted him. The magpie was perched on Lady Marchwell's wrist as she smiled down at them from the top of the staircase. Juliet's aunt was dressed as Cinderella's Fairy Godmother, in a voluminous blue cloak over a white gown, with a tall pointed hat that completely concealed her graying curls. "May all your wishes come true, *mes enfants,*" she declared amiably, waving a rather gaudy wand as she began to descend.

Jack's presence marked Lady Marchwell as something out of the ordinary run of ladies. No sweet, twittering canary or lovebird for her, instead she chose a raucous, cheeky, exceedingly ill-mannered magpie that would have stolen the world itself provided it glittered enough.

As she reached the foot of the stairs Juliet's aunt smiled again. "Welcome back, Charles."

"I'm glad to be back, Lady M," he replied warmly, but Juliet knew he was annoyed about the interruption. And maybe he was annoyed to be here, instead of with . . . whoever it was.

"I trust you mean to change into costume before attending the ball?"

"Naturally, for what is Titania without her Oberon?" he replied.

What indeed? Juliet thought, for his words seemed a little too close for comfort.

Charles eyed Jack as the bird fluttered and then swayed on Lady Marchwell's wrist. "Is that scoundrel drunk again?"

"He's had a festive sip or two," she admitted, "but only to toast the season."

"Be honest, Lady M, he has some excuse or other to toast every day of the year, and twice on Sundays."

Juliet would once have joined her aunt in laughing at this, but today she simply could not; indeed, she couldn't even remain at his side, and moved away under the pretext of rearranging his greatcoat on the chair. The coat would provide a moment of distraction; a moment to compose herself a little more. She felt him turn quickly to briefly stretch out a hand that he immediately snatched back, and she sensed that his reaction had nothing to do with her leaving his side but everything to do with where she moved to. Why? What prompted such an undoubtedly nervous response on his part?

Any hope she had entertained of regaining her composure was forgotten, for the very act of moving the coat brought about a denouement that shattered everything. A dainty golden chain dangled from the coat's flapped pocket, and began to glitter and flash in the firelight. It immediately caught Jack's single eye, and with a delighted chatter—*chak-chak-chak*—he launched himself from Lady Marchwell's wrist and dove upon the shiny object. For a few seconds he fluttered furiously against the coat, then flew off with his trophy, a costly gold locket that Charles's conscience had bade him purchase for his betrayed wife. Finding a safe perch among the evergreens garlanding the gallery balustrade at the top of the staircase, the wobbling magpie brandished the locket and chain triumphantly in his beak.

Voices sounded from the floor above as the first guests emerged to go down to the grand parlor, although as yet no one had reached the staircase.

Lady Marchwell was dismayed with the magpie. "Oh, Jack, you bad bird! Bring it back this instant!"

But the bird's antics were no longer of any interest to Juliet and Charles, for the locket was not the only thing to have been dislodged from the greatcoat pocket. A crumpled note had been pulled out at the same time. Charles moved swiftly to retrieve it, but his wife's fingers closed over it first. She heard his sharp intake of breath, saw the guilt written large in his eyes, and knew this was his moment of nemesis. Had he made no move or sound she would simply have pushed the note back into the pocket and thought no more of it; instead she held it tightly in her hand as she studied her husband's face, which was suddenly pale beneath his tan.

He swallowed, then cleared his throat and tried to make

light of things. "It's nothing, sweeting," he said, and held out his hand for the note.

She stepped back. "What's going on, Charles? Why don't you want me to see this?"

"It's nothing at all," he repeated, but his tone gave the lie to his words.

Lady Marchwell's attention was now riveted upon her niece and her husband.

"Then you will not mind if I look at it?" Juliet went on.

He didn't reply.

"Charles?"

"I would prefer you not to," he said then, at last meeting her gaze properly.

Time seemed to suddenly stand still, and all she could hear beyond the thudding of her heart was Jack's pleased little noises as he deposited the locket amid the greenery and subjected it to a close, single-eyed examination. She knew too that a little gaggle of guests were at the top of the staircase, having paused there in some embarrassment as it was realized there was a scene of some sort taking place below.

"What is the matter, Juliet? Charles?" Lady Marchwell was anxious, especially now there were other ears to hear.

Charles tried to smile reassuringly. "Nothing, Lady M, nothing at all, although I fear I may have given Juliet the opposite impression. It's merely a note from a fellow member at White's challenging me to a match next spring between his brown colt and my bay filly. He suggests Newmarket, and I am agreeable. That is all. The sum involved is rather more than I usually wager, and in all honesty I'd prefer Juliet not to know how much I am prepared to risk on my filly's unproven talents."

Experience not only told Lady Marchwell he was lying, but also the likely truth. Her natural impulse was to shield her niece by pretending to accept his explanation, not least for the benefit of the eavesdropping guests whose numbers increased by the moment. "There you are, Juliet. Gentlemen will always be gentlemen, and they will always wager upon anything, so don't be a ninny, just give it back to him." The underlying advice was plain enough. *If you read that note now the whole house will soon be party to its contents; better to play the ostrich, prevent gossip, and save your marriage.*

But Juliet could brook no such double standards, and didn't care about the faces gazing from the floor above. To have simply returned the note to him unread might bring the immediate awkward moment to a close, but it would also ensure countless other such moments as her wretchedness refused to let the matter lie. She *had* to see what the note really said, for she could not continue as she had these past months.

There was a stir from the landing and staircase as with trembling hands she began to smooth the paper.

3

"Please don't read it, Juliet," Charles pleaded, "for I swear that it contains nothing over which you need concern yourself."

Juliet moved farther away from him, fearing he would snatch it from her, but he remained where he was. At last the few handwritten words were quite legible. She read them aloud. "My darling Charles, I yearn for you to come to me again, and pray to be in your arms tonight. Your adoring mistress, Sally."

There were gasps from the onlookers, and Lady Marchwell closed her eyes. Charles stood as if carved from stone, his face ashen, his eyes tormented with remorse. The note slipped from Juliet's numb fingers. A mistress? "Oh, Charles, how could you do this . . .?" she whispered.

He was stricken to the core, and his voice was choked. "If you want me to say that I am sorry, then I say it with all my heart. If you want me to say that it will never happen again, then that too I say with all my heart."

Something seemed to shatter within her, and her air of calm disintegrated into fury. "What I want you to say is that this hasn't happened! That you are not the Charles to whom those words are directed! That you don't keep some tawdry *belle de nuit* for your pleasure?"

A rustle of whispering passed among the watching guests, whose numbers had now swollen to include almost everyone staying at the house, or so it seemed to Lady Marchwell. Charles was now as beyond considering an audience as Juliet. He turned away, his hands momentarily hiding his face, then he dragged them away again to make himself confront the bitter accusation in his wife's eyes. "Oh, my darling, would that I *could* offer that reassurance, but I cannot."

"How long have you been making me the laughingstock of society?" she demanded, her green eyes shimmering with tears, her fists clenched as she forced her fingernails into her palms in an effort to cling on to the remnants of self-control.

"I haven't made a laughingstock of you, Juliet, so please do not think that I—"

"Then simply tell me how long you have been indulging in this sordid liaison." At least let him be truthful about *that!*

"Not long."

"Liar!" she cried. "You first broke your vows at the beginning of this year, and you have clearly been doing it ever since! You've been making love to your doxy, then leaving her bed to come to mine! How *could* you? How could you . . . ?" The last two words were only whispered, for a great wave of misery washed over her and she broke down in tears.

He stepped instinctively toward her, but she struck him on the face, her fingers leaving red marks. "I suppose the locket was a sop for your conscience, a loving trinket to allay suspicion?" Her voice was almost shrill with emotion, and the watching guests ceased to whisper but chattered loudly about the incredible fracas they were witnessing. Their voices fell away into silence again to listen to Charles's reply.

"Juliet, my dearest darling . . ." But he couldn't say any more, for he was guilty. *Guilty!* He closed his eyes, wishing hell and damnation on the thieving bird that had brought this about.

"I want you to leave this house," Juliet said then, her voice suddenly becoming oddly calm.

Lady Marchwell spoke up quickly. "Never do anything in the heat of the moment. Juliet, my dear, I know this is a horrid bolt right out of the blue, but—"

"But it isn't completely out of the blue, Aunt M," Juliet interrupted, her gaze still fixed upon Charles. "I've suspected for a long time, and this has merely confirmed my fears."

Charles was tormented. "Forgive me, I beg of you! Forgive me everything, for I vow I will never hurt you again. I love you, Juliet, and if you would but give me the chance to explain—"

"What is there to explain? You keep a mistress, her name is Sally, and she wishes you to be with her. I only hope she is worth it, because you are not welcome here. I want you to leave because I cannot bear to be with you anymore."

Lady Marchwell was desperate to prevent the matter sliding further into the morass of rage and recrimination. "Juliet, my dear, this is my house, not yours, and if—"

"And if he stays here, then *I* will leave," Juliet said quietly, "and it will not be to return to Somerset, for I will never set foot in Neville Castle again. Nor will I go to Grosvenor Square." Everything she held dear had been dashed aside, and Charles was solely responsible. *He* had broken his vows, and with them her heart. She couldn't and wouldn't forgive him.

Still Lady Marchwell endeavored to pour oil on troubled waters. "My dear, you are hurt and bitter right now, but I am sure that you and Charles still love each other enough to—"

"I despise him," Juliet broke in softly, for in that moment she did.

So did a young lady guest garbed as Puss in Boots. "Hear, hear . . ." she cried, her own husband having similarly deceived her.

Charles spread his hands. "Please find some forgiveness in your heart, Juliet," he whispered.

"Were you forced to commence your liaison?"

He didn't want to reply, but had no choice. "No."

"Then I have no forgiveness."

"Nor I! Nor I!" cried Puss in Boots, brandishing a dainty fist.

Lady M spoke up quickly. "Juliet, my dear, you must not be rash. Many a man strays from his marriage bed."

"Yes, and many a wife endures such infidelities, but I think more of myself than to allow anyone to walk over me as if I am of no consequence." Juliet tossed a heartbroken glance at Charles.

He was appalled by the image her words created. "I would *never* do that!" he cried. "I may have failed you, my darling, but I have never ceased to love and cherish you."

"Shame! Shame!" was heard from several of the guests, and Puss in Boots was so indignant that she had to be restrained from rushing down to confront him.

"And never ceased to pat yourself on the back for having so cleverly pulled the wool over my trusting eyes," Juliet replied. "Please go, Charles, I don't want to see or speak to you again!" She struggled with her wedding ring, tore it from her finger, and hurled it at him. It arced through the air, then struck the floor with the clarity of a little bell. Shining brightly, it rolled over the tiles and came to rest beneath the table upon which stood the bowl of holly. Juliet caught up her skirts and fled toward the staircase, at the top of which the guests parted like the Red Sea.

Lady Marchwell was unutterably dismayed. "Please don't go like this, Juliet! Stay, I beg of you, for I'm sure this rift can be mended."

Charles took several steps after his distraught wife. "Don't reject me, my darling! Let me prove that you are the one I love, the one I've always loved."

"Monstrous liar!" cried an indignant dowager whose Cinderella costume fitted her ample figure a little too well.

Juliet paused to glance coldly back at him. "You've *always* loved me? Charles, I will never again believe you ever loved me at all."

She began to run up the staircase, hardly aware of those

gathered at the top, and certainly not aware of Jack. The magpie was still on the garlanded rail, and had been jealously guarding the locket from any light fingers, not that anyone had dared to chance a peck from his powerful beak. Now, however, the bird's attention wavered from the locket to the wedding ring, which shone so enticingly on the floor of the hall. He was torn between the two prizes, but his mind was made up when Charles stepped to retrieve the ring. With a fusillade of jealous squawks, the magpie abandoned the locket and flew down to whisk the ring from Charles's outstretched fingers. This time the magpie made certain of his ill-gotten gain by disappearing with it into the adjacent grand parlor.

In that moment Charles could willingly have strangled the unprincipled bird. All he wanted was to return the ring to Juliet's finger, as if that would miraculously put his marriage in order again, but when he dashed into the grand parlor, set upon strangling the wretched magpie if necessary, Jack had disappeared.

Lady Marchwell knew she must play the firm hostess, so she smiled up at the hovering guests. "Come now, ladies, gentlemen, and children too, of course. I believe this part of the entertainment is at an end. Pray come down so the ball may commence." With that she looked into the ballroom and nodded at the small orchestra she had engaged for the occasion. The jaunty but rather inappropriate notes of the "Our Love Will Never End" reel immediately began to sound.

Lady Marchwell frowned at such a choice, but had to make the best of it. She smiled and nodded graciously at the guests as they passed, and took Puss in Boots by the arm as said young lady showed every sign of subjecting Charles to some remarkably feline scratches. "Not now, Hermione, there's a dear cat," Lady Marchwell murmured, steering the furious young lady into the grand parlor, and giving her into the care of a rather frail and elderly Ali Baba.

When all the guests had gone into the grand parlor, Lady Marchwell drew Charles to one side. "Perhaps it would be better if you do as Juliet wishes," she said with a long, sad breath

"And leave? But if I do that—"

"Right now she is not open to reason. Oh, Charles, *why* did you do it? I really thought that your marriage was stronger than this."

He ran his hand agitatedly through his hair. "Pathetic as it sounds, I was jealous of my friends' freedom to do as they pleased."

"If that is your reason then you are far more immature and feckless than I ever dreamed."

"I don't love Sally, nor does she love me, although she is determined to keep me simply for the kudos of having a titled protector. She has been threatening to tell Juliet if I try to end things."

Lady Marchwell raised a scornful eyebrow. "Oh, poor you."

He colored at the sarcasm, and returned to her. "I suppose I deserve that."

"Yes, you do, sir. I suppose your next whine will be that the liaison never meant anything and so you ought to be granted absolution."

His flush intensified. "Well, it *didn't* mean anything, it was something I started then could not stop."

"How very unfortunate for you."

"I know I have sunk in your estimation, but—"

"But nothing, sir, for you have sunk almost without trace," Lady Marchwell said tartly. "How dare you say this year-long liaison has meant nothing! That response has been the bleat of faithless males throughout the ages. Why is it that men regard as irrelevant a physical act their wives deem an expression of love? A woman does not give herself lightly, but it seems the men think nothing of it. Why then should your wife think you've ever meant any of the kisses you shared with her? Reason tells her you didn't."

"But I did! Damn it all, Lady M, I *adore* Juliet!"

"Oh? Yet you have acquired a mistress. But I was forgetting, she means nothing to you, does she? It is a veritable torture for you to lie in her arms, and anyway, it's all of no import." Lady Marchwell pursed her lips and eyed him. "Tell me, Charles, if the shoe were on the other foot now, and it was Juliet saying all the things you are saying, would you accept that it meant nothing and take her back into your arms?"

"Well, I . . ."

"The truth, sir, no shilly-shallying."

Charles took a long, unhappy breath, and shook his head. "No, of course I wouldn't."

"Exactly. You would be crushed to a point you would fear was beyond redemption, and you would certainly need time to recover from such a blow to your heart, your pride, and your faith. So kindly have the grace to accept how Juliet feels right now. I'm afraid you will simply have to wait and hope that she comes around."

He looked anxiously at the older woman. "She will, won't she? I—I mean, she won't spurn me forever?"

Lady Marchwell didn't know the answer. "That is in the lap of the gods, Charles. One thing I will say is that you have much growing up still to do. Boys do not make good husbands, and I fear that your particularly infantile behavior has forced Juliet to reassess everything. Maybe you stand no chance of winning her back until you are a man in every meaning of the word."

"If I leave, where should I go? Back to the Retreat?"

"Certainly not, for that is Juliet's territory." Lady Marchwell's mouth twitched. "Your present destination is your problem, sir, but if you wish there to be any hope of a reconciliation with Juliet, I suggest you stay well away from your mistress. Grosvenor Square will not do for obvious reasons, so I suggest you hie yourself back to Somerset. Neville Castle is a bolt hole par excellence."

"So is Hades itself," he remarked in a wryly resigned tone.

Lady Marchwell smiled. "I think you are already in that

particular place, Charles. If there is to be an ultimate destination, I pray it will be somewhere that will guarantee you mature from the callow boy you reveal yourself to be right now. Whatever you do, I cannot emphasize enough that you rid yourself of your unpleasant mistress, whose blackmail can surely hold no threat now that Juliet knows the worst. Who is this other woman, by the way?"

He responded reluctantly. "Her name is Sally Monckton, and she is an actress at Astley's."

Lady M recoiled. "Astley's? Oh, *Charles*! You might at least have had the discernment to find someone at the Theatre Royal or Covent Garden!"

"I would have thought a mistress was a mistress, no matter whence she came."

"Your words, not mine. Now, be gone, for the sooner you are no longer beneath this roof the better."

"I will return tomorrow, and the day after, and the day after that."

"I cannot prevent you, but if Juliet requests me to have you ejected, you may be sure I will carry out her wishes. I have always liked you, Charles, but I am first and foremost Juliet's aunt, and she is my sole consideration in this particular matter."

He nodded. "I understand."

Minutes later he had ridden away from Marchwell Park and returned to London, not to the Grosvenor Square town house but White's club in St. James's, where his lack of female companionship could not only be guaranteed, but could be confirmed by any number of witnesses. It had also to be said that being an all-male preserve, the club was free of those feminine touches that were bound to make his pain and remorse all the worse.

He gave Sally her congé that very night. It was a disagreeable meeting, during which she revealed that behind her charming exterior there lurked a common vixen who had managed to stay completely out of his sight until now. She berated him as being every vile thing under the sun, except that her vocabulary was far more shocking and colorful than that. It seemed that Astley's Amphitheatre was nothing if not educational.

The past faded and it was 1819 again. Juliet placed her empty cup on the little table beside the sofa, next to the decanters of sherry and brandy that were always kept there, then she leaned her head back. Had she been foolish to refuse all Charles's pleas six years ago? Had she been a mule not to listen to Aunt M's commonsensical arguments? Would he have been faithful ever after if they had been reconciled? Or would he have known her for an incurable gull and broken that same commandment again and again?

It was too late for answers now, because he had gone to Bengal—Madras itself, she believed—and before leaving he had intimated that he did not intend to ever return to England. For several minutes more Juliet gazed into the fire, dwelling on it all. She was warm and drowsy from the flames and the hot chocolate, and gradually her eyes began to close. As she slipped into sleep her last thought was to wonder what had happened to the wedding ring that Jack had hidden so securely that it had never been found.

4

*C*harles paused at the library door to glance back at the entrance hall. For a moment he saw again the misty figures of 1813, like actors placed upon a stage, with their audience of Christmas guests gazing down from the top of the staircase. He took a defiant breath. Those events had not brought the curtain down on his marriage, but had merely been a temporary setback.

There was only firelight inside as he entered the library, which to his relief was deserted. He became aware of the slow ticking of the long-case clock as he closed the door behind him, then looked around at the holly-decked shelves where gilt-embossed book spines shone in the dancing light. Had any of the more learned tomes been opened since Lord Marchwell's demise? Probably not, for Lady Marchwell preferred novels. He almost feared to let his eyes wander above the fireplace, where the portrait of Juliet had always hung, but at last he gazed again upon the gentle face that haunted him.

It was so exquisite a likeness that the living, breathing woman might be on the point of stepping down into the room. She was wearing a low-cut white silk gown and the emerald drops and necklace that had been his wedding gift. Behind her the grounds of Marchwell Park reached to the Thames, where Magpie Eyot and the Retreat were clearly depicted. He went closer and reached up to touch the canvas. "Oh, Juliet, my dearest darling, I was such an eeyot; such a very great eeyot . . ." he murmured.

A slight movement in the corner of the room made him turn sharply, fearing he wasn't alone after all, but all he saw was Jack the magpie perched on the lip of a silver tray endeavoring to dislodge the stopper of a decanter of dark amber liquid. For a moment man and bird looked at each other in the firelight, then the latter returned his attention to the stopper.

Suddenly finding himself face-to-face with his old foe— or should that be face-to-beak?—Charles was surprised to realize that his animosity toward the magpie was not as virulent as might have been expected. "So you're still around, you plaguey old cyclops, and still possessed of a taste for Lady M's best sherry."

Jack ignored him, the stopper being of infinitely greater importance, and Charles watched resignedly. What point was there in blaming a magpie for his woes? If he, Charles Neville, had not strayed so shamefully from the marriage bed there wouldn't have been any unsavory secrets to expose. As this thought struck him, he went to the table, removed the stopper, and poured a measure into one of the crystal glasses on the tray. "There you are, since you've probably been wrestling with that decanter for the past hour or more you deserve a reward for your endeavors. Merry Christmas and *pax vobiscum* for the New Year."

The magpie blinked his one eye, as if fearing to awaken at any moment and discover the stopper wedged in more tightly than ever.

"Well, go on," Charles urged.

Needing no further bidding, the bird plunged his beak into the glass and took a long draft, tilting his head back with pleasure as the sherry trickled down his throat. Charles didn't hear Lady Marchwell enter the room, and knew nothing until her sharp voice suddenly addressed him. "So you have the audacity to still behave as if you reside here, do you, sir?"

Once again he turned quickly, his heart sinking at her tone, which did not bode well for his chances. Somehow he managed to execute what he hoped was a suitably respectful and placatory bow. "The compliments of the season to you, Lady M."

Juliet's aunt, dressed as Queen Elizabeth to the very last curl of her elaborate red wig, inclined her head civilly, no more, and her sapphire-and-silver brocade gown, stiff with a farthingale, rustled as she advanced from the door. "Why have you returned after all this time?" she inquired coolly.

"To make full atonement."

"Then you may not be comforted to know that Juliet hasn't intimated a change in her attitude toward you."

His heart sank more. "She still despises me?"

Lady Marchwell went to scoop the reluctant magpie onto her finger. "That's enough of that, you drunkard," she muttered, and Jack hung his head forlornly as he realized his tippling had been curtailed for the moment. Lady Marchwell stroked the bird's gleaming back as she looked at Charles again. "Juliet has never *despised* you, Charles, she has simply been unable to forgive you for hurting her so much."

"I know the extent of my sins, Lady M, but I also know the extent of my love for my wife. It is endless, believe me, and I have come back to try my damnedest to win a reconciliation."

"Have you indeed?" Her attention wavered again as Jack, deeming her attention to be sufficiently diverted, hopped back to the tray and took another swift sip. Lady Marchwell was incensed and tapped him imperatively, at which he gave an indignant squawk and flew up to a holly-swathed bust of the Emperor Tiberius that was set in a niche above a topmost shelf of books. Some sprigs of holly were dislodged, and to show the extent of his annoyance the magpie threw the rest down as well, then shuffled about, muttering horribly.

Lady Marchwell ignored her pet's wrath as she addressed Charles. "When you and my niece were married I believed yours to be an indestructible love match. You didn't seem separate people, but one entity, sharing every thought and sensation, anticipating each other's words, knowing all there was to know. Juliet entrusted you with her heart, but learned most cruelly that you were merely *pretending* to entrust yours to her."

"It was no pretense, Lady M," he broke in quickly.

Jack made a rude noise from the safety of the emperor's head, and Lady Marchwell's eyebrow quirked. "My sentiments exactly," she said wryly, holding Charles's eyes. "It had to be pretense, sir, or you would not have taken up with Sally Monckton, whom I believe to have had five further protectors since your departure from the scene. Off with the old and on with the new is her motto, it seems."

Charles was offended. "Lady M, I do not regard this as a matter for amusement. Surely you can find it in your heart to forgive a little? It's Christmas, the—"

"The season of goodwill?" she said quickly.

"Yes."

"It was Christmas six years ago too," she pointed out, and Charles's resentful glance went to the magpie.

"So it suits you to blame Jack, does it?"

"I did," Charles admitted, "and I suppose it is only habit now, for I fully realize that if I had behaved myself there would not have been an incriminating note to be discovered."

"Very true."

He looked imploringly at her. "I crave another chance with Juliet, Lady M, another chance to place this ring upon her finger." He fumbled inside his shirt and pulled out the wedding ring on its purple ribbon.

Lady Marchwell stared at it. "Is . . . that Juliet's ring?"

"Yes, of course. How can you doubt it?"

"Because we thought Jack had hidden or lost it forever."

"Ah."

Her eyes moved to his. "How enigmatically you say that."

"Perhaps because the way it was returned to me was rather enigmatic too."

The long-case clock near the door began to whir, and then chimed the hour. It was nine o'clock. Lady Marchwell went to a large upright chair and sat down carefully, mindful to be decorous in spite of the farthingale beneath her regally sumptuous royal costume. "Very well, Charles, you have ten minutes in which to convince me that I should help you. When you have said your piece I will consider whether to grant you your wish or have you thrown out. But first you will explain the matter of the ring. Be quick now, sir, for the seconds are ticking away."

For a moment he couldn't find words. He went to the fireplace, and rested a hand on the carved stonework above it as he looked up at Juliet's portrait. "The ring was returned to me in February 1814, on the very eve of my departure for India. I had at last given up trying to gain admittance here, and given up writing letters that I feared were never opened."

"Oh, I saw that Juliet received every one," Lady Marchwell interrupted, "but she did not change her mind, especially as the sorry tale was still very much in circulation, and Sally Monckton was doing all she could to blacken your name in the scheme of things. Eventually Juliet desired that you be informed she was no longer here at Marchwell Park, and that I was yet to be informed where she had gone. I complied with her wishes."

He looked around at her. "She was here all the time?"

Lady Marchwell nodded. "But we digress, sir, for you were telling me of the ring's return."

Charles looked at the portrait again. "In February, having decided to forget my sorrows by going to Bengal, I settled all my business here and made every possible arrangement for the running of my affairs during my absence. I also saw to it that Juliet received a handsome allowance, as always she had."

"I know."

He gazed at his wife's face on the canvas. "On the eve of my departure I endeavored to sleep in the private room I had taken at White's. It was midnight and the night one of the coldest of that unbelievably bitter winter. A fire burned in the hearth, but even so there was ice on the inside of the window. I wasn't relishing the coming journey, or indeed leaving England, for I was leaving Juliet as well, but I had accepted that she would never forgive me. Suddenly I heard a tapping at the window. I confess I was alarmed, for it was on an upper floor with a sheer drop. I went to melt a little of the ice on the glass with my hand in order to look out, but I saw nothing. Even so the tapping came again, so I wrestled with the frozen window, which at last gave up its resistance."

Lady Marchwell's hand crept to her throat. "What did you find?" she asked, her eyes a little wide.

"Jack."

"Jack? But that's not possible, he never leaves the park, and certainly would not have ventured anywhere at night in that awful winter, let alone all the way to St. James's. And anyway, how on earth would he have known where you were?"

"It was he, make no mistake, for how many one-eyed magpies are there that also reek of sherry? Not many, I fancy. What's more, he had the wedding ring in his beak, so it could not possibly have been any other specimen of *Pica pica*."

As if knowing what Charles was saying, Jack claimed full responsibility from the niche. *"Chak-chak-chak-chak."*

Charles continued. "He stood on the thick crust of ice and snow on the window ledge, just looking at me, then he put the ring down and flew off. Ever since I have worn the ring on a ribbon around my neck, and it has been my constant wish to one day see it returned to Juliet's finger."

"Chak-chak."

Lady Marchwell recovered a little from the tale of her pet's extraordinary conduct, and regarded Charles thoughtfully. Had he turned he might have seen the compassion in her eyes, and the gentle sympathy playing upon her lips. She was not by any means set against him; indeed it was her opinion that his estrangement from Juliet had gone on for far too long. He had done wrong, but should he be punished forever? Ah, that was the question. "What did you do in India?" she asked suddenly.

"Do?" He smiled. "I made my fortune, or at least I made *another* fortune. I rival Croesus now."

"How lucky you are."

"Maybe, except that like Croesus I am cursed. Outwardly I seem to lack nothing, yet in truth I lack everything, because the person I yearn for, hunger for, has rejected me these past six years." He turned. "Is she here?" he asked directly.

Lady Marchwell hesitated, and then shook her head. "No."

His heart sank. "Please do not play me for the fool again by saying you do not know her whereabouts."

"Oh, I know, but I am in a quandary." Lady Marchwell rose from her chair and carefully tweaked her voluminous Queen Elizabeth skirts. Then she held up a hand for Jack to fly to her, which he duly did, rocking for a moment before gaining his balance. The bird's handsome head cocked to one side as for the first time he perceived the wedding ring. Opportunist magpie thieving was the last thing Charles desired right now, and as he pushed the ribbon hastily back inside his shirt, Lady Marchwell continued to speak. "You see, Charles, although you have convinced me that you deserve another chance to see Juliet again, I—"

"You have?" Charles was so delighted he could have rushed to hug her, but given the circumstances, such familiarity was hardly fitting.

"Yes, I have," she confirmed. "Six years ago I was dressed as a fairy godmother, which I fancy was well suited to the granting of a wish. Queen Elizabeth may not carry a wand, but her royal power will no doubt serve the same purpose. I will do what I can for you, Charles, but have to warn that I do not think Juliet will want to see you. She has become settled, and—"

"Settled?" he broke in quickly. "There is someone else?"

She smiled. "No, not with someone else. She is her own woman, no one else's. But I *will* approach her for you."

Relief almost swamped him. "Tonight?" he said quickly, wanting to rush her.

"Certainly not. It's Christmas Eve, for heaven's sake. You will have to contain your impatience."

Where was he expected to stay in the meantime? he wondered as visions flashed before him of disgruntled postilions, icy roads at night, and every Windsor inn filled to overflowing.

Lady Marchwell went toward the door, then halted. "I am not cruel enough to send you away again while I deliberate, but I fear the house is already too much of a crush with guests. However, there is room at the Retreat."

He was taken aback. "But . . . isn't that considered Juliet's territory?"

"If she were here, yes. But she is not."

"I saw no lights there as I arrived, and presumed it was closed for the winter."

"Not closed, exactly, but rather in a state of readiness. Guests *were* expected, you know them actually, my grandniece Rebecca, her noisy husband, and singularly ill-behaved brood. For the sake of my other guests I decided such an undisciplined faction should be confined to the island, and until this evening I still imagined they might still arrive. Then a message came a short while ago to say that young Theophilus has the measles, so they are all staying at home in Daventry. I haven't yet had time to send word to the servants at the Retreat, so right now they still expect to have work to do. So they may as well attend to you instead. If, that is, you find yourself able to stay there. After all, it is full of memories."

"I have no quarrel with memories, Lady M, for they are

all I've had for a long time now. Besides," he added shrewdly, "I do not doubt that if you so desired it some closet or attic here in the main house could be found for me, but your other guests have memories too, and my face is bound to stir whisperings you would prefer not to hear again."

"I don't deny such selfish motives, for I would rather *not* spend Christmas with the household raking the coals over, or the New Year with the *monde* of London fanning the embers." Lady Marchwell gave him a faint smile. "So the Retreat is agreeable to you?"

"Yes, of course."

"Very well, I will make arrangements for you to be rowed across."

"I am capable of rowing myself, Lady M."

She smiled. "Maybe, but the river is running a little high, and it is some time since you last made the crossing, brief as it is. A scandal about your watery demise would not please me either, so I would prefer James to attend to your safe arrival on the island."

Good old James, Charles thought sourly.

"Wait here, and when all is in readiness James will come for you. You have luggage, no doubt?"

"Yes."

"Everything will be taken care of." With that Lady Marchwell went out with Jack, leaving Charles alone with the ticking of the clock.

5

*T*he rowing boat bobbed halfway between the shore and Magpie Eyot, and Charles huddled in the stern with a lantern that threw little light as the storm raged mercilessly over the southern counties. The Thames was not only swift and strong, but choppy too, obliging James to work mightily upon the oars to prevent the boat from sliding downstream with the current.

Charles was uneasy on such deep, dark, swift water, especially on a night as cold and inhospitable as this. The joy and merriment of Christmas seemed a universe away, and danger brushed so close that England suddenly seemed more alien and hazardous than the Bengal climes he had known these past years. The swollen river sucked and gurgled along the bank, and gusts of snow stung his face as he listened to the wind rushing through the slender fronds of the great willows, the lowermost branches of which dragged in the water. Ahead lay Magpie Eyot, where the storm was in full cry through the tall Scotch pines.

How far away now that balmy summer day not long after their marriage, when he had rowed Juliet on the sun-dappled river, and gently maneuvered their little boat beneath the willows so he could kiss her in the secrecy of the leafy bowers . . .

*   *   *

"We really ought to return to the lodge, Charles, for everyone will be there by now and will be wondering where we are." Juliet lay back lazily on a mound of cushions in the stern of the rowing boat, twirling a bright pink pagoda parasol over her shoulder. She wore a cream lawn gown, frilled and beribboned, and brown ringlets tumbled from beneath her straw bonnet.

"No one will even notice our absence," Charles replied, handling the boat into the cool green shadows of the willows. "When Lady M invites her Whig friends to an afternoon at the Retreat, the gentlemen expect to spend all their time talking politics while attempting to rob the Thames of all its fish. The ladies desire only to sit in private little groups discussing—and inventing, I might add—matters of as scandalous a nature as possible."

"Maybe they will think *we* are suitably scandalous for slipping away like this."

He laughed. "Never! We will always be dull fare for gossips because we are so married and in love that we think only of each other." Shipping the oars, he quickly rose to catch a sturdy bough that projected from a lightning-blasted tree, then made the boat fast to it. The little craft swung gently around on the current before lodging safely against the tree.

Juliet dipped her fingers into the shining water, her face suddenly thoughtful. "Will we really?" she murmured.

"Mm?" He paused as he took off his coat. "Will we really what?"

"Always be dull fare for gossips?"

"Of course." But inside he was aware of a flicker of something, a vague restlessness perhaps. Whatever it was, it touched him now, reminding him of how young he and Juliet were to be man and wife. He had loved her for a long time now, to the exclusion of all others, with the result that while he devoted himself solely to her, his friends indulged in all the passions and peccadilloes young men do. Did he resent that? The thought shocked him, but could not be dismissed, for if of no importance why had it entered his head at all?

"Charles?"

He looked into Juliet's lovely green eyes. "We love each other too much to be scandalous, my darling," he said reassuringly, but was still pricked with a sliver of guilt, even though he had done nothing. Doubt had been raised in his innermost self, and he had to force a light laugh as he got down on the cushions with her. "I am certainly thinking of loving you right now, Lady Neville," he whispered, leaning over to kiss the tip of her nose.

"And I am thinking of my new parasol, which will surely be consigned to the Thames unless I am able to set it properly aside."

"How easily you attempt to dampen my ardor," he replied, taking the parasol and tossing it behind him in the boat.

She was flirtatious. "Is your ardor so delicate that so small a thing as a parasol becomes an obstacle?"

"Fie on you, madam, are you challenging my manhood?" He moved over her, supporting himself on his hands as he gazed down into her eyes.

Voices carried from a crowded pleasure barge that sailed downstream only yards from their secret place amid the willows. Juliet's breath caught nervously. "Sssh, Charles, they may hear us," she whispered.

"There will be nothing to hear if you kiss me," he replied.

She knew the look in his eyes, and was a little shocked. "Here? Oh, Charles . . ."

"Why not here? Where better to make love than on the river, beneath a canopy of leaves? Have you no spirit? Don't you relish the risk of being caught?"

She gazed up at him for a moment, and then smiled. "You are leading me astray, Sir Charles."

"Ah, so you *do* relish it," he breathed.

"I would be an eeyot not to," she said softly as he sank down to gather her into his embrace. Their lips came together, and she linked her arms around his neck, her body arching against his. And so they made love in the boat, their passion and pleasure taking them into another realm entirely. As Charles was lost in the ecstasy of the moment, the insidious uncertainty, so briefly presented, slid ashamedly away into the leafy shadows.

Charles raised his face to the storm, remembering how the uncertainty had returned again and again, gradually changing into an obsession. Oh, fool, fool! Why could he not have been content with the riches Fate had poured into his lap? He'd had everything, but had thrown it away because he was too immature to appreciate his good fortune.

With a heavy heart he gazed ahead, wishing the crossing was over and done with, for he longed to rest his head on a pillow and sleep. After eating, of course. As he looked at the island, something suddenly occurred to him. The charmless postilion had been paid for his trouble, and the luggage already taken across to the Retreat, or so James had assured him, so it was a little puzzling that there were still no lights at the lodge. "James, shouldn't there be lights on the island?" he shouted above the storm.

"The servants are probably dozing in the kitchens, sir," the footman called back between the grunts of pulling on the oars. "They'll be hoping no one's going to arrive at this late stage."

"How can they hope that if all my luggage has arrived there?" Charles's voice was buffeted by the storm.

James didn't reply, but glanced over his shoulder to be sure of navigating the frail craft to the upstream side of the jetty, where another rowing boat tugged at a mooring rope. With a skill and dexterity born of years of practice, the footman edged to the jetty, and quickly grabbed another rope. Pulling mightily on it, he forced the rowing boat alongside the wooden structure. "Best jump while you have the chance, sir!" he yelled, straining to keep closed the gap between boat and landing.

Charles obeyed without thinking, holding the lantern as carefully as he could as he scrambled thankfully onto the wet, slippery planks.

"You go on up to the lodge, sir, while I make things secure here," advised the footman.

"Don't you need a little help?"

"No, I can manage well enough," James reassured him.

"As you wish." Tugging his top hat low, and hunching his shoulders against the wind, Charles began to hurry along the jetty and on to the blessedly firm grass of the island. Something made him pause and look back, and to his astonishment he saw James reaching over to untie the second rowing boat. Then, with the other craft tied firmly to the stern of his own, the footman calmly pushed an oar against the jetty, and slid downstream on the current for a few yards before he was able to use the oars again.

Dumbfounded, Charles stared after him, so surprised that for a moment he couldn't move. Then he ran back onto the jetty. "Hey! What are you doing? You're marooning me here!"

"Lady Marchwell's orders, sir," James shouted back. "She said something about being your fairy godmother."

Charles was obliged to cup his hands to his mouth as the two boats edged farther and farther away. "I don't give a damn what she said, I order you to come back here this instant!"

"Happy Christmas, Sir Charles!" the footman yelled back a little cheekily.

"Damn your insolent hide! When I get my hands on you next, I'll—" But there was no point in elaborating upon the intricacies of James's punishment, for the footman was almost out of earshot and clearly didn't care anyway. He obeyed Lady Marchwell and *only* Lady Marchwell.

Incensed that Juliet's aunt should play such a trick upon him, Charles stood there in the windswept darkness. Well, she wanted to avoid the revival of old scandals, and this was one way of achieving it. With him safely on the island, her entertainment at the big house could proceed serenely without unwelcome interruption. The absence of lights at the Retreat now began to assume a different meaning. Dear grandniece Rebecca and her entourage had probably never been expected, therefore there weren't any servants on the island, and if he wished to eat he would have to wrestle with the store of Durand's canned food that he hoped was still kept in the kitchens. If not, he would be reduced to a diet of bottled fruit until her ladyship saw fit to set him free. Dear God, he was hungry enough to eat a mountain of the hottest curry Madras could provide, but he'd settle for anything to fill the yawning pit in his stomach. Resigned to his fate, he began to walk up the gently sloping grass toward the dark outline of the fishing lodge.

Back at Marchwell Park, Lady Marchwell was using a spyglass to observe proceedings on the river from the window of her private apartment on the second floor. She smiled as James left Charles stranded on the island, and only straightened from the spyglass as the latter's lantern began to bob slowly up the island lawn toward the Retreat.

"Oh, Jack, I do hope I'm doing the right thing," she murmured to the magpie on her shoulder, and the bird tilted his head to one side, as if listening. "I could not in conscience stand in Charles's way, even though I know how Juliet feels. After all, a Christmas wish is a Christmas wish, is it not?"

"Chak-chak." The sounds were uttered sympathetically.

"I know you understand," she said with a smile, and put a hand up to touch the bird's glossy plumage, but Jack fluttered down onto the window ledge and tapped at the glass. "You want to go out?" Lady Marchwell said in surprise. "But it's hardly the night for a little stretch of the wings."

He tapped the window again and fixed her with his single eye, so with a shrug she leaned forward to open the window. "Very well, off you go, sir, but don't you get up to any mischief, do you hear? Stay away from the Retreat, for I doubt if your presence will be welcomed."

With a staccato volley of cries, the magpie launched himself into the windswept night.

Charles continued to make his way toward the lodge. How many times had he walked here in the past? How many times hand in hand with Juliet? Refreshing spring days of new green leaves and daffodils; lighthearted summer days of love, sunshine, and roses; crisp autumn days of gossamer and Michaelmas daisies; and joyful winter days of snow, Christmas, and holly berries. Yet here he was, lonely, cold, and empty, trudging through a vile December storm to a cottage orné that was also lonely, cold, and empty, and all without the guarantee of being able to see Juliet. Some Christmas this promised to be.

Magpie chattering echoed through the air behind him, and Jack descended from nowhere to flutter onto his shoulder. The bird dug his claws into the greatcoat's costly astrakhan collar, then huddled close to Charles's head, as if to shelter beneath the brim of his top hat.

"What are you doing out here?" Charles muttered, in half a mind to brush the bird away, but then taking pity on the shivering bundle of black-and-white feathers.

"Chak-chak." If a magpie could sigh, then Jack did.

"The same to you," Charles muttered. "Well, in spite of Lady M's assertion to the contrary, it would seem you do indeed go abroad at night, but at least you'll be company of a sort for me, I suppose, and if she forgets I'm here, I can always eat you."

"Chak-chak."

"Aha, my friend, you think I'm joking, but I'll have you know that spitted magpie is a great delicacy."

Snowflakes patted Charles's face as he continued toward the fishing lodge, and he marveled that he was actually glad of the bird's presence. "You can be Man Friday to my Robinson Crusoe," he informed the bird.

As if not thinking much of the role expected of him, Jack

uttered a loud squawk and flew off again. Charles did not see where.

Meanwhile, Juliet continued to slumber on her warm sofa. Memories of Charles had slipped away, and she heard nothing as a log shifted in the fireplace and sent countless bright sparks up the chimney toward the stormy heavens. A glowing pinecone rolled onto the hearth and lodged against the polished brass fire screen just as Jack came to perch beside her. The empty chocolate cup rattled a little in the strong draft of the magpie's wings, and Juliet sat up in confusion, still trammeled with sleep as she pushed her hair back from her face. "Jack? What on earth are you doing here?"

"Chak-chak." The bird shuffled around the table, then quite deliberately pecked at the cup until it fell over. Thankfully the costly Wedgwood didn't shatter, but Juliet distinctly heard an odd tinkling noise, as if there were something small and metallic inside. Puzzled, she moved the cup, and there, shining in the firelight, was her long-lost wedding ring! Thunderstruck, she was about to pick it up when suddenly it vanished, and so did Jack.

With a gasp Juliet awakened properly. The cup was standing as she'd left it, and she knew the magpie had never been there. She had been dreaming. Tears sprang to her eyes as she realized her wedding ring had not reappeared after all. Oh, eeyot, eeyot . . . Fighting back the tears that were always so close at Christmas, she got up and went to her bedroom.

6

Charles paused before stepping up onto the verandah that encompassed the entire ground floor of the Retreat. What he'd said so bravely to Lady M about staying here was one thing, the qualms of the secret Charles Neville something else entirely. Juliet had seemed to be everywhere from the moment he set foot on the island. She sighed through the trees, trod the grass beside him, or watched from the jetty. Now it was as if she were hiding in the lodge, peeping from a darkened window, dreaming in the bed they had once shared, or perhaps waiting reproachfully behind the door through which he must enter.

Guilt, as immediate and painful as it had ever been, had him in its grip as he made himself go inside. The small lobby was lit only by the faint glow of a fire that had been banked up for the night and protected by a screen. His eyes, already accustomed to darkness, immediately perceived that nothing had been changed since last he was here. Even the Christmas decorations were arranged the same way, bunched and festooned as Juliet had always liked them. The red-tiled floor was scattered with finely woven rush mats, and the whitewashed walls still boasted the same dreamy Thames fishing scenes, the river caught forever at moments of late summer sunset.

His glance returned to the fire, for the fact that it was lit at all suggested to him that Lady Marchwell had not fibbed about guests having been expected. He was relieved, for that meant there was bound to be more to eat than Durand's cans or bottled fruit. Oh, to enjoy a fine rare beefsteak, a liberal dollop of Tewkesbury mustard, and a chunk of fresh crusty bread, all washed down with a brimming tankard of sharp cider from his family's Somerset orchards. How he had dreamed of that particular meal, which was what had been set before him at the harvest supper the night when he first realized he was in love with his childhood friend and neighbor, Juliet.

Well, best to alert the servants to his presence, he decided, entering the drawing room where he knew there was a rope-pull that rang a bell in the kitchens. Firelight danced here, the flames for some reason not banked as in the lobby, and as he strode toward the rope that hung beside the mantel he was conscious of the much-loved room around him. There was also a sweet perfume in the air. What was it? Chocolate? Yes, that was it, the delicious fragrance of chocolate recently consumed from the cup on the table by the fireside sofa. How impertinent of Lady M's servants to not only drink such a costly beverage at her expense, but to do so in the drawing room out of her best Wedgwood!

Reaching the fireplace, he jerked the rope, then held his hands to the fire. He yawned, the long day on the road, to say nothing of the months of travel since quitting Madras, suddenly catching up with him. He removed his greatcoat and tossed it over the back of a nearby chair, then sat on one of the blue-and-white sofas to tug off his boots, there seeming little point in ceremony. That done, he glanced around. His reflection glanced back at him from the mirror panels on the walls, reminding him of how strange it was to be here again, where there had once been such happiness, laughter . . . and love.

He loosened his neckcloth and shirt, and removed the wedding ring on its purple ribbon. The gold shone in the firelight, and the metal was warm from his body. Drawing it to his lips he kissed it gently, vowing that heaven and earth itself would be moved in his efforts to replace the precious band of gold on Juliet's finger. Still holding the ribbon, he put his head back and closed his eyes. It vaguely occurred to him that the servants were an unconscionably long time answering his summons, but sleep was overcoming him swiftly now. He yawned again, then again, and before long he was in a deep slumber.

He didn't hear distant church bells greeting midnight, nor did he see the leap of candlelight as a sleepless Juliet came downstairs to make herself a drink of hot milk in the kitchens. She didn't look into the drawing room as she passed the door, and soon there was no movement in the lodge as the estranged husband and wife slumbered separately. They were as unaware of each other's close proximity as they were of the storm dying away outside, nor did they see the silver light of the Christmas Day dawn steal across the heavens.

Stillness settled over the countryside as snow began to fall in earnest, covering everything with truly seasonal white. But a certain magpie was not asleep. Far from it. Finding his way in through the ill-fitting space between washhouse wall and eaves, he fluttered at leisure from room to room, perch to perch, checking this and that, to be sure all was as it had been when last he was here. He soon came to the drawing room, where his acquisitive gaze was drawn as if by a magnet to the wedding ring Charles still held as he slept.

A pensive glint entered the magpie's eyes, and not even a tiny sound passed his beak as he glided quietly to the sofa. For a longing moment he eyed the decanters on the table, but he knew an impossibly tight stopper when he saw it. No amount of pecking would shift either of these, so her ladyship's sherry and brandy were safe enough. After deftly disentangling the purple ribbon from Charles's fingers, the bird held it tightly in his beak, and flew off with his loot. He searched high and low in the lodge for a suitable hiding place, and when he found it he congratulated himself on his cleverness, although to be sure he ended up more or less back where he started, and might have saved himself a great deal of wasted effort.

A mixture of bright sunshine and magpie din aroused Charles the next morning. Jack was in fine feather, squawking loud felicitations as he shuffled obviously around the sherry decanter, hoping that as a measure had been put at his disposal the night before, the same might happen again now.

"The first tot of the day, eh?" Charles murmured, tugging the virtually jammed stopper free. There wasn't a glass to hand, but the Wedgwood cup was still there so he used that instead. "God rest ye merry, Magpie," he said as he got up to stretch.

The groan of his stomach reminded him that food was now a much more pressing problem, and he had better rectify the situation *tout de suite* if he wished to physically survive this Christmas, if not mentally. It was then that he noticed the fire had gone out, leaving just ashes in the hearth. If it weren't for the sunshine flooding in, the room would be cold. What were the damned servants about? If they'd come to his call last night they certainly hadn't awakened him, and now they had omitted to attend the fire. He listened for a moment, expecting to hear something that might indicate the activity of a housemaid. But there was nothing, except for the busy tapping of Jack's beak in the Wedgwood.

Frowning, Charles went to jerk the rope-pull, but just as his fingers closed around it he caught sight of the reflections in the mirror panels, and froze. There in the doorway, staring at him as if at a ghost, was Juliet. She was wearing a fur-trimmed emerald green cloak over a crimson merino gown, and her hood was raised over her pinned-up curls. It had been her intention to walk in the sunshine and snow, instead she had been arrested by what she saw in the drawing room. Lips parted and eyes wide, she could only stand there.

He was equally robbed of wit, but at last managed to face

her properly. "Juliet, I—" Instinctively he took a step toward her, but she recoiled.

"What are you doing here?" she whispered.

"I need to see you." He feasted his gaze upon her. How little she had changed, but how little encouragement there was in her eyes . . . He felt a fool, standing there bootless, in crumpled clothes, his hair an uncombed thatch that probably made him look half wild. What must she think?

"Why have you come?" she asked again.

"I came because I love you, Juliet. You are all I've thought of these past six years."

She hesitated, a flush of color touching her cheeks.

"Can we at least talk?" he begged, sensing that she was within a heartbeat of turning on her heel.

Somehow his words decided her against him. "If you imagine you have me cornered here you are very much mistaken. The servants may have been dismissed for Christmas, but I am quite capable of returning to Marchwell Park on my own. Aunt M will have you thrown off her land."

She fled before he could answer. Her little ankle boots sounded on the lobby floor, then the main door slammed, the noise resounding through the lodge as if through a castle. In spite of having anticipated her flight only moments before, Charles was caught completely off guard, so dumbfounded that for several moments he couldn't move. Then he was galvanized into action. "No, Juliet, you can't get across the river!" he shouted, grabbing his boots and hopping around frantically as he hauled them on. Then he snatched his greatcoat from the back of the chair and ran after her, still putting it on.

The cold air caught his lungs as he dashed outside and over the snow-covered lawn. He could see her ahead of him, her green cloak flapping to reveal the crimson gown beneath. Her hood had fallen back, and her brown curls had fought free of their pins. "Juliet! There isn't a boat!" he shouted.

But she took no notice, and in another minute had

reached the jetty, where she stopped in confusion as she found no boat. Charles ran on to the jetty just as she tried to leave, and she lost her balance. With a frightened scream she teetered above the swift gray Thames, and would have fallen in had not Charles's hand shot out to seize her wrist. He pulled her back from the brink, and crushed her into his arms.

"This is foolishness, my darling," he breathed, pressing her close. "All I desire is that you talk to me. Just talk to me. Nothing more."

She struggled and pulled away. Her cheeks were pink, her green eyes bright, and her hair now as much of a tangle as his. "What have you done with the boats?" she demanded.

"Me?"

"Yes. You must have done something, for how did you get to the island if not by boat?"

"Your aunt dispatched James the footman to row me over, and unknown to me she instructed him to maroon us both here."

Juliet stared in disbelief. "That cannot be so. Aunt M would *never* allow you to come here."

"On the contrary, she not only permitted me to come here, she made damned sure I stayed. And before you call me liar again, let me assure you that I didn't even know you were on the island. I thought I was coming here to await your response to my request to see you."

"Why would my aunt thrust us together? She *knows* how I feel about you."

He searched her lovely eyes, so angry and accusing. "Perhaps I persuaded her that I deserved—"

"You don't deserve anything," she pointed out quickly.

"Everyone deserves a second chance, Juliet, even a faithless husband. Lady M thinks so too, and is being the fairy godmother who grants my wish."

"Wish?"

"Yes. I have yearned for a reconciliation ever since you

so rightly spurned me. The chance to speak to you again has been my single prayer throughout the past six years. I cannot go on without striving to win your heart again, and that is why I am here. I laid bare my heart to Lady M, and my presence here on the island is the result."

Emotion got the better of him, and he put his fingertips lovingly to her cheek, but she brushed his hand aside. "I don't want your caresses, Charles."

"Maybe not, but it's Christmas Day, Juliet, and I love you deeply. Have you no mercy? We once meant everything to each other, and to me you still do, so if we let this opportunity pass by we will both be eeyots."

Tears sprang to her eyes. "Don't use that word."

"I must use every weapon at my disposal if I am to win your hand again."

"If I agree to talk, I don't want you to think that it necessarily follows that we will be reunited. What you did was despicable, and I do not know that I will ever be able to trust you again. Without trust there can be no future happiness. You do understand that?"

He nodded. "Of course."

"I will never, never be the sort of wife to accept a husband's unfaithfulness."

"I know." Oh, how he knew . . .

She held her head haughtily. "Do you accept my terms for talking?"

"Yes."

She relaxed a little. "Very well. Shall we walk awhile?"

Walk? His stomach was rumbling like an earthquake, but he dared not let any opportunity to be with her pass by, so he nodded. "Yes, of course." He offered her his arm, but she shook her head.

"There must not be any misunderstanding, and if I take your arm I fear there will be. Let us simply walk around the island."

With that he had to be content.

The little scene by the jetty had been observed from

Marchwell Park, where Juliet's aunt was again at the window with the spyglass. Magpie Eyot had been under such close scrutiny since dawn that she had left her Christmas guests to their own devices; indeed, she'd hardly given them a thought. Her prime consideration was the pair at the Retreat, and whether or not their broken marriage could be satisfactorily repaired.

As she peered through the glass, she saw a familiar black-and-white shape winging toward her. So *that* was why she hadn't seen him yet this morning, he'd been out all night. She quickly opened the window for the magpie to come inside, which he did, scattering powdery snow into the room as he landed on the ledge.

Lady Marchwell was all concern. "My poor, darling boy, you must be *frozen!*" she cried, and hastened to send her maid for a glass of sherry. Jack had long since learned that wonderful word, and knew exactly when to play upon his mistress's emotions. He shivered and looked forlorn, so that she hurried to place a velvet cushion in front of the bedroom hearth. "Here you are," she said, denting it to make a nest. In a trice the magpie was warmly ensconced. No fool he! All this and sherry on its way too? Oh, how he loved this time of year.

But Lady Marchwell was eyeing him thoughtfully. He had, she decided, become a little too attached to drink, which could not, in the long run, be very good for him. A New Year's resolution was necessary to return him to a desirable state of decorum and sobriety.

7

*C*harles and Juliet walked side by side through the snow, following the path that led around the island at the very edge of the Thames, although from time to time the swollen river covered it completely and they had to make their way through the trees instead. The path was one they had walked countless times in the past, always hand in hand, always pausing to kiss, always in love. Today, although their hands occasionally brushed, there was a yawning chasm between them. Could it be bridged? Charles prayed so with all his heart.

Such a morning was perfect for Christmas Day, with the distant bells of Windsor ringing across the countryside, children building a snowman outside a cottage on the far bank, and bright red berries shining on all the holly bushes that flourished on the island. Magpies chattered in the pines, their black-and-white plumage sharp against the blue of the sky, and now that he was with Juliet again, Charles found that he no longer found the birds' noise quite so abhorrent.

They talked of this and that, harmless topics that were nevertheless reminders of how things had once been between them. Mannerisms, occasional smiles, and even an occasional sprinkling of laughter served to arouse shades of the happier past, before hearts and vows had been broken. It was when Juliet asked about Bengal that the hitherto tentative conversation became more serious, for although she was clearly fascinated by the wonderful things he had seen there, and put many questions to him, it was the questions she didn't put that lingered in the crisp air.

He knew she was wondering what women he had known during his years in Madras, and how intimately, but she was too proud to ask. It was up to him to tell her, if only so that he could in turn ask her about the men in her life during the past six years. Truth to tell, it did not matter how reassuring Lady Marchwell had been on that score, he needed to hear it from Juliet herself.

If he had but known, Juliet was at that same moment struggling to put her unasked question into words. A fear lurked within her that there had been another Sally Monckton in Madras. It was something that had preyed upon her mind since they parted, for if he had taken a mistress while their marriage was happy, then surely he had no reason not to take another when bitterness and thousands of miles separated him from his wife.

As these private anxieties become harder and harder to subdue, they suddenly halted and turned at the same time.

"Juliet, I—"

"Charles, I—"

They both broke off, their eyes meeting self-consciously, then they both demurred.

"After you," he said.

"You first," she said.

This time they both laughed, and for a second her glance brushed his with the playfulness of old. "All right, I'll ask first, although . . ."

"Yes?"

"Although I am embarrassed to mention such a thing to you."

"Ask what you will," he urged.

Her cheeks filled with color, and she cleared her throat as she looked down the Thames toward Windsor. "Did you meet anyone in Madras? I . . . I mean, was there someone you loved?" For a moment she could not meet his gaze, but then looked him full in the eyes. "The truth, Charles. I must know the truth."

"My days of lying to you are at an end, Juliet. Yes, I met many women in Madras, some of whom made their availability quite plain, but I did not take any of them to my bed. Nor indeed, should you think that an ambiguous answer, did I go to anyone else's bed. I made love to no one, desired no one, because all I could think of was you."

"You haven't been with *anyone* at all?" Astonishment lit her eyes.

"That's right."

She didn't know what to think, for the Charles Neville she knew was a passionate man who had proved his ardor for her both on going to bed and on awakening again the next morning. For him to be celibate for six long years . . .

"Juliet, guilt and heartbreak are sovereign cures for lust, unless it be for the one for whom one feels the guilt and heartbreak. I have made love to you a thousand times over in my imagination."

The color on her cheeks deepened, and she had to look away, for in her dreams she had made love to him too. A thousand times over.

"Do you believe me, Juliet?" he pressed.

She nodded. Of course she believed him, because she had been the same.

"Juliet, I must ask you . . . ?"

"If I have taken a lover? Or lovers, maybe?" Her glance swung back to him. "Like you, I have not been without offers, but also like you, I have not desired any of them."

He reached out to take her hand. "Do you love me still, Juliet?"

"I don't know, Charles. At this moment I feel so overwhelmed and confused that it is an impossible question to answer."

He smiled, for at least she had not dashed his hopes completely. "I am content with such an answer, for I have no right to expect any more. But know this, I still love you, and if you would have me back again I would surely be the happiest of men."

"You go too fast, Charles."

"I know." He smiled again. "I also know that I'm getting damnably cold out here. Can we please continue at the lodge? I'm so hungry that I could even contemplate shinning up one of those pines for some cones."

She gave a quick laugh. "There is no need to do that, for I am sure the Retreat's kitchens can provide better fare than that, and a warm fire too. But no servants to attend to your needs. What you eat must be prepared yourself."

"That is no hardship to me. My wanderings in Bengal prepared me for most things."

They turned and made their way back to the lodge, where the kitchens were delightfully warm, the fire there being much larger and staying alight much longer than in the rest of the house. Soon there were fresh flames as Charles poked the winking embers and then added a holly log that spat and crackled as the fire grew stronger. The dancing light shimmered on the many copper pots and pans that hung around the fireplace, and the blue-and-white crockery on the wall dressers was turned to pink and mauve.

The cooking of simple but substantial meals was nothing to Charles, and soon the smell of toasting bread and scrambling eggs filled the air. When the singing of a kettle in readiness for tea was added to the mix, the atmosphere between the estranged couple soon mellowed into a more mutual desire to talk. Juliet so far forgot herself as to giggle when he placed an exceedingly hearty breakfast before her on the scrubbed table. "Why, Charles Neville, I would *never* have believed you capable of cooking!"

"Nor would I. The brief perusal of a White's menu card was once my sole contribution, but when the Devil drives . . ." He smiled as he drew out a chair and sat opposite her. "I have to say that scrambled eggs are enhanced to an unbelievable degree by certain eastern spices, none of which is available in this particular kitchen, but one day soon I will see that you sample what I mean." He colored a little as he finished, for the sentence presumed there was going to be a happy outcome.

She poured the tea. "Aunt M always says that fresh thyme leaves are the best complement to scrambled eggs," she said almost absently.

"Or perchance a little of the ketchup made from her secret recipe by Mrs. Fellowes, the cook at Neville Castle."

Juliet nodded. "Yes, a little of that too." She watched as he applied himself to the food, and when he had finished pushed her own plate toward him. "Have this as well. I'm not really very hungry."

"I suppose I have ruined your appetite," he replied a little ruefully.

"Well, I confess to being a little nervous and bemused to find myself breakfasting with you again," she admitted, then raised an eyebrow at the vigor with which he set about her portion as well. "Just how long is it since you last ate?"

"It feels like a week, but I suppose it was early yesterday afternoon. A Basingstoke inn, as I recall. Indifferent fare."

"You could have cooked better, no doubt," she replied with a faint smile.

"Indeed I could."

Their eyes met, and this time she did not look away. "Why did you turn to Sally Monckton?" she asked quietly.

He exhaled slowly. "My reasons were shameful and callow, and reveal me to have been little more than a boy masquerading as a man." He explained exactly how he had felt at that foolish time, and with each word he felt more humbled and dishonored. He did not leave out a single detail, or spare himself by making excuses, so that when he finished he could truthfully say that she now knew everything. He stripped his conscience bare, and there was nothing more he could do to convince her of his remorse.

She said nothing when he finished, and he became anxious. "Juliet, it would not happen now, believe me. Six years is more than time enough to reflect upon all that I so stupidly threw away."

She toyed with her teacup. "I believe all you've told me, Charles, but you have to understand that your actions proved I could not trust you. I'm sure that if I were the one explaining my infidelity, you would also find it hard to trust me again."

The words echoed Lady Marchwell's. "It would be deceitful of me to deny it, for I could not bear to think of you in someone else's arms."

For a moment she was silent again, then she glanced at him and away again swiftly. "Did you ever love her? I mean, really love her?"

"No." It was the truth.

"That at least is consolation."

He saw a lifeline in such words, and clutched at it. "You *can* trust me again, Juliet, for I swear that I am now the man I ought to have been then." He rose and went to a window to look out over the snowy island. "I can only say that the past six years have been my punishment, and that every day I have awakened yearning to find it was a nightmare, and that you will be beside me again, just stirring from sleep, puzzled to know why I am so overjoyed. Juliet, if I could turn back the clock and make things as they were before I let you down . . ."

"But we're different people now, Charles," she interrupted quietly.

He went back to the table, his eyes imploring. "*I* am different now, Juliet, but you are the same sweet, gentle, kind, adorable woman you always were."

"The same gull I always was too?"

"That is not what I said, or indeed what I meant." Now his was the gaze filled with reproach. "You see before you a new husband, a better husband, a *true* husband, who believes to the depths of his soul that we can start again. All you have to do is wear my ring again, and let me prove that I am worthy of you."

The light in his eyes, the fervor in his voice, and the urgency in his manner, all combined to quicken her heart. More and more glimpses of past happiness jostled at the edge of her consciousness, reminding her just how much love and joy she had shared with him.

"Please, my darling," he whispered. "See, I have worn the ring all this time . . ." He reached inside his shirt for the purple ribbon, but of course it was not there.

Juliet was puzzled. "My wedding ring? But that's impossible, for Jack lost it."

"No, he didn't, he brought it to me at White's." Charles delved everywhere in the shirt in case the ribbon had somehow come undone. Then he remembered taking it off in the drawing room the night before, and without further ado he strode from the kitchen to get it.

Juliet hurried after him. "This is nonsense, Charles. Jack can't possibly have taken the ring to you, White's is *miles* away from here!"

"Nevertheless he did, and I have kept it around my neck for six years," Charles shouted over his shoulder as he entered the drawing room. But when he went to the sofa, he found neither ribbon nor ring. He moved the cushions, shoved a hand in every corner, and even looked underneath, but there was no telltale sheen of purple satin or rich glint of gold. Dismayed, he cast around the rest of the room, but no matter where he searched, he found nothing.

Juliet, meanwhile, watched patiently from the doorway. She could see a great deal of the room, far more than Charles could, and what she saw made her smile. Charles had always been comical when he'd lost something, especially when so often he failed to see what was right under his nose. Or right above it. Fondness warmed her eyes; no, much more than fondness . . . "Do you remember when you lost that letter opener your great-aunt gave you for your birthday?"

"That was not funny, for she was coming within the hour and was bound to want to see I'd received it safely." Charles ran a hand through his hair, and glanced around in bewilderment. Where on God's own earth was the ring? It had been here last night, but now it had disappeared.

"I remember you found the letter opener in the nick of time, only for her not to mention it anyway," Juliet went on.

"Which, as I recall, afforded you much hilarity at my expense."

"Of course." She paused, knowing she loved him still, and that ring or not, she would be his wife again. How could she not? She had not been able to forget him, and if she'd wavered at all these past six years it was pride's doing. But the future was a long time to spend alone, and now that she was with him again she knew she wished to spend it with him. Sally Monckton should not be accorded the importance of keeping Sir Charles and Lady Neville apart a moment longer, especially when the ring he sought so desperately was only a few feet from where he stood. "Charles, you must forgive my mirth, but if you will keep giving me cause . . ."

"Cause? What do you mean?" He was cross with her. "Juliet, I have been waiting six years to put that ring back on your finger, it has been my greatest wish, and now that I am with you again the damned ring has disappeared and *you* appear to think it amusing!"

"Perhaps because it is. Think now, sir. How did the ring disappear six years ago?"

"You know how, your aunt's brigand of a magpie took it."

"Exactly." She could barely hold back her laughter.

Realization dawned, and at last Charles began to look higher than the furniture and floor. Sure enough, entangled amid the greenery on the chimneypiece was the purple ribbon and its precious band of gold. Without further ado he seized a nearby upright chair and dragged it in front of the fire.

Juliet was perturbed. "Oh, do be careful, Charles, for that chair is—"

But it was too late. He stepped up, and as he stretched out a hand to the purple ribbon, the chair collapsed. For a moment he flailed in midair, but managed to get hold of the ribbon before he, the chair, and the greenery crashed to the floor.

Winded, he lay in the wreckage of the chair, with sprigs of holly and pine scattered all over him, but he brandished the ring triumphantly aloft. "I have it! I have it!" he managed to gasp.

Helpless with laughter, Juliet knelt beside him. "Oh, Charles, what a catastrophe! Whatever next?"

He seized her left hand. "Whatever next? Why, this, my lady, this!" He pushed the ring, still entangled with the ribbon, onto her fourth finger. Then he enclosed her hand in both his, his eyes silently pleading.

She hesitated, and then with her other hand plucked a holly berry from his blond hair. "Do you really wish us to begin again?" she asked softly.

"How can you doubt it? You are the only woman for me."

"Then the ring will stay on my finger," she whispered.

The gold already felt as if it had never been removed at all; indeed, the terrible rift might almost never have been as Charles drew her down into his arms and her lips to his. Their first kiss for six years healed a great deal of the pain, although only time would repair the wound completely. This Christmas was the beginning, but already they both knew how very much they wanted to spend the rest of their lives together.

In Lady Marchwell's bedroom, Jack snuggled cozily in his velvet nest in front of the fire. He was in a rosy glow of the highest order, the room swam pleasantly before his unfocused eye, and he was happily contented. Of course, if he had realized that sobriety was to be his lot in the coming year, he would probably not have been quite such a merry magpie. But for the time being . . . He gave a delicious sigh, closed his eye, and fell asleep.

Best Wishes

by Edith Layton

"*I* wish I'd never laid eyes on you!"

His head shot up. "Indeed?"

The nostrils on his long elegant nose pinched. That was the only outward sign of any emotion. His lean face was expressionless. He put his book down on the coverlet and stared at her.

"I might say the same, my dear," he said after a second, picking up his book again. "But I am not histrionic. And I believe this is a tempest in a teapot. I think if you considered it, you would agree."

All she could think was that he ought to be glad she didn't have that teapot the tempest was in at hand. She'd throw it right at his head.

"I *have* thought about it," she cried, stamping her foot. "It is *not* a tempest, it's a reasonable request."

He looked down and pretended to be reading again. She knew it. How could he read when she was standing by the bed, screaming at him? He was probably shamming it just because she was screaming, she realized. He never shouted and so doubtless thought she was beneath his contempt for raging the way she was. But the fact that he just sat there in bed, holding the cursed book, seemingly calm and deaf to her arguments, made her even wilder. He could at least tell her how shocked and disappointed he was with her. Then she could tell him exactly how shocked and disappointed she was in him.

She fought for composure.

"I do not wish to go to the Fanshawes' for Christmas," she said again, only this time woodenly. "I do not like them. I do not like their friends. And I do not want to spend my holidays with them."

He turned a page. "We are promised to them."

"*You* are promised to them!" she shouted, losing all pretense of composure. "And what's more, I believe because you probably promised far more to her! I don't want to go and I won't. *I will not!*"

She thought she saw him wince, but it was likely only an illusion from the flaring of the lamplight. It was probably feeling a draft. She'd shouted loudly enough to crack the glass that sat over the candle.

"You are my wife. I have given my word. We are going," he said, and turned the page again.

She was pleased to see that the pages were turning like leaves in a storm, and he didn't seem to notice. That was the only thing that pleased her. She wondered if she'd actually have to throw something at him to get any other reaction. It was like fighting with a damp feather pillow. If he'd raise his voice, she'd know what he was really thinking. But he was too civilized. The hotter she got, the colder he grew. It just made her more frustrated, and so even angrier.

This was only the third fight they'd had. The first two had been so foolish she thought they'd fought only to be able to make up again, as they had, delightfully. They'd been married three months now and she'd never been angry with him before. Not really. Oh, she hadn't liked little things he did here and there, now and again, but she never mentioned them. They were, after all, trivial and no one was perfect. For example, he ate kippers for breakfast and the scent made her ill at any time but especially made her breakfasts unpleasant; he didn't love music as much as she did, so they didn't go to as many concerts as she'd like; he kept dogs but not cats. And he never raised his voice, even when he was annoyed.

These were, admittedly, little things. Doubtless he'd had the same sorts of minor complaints about her.

But this was enormous, in her eyes. Worse, she suddenly realized he *did* have minor complaints about her, but he told her about them and they laughed over them together. She'd never complained about him, to him. Until now. But now she had a lot to complain about and could not let it go.

She straightened her back. She was very angry, and if he was surprised she was capable of such fury, it was only his own fault. There were many things she felt deeply about, and if he'd known her longer he'd have seen evidence of them before this. Her family was not a fractious one, but they had words, and sometimes those words were loud. It helped clear the air. The air in here was getting heavy and thick with unspoken resentment. She didn't know how to fight with raised eyebrows and curling smiles, the way he and his set did. She wanted to have it all out in the open. But he didn't know that. How could he? It wasn't her fault they hadn't disagreed about anything before they were married. They'd married so quickly.

He was the one who had wanted an immediate wedding. She'd only instantly agreed. They'd met in May and married in September. True love, their friends said, such love needed consummation, not more time to come to fruition. It had seemed so at the time.

She'd had some reservations, but they never gave her more than a moment's pause. He was eight years her senior. But her own father was that much older than her mama, and they had a wonderful marriage.

Jonathan was so clever and worldly wise, and she had only book knowledge of the world. But she was as smart as he was, or at least she always felt she had a great deal of knowledge, if not experience. Also true, and most significant, her new husband, Jonathan, Viscount Rexford, was a reserved fellow, distant, even with her.

But that was an essential part of his charm. He was the very paragon of a perfect gentleman. Handsome in classic fashion, he was tall, lean, and elegant, a study in dark and light with his inky close-cropped hair and steady slate eyes. He was sophisticated, with a famous dry wit and a signature style that was cool and reserved. His smile was hard-won, but once won, unforgettable in its warmth and charm.

Everyone said they were surprised to see him tumble into love with a pretty little thing from the countryside. She knew they always said, "Good family" when they talked about her behind their hands, but she also knew they then added, ". . . of no particular distinction."

"She was new to town, and fresh as the morning," she'd overheard one buck say about her to another just the other week at the theater, when they didn't know she was behind them. "That's what probably accounted for that surprising marriage. Damned pretty filly, though, with such a sweet little ars . . ." He'd stopped talking abruptly when he'd seen Jonathan's eyes on him.

Well, she'd thought, who wouldn't freeze under that stare? Such cool gray eyes Jonathan had, they were what first attracted her to him—when she'd seen them light with silver when he laughed. Tonight, as that night at the theater when he'd overheard the improper remark, those gray eyes were flinty, cold as the surface of an icebound lake. The foolish young buck who had been overheard had turned pale and quaked, before he'd fled. But she was too angry to be afraid.

"I won't go," she said again.

She stood at the foot of their bed, staring, sure her eyes were burning holes in the back of the book he still held.

He put a long finger into the book to keep his place—if he even remembered what book he was reading now, she thought spitefully.

"I see. Am I to assume you are going back on your word?"

"I never gave my word. I don't remember being asked."

"I remember telling you."

"Aha!" she cried. "There it is! There you are! You *told* me. You never asked."

Was that a shadow of surprise she saw on his face? It was gone before she could tell.

"I recall our discussing it."

"So do I. We discussed it. We did not decide it, or anything. I read you Mama's letter asking if we were coming home for Christmas. I told you how much fun it was and how much you'd enjoy our traditions. You mentioned your invitations, including the one to the Fanshawes'. I made a terrible face. You laughed. We talked about other things. So, where is the word I gave, eh?" She tossed up her head, triumphant.

There was a silence.

He turned to his book again. "I said we were going. I assumed you agreed . . ."

"You had no right!" she cried.

"Pamela," he said, snapping his book shut and putting it down with finality. "Whether or not I asked—and I do recall asking, but if you don't it is possible there was a misunderstanding—the point is that I wrote to accept and said we were going. And so that is the end of that. Now, are you coming to bed?"

She stared. He'd said that in a conciliatory tone, in the deep smooth voice she'd fallen in love with. And he lay in their bed, waiting for her. The room was strikingly chill now that the fire in the hearth was dying, and the great bed was covered with a huge, plump, feather-filled silken coverlet that warmed a person within minutes. His body would be even warmer and would heat her even faster. It did even now, just thinking of it. She knew the warmth of the man behind that cool façade and knew that the slender body under those heavy coverlets was all supple well-knit, smooth, hard muscle. She knew how clever those long sensitive hands could be on a woman's body, and knew very well the sighs he could win from her with them.

But she also wished she could see that strong handsome body of his better; she often wished she weren't still so shy with him. She wished she could bring herself to ask him to leave the lamp on sometimes. He was a wonderful lover. At least, since she'd had no other, she believed him to be so, because he drove her mad with desire and pleased her very much. But she sometimes wondered if he could please her a little more. She dearly wished she could ask him, sometimes, to do *that* more, or *this* a bit less, and could she do *that* to him . . . ?

The truth was that she was still reticent with him about their lovemaking, as well as other things, and unsure of herself with him and his world. She'd thought that in time . . .

But now this! Her anger flared again.

"I will go to bed," she said stonily. "But not with you, thank you very much."

His eyebrow rose in his signature expression of surprise. She wished she could say something to make both of them fly up. "Indeed?" he asked, and now his nostrils flared.

Too sad, she thought angrily, that his nose was his most expressive feature tonight.

"Indeed!" she said, and hesitated.

Because she didn't know where she could sleep if she didn't go to bed with him.

They shared a bedchamber, rare for a couple of their noble standing. She'd loved the closeness of sleeping beside him through the night and waking with him in the morning. Because of that, she couldn't leave the room tonight. That would be an irrevocable declaration of war to the world. She was of good birth, but didn't come from a high-nosed, care-for-nothing family with centuries of aristocratic training; she cared about what servants thought. If she now left this room to go to any one of the dozen other bedrooms in this great house of his, all his servants would know it.

She didn't think she could bear the speculation in everyone's eyes tomorrow morning. And that would be literally everyone in the immediate vicinity, because she knew how servants loved to gossip about their masters. Even at home, let Papa and Mama have a shouting match and the whole neighborhood knew about it the next day.

So where could she go now?

He realized her problem, of course. She thought she saw a ghost of a smile on his lips. That decided her.

There was the dressing room. It was small, but there was enough space for a person to sleep. Unfortunately, she remembered, there was no cot or couch to sleep on. She glanced at him. The smile looked larger. It looked a great deal like a dawning gloat. She'd rather sleep on the floor than near him tonight.

She walked toward the bed. The smile on his face grew warm and welcoming.

She grabbed the bottom of the silken coverlet in both hands and pulled, dragging it from the bed. It slid off into her hands before he could snatch it back. His eyes widened, and she wondered if he would try—but realized he probably believed fighting for his covers was beneath his dignity. That might have turned into a tug-of-war, which could have turned into . . . anything. No matter, she had it all. She gathered up the coverlet, turned, and marched toward the dressing room, trailing it behind her. Then, with the swirl of red silk half enveloping her, she turned around and faced him again. She held her head high.

"I will sleep in there," she announced. "And there I will sleep every night henceforth. I will not spend Christmas with your mistress. Bad enough I must know of her."

"My ex-mistress," he said through clenched teeth. "My one time, a long-time-ago mistress, and I wish no one had ever told you about her. She is entirely respectable now."

"Unlike your other ex-mistresses?" she asked sweetly.

"I was not aware you wanted a husband straight from a monastery."

"I wanted one with a bit of discretion. I think it is the outside of enough that you still wish to share your holidays with her. And God knows what else."

"Only the holiday," he said with outsized patience. "She has not been anything but a friend to me for over a decade. So why are you distressed? A decade ago you were too young for my attentions," he added with a faint, amused smile.

"I wonder if I am not still too young for you now," she said, just to erase that supercilious smile, "or at least not jaded enough to appreciate your dissolute ways."

"You did not think so last night."

She flushed. "I did not know you were planning to run to your mistress for the holidays then."

"I am not running to her," he said in bored tones. "We will take the traveling coach and arrive in slow and splendid style. Come, what is your real objection?"

"My real objection?" she asked, incredulous. "Apart from the fact that I wanted to be with my family, aside from the fact that I never said yes to your plan? Or that I wonder how you can want to take your new wife to celebrate Christmas, of all holidays, with a woman you used to make love to? Or that I am aghast at the thought that you can wish to sit at a holiday table beside two women you have bedded? Do you want to compare how we each responded to your touch, your kisses? I find that . . . loathsome."

He sat frozen. Before he could answer, she went on, unsuccessfully trying to keep her voice from breaking. "I don't understand you or that set of your friends, my lord. I thought you'd be done with such when we married. But to go to a house party with such people! From what I hear, half of them will spend half their nights in the wrong beds; the other half will spend the next day making jokes about it. That is not my idea of Christmas."

"Well," he said in a hard, cold voice, "there you are. You obviously don't understand, and clearly pay undiscriminating attention to foolish gossip as well. We are not going to an orgy. They are just my friends. That is all I am to Marianna Fanshawe now. And no, I do not compare—the very idea is repellent. I would never have thought of doing so.

Ten years is an eternity." He added, very much on his highest ropes, "The thought of such comparisons or activities is absurd. I am looking forward to intelligent conversation with old friends, and thought you might like to get to know some of the kingdom's finest minds."

"And bodies?" she asked sweetly.

"I would not have married you if I wished to share you," he said icily. Seeing her hesitate, he added, "I thought you'd enjoy it. Yet here you are, acting like an outraged virgin invited to a Roman revel. At least I considered your feelings. I wonder if you considered mine at all? You think passing the holidays in a merry round of sticky sweets and stickier infants, discussing the childhood colics of all your assorted nieces and nephews, as well as rehashing all the childhood pranks of your brothers and sisters, would be 'great fun,' as you described it, for me?"

She sucked in a harsh breath. "I tell you what," she said, holding her head even higher so the tears wouldn't slide down her cheeks to betray her. "You go to her for Christmas, and make merry, or whatever else you want to make with her. And I will go home."

"This is your home," he said, but she slammed the dressing-room door behind her, and he wasn't sure she heard him.

He was sure he was cold, though, through and through, body and soul. She'd taken more than the coverlet with her.

He looked down at his toes. They looked very foolish sticking up, big, and bare, and doubtless turning blue. He probably looked like a fool altogether, he thought bitterly, lying on a big empty bed in nothing but a thin dressing gown on this cold December night. He'd been planning to surprise her the moment she got into bed by shucking out of his dressing gown and taking her in his arms so they could set fire to the night. She'd turned the tables on him, carrying on like a fishwife cheated of a penny. His soft-spoken shy bride? He never knew she could screech like a murdered cat.

He muttered a curse, drew up knees, and turned on his

side. The dressing gown fell open. He shivered and pulled it closed again. That didn't help. The room *was* cold. The feathers beneath him were warmer than the air around him. He'd slept on the ground in Spain when he'd been with the troops, and had slept like a dead man every night. But he'd been younger then, and full of courage—exhausted every night as well, and probably too full of patriotic fervor, fellowship, and good red wine to notice things like temperature. Besides, Spain had been warmer.

He was sure there was another coverlet somewhere nearby, but he couldn't call the housekeeper or his valet to get it or tell him where it was. He stepped out of bed and went to the dressing room to get a greatcoat or such to fling over himself, and stopped at the door. She was in there. He'd be damned if he'd give her that satisfaction. Especially when he'd been cheated of the satisfaction he'd wanted to give her.

He stormed back to the great bed, until he realized she could probably hear him, and then he went soft-footed. He crept into bed and curled up in a knot. Damn. He wished he knew what had set her off.

She'd known they were going to the Fanshawes', he'd swear to it. And why should she carry on, even if she hadn't? He hadn't slept with Marianna for a decade, and didn't want to again. She'd been a fascinating older woman then; she was just a jolly old friend now. Compare her to his bride? That was obscene. He was outraged at his wife's accusation—but then he stilled. In truth, when he'd been younger, he supposed he had compared his intimate experiences of women, at least in his own mind, rating them, grading then, remembering them when he'd see them again. It was inevitable, it had been eventually depressing.

In the old days, in the days he now considered his cold days, he sometimes might find himself at a social affair with one or more women he'd bedded too. At first, he'd been appalled by the unforeseen occurrence, almost as much so as his bride had just been. But in time, he admitted, he'd felt a frisson of pride. It had shocked and disappointed him, making him aware that he was in danger of becoming someone he didn't care for.

That was one of the reasons why he'd been so eager to marry Pamela. One look at Miss Pamela Anne Arthur and he knew he had met his match. The daughter of a country squire, she was young, but had two seasons and so was not an infant. He'd been out of town for her first season and the moment they'd met he'd been determined that she not spend another in London without him at her side, and in her bed.

She was well born but not infatuated with her heritage, as he'd found too many other young women in the *ton* to be. She was educated, but neither a bluestocking nor a pedant. She was fresh and unspoiled, candid and honest, nothing like any woman he'd ever known. Since he married her he'd discovered she was nothing like any woman he'd ever had and he'd known how right he'd been to hasten her into marriage. Because he'd never want any woman but her again.

Or so he'd thought, before tonight.

But damn it, she was wrong about this. He didn't want Marianna anymore, and actually felt a little queasy remembering their intimate moments. They'd been hushed and rushed and though carnally fulfilling, totally unsatisfactory in all other ways. At least, so they seemed to him now. Now he was married to a female who thrilled him in ways he'd never dreamed about then.

Lord, but his wife was lovely! Even tonight, as she'd stood there screeching at him at the foot of his bed, backlit by the hearth fire, he'd seen her magnificent breasts heaving with distress and had a hard time remembering what she was so distressed about. A very hard time, literally.

She was as desirable in her fury as she was when she lay there smiling up at him with warm welcome. It went beyond beauty, though she had that in plenty. She had milk white skin and dark russet curls, and a shape to make Venus on that clamshell look like a dried-up winkle left on the shore. She was full-breasted, slim-waisted, with a firm pert bottom that could not be ignored. He'd have called out that young fool for talking about her adorable bottom the other day, but not only would that have made the remark famous, the truth was she had the best one he'd ever seen or been privileged to hold.

He'd known greater beauties whose faces hadn't captivated him half as much, perhaps because they hadn't held half as many expressions as her lovely face regularly showed. Pamela's features were small and even, except for those huge brown-gold eyes of hers. And she had the most remarkable mouth, with a slight overbite that showed off that plump, tilted upper lip that drove him mad.

Above all, the woman who owned that beautiful face, the one who dwelled in that extraordinary body, was herself as remarkable: clever, intuitive, and, best of all, she could always make him laugh. He thought he had a fair sense of humor, he appreciated a good joke and could make clever comments. But he wasn't a merry fellow, he knew that. He just wasn't lighthearted. It would have been amazing if he were. Heir to an old title and considerable fortune, he'd been brought up to shoulder responsibilities, and was sent off early to all the proper schools by disinterested parents. Although he had a brother and a sister, he'd never really gotten to know them and still did not.

He'd always been drawn to laughter, as though he could warm himself at it. That was how he had found his bride. He'd been at some foolish affair in London, bored to extinction—until he'd heard a woman's full, rippling laughter. He'd turned to see her, and been caught. She'd seemed like a bonfire, a beacon, a bright and shining, warm and giving lady. So she was, or had been, until tonight. She'd been a delight to talk to, a pleasure to make love to, a perfect bride, an astonishing lover, reserved until he touched her, and then turning to flame under his hands and lips.

Yet he sometimes wished she weren't so very obliging with him. At times he caught a vagrant hint of some wish on her part that was unexpressed. She sighed and moaned most agreeably when they were making love, but never spoke. He didn't know how to deal with someone so tender and un-tried, so he continued to be gentle and careful with her, hop-ing experience would tell him what she could not as yet. He felt time would loosen her lips.

It had, tonight, and with a vengeance.

Hesitant with him? *Ha!* he thought, flopping over to his other side. She'd pinned his ears back. Which was just as well, because if she hadn't she'd have shattered his eardrums.

Jonathan, Viscount Rexford, lay alone in his great bed and shivered with the cold. He thumped over to his other side again to capture a hint of heat from the feathers he'd just deserted. He missed his wife for more than her warmth. They hadn't spent a night apart since they'd married. Amaz-ing how fast a fellow became accustomed to comfort and pleasure.

He was tempted to go to the dressing room, fling open the door, take her in his arms, carry her back to bed, and tell her to forget the plans to go to the Fanshawes' for Christmas, before he made amazing love to her. He suspected all would be forgiven if he just capitulated.

But he wasn't good at surrender. And he'd given his word. And she was his wife. And, damn it all, she was wrong. He turned again, and tried to think warm thoughts. But they were all about his wife, so he sought a solution to his insolvable problem instead.

His wife, in the dressing room, turned over again. She was very warm and comfortable, physically. The doubled silk of the great feather quilt upheld her, with enough left over to cover her. But she was cold to the heart. She missed her husband. She hated his being angry with her. She shiv-ered at the thought of his disdain for her. She wished she could just get up, march into the bedchamber with the cov-erlet, throw it on the bed, along with herself, and beg for his forgiveness, his lips, and his love.

But he was wrong, and she had nothing to be sorry for. Except for her marriage, her disappointment with her husband, and Christmas, which had always been such a joy and might now become the ruination of all her dreams, and her love, and her lovely marriage.

Pamela woke yet again from the fitful slumber she'd finally fallen into before dawn. She hadn't heard Jonathan moving around in the bedchamber, so she rose and slowly cracked open the dressing-room door to put an eye to it to see if he was still sleeping. The sun wasn't full up yet. But in the night she'd realized how embarrassing it would be if her maid came in to bring her morning chocolate as usual, only to find her mistress sleeping on the dressing-room floor. She had to get back into bed before anyone realized where she'd passed the night, but not until after he'd left it.

The floor was cold under her bare feet, and her heart felt colder as she tried to see into the great bed. It was empty. As was the room. He was obviously already dressed and gone.

She quickly went into the room, threw the coverlet back on the bed, and scurried under it. She only meant to do it for appearances, but when her maid came to open the curtains at noon, she was still soundly asleep.

Pamela awoke, stretched and yawned . . . until she remembered the night and the nightmare that had not been a dream. Then she stared dully at the ceiling. She'd had an inspiration in the night, sometime between headache and turn over again. But she didn't know if she had the courage to carry it out today. She'd dress and go downstairs. Then time would tell if she had found a solution, or would instead spend the Christmas holiday all by herself. That seemed to be her only option unless they came to some sort of resolution.

She couldn't just capitulate, and of course he wouldn't drag her along with him. He had far too much dignity. And she wouldn't go home without him; she couldn't bear the shame of it. So unless they spoke and worked it out, Christmas would be a disaster and likely the beginning of an unimaginably bigger one, one that might not ever be mended.

Pamela tried to swallow the lump in her throat, waved away her maid's offer of morning chocolate, and slid out of bed to prepare to test her fate and her future.

He was in the breakfast room, looking as heavy-eyed as she felt.

She slipped into her chair and asked the footman for some tea and toast. She didn't think she could pretend to eat anything else.

"Good morning, my dear," her husband said in his normal cool accents.

"Good morning," she said, looking at her plate.

"Did you sleep well?" he asked.

"No," she said.

He hesitated. "Nor I," he said.

She looked up at him.

His smile was wan. "I had a thought in the night," he said slowly. "Since we've received competing invitations for the holidays, promising diverse pleasures, what say we take advantage of both? That is to say: we spend half the holiday with my old friends, the Fanshawes, and the other half with your family?"

She blinked. "Why, yes," she said, with rising enthusiasm. "That sounds equitable. The twelve days of Christmas divided. Six with your friends, and six at my family home. Oh, Jonathan, what a lovely idea!"

"Actually," he said, smiling back at her, "five and five, because we need two days of travel to get from the Fanshawes to your family home."

"Oh, Jonathan!" she cried. Forgetting the servants, she rose from her chair and rushed round the table to him—and into his opened arms.

But it was after they'd kissed and gone back to their

places, with their servants still hiding their smiles, that she realized that still meant five days with his mistress.

And he remembered that an armistice was not exactly peace.

"Their manor is historic," Jonathan said, looking out the window at the stark gray pile that was Fanshawe Manor as their coach went up the long and winding drive to the front door. "It dates from Charles II's day."

"Yes," Pamela said in a pinched voice, looking down at her guidebook. "So it says here. Evidently Charles gave it to a mistress for services rendered. Interesting how heredity holds true."

Jonathan's lips thinned. "He gave it to a Fanshawe, not to one of Marianna's ancestors," he said patiently.

Pamela sniffed. Her husband chose to believe it was because the swansdown that trimmed her pretty bonnet had got up her nose, and not because of what he'd said.

Their coach rattled up the front drive. Jonathan tried to see the manor as it might look through his wife's jaundiced eyes, and had to admit it didn't seem to be the cheeriest place to spend a Christmas holiday. Fanshawe Manor was an ancient and impressive house, but the overall impression was stark and bare. It was a great box of a place perched on a sloping hilltop. Landscape was something that occurred miles behind it, like the background of a picture. Odd, but when he'd first seen the manor all those years ago, it had looked like a fine place to spend Christmas. That had been because it was his friend Tony's ancestral seat, and being able to spend Christmas with a family had been a welcome new experience for him.

He hadn't known that Tony's widowed cousin Marianna would enliven the holiday for him in ways he couldn't have foreseen. Much his senior, but still comely, jolly, plump, and pretty, the widow had given him several fine Christmas surprises, gifts of herself that she kept on giving well into the glad new year. They'd kept up their association until he'd had to go back to university. When summer came, he went off on his grand tour, with Wellington's forces. While he was away, Marianna had become Tony's uncle's second wife, and a permanent resident of Fanshawe Manor.

Tony had fallen at Salamanca. But Jonathan had seen Marianna since, always with her husband. It was hard to avoid them if one was at large in London, and he'd never seen a reason to try to keep out of their way. The affair was ancient history, one he never gave a second thought. Both he and Marianna, and their world, had changed out of all recognition. Marianna and Fanshawe were a well-matched pair, of a similar age and easygoing disposition. It was true he didn't pass much more than the time of the night whenever he met up with them when he was on the town, and further true that he hadn't seen them for a while.

When their invitation had come he thought it a fine way to introduce himself and his bride as a couple to the *ton*. Where else could they have gone, after all? Christmas was a holiday meant for sharing, and he was now an orphan. His brother was abroad, his sister lived in the north, and nothing in either of their histories or attitudes made him think they wanted, much less required, his presence. His closest friends, those who had survived the wars, were war-weary and reclusive. His newest friend was his wife. Spending the holiday with her relatives did not appeal. They were a clannish bunch who only made him feel more of an outsider. But the Fanshawes, he remembered when he read the slip of vellum requesting the honor of his presence in their home for Christmas, knew everyone.

He'd married with haste and had a delicious protracted honeymoon with his bride. That had been wonderful, but when the invitation had come he realized she knew few people in London's *ton*. What better way to remedy that than to take her to a hotbed of social activity for the holidays?

But now the word "hotbed" itself gave Jonathan a frisson of unease. The Fanshawes *were* part of a rackety, pleasure-loving set. Precisely because of that, they entertained some of the best minds in the land, from poets to politicians. Pleasure was a much sought-after commodity these days, the recent wars having left scars only pleasure seemed to heal.

Jonathan suddenly found himself hoping the Fanshawes and their friends wouldn't leave any scars on his lovely bride's tender, unsophisticated sensibilities. He'd just have to continue to keep close watch over her. At least that, he thought, glancing at his wife and remembering last night and their wonderful ongoing reconciliation, would be a pleasure.

The coach drew up at the bottom of a long wide fan of stairs. As a footman opened their coach door and Jonathan stepped out, the doors of the manor flew open.

"Coo-whee!" a voice sang out. "Look who's here, Fuff!"

Pamela paused on the carriage stair and looked up, as did Jonathan. A plump old woman dressed in cerise, with a mop of hennaed hair festooned with plumes, stood at the front door of the manor, wreathed in smiles. A fat little gnome of a gentleman with a red waistcoat stood by her side.

Jonathan breathed a sigh of relief. The frumpy-looking female was the once-voluptuous Marianna Fanshawe. The fellow who resembled Father Christmas was Fanshawe himself. They'd both aged even more since he'd last seen them, and not well, except for Jonathan's own purposes. They looked about as rackety as a pair of Christmas elves.

Jonathan looked at his wife and smiled. Now she'd see what he meant about a tempest in a teapot, and would be a little humble, perhaps, because of how she'd carried on.

"It's Rexford and his new lady!" Marianna caroled in a voice that must have carried into the next county. "Now don't be jealous, Fuff, my sweet. Remember, though he's still handsome as he can stare, I gave him up years ago! Sorry, Rex, my old dear, but Fuff is a possessive fellow."

"Yes, indeed," Fanshawe said on a merry chuckle as he started down the stairs. "Welcome to my home, my lord. You're welcome to anything in the house, old fellow—except for my lady wife, of course."

*   *   *

"Senile, I suppose," Jonathan said as he watched his wife pace furiously around the guest chamber they'd been shown to. "But we can't just turn around and go, even if they are."

"Not senile," she said stormily. "Just careless. I wrote and asked my brother Charles. He knew about them. Careless of morals and manners, he says. Everyone says so."

"Look, my dear," he said in his best voice of reason, "you refine upon it too much. My association with the woman was over a decade ago. I imagine Marianna likes to remember our past association only because she hasn't much else to cheer her these days . . . Now, wait!" He stepped back from the force of his wife's outraged glare.

"*You,*" she said frigidly, glowering at him, "are as bad as she is. You made love to her." She swallowed hard before she went on. Horrid to think that dreadful woman had kissed those firm lips of his, stroked that hard muscled back, delighted in his heat and strength, known the feeling of his most intimate embrace. What words of love had he whispered to her? She couldn't bear it.

"You had biblical knowledge of her, and who knows what other kind," she went on. "*She* remembers it fondly? And you? How do you remember it? Oh, I forgot, you're too much of a gentleman to say, even to your wife. So what am I supposed to think? And what am I to do? Agree with her? *I* am appalled. I didn't expect that you had no experience before we met. However, I didn't expect to have to hear about that experience."

"It means nothing," he said. He didn't know what else to say. Tell her that he'd never made love to Marianna, or any woman, as he had to her? That aside from that, he'd been young and overeager, and so overwhelmed by what seemed like his incredible good luck that he'd only taken, and never tried to give pleasure? That they hadn't shared anything but a pillow? That it was a wholly other experience from what he shared with his wife?

All of it was true. But the codes he lived by made it impossible for him to say any of it. A gentleman did not discuss previous lovers with anyone. A fellow did not discuss his sexual experience with his bride. And a man had to stand by his given word. "It meant nothing," he repeated.

"It does to me," she said. "And I don't like her, or it, or you."

"That," he said, "is childish."

"So be it. I want to leave."

"We will, but for now, we cannot. It is only for five days."

She turned her back on him.

There were twenty guests seated at the long dinner table in the grand dining room at Fanshawe Manor. Twelve of the guests Pamela, Lady Rexford, knew to be infamous. Thirteen, she thought, considering that her husband would have to be included now. Because Lord Treadwell, husband to a gaunt and raddled blonde of a certain age, had just informed her that his wife had also shared a bed with Jonathan, once upon a time.

Pamela now felt so justified, so right about her previous indignation and refusal to come here, that she wished she could find a lonely, windy moor where she could celebrate her glorious vindication.

"Your rib is some kind of bruiser!" the gentleman at her right side had just said with admiration, before Pamela could introduce herself to him. "A hard goer and a tireless one. At least, so m'wife says."

"Indeed?" was all she said as she stared cold-eyed at the lady's husband, taking a page from her own feckless husband's book of callous noncommittal expressions.

"Right," he said, and continued chewing whatever he'd pushed into his mouth right after he'd let out his killing words.

He had wide light blue eyes with scant lashes, which gave his round face a perennially surprised look. Otherwise, he looked like any number of other fattish, balding older gentlemen, except that he was sitting at this table, which meant he was both rich and titled. The fact that he liked to sprinkle his conversation with thieves cant, like a lad down from university, gave Pamela some clue to the weight of his mind.

"My rib and yours, y'see," he went on after he swallowed. "Thick as inkle weavers that whole summer ten years past, the pair of 'em. She says she knew she'd have him in the hay and begging for mercy in an hour, and so she did."

"And you're pleased with that?" she exclaimed before she could stop herself.

"I should say!" he said. He pointed a fork at her to give weight to his point. "Not many chaps have a wife who can get 'round a young gent like my lady can. It ain't all ancient history, neither. Wouldn't be surprised if she gets him again this very night."

Pamela sucked in a hard breath. There was now only one question in her mind. Should she get up and leave this place, and her marriage, immediately? Or wait until the company left the dinner table? She couldn't believe Jonathan would be so lost to propriety that he'd take up with another woman under her very gaze. But she couldn't believe what this fellow had just said either.

They didn't look like a raffish crew. The lovely old manor was filled with merry guests. The younger ones were definitely fashionable, the older ones seemed unexceptional. It was true many of the ladies had improbably bright hair and cheeks that obviously owed their blushes to rabbits' feet and not compliments. But most of the gentlemen seemed more interested in falling on their dinners than any other kind of flesh.

Yet, now this!

"You're saying you think they'll . . . do it again this very night?" Pamela found herself asking in a shocked whisper.

"No, didn't mean to be so literal, milady. Not tonight, a'course," the fellow said as he crammed in another forkful of food. "But I'll wager a pony they'll be at it by dawn."

Pamela sat and stared at his working jaws.

"Likely, we will," Jonathan commented from where he was seated at her other side.

She swung her head around and gaped at her husband.

He smiled. "If your lady is up to a dawn ride, I'm her man," he told the gentleman. "I mean to get back my own this time."

"Ha!" the fellow said happily. "Prepare to lose another monkey. Neck or nothin', that's her. She'll be up and over any obstacle you name before the word's out of your mouth. She said she'd fly over the old barn and so she did. Left you panting in the hay and that's a fact, my lord. Bruising rider, that's m'girl!"

"Oh . . . *rider*," Pamela breathed.

"'Oh, rider,' indeed," Jonathan said into her ear as he leaned to whisper to her, the smile in his voice palpable. "The lady is a steeplechase rider, and I don't doubt she can still beat me at it. But I'm game to try again. Oh, ye of little faith. *Honi soit qui mal y' pense*," he added, and translated, "Evil is who evil thinks, my dear."

And then, because it wasn't polite to keep speaking to one's own wife at a dinner party, he turned to the lady on his other side.

The raddled blond steeplechase rider leaned across her husband's plate and gave Pamela a huge wink.

When the ladies left the room to give the gentlemen time to empty their bladders and fill them up again with port, the blond lady seized Pamela's arm in her sinewy hand as they strolled into the salon.

"My husband gave you a turn, did he?" she laughed. "Don't deny it. You went the color of whey. Thought I was after Rexford, did you? Well, I would be if I could be, but he never did take me up on anything but a race and he isn't about to start now. Not when he has such as you on his arm."

Pamela smiled, uneasily.

The lady patted her cheek. "Pretty as you can stare, and

he keeps staring at you. Gather ye rosebuds, love. They don't last long, you know."

The evening went much better for Pamela after that.

"In fact," she said as she brushed out her hair after she'd dismissed her maid later that night, "I actually had fun!" She saw Jonathan's look of surprise. "Their jokes were old, and they were all so tipsy that they enjoyed those jokes more than anyone else did, but they were a jolly crew. They've known each other so long it's almost as if they're a big family. No wonder they like to spend the holidays together. The ones I got to know were delightful. Baron Oldcastle is a dear, and Mr. Vickery has such a sly sense of humor, and though Lady James is hard of hearing, she's charming. Her risqué comments are adorable rather than shocking."

Jonathan took the brush from her hand and leaned over her. "I'm glad you've reconsidered," he said as he ran his lips along the line of her jaw. "But it's early days. Reserve judgment. Oldcastle is more than a dear, and Lady James can be much less than charming. And more company will be coming. Now, as for the rest of tonight . . ."

"What a silly I was," Pamela exclaimed, rising and wrapping her arms around his neck. "To make such a fuss about nothing. You were right . . . no!" she said, clapping a hand over his lips. "I'll never say that again, so be still and treasure it. I think I was a bit inflexible. I did listen too much to gossip. I ought to have known you'd never do anything to expose me to embarrassment or humiliation. Your friends have been everything kind to me and have done all they can to make me feel at home."

"I'm glad you're having a good time now," he murmured against her warm palm before he gently teased the fleshy base of her thumb with his teeth.

"Who wouldn't?" she asked, with a delicious shiver at the feeling of his teeth nibbling at her palm. "Such friendly people. It's true they don't keep to any Christmas traditions that I know, so one would almost forget the holiday's approaching. Although they *are* very fond of wassail."

"Minx!" he said appreciatively as he dropped her hand and drew her closer. "You are doing well here. Perhaps too well. You've already learned to turn a compliment like a knife."

"I almost regret having struck our bargain and leaving before Christmas itself," she said with a sigh. "But I should like to see my family."

He stilled. "And so you shall see them." He hesitated. "Look, my love, there's no need for utter surrender, you know . . . except to me, this way, at least." And then he changed the subject, without saying a word.

The great dining room was full, all the guests had arrived. The conversation was loud and incessant, the toasts frequent, and even more so after the ladies had left the gentlemen to their port. That was why not a few of the gentlemen had to hold on to the wall in order to leave the room to join the ladies again.

But Jonathan had a hard head, and besides, he was not quite as merry as some of the company tonight.

"What? You've got the morning after headache already?" Sam Gregory, a fresh-faced young gentleman, asked when he noticed Jonathan's faint frown. "Without even having had the pleasure of earning it?"

Jonathan smiled thinly. "No such luck, or bad luck. It is only that I had forgotten what these house parties were like. I've been abroad a long time, you see."

"It's not that," Lord Montrose, a high-nosed worldly gentleman, commented softly as they watched some other guests staggering out into the hall. "I've never been to such a Christmas party myself. The jests are a bit warmer than one would expect to hear in mixed company," he explained to puzzled young Sam Gregory as Jonathan nodded. "Indeed, the mixture of company itself is unusual. Some, quite *comme il faut.* Others? A trifle raffish, perhaps? Present company excepted, of course," he added.

"So I thought," Jonathan murmured.

"Not quite the thing, perhaps?" Lord Montrose went on. "At least, not mine for the Christmas holiday. It almost makes me wish I'd accepted my second cousin's invitation. But the prospect of being entertained by their five lively infants dampened my holiday spirits somewhat."

Jonathan laughed. "Understandable. I was hesitant to visit my wife's family for the same reason. Still, we're leaving here in a few days for just such romps."

"I doubt it," Lord Montrose said serenely. "My cousin's also expecting another addition at any hour. Mind, I don't mind having to boil water, but only to add to my punch."

The men laughed, though the younger gentleman's face flushed.

"Astonishing," Lord Montrose said, raising his quizzing glass and peering at the younger man. "You color at a hint of a medical reference, and yet I didn't see a trace of embarrassment when those questionable tales were being told tonight."

"And those references," Jonathan said, grinning, "all had to do with getting a female into such a situation in the first place."

"Well, but one's fun, and the other is . . ."

"Reality," Lord Montrose said.

"At any rate," Jonathan told Lord Montrose, "I'm glad it wasn't only my perception. I mean, about this gathering. I did think it was getting rather warm in here tonight and have been wondering at the wisdom of my bringing my bride to such a gathering."

"Take heart. It likely was an aberration, not due to the spirit of the holiday but rather due to the spirits of the season," Lord Montrose said with an admirably straight face.

Jonathan smiled, as expected. But his smile didn't reach his eyes.

* * *

"Tonight, my friends," their hostess declared when all her guests had assembled again in the salon after dinner a few minutes later, "we'll have a scavenger hunt! With prizes!"

The company gave out a ragged cheer. Pamela smiled. Last night, she'd won at charades. The night before, she'd won at cards. She shot Jonathan a smug look and sat up straight in her excitement.

He did not return her merry glance, but rather stroked his chin and looked thoughtful.

"Now," Marianna said as she handed out slips of paper to her lounging guests, "here's the list. Everyone must find the objects written on their list and return them here before cock's crow, if not sooner. Now you must all choose a partner. No, no," she said, shaking a plump beringed finger at Pamela, "not your own life's partner, if you please. Wives and husbands know each other too well, and so work too well in tandem, giving the married couples an unfair advantage. So we will re-pair the company and have a more interesting hunt." She told Pamela, "Now, you, my lady, will be partnered by . . ."

"Me," ancient Baron Oldcastle called out. "I need a supple lass to help me bend and seek."

"No, me," Lord Ipcress cried. "The lady's a winner, and my luck's been out of late."

"If you please, youth goes to youth, so it's me," handsome Mr. Burroughs insisted.

Other gentlemen put in their claims as Pamela blushed with pride. She'd always been good at games.

"It's only right to handicap a constant winner," Marianna said. "So she gets my dear Fuff, because there never was such a fellow for not finding his own nose in front of his face!"

A great many mock groans met this announcement. Lord Fanshawe, or "Fuff" as his friends called him, grinned and waved at his guests. Pamela smiled. The old fellow didn't make much sense, but she could have gotten a worse partner. Though she liked most of her fellow guests, she had to admit she didn't like the looks some of the gentlemen shot at her. She now thought that because she'd been so relieved not to find monsters of depravity at Fanshawe Manor, she'd perhaps been too hasty in her praise of her hosts and their company. She tried not to be a prude, but felt that a gentleman oughtn't to look at a married lady with such naked assessment as she'd been treated to since she'd arrived at the manor. Her elderly host's admiration, though apparent, was not objectionable.

"And I shall have Rexford," Marianna announced, "which is very much like old times." As Pamela blinked, she went on, "Now, as for the rest of you . . ."

Honi soit qui mal y pense, Pamela reminded herself. It wasn't her hostess's fault that she so resented her so much she could scarcely exchange a word with her. But however much she knew she had to try to be more flexible now that she was a married lady, and even if her hostess was now somewhat the worse for years, still Pamela couldn't get over the fact that the woman had been her husband's lover. She didn't know if she ever could. The best part was that she didn't have to. Two more days and she'd be gone from here. It was good to see she had no dragons to fight after all, but she didn't think she'd ever care to return. And from what she could see, neither would Jonathan. He might consider these people his friends, but she noticed he'd spent all of his time with her.

"And, Montrose, you go with Lady Simmons," Marianna said as she continued pairing up her guests. "My lord Oldcastle, you have Miss Chudleigh—oh, very well, don't start complaining. Miss Chudleigh may go with Lord Dearborne, and you will be partnered by her friend Mr. Barrow. Happy now? Very good. And my lord Billings . . ."

"Off we go then, eh?" Lord Fanshawe said from the vicinity of Pamela's elbow.

She looked down at him. "Not yet," she said, showing him the list. "First we have to see what we're looking for, then plan how to get them." She frowned. "The thing is that

I don't know if this is fair. I'll still have the advantage. After all, you know where everything is."

"Consummately unfair," Lord Ipcress commented from where he stood behind them, watching.

"All's fair in love and war," Marianna Fanshawe said on a laugh, taking Jonathan's arm. "Now, let's get on with it, there's darkness being wasted."

Jonathan didn't budge. He stood watching Pamela peruse the list as the other guests formed pairs and began to leave the salon.

"A painted thimble," Pamela told Lord Fanshawe. "Let's start with that. We just have to go to the housekeeper, don't we?"

He nodded. "Very, yes, indeed, that's the ticket. Off to the housekeeper then, shall we?"

"Yes, but then we have to get a rag doll," Pamela said as she started to leave the room with her host.

"In due time," he said, taking her hand in his plump little paw. "First things first. This will be fun, what?"

The manor was a rabbit warren of rooms, and Pamela found herself utterly lost as her sprightly little host pulled her along dark corridors. It was a warm, crowded darkness, because the old place was furnished with what seemed to be the relics of a dozen generations of Fanshawes. Her host held one of her hands. Pamela kept the other stretched out in front of her so she wouldn't bump into bureaus, tables, chairs, or walls. That way she didn't collide with them all, just most of them.

One would think they'd light more lamps for the scavenger hunt, she thought as she nearly missed colliding with another armoire. She was sure she'd show bruises on her shins in the morning, and wondered how the other guests, who didn't have the help of a resident of the manor, would ever get back to the main salon when they were done.

"Here!" Lord Fanshawe finally chortled, and abruptly stopped.

Pamela looked around. They stood in a dimly lit room

filled with massive pieces of furniture. Most notably, an enormous canopied bed.

"The housekeeper lives here?" she asked in confusion.

"Hee hee," her host chortled, tugging on her hand. "We can forget that air of innocence now, what?" He grabbed her and tried to drag her closer to his portly little person.

Pamela was as furious as appalled by her host's sudden display of grappling arms, and soon made even angrier by the wet kiss that slid along her chin as she struggled with him. But she didn't struggle long. She was country bred, and came from a large family with protective brothers eager to share their knowledge of self-defense with an adored little sister.

"Stop that!" Pamela puffed, and shoved him hard. It was like trying to shove one of the armoires she'd careened into earlier in their journey through the manor. He was old and fat and short, but sturdy as a tree trunk. She didn't want to kill the old fellow, but she did mean to disable him. So she stomped on his foot and hooked an ankle around the other one that he immediately hopped to, and then she pushed him hard again. This time, he toppled.

"Outrageous!" she huffed. Leaving him sitting on the floor, she turned on her own heel to find her way back from what she now realized must be her host's bedchamber.

She stormed out into the hall, and straight into another pair of arms and a hard chest.

"I thought you'd give him the slip," Lord Ipcress said on a laugh as he wrapped her in an embrace. "Old fool, to think a prize like you would dally with him. I saw where you were really looking."

This gentleman was wearing boots instead of evening slippers, so he didn't even notice a foot slammed down on top of his. He was too close for a raised knee to do anything but encourage him, and not only was he able to catch her flailing hands, but he stood some inches taller than Pamela and had impressive muscles. So she resorted to throwing back her head and letting out a fearsome screech. It made

Lord Ipcress wince, which made him close his eyes, which also meant that he didn't see the fist that connected with his jaw.

"Get up so I can knock you down again," Jonathan said through clenched teeth.

Lord Ipcress either didn't hear him or decided to let things literally lay where they were for the moment.

"I'm sorry," Jonathan told Pamela as he drew her close. "I didn't know and didn't believe what I thought I began to see. We'll leave at first light. Pamela, I'm sorry."

"You needn't be," she said breathlessly.

"Of course I need be," he said impatiently. "I wish I'd listened to your fears and given them more credence, instead of assuming I knew best. By God!" he said with an angry look at the man who lay at their feet. "I'd no idea of what passed for amusement in this set; my experience of these people was out of date. When I saw the way the guests were being paired off, and how they reacted, I remembered your suspicions, and followed. Where's that wretched Fanshawe?"

"I knocked him down," she said.

"Too bad. I'd have liked to do it."

"Where's . . . Marianna?" she asked.

"God knows," he said bitterly, "and only He cares."

"I'm sorry," Jonathan said again. He stared out the coach window as they drove down the frosty country lane toward the main highway again. "What a ghastly way to start a Christmas holiday. Forgive me."

"They all weren't awful," Pamela said generously. "I quite liked some of them. The Whitleys and the Gordons, and Mr. Ames and Lord Montrose also left this morning, you know."

"Yes, and Sam Gregory as well," he said. "But that only means we weren't the only ones foolish enough not to look before we leaped." He avoided her eyes and cleared his throat, very glad that he'd sent her maid with his valet ahead in another coach.

"I spoke to Lady Fanshawe this morning," he said. "We'll never see them again. I can only think that losing her looks made her also lose her good sense. Although, now in retrospect, I have to admit that a grown woman who found it amusing to seduce a green lad never really had good sense. What could I have been thinking? There was gossip, but I discounted it in my eagerness to see you established in the social whirl. I've been away at the wars too long, Pamela. I'd forgot not only who was important in the social world, but also my own good sense. Forgive me. We'll make new friends, decent friends, together. I'll not impose my preferences on you either."

She nodded, and smiled widely. He was anxious to win her over, but he was only human. She was drinking in every penitent word, and he supposed she had the right. But he was tired of apologizing.

"Do you think our arriving days early will upset your family's plans?" he suddenly asked.

"I think they will be ecstatic," she said.

She thought she heard him sigh. So she moved close to him and rested her head on his shoulder. "We'll have a happy Christmas," she said. "You'll see."

He took her hand. "I hope we shall. I only wish my part of it had turned out differently."

She didn't like her new husband when he was arrogant. But she discovered she didn't like him when he was this repentant, either. So she kissed him, and they forgot sadness and apologies, and Christmas itself, for a while.

Jonathan smiled. His wife had her nose pressed to the carriage window, like a child at a sweet shop.

"It looks just the same!" she caroled as she stared out at the old farmhouse they were approaching. "Oh! But I've so missed this place."

Her husband's smile slipped.

"London is wonderful," she went on, "but this is home!"

"Indeed," he said. He had a home in the Cotswolds as well as the one in London, an ancient manor house that his wife had said was lovely, the one and only time they'd visited it. His estate was older, more beautiful and historic than the house they approached. But she'd never greeted it with half so much pleasure as she now showed as they neared her parents' rambling country home.

"Oh—there's Papa!" she cried as the coach slowed in the front drive. "And Mama! And Bobby and Elizabeth—and Cousin George! That means that Mary must have had the baby. And that little love with the basket of holly must be Harriet's youngest, only look at her curls. Oh, my, how lovely, all the children standing waiting for us, isn't that sweet? They've grown so much I vow I can't tell whose child is which. Look! There's Kit and Harry with different hairstyles! Oh, good, they must have finally grown up and decided being the terrible Arthur twins is passé. And could that be Cecil? No! But it is! He's home from the sea at last. Oh, Jonathan," she cried, turning to give him a quick hug, "we're here! I'm home!"

There was nothing he could say. No one would have heard him anyway. The coach slowed, and the door was pulled open, and his wife flew into the many welcoming arms of her enormous family.

"Rexford," a tall, thin, dour gentleman said when he saw Jonathan descending from the carriage.

"Laughton," Jonathan said, acknowledging his wife's brother-in-law with a nod. He watched as her adoring relatives engulfed his wife. "Been here long?"

"A week," Laughton said glumly. "You're just in time. You missed the traditional family musicale, where the children show off their progress on the flute, pianoforte, and harp. Tonight they're holding the traditional charades party. The costumed pantomime's tomorrow night. Got an evening of dancing set for after that. Parties every night until Christmas, and then there's the round of visiting to be done."

"Yes, I see. So Pamela said it would be." Jonathan didn't have time to say more. His wife flew out of the pack of her relatives, grabbed his hand, and dragged him to them in order to reintroduce him to everyone he hadn't seen since his wedding. With her six siblings and their spouses, their children, a covey of cousins, aunts and uncles, and old family friends to be greeted, it was snowing heavily by the time the introductions were done. No one but Jonathan seemed to notice.

"And you'll be my king," Pamela said as she adjusted her paste tiara.

"I should rather not," Jonathan said, picking up his pasteboard crown and staring at it. "That is to say, I'm really not very good at pantomimes."

"You must," she said firmly. "Everyone will be in costume . . ." Her eyes grew wide. "I mean, I wish you would try. Please do put it on. You don't have to act in the pantomime but you do have to look as though you'd take part." She raised the crown and set it lightly on his head, then tilted it so it sat rakishly on his close-cropped curls. "Oh, don't you look regal! Far better than any of the Hanovers."

He smiled. "That's not much of a compliment."

"Oh, please," she said. "It means so much to Mama. If you don't, she'll take it as further evidence that you don't like her. Try as I might, I can't convince her that is just your way."

"What is just my way?"

"You know," she said, twitching a shoulder, making the filmy gauze of her princess's costume seem to float around her, "your reserved manner. We're a convivial group, and she thinks anyone who doesn't talk sixteen to the dozen is disapproving." She glanced up at his reflection in the mirror before her. "You don't disapprove, do you?"

He put his hands on her shoulders and dropped a kiss on the tip of her nose. "No, I do not. What is there to disapprove of? All right, I'll be a king. And I'll try to talk more. Are you happy?"

She spun around and hugged him. "Oh, so very happy now, my dear! Isn't this the best Christmas?"

He didn't answer. It was not. It was very far from it, at least for him. But she was ecstatic, and that actually made him even less happy. This was their second day at her parents' home, and she'd been busy from morning to evening, visiting with her family. There was room for all of them, and it was a huge family. The manor was a rambling old house, made up of rooms that had been cobbled together by her ancestors as the spirit moved them and their family increased. They had been fruitful and so the house had multiplied, until now it was a welter of styles. It was not, Jonathan supposed, uncomfortable. But neither was it the sort of place that he had ever called home, or wanted to. It lacked grace and style, both of which were things he always sought.

Though his wife was clearly thrilled to be there, Jonathan felt severely out of place. He often found himself wondering how such a bright and lovely person as his bride could have sprung from such beginnings. This made him feel guilty, because he didn't like to think of himself as stiff, or cold, or an elitist, and everything in this house made him feel more like one.

Viscount Rexford knew he was a man of consequence, but also knew that it was a damnable thing to be aware of that consequence. So he tried to fit in, but the longer he stayed at his in-laws' home, the more of a stranger he felt. He didn't mind the myriad sticky-fingered infants, and actually enjoyed the time he passed with the older children. But there were so many of them, and they had so many activities and friends present, that he didn't see them that often or for that long. Which was too bad, because they were the only ones here he could have a good conversation with, or at least conversations that didn't involve something that had happened the last time Christmas had come to the squire's home. And his wife had no time for him at all.

He didn't even have the solace of her company. When they chanced to be in the same room, she was lost in conversations with this brother or that sister, or was busily trading stories with one old friend or another. When he didn't see her surrounded by laughing men, he saw her giggling with women, or cuddling a baby, or kneeling to have earnest discussion with a toddler. And not one of those conversations was one he could share.

He hated to be selfish, or at least to be aware that he was, but he sometimes wondered if she remembered he was there at all. Then he reminded himself that he'd brought her to the Fanshawes' over her objections, hadn't he? And she'd been molested there. He owed her more than courtesy in this. After all, the most dire thing that could happen to him here was to be bored to death.

And it was only three more days. He paused. *Damnation!* No, it would be five more days, because they'd come early when they'd escaped from the blasted Fanshawes. He picked up the ancient moth-eaten robes that a generation of his wife's ancestors had worn at their Christmas pantomime, repressed a shudder, and prepared to be king for a night.

"She was the sweetest babe," the old woman dressed up as a fortune teller told Jonathan. "Never a cry out of her. Why, didn't Betty, she who was wet nurse for both Pamela and Eugene, didn't she say that sweet Pamela could be stuck with a pin and she wouldn't cry?"

"No, I don't think so," the other wizened old woman she was sitting with said. This one was dressed in so many shawls Jonathan couldn't tell if she was supposed to be a mummy, or was actually an invalid. "It wasn't Betty who nursed Eugene, Elizabeth," she said thoughtfully. "It was that Tolliver woman from Frick's farm."

"I think not!" the fortune teller said on a laugh. "I'd forget my own name before I'd forget that. It wasn't that Tolliver woman. She had a wart on her chin. Remember, it frightened young Arthur and made him cry? He said she was a witch, and wasn't there a fuss when Mary found out about that! She never was one to let the children be impudent to the servants. No, I believe it was Betty. Here, Mary?" she called, snatching out at a nearby shepherdess's gown. "Wasn't it Betty who nursed Eugene?"

Pamela's mother left off talking to one of her daughters. She went over to where her two old aunts were entertaining her new son-in-law.

"Why no," she said. "It was Mrs. Fairchild, from Hildebrandt's farm."

"So it was!" the fortune teller exclaimed. "She was the one with the mole. Mrs. Tolliver had the crooked teeth. Where is my head? So, she was the one who was Pamela's nurse too."

"Oh, no," Pamela's mother said. "That was Betty. She nursed Pamela."

"How fascinating for Rexford," a slender young gentleman dressed as a devil said with a laugh. "Regaling him with wet-nurse tales. Fie, Mama! Trying to bore your new son-in-law to extinction? Come along, my lord, we've some hot punch and a few warm tales for you."

"Very well," Pamela's mama said. "Take him and entertain him royally. But be back for the pantomime, if you please."

"You must think we're a pack of regular country bumpkins, a pack of Johnny Raws," the young man said as he bore Jonathan off to join a group of costumed men standing by a punch bowl in the corner of the room. "I'll wager they've filled your head with baby stories until you're ready to howl like a babe yourself. Here, gents, I've rescued our new relative."

Jonathan was handed a cup of punch. "More in this than a stick of cinnamon," Pamela's father, dressed as a Roman senator, said with a wink. "So, tell us, Rexford. What's new in London?"

"Town was pretty thin of company with Christmas coming," Jonathan said, searching for a subject that would interest his host. He scarcely knew the man, but remembered Pamela said he was an ardent sportsman. He himself didn't hunt, and only fished in order to find solitude. Although he had plans to raise horses now that he was married and ready to live at his country estate, he didn't wager on them. He cudgeled his brain to think of something that might interest his father-in-law. He did fence, but didn't think that would fascinate a country squire. He did spar at Gentleman Jackson's salon! "Ah, yes," he said, "the latest rumor is that Cribb is going to fight Molyneaux again in the new year."

"I doubt it!" his father-in-law exclaimed. "Twice was enough, I'd think. At any rate, Molyneaux had his jaw broken by the Champion in September, and I daresay that will take a while to heal. Don't know if the Moor would care for another taste of that kind of punishment, either."

"Were you there?" Jonathan asked.

"No, but I'd have given a pretty penny to have been! I did see Molyneaux destroy Rimmer, though, earlier in the year. Now, there was a match to remember."

"Aye," another noble Roman said, "so you said. And you told me that I had something of the Champion's style when Nick and I went at it that time after I thought he'd insulted that barmaid in town, you remember, the one I fancied."

"Ho!" Pamela's father said. "But you fancied every barmaid, Charles."

The men laughed. Charles smiled. "So I did. Wasn't she the wench though? Lord! She had half the boys in the district sniffing after her. When they weren't fighting over her, they were planning on how they could snare her. She finally ran off with young Fairchild, didn't she?"

"Her? No," a fellow clad as a Gypsy put in. "She ran off with a tinker, I heard."

"Heard wrong," another gentleman, this one in motley pirate's garb, protested. "She never. Harry here had the right of it. She run off with young Fairchild, and his father had to pay a pretty penny to be rid of her. Almost got to Gretna too."

"No, that was Fairchild and Dylan's daughter who got intercepted on the road to Gretna," Pamela's brother Kit said.

"Aye, that's right," a man got up as a harlequin in patches said. "And then they up and ran to Scotland, and never looked back. Anyone hear what happened to them?"

"You ask every year, Godfrey," another man said. "And no one ever knows. Did you fancy her yourself?"

"Why, so I did. Who wouldn't?"

"There's truth in that, she was a pippin. But then what happened to the bar wench Nick fought over?"

"She went to London by herself," the harlequin said. "What happened after that, I don't know, but that I do remember."

"I remember that you fancied her too," the Roman said slyly.

That evening Jonathan also learned, yet again, that it was possible for a man to sleep standing up, with his eyes open, and without falling down.

He opened his eyes. Now that he was finally in bed, Jonathan couldn't sleep.

"Can't sleep?" his wife asked from the next pillow.

"How did you know?"

"I can't either," she said.

"Well, as it happens, you lucky lady, I happen to have a cure for that," he said softly, and reached for her.

She scooted back and sat up against her pillow.

"What's this?" he asked on a laugh, drawing back. "I bathed and cleaned my teeth." He raised his arm and pretended to sniff at his underarm. "I'm fragrant as a rose."

She said nothing.

His voice became tender. "I'm sorry. Are you unwell?"

"No," she said tersely.

He was still for a moment. He'd been pleased to find her awake in the deep of this lonely night and had looked forward to her intimate company. He'd been willing to settle for good conversation. But though he'd only been married three months, he wasn't slow at recognizing storm signals flying.

"I see," he said slowly. "So, what is it then?"

"You," she said deliberately. "I believe you are the one who can tell me what it is."

"I can?"

"You ought to," she said. Like steam escaping from a kettle her words rushed out. "You should! I mean to say, why else would a man stand mute as a clam all night, if he didn't have some issue or another that was bedeviling him?"

He was honestly perplexed.

"You did not say two words together to anyone tonight!" she cried. "Not to my mother or father, or any of my sisters or brothers. You stood like some . . . icy paragon, looking down your long nose at my family!"

He tried to remember just whom he had conversation with. "I wasn't looking down at anyone," he said defensively. "There was just nothing for me to say."

"Nothing to say!" she echoed with vast frustration in her voice. "You, who reads every news sheet and magazine, and keeps up on politics and literature, theater and . . . and everything going on around you, had *nothing* to say to my family? I think not, and I tell you that I take it badly. If I could go to those frightful Fanshawes and pretend to be enchanted by their dissolute and vulgar company, the least you could do was to pretend to be entertained by my family. But I suppose they are too decent for you."

His head went up, and now he did look down his long nose at her. It was just too bad, he thought, that she probably couldn't see it in the darkness. "My friends let you speak," he said icily. "I, on the other hand, had no chance to say anything. My friends included you in their conversations and their games . . ."

He belatedly realized his misstatement. He almost heard her mute satisfaction with his poor choice of words, and hurried on the attack. "But no one here pays the least attention to me," he said. "Since I did not have the same wet nurse as anyone present, or the same nursery maid, nor shared in any of those interminable convoluted escapades your family never tires of repeating, they had no interest in anything *I* had to say."

His voice, she noted with interest, was growing loud. That was something she hadn't heard before. It pleased her. "I don't believe you tried, my lord," she said with haughty disdain. "You didn't even speak with Laughton and he is the most congenial chap. Nor can you accuse him of rehashing old tales. He couldn't. He's only been married to my sister for a year."

"He collects *beetles*," Jonathan said with weary patience. "He earnestly collects them. There is not much else I can bring to a conversation that might interest him."

"I do not believe you tried," she said again.

"I see," he said. "And you know because you were at my side every moment? How very odd that I didn't see you there. Dear me, can I be growing shortsighted?" he asked with a curling lip. "But how is that possible? I clearly saw you across the room, giggling with your sisters and friends; I saw you dandling every infant in the county on your knee at one time or another during the interminable evening, I saw you swapping those same shared tales with your brothers and cousins. I did not see you with your husband, though. In fact, if one were a visitor here, one would be hard-pressed to realize you *were* married. I remind you that *I* never left your side when we were at Fanshawe Manor."

She was still, because she was stung. What he said was true, and the realization hurt. She had neglected him. She opened her lips to murmur an apology. But he sensed his victory, and spoke too soon.

"A very jolly Christmas this is turning out to be for me," he said loftily. "I might as well have stayed at home by myself with a good book, and shared a toast to the season with the butler. He, at least, knows who his master is."

"His *master*!" she cried, pouncing on the word.

He realized his error, and winced.

"Well, I take leave to tell you that you are not my master," she raged. "You are my husband, and I also tell you that I have never so regretted it!" She rose from the bed, and stepped down to the floor. "Nor will I sleep next to either my master or my husband tonight! After all, a master does not wish his servant in his bed and I do not believe a husband who deems himself my master deserves me at his side!"

Once again he realized her predicament before she did, and watched with interest.

She understood a second later, and stood irresolute. If she left the room, her family would be scandalized. They'd want to know the reason for any discord. They'd take sides and the quarrel would become everyone's entertainment, and the bane of her existence however it turned out. She knew this house like the back of her hand and yet knew she could not step out the door. And this bedchamber did not have a dressing room.

It did, however, have a chaise in the corner, against the wall. She stormed over to a chest under the window, flung it open, pulled out a blanket, flung herself on the chaise, and dragged the blanket over herself.

The room was still.

She heard a sigh, and saw his outline as he rose from bed. He walked over to her. She froze, and held her breath. She doubted he meant to do her an injury. But what would she do if he dared embrace her? Could she return his kisses? No, she thought with a kind of thrilled panic, she didn't think she could. So, what should she do?

He leaned over her and her breath caught in her chest. He reached down, picked her up, and carried her to the bed in a few swift strides. He deposited her there and in one swift movement stripped the blanket from her, causing her to roll right out of it. Then, as she lay tumbled, watching him in newborn fear and vast surprise, he marched back to the chaise, lay down, and covered himself with the blanket he had taken.

"Good night," he said, and turned his back to her.

He'd won, she realized. Being a gentleman had utterly trumped her. That rankled. But that wasn't what kept her up half the night. What did, was the slow dawning realization that he'd had a point.

He stayed awake awhile, feeling very ill-used. But he knew he'd won, and also that whatever else his wife was, she was fair-minded. And so he finally fell asleep with a smile on his lips, wondering what the devil she'd do in the morning. His bride might not be reasonable, he thought as he drifted off, but by God, she was interesting! He hadn't felt so alive in years.

"I apologize," Pamela said.

Jonathan opened his eyes all the way, and saw her seated at the dressing table.

"I should not have left your side last night," she said, looking at his reflection in her mirror. She'd been waiting for him to wake up and had spoken the minute she'd seen those thick eyelashes of his flutter and open. "I suppose I was just so pleased to be with my family again that I forgot it was my duty to make sure you were as comfortable as I was. Forgive me for that."

He sat up. Holding his blanket over his naked body, he rose and came to stand beside her. "I do," he said, gazing down at her. "And I earnestly ask you to forgive me for my poor choice of words. I never want to be your master. But I do wish I could have you as my partner in this new life of ours."

His blanket was not very securely held. They were late for breakfast.

They came down the stairs to see the manor had been transformed in the night. Evergreen branches were swagged over every mantel, and were twined around the chandeliers. The staircase was decorated with ropes of rosemary and pine, enlivened by strings of nuts and bright winter berries.

"Greetings!" her father called when they entered the dining room. "We've been at work for hours, sleepy heads."

There were a few murmured comments about newlyweds from among the others in the room that made Pamela's cheeks grow as rosy as her much kissed lips.

"Did you forget, puss?" her father asked.

She frowned in incomprehension as she took a seat at the table.

"Marriage has addled your wits." Her brother Kit laughed. "We always get up at dawn to start decorating the old place on Christmas Eve. Remember?"

"Oh!" she said, round-eyed. "Is it the twenty-fourth today?"

"Aye. But don't worry, we haven't hauled in the Yule log yet."

"Not that we haven't picked it out," her sister Rosemary said. "Father has had his eye on it for months. And the children are on tenterhooks, waiting for us to finish breakfast so we can go out with them and help them bring in the rest of the bunting. We still have yards of holly and ivy, to say nothing of mistletoe, to harvest."

"Not that those two need any mistletoe," a cousin called out, and made everyone laugh.

"We can't put any holly, ivy, or mistletoe up until tonight," her mother cautioned them, unnecessarily, because they all knew it so well. "Bad luck to set so much as a pinch of any of them inside until dark. But we can and will collect it today. First, we'll go watch you gents cut the Yule log. Then, while you haul it home, we'll get our holly and ivy. You men can come help us pull down the mistletoe. We're all ready to go, so finish your breakfast and we can get started," she told Pamela. "But be sure to eat enough to keep you warm, it's very cold today. We can have another cup of tea while we wait. We didn't want to start out without you. It would be a hard thing to have you to come all this way and miss all our fun."

"I'll say!" Pamela's brother Harry exclaimed. "Remember how vexed Charles got that year when he overslept and missed dragging the Yule log back?"

"Didn't I just?" Charles declared. "I still get hot when I think about it. How could you let me sleep past that? I was looking forward to it, and only overslept because I was so overactive the day before. Remember? We had that horse race *and* a foot race, and I was so tired I couldn't wait to fall into bed. I still believe it was because I was the one who found the log that year, and not Kit, that he deliberately let me oversleep."

"Hardly," Kit said. "You were overactive at the punch bowl the night before, if you remember."

"Me?" Charles laughed. "And what about you and your friend Wilson? Didn't I hear something about the flask he enlivened the punch bowl with that night? Or don't you remember?"

There was much laughter, and soon others at the crowded table began to offer other versions of the reason why Charles had missed dragging home the Yule log that year. Then they started to talk about the year before, when they'd chopped the chosen log only to find it rotted at the heart and how they'd had to scurry to find a new one.

Pamela laughed as she remembered. Wanting to share the fun, she looked at her husband, at her side. He sat with a faint, agreeable smile on his lips. But his eyes were glazing over. She shot a glance at Laughton, her sister's husband, and saw a similar expression in his mild brown eyes. Her own widened as she realized every second word she was hearing was "remember?"

"Come now!" she said into the first moment of silence that presented itself. "This is hardly fair! Neither Rexford nor Laughton was here then, and they can't help but be bored to flinders by our reminiscences."

Her sister shot her a grateful look. But her brothers jeered.

"What?" Harry asked, incredulous. "Speak for yourself, sweetings. Who could resist that tale?"

"And we tell it so well they'd have to see the point. Don't you, my lord?" George asked. "And you, Laughton?"

"Indeed," Jonathan said as Laughton also hastily agreed.

"You just don't want us telling them about that time you ate the mistletoe berries instead of chucking them over your shoulder when you made a wish, as you were supposed to do, Pam. Gad!" Kit said with a shudder. "I'll never forget how sick you were. Not from the berries, I doubt they had time to sit in your stomach long enough. But from that brew Mama kept pouring into you to get you to relinquish them."

"Now, now," his father admonished him, "no more of that, sir, if you please. Some of us are still eating breakfast."

"What?" Kit cried. "And you with an iron stomach? Taking her part, are you, Father? Don't you want Rexford to hear what Pam said to Mama—when she could speak again, that is. Well, I remember. She said she never knew she was supposed to pluck them after a *kiss,* she thought it was after a wish!"

"Worse than that," Harry said with a grin, "she thought she was supposed to eat them, not toss them over her shoulder."

"She never could resist a berry," Kit laughingly agreed. "We told her they were poisonous, but would she listen? Never. Remember?"

"I remembered," his mother said, shaking her head. "That's why I told Dr. Foster to check her ears as well as her stomach when he got here."

The company roared at the old familiar story and Pamela smiled at the memory in spite of herself. She was relieved to see that her husband seemed genuinely amused as well. She was grateful, though she felt uncomfortable now. Her unease wasn't about any embarrassing tales her loving family could tell him, but because she finally realized what a dead bore he must find them all.

Now that she was aware of the problem, her joy in the day was ruined. The situation didn't improve as the day went on.

The trip in the sleigh to get the Yule log was enlivened by stories of every other such trip they'd ever taken, back to the first Arthur ancestor who ever strode over English soil, or so Pamela thought in despair. The ho ho ho's were louder than the thuds of the axe as the Yule log was cut, as the merry company remembered the time Grandfather almost lost his thumb at the same task, and what he said in his own defense.

She and her sisters and the children went on to cut mistletoe, and she had to hear the story of her unfortunate taste in berries again. She was sure someone was telling it to Jonathan too. Then, when the men rejoined them, after they'd hauled the log into the front hall and wrestled it into the hearth in the main salon, she had to watch him endure the stories about how Percival had fallen out of the oak that year when he'd reached for an elusive strand of mistletoe. Then he was regaled with tales of little Cousin Orwell and the mishap in the holly bush, young Mary and her strange reaction to the ivy crown she'd insisted on wearing, and yet again, the story of how her mama and father had met under a ball of mistletoe at a local dance. The story still brought a fond smile to her lips, but she couldn't help realizing it might not be as fascinating to her husband.

How tedious and unsophisticated he must think her family, she thought sadly as she watched her husband smile at a story her father was telling. Jonathan was so urbane that her father would have no idea that his listener was being bored to flinders. She herself would not have known if he hadn't told her. She might get angry when her husband responded to anger with that insufferable icy calm, but now she realized concealing his emotions was a gift as well as a powerful weapon. She felt hopelessly outclassed. How could she ever measure up to him?

How unfair he must believe her to be as well, she thought. And with good cause. She resented his highhandedness in forcing her to share the holiday with a previous lover. But here she was, insisting that he pass the holiday with her family, being regaled with stories of family and simple country folk he didn't have a thing in common with. She'd trimmed his hair because she'd had to endure those nights with the Fanshawes, even before they behaved so badly. He hadn't said a word of criticism of her family, except in his own defense.

Pamela was subdued as she dressed for dinner that night. Her maid had been given the night off to celebrate with the other servants, and so Pamela frowned as she tried to anchor a rosy camellia in her curls, to top off her holiday garb.

"Why are you scowling?" Jonathan asked as he came into the room. "You look lovely. No, better than that. You look like the very spirit of Christmas."

She wore a simple green silk gown with a golden stole, and looked so fresh and lovely, so innocent and yet desirable that he caught his breath. But they had such problems of late that he was reluctant to drop a kiss on her bare shoulder as he longed to do—as he would once have done without thinking.

She shrugged, causing her breasts to rise and fall, along with his pulse. "I always wear green and gold at Christmas," she said diffidently.

She glanced at him from under her lashes. He looked elegant tonight, as always. He wore a gray jacket and slate unmentionables, both matching his cool steady eyes. His waistcoat was a symphony of burgundy and green. He looked so handsome, yet so immaculate and untouchable, that she wanted to weep.

"What?" he said quickly, and took her in his arms.

She shook her head, unable to speak. It suddenly was too much. She couldn't go on like this. He was so near and yet so far, and growing further away from her every hour. Bad as it would be at any time, the comparison of all her past happy Christmas memories and the awful reality of this sudden impasse with the man she loved most was simply unendurable. She needed joy now, at this important time of year. She needed closeness, and love, and him. The only thing left to do was to offer him the only thing she could give him: truth.

"Oh, Jonathan," she sighed against his chest. "I feel so . . . I have to apologize to you," she said, pushing him away, and holding him literally at arm's length. "I carried on like a shrew because you took me to the Fanshawes'."

"You were right to do so," he said, frowning because of the tears he saw starting in her eyes.

"Well, yes, and no," she said. "Later, in retrospect, I suppose I was. But not at first. At first, they couldn't be nicer to me. And yet I carried on like a madwoman before I even found out what they were like, without giving them a chance. But you! Here you are, in the heart of nowhere, bored to bits by my family, and you haven't said a word. Not one word of complaint, not once wished to go home."

"Yes, I have," he said. "And yes I did."

"Well, yes," she conceded. "But only after I attacked you. In retaliation, I'm sure. I think you'd have borne it all in silence, otherwise. I'm glad you didn't, because otherwise I wouldn't have seen it. I'm so sorry I didn't pay attention to you. But the truth is that when you're so polite when I get angry, it only makes me madder."

"In future, I'll try to bluster, shout, and scream," he said humbly.

"Would you?" she asked.

"If you wish."

"I do!" she said. "When you're so quiet it just makes me want to stick you with a pin. I'm not used to silence."

"I grew up with nothing else. I promise I will shout the house down the next time you vex me," he vowed.

She giggled. "I can't imagine that! But I wish you'd try. Then I'd know where I stand. Please, let me get on with my apology. Because if carrying on is necessary for me to clear the air, and it is, you must understand that a total apology is as important to me in order to make amends. It's what I'm accustomed to. We are a very dramatic family, you see."

"I begin to understand," he said with an admirably

straight face. "Carry on. Literally or figuratively. I am at your command."

"Well," she said, "only today did I allow myself to see what you have suffered since you got here. You're far too polite! I let you know how I hated being at the Fanshawes' immediately, even before I got there."

"I should have listened to you, and we would never have gone there."

She shook that off. "It doesn't signify. At least, maybe it does, but that's not what I'm speaking about now. You see, it was only after we were here that you showed me your discontent with being here at all."

"No, that's not true. I didn't want to come here."

"Well, yes," she admitted. "And I do think that was wrong of you. Even so, we are here, and you suffer. I know that's so," she added before he could speak. "My family means well, but we don't consider what it is to be an outsider, and I suspect that even though we're married it will take some time before you're part of our inner circle. That is, if you even wish to be."

"I do," he said, as solemnly as any bridegroom.

"Thank you. I don't know why you should! Now I see that whenever we get together, and at Christmas, especially, the same stories get told, the same things are done. It's comforting for us, but you must be at wits' end! I know we couldn't have stayed at the Fanshawes', but surely, this isn't much better for you than their house was for me. Well, safer, of course," she said thoughtfully. "But not better. My family forgets everything and everyone but their own history, and if you weren't there when it happened, hearing it retold cannot be a treat. And that is mostly what we do. You must have felt so alone. Even when I was so misused by the Fanshawes, I had you as my ally. Your only ally here has been my beetle-loving brother-in-law. Perhaps as the others marry it will get better, but as for now? I do apologize."

He smiled. "Don't," he said. "It was churlish of me to complain. I think I only did so in order to have my own back at you. Because you were so very right, and it's hard for me to admit I was wrong. Listen, my love," he said, his hands on her shoulders as he looked down into her eyes. "There's not a thing wrong with your family. I didn't really have one, not as such, and so I didn't understand. I wasn't hatched from an egg, but what I grew up with was nothing like this! I had nurses and governesses, and then I was sent to school. When I came home for the holidays—*if* I came home for the holidays—it was to be left by myself in the nursery.

"Your family is a tightly knit group of people who dearly love each other," he said. His gray eyes warmed to the color of a summer's fog as he smiled. "That's both wonderful and remarkable to me. I can only hope that in time I do something foolish enough, or downright stupid enough, to be included in your family's ongoing chronicles."

His voice became slow and serious, and his eyes searched hers. "You wouldn't be as bright and open as you are if you'd come from a family like mine. I thank your mother and father for nurturing you the way they have done. You screeched at me the other day, and I admit, I was appalled. At least I was until I realized it was because I never learned to love loudly enough. Don't apologize for your family, be proud of them. I wish we could create the same sort of family together, you and I. I think we only need time enough to do so. Time and love and caring enough. Then, eventually, we will have our own myths and legends and lore to bore our children's spouses with. If, that is, you'll bear with me long enough?"

"Oh, Jonathan," she cried, and went into his opened arms. She hugged him, hard. "I so wish I hadn't been such a fool."

"I'm so glad you were," he said against her hair.

She reared back and glowered at him. "You don't have to agree!"

He laughed. "Yes, I do. Shall we have another fight? Where will you sleep tonight? You're running out of sanctuaries, you know, and December is such a cold month. Now, there's the stuff of stories to keep telling our descendants!"

She smiled. "Yes. True. Jonathan?"

"Mmm," he said as he dragged her close again and inhaled the camellia she'd pinned in her hair.

"I wish we hadn't argued."

"If we had not, how would we have come to this?"

"What have we come to?"

"A beginning," he said. "I now understand that I must roar at you when I am cross with you, which I imagine I shall be again, in due time. You now know that I freeze solid when I am most upset. Fire and ice. We are a perfect December match, you and I, the very spirit of a wonderful Christmas night—if we can just remember to always add faith and love and joy. We can learn to live with each other, my love. We will." He bent his head to see her expression. "What do you think?"

"Yes," she said simply. "We must. For I do love you so much that I cannot bear it when we are at odds."

"So we shall," he said. "And as for now? We'll spend this Christmas with your family, and then, next year, we'll have them all come and start a new tradition with ours. What do you think?"

She nodded. "I think that's a grand idea. But it will take more than one new baby to make them give up their traditions. I think we'll have to come here next year and add to their tradition. All three of us."

She felt his breath catch.

"It's so?" he asked.

"Well," she said, keeping her head down so he couldn't see her smile. "It might be. It could be. I do wish it would be."

They were late to dinner.

But they didn't waste the mistletoe. And this time she used it just as she should, for kisses and wishes. He was delighted to share them with her.

     *   *   *

They were both smiling when they finally went to dinner. But Pamela found her spirits sinking as she came down the stairs. It was one thing to say she understood her husband's feelings, because now she did. It was quite another to actually have to watch her family ignoring him, as well as to see how he bore up under it, however stoically.

"Here they are!" one of her cousins trumpeted as they went into the salon.

"Now we can get on with it!" her father said.

"Oh, sorry we're late," Pamela said, feeling her color rise. "But you didn't have to wait for us. Though it was kind, because I did want Jonathan to see how we light the Yule log."

"Couldn't start without you," her brother Kit answered. "We need the newest member of our family to help light it, remember?"

"What?" Pamela asked. "But why us? Little Gwyneth is our latest addition, she's only been with us for two months," she added, smiling at Gwyneth's proud new mama.

"They refused to wake her for our pyrotechnics," Kit's twin, Harry, explained, laughing. "That leaves Rexford."

"Surely not," Pamela said in confusion. "That leaves Laughton."

"Not I," that gentleman said quickly. "I had the honor last year, remember?"

She hadn't. But that wasn't why she looked distressed. It was because that was still another "remember" that her husband did not.

"And weren't you wary of doing it?" Charles asked Laughton.

"Aye!" Cousin Godfrey agreed merrily. "I think it was because he was afraid he'd set fire to one of his little friends. But so he did. Remember how many of the little beasties came scurrying out of that log as soon as it started blazing?"

Laughton smiled as everyone laughed, even Jonathan. Though he hadn't been there, he knew his brother-in-law's penchant for beetles.

"I didn't see one rare specimen in the scramble," Laughton said good-naturedly. "And so I didn't mind the mad fandango you did on the escapees when they came near you either, Godfrey."

"Yes, it's Rexford's turn," his father-in-law said over the laughter that filled the room. "And high time he had a turn at something. Sad stuff this Christmas must be for you, my lord," he told Jonathan. "We all go through our paces every year like trained ponies, doing what we always do, and enjoying it for just that reason. It has to be a dead bore for you, though. I know, you're far too polite to agree. But now you get a chance to add your own bit and become part of our pageant. Then next year, you can share your experiences with the next in line."

His voice became solemn. "Lighting the Yule log is very important for good luck in the new year," he told Jonathan. "Now. I shall light the last bit of last year's log that I saved for this year. And then you start us off anew."

He took a thick charred stick of wood from where it had been propped at the side of the hearth, and ceremoniously lit it. Once he got it burning like a taper, he held it high to show the assembled company, and then solemnly handed it to his new son-in-law.

Jonathan took the glowing brand and bent to the hearth. He knelt, and set the blazing stick to the tinder surrounding the new Yule log, touching it in several places so that it would catch evenly all round the log. He blew on the tiny flames, fanning them until the tinder was burning brightly.

But the log wasn't. It was huge, dark, and sullen-looking, a great brown lump surrounded by masses of easily leaping flames that were quickly consuming the tinder. Jonathan thought he'd never seen a less combustible piece of wood. It looked like it would never catch. The watching company seemed to hold their breath just as he was doing. Fine thing, he thought nervously, if the damned thing didn't catch fire. What would that mean to his wife's family? That he'd ruined their luck in the new year? Would he be the first new addition to their family in all its long history to be unable to light their new Yule log? Gads! What would poor Pamela think of him? It was a greater responsibility than he'd guessed. Was it a test? He reached for the bellows . . .

And then he saw a single sheet of flame flare up on the right side of the log. Then another erupted from the middle of the log, along with a thin plume of smoke that went straight up the flue. The log was suddenly surrounded by a flickering transparent blue aura. Then, with a loud snap, blue and orange flames began licking up and down the length and width of the great log. It popped, it hissed, it flared. The log was definitely on fire.

A crackling blaze roared in the hearth, and Jonathan's face, illuminated by its ruddy light, showed a relieved smile. When he finally straightened he felt that he'd accomplished something, and grinned as he bowed to the company's loud cheers and applause.

"That's a relief. Your face when it just sat there smoldering, Rexford!" Cousin William said. "A study in frustration. Can't blame you, indeed I felt for you. You did far better than I did. Remember the night I tried to light it?" he asked the company.

There was much laughter. "Not your fault, old fellow," Kit said, clapping William on the back. "Don't you remember? No one realized the log had been sitting in the damp for weeks. Couldn't have lit that blasted thing with a torch!"

"Well, how was I to know the window the log had been stored under had been broken and the rain the night before had got in and made the thing damp as a moat?" Pamela's father asked. "We were lucky. We used another and no harm befell us. This year we have nothing to worry about. It was touch and go there for a while, but the log is lit, and burning brightly."

Jonathan felt relief and amusement as he realized his own story was now doubtless part of the family chronicles.

"Yes!" His wife suggested, "The Yule log is lit. Come, let's move on!"

Jonathan's new relatives burst into song. He went to stand by his wife, put his arm around her, and joined in. He knew the tune. It was a traditional one. Pamela looked up at him and smiled as he added his deep, true baritone harmony to her clear soprano.

The front door was opened and the neighbors who had been waiting on the steps trooped in, singing the same song, as they did every year.

The wassail was brought in by a pair of beaming servants, straining under the weight of the great basin filled with hot punch that they carried. It was carefully placed on an ancient trundle table. Cups were dipped in and toasts were raised to good health, good luck, and happiness. The house smelled of fresh pine and wood smoke, candle tallow, rum, cinnamon, and the various heady scents of roasting meat, poultry, and pies, the whole laced with gusts of cold clean air from the opened door. Then the door was closed and more toasts made, more food brought in, and more carols sung.

His father-in-law introduced Jonathan to the neighbors. Pamela's brothers whispered the latest, as well as the oldest gossip about each one of them to Jonathan after each passed along to greet other guests. Jonathan soon knew that Mrs. Tansy liked the rum punch a jot too much, or at least she had last year. Mr. Fairbanks liked his dinner too much too, because he was at least a stone heavier than he'd ever been. And his wife liked that too little, just get her started on the subject—or rather, don't, Jonathan was warned.

Jonathan learned that the vicar was afraid of dogs and the baker's wife, of thunderstorms. He heard stories about every member of the increasingly merry party, and by the time the neighbors and townsfolk trooped out again, he felt as though he'd known them for years and, moreover, was interested in them and their future as well as their past.

Jonathan realized he was actually enjoying himself.

Was it that he was now ready to meet his new family? he

wondered. Or was it that they realized it was time to truly admit him to their ranks?

He never knew.

He only knew that the dinner was sumptuous and the company warm, welcoming, and delightful. When he finally went to bed, and at last was able to hold his dear wife close in his arms, he went to sleep with only one wish in his heart for the holiday: that every one from now on would be as merry and bright as this one had been.

Pamela smiled in her sleep, and curled closer to him with a sigh. She'd made the same wish, and believed it would come true.

It did. For them, at least.

The story of their first Christmas, when suitably edited, made a wonderful story with which they regaled their increasingly enormous family on every Christmas Day. Of course they were to fight again on each and every one of those holidays, but always with as much joy and zest as love and laughter. Which was to say, a very great deal of it, for all their happy Christmases ever after.

Let Nothing You Dismay

by Carla Kelly

*I*t was obvious to Lord Trevor Chase, his solicitor, and their clerk that all the other legal minds at Lincoln's Inn had been celebrating the approach of Christmas for some hours. The early closing of King's Bench, Common Pleas, Chancery Court, and Magistrate's Court until the break of the new year was the signal for general merrymaking among the legal houses lining Chancery Lane. He had already sent his clerk home with a hefty bonus and a bottle of brandy from his stash.

Trevor had never felt inclined to celebrate the year's cases, won or lost. He seldom triumphed at court because his clients were generally all guilty. True, their crimes were among the more petty in English law, but English law always came down hard against miscreants who meddled with another's property, be it land, gold bullion, a loaf of bread, or a pot of porridge. A good day for Lord Trevor was one where he wheedled a reprieve from the drop and saw his client transported to Australia instead. He knew that most Englishmen in 1810 would not consider enforced passage to the Antipodes any sort of victory. Because of this, a celebration, even for the birth of Christ, always felt vaguely hypocritical to him. Besides that, he knew his solicitor was in a hurry to be on his way to Tunbridge Wells.

But not without a protestation, because the solicitor, an earnest young man, name of George Dawkins, was almost as devoted to his young charges as he was. "Trevor, you know it is my turn to take that deposition," the good man said, even as he pulled on his coat and looked about for his hat. "And when was the last time you spent more than a day or two home at Chase Hall?"

"You, sir, have a family," Trevor reminded him firmly. "And a wife eager to see her parents in Kent."

Dawkins must have been thinking about the events of last Christmas. "Yes, but I could return for the deposition. I would rather not . . ." he paused, his embarrassment obvious.

". . . leave me alone here, eh? Is that it?" Trevor finished his solicitor's thought.

The man knew better than to bamboozle. "Yes, that's it. I don't want to return to . . . Well, you know. You were damned lucky last time."

Not lucky, Trevor thought. I thought I was home free. Damn those interfering barristers in the next chamber. "I suppose. I suppose," he said. "I promise to be good this year."

His solicitor went so far as to take his arm. "You'll do nothing besides take that deposition? You'll give me no cause for alarm?"

"Certainly not," Trevor lied. He shrugged off his solicitor's arm (even as he was touched by his concern), and pulled on his overcoat. He looked around the chamber, and put on his hat. Nothing here would he miss.

He and his solicitor went downstairs together and stood at the Chancery Lane entrance to the Inn. He looked up at the evening sky—surprisingly clear for London in winter—and observed the stars. "A rare sight, Dawkins," he said to his employee.

As they both looked upward, a little shard of light seemed to separate itself from a larger brightness, rather like shavings from some celestial woodcarver. Enchanted, he watched as it dropped quickly, blazed briefly, then puffed out.

Dawkins chuckled. "We should each make a wish, Trevor," he said, amusement high in his voice. "Me, I wish I could be more than five minutes on our way and not have one of my children ask, 'How much farther, Papa?'" He turned to Trevor. "What do you wish?"

"I don't hold with wishing on stars," he replied.

"Not even Christmas stars?"

"Especially not those."

But he did. Long after his solicitor had bade him good night and happy Christmas, and was whistling his way down the lane, Trevor stood there, hesitating like a fool, and unable to stop from staring into the heavens. He closed his eyes.

"I wish, I wish someone would help me."

"Miss Ambrose, do you think we will arrive in time for me to prevent my sister from making this Tragic Mistake that will blight her life and doom her to misery? I *wish* the coachman would pick up speed!"

Cecilia Ambrose—luckily for her—had been hiding behind a good book when her pupil burst out with that bit of moral indignation. She raised the book a little higher to make sure that Lady Lucinda Chase would not see her smile.

"My dear Lady Lucinda, I have not met her, but from what I know of your family, I suspect she is in control of her situation. Is it not possible that your sister welcomes her coming nuptials? Stranger things have happened."

Her young pupil rolled her eyes tragically, and pressed the back of her hand to her cheek. "Miss Ambrose, in her last letter to me she actually admitted that Sir Lysander kissed her! Can you imagine anything more distasteful? Oh, woe!"

Cecilia abandoned her attempt at solemnity, put down the book after marking her place, and laughed. When she could speak, she did so in rounder tones. "My dear little scholar, I think you are lacing this up a bit tight. If the wicked stage were not such a pit of evil and degradation, you would probably be anointed a worthy successor to Siddons! It is, um, possible that your sister doesn't consider kissing to be distasteful. You might even be inclined to try it yourself someday."

The look of horror that Lucinda Chase cast in her direction assured Cecilia that the time was not quite ripe for such a radical comment. And just as well, she thought as she put her arm around her twelve-year-old charge. "It is merely a suggestion, my dear. Perhaps when you are eighteen, you will feel that way, too." It seemed the teacherly thing to say, especially for someone into her fifth year as instructor of drawing and pianoforte at Miss Dupree's Select Academy for Young Ladies.

Her young charge was silent for a long moment. She sighed. "Miss Ambrose, I suppose you are right. I do not know that Janet would listen to me, anyway. Since her come out she has changed, and it makes me a little sad."

Ah, the crux of the matter, Cecilia thought as the post chaise bowled along toward York. She remembered Miss Dupree's admonition about maintaining a firm separation between teacher and pupil and—not for the first time—discarded it without a qualm. She touched Lucy's cheek. "You're concerned, aren't you, that Janet is going to grow up and leave you behind?" she asked, her voice soft. "Oh, my dear, she will not! You will always be sisters, and someday you, too, will understand what is going on with her right now. Do trust me on this. Perhaps things are not as bad as you think."

Her conclusion was firm, and precisely in keeping with her profession. Lucy sighed again, but to Cecilia's ears, always quite in tune with the nuances of the young, it was not a despairing sigh.

"Very well, Miss Ambrose," her charge said. "I will trust you. But it makes me sad," she added. She looked up at her teacher. "Do you think I will survive the ordeal of this most trying age?"

Cecilia laughed out loud. "Wherever did you hear that phrase?"

It was Lucy's turn to grin. "I overheard Miss Dupree talking to my mama, last time she visited."

"You will survive," Cecilia assured her. "I mean, I did." Lucy stared at her. "Really, Lucy, I *was* young once!"

"Oh! I didn't mean that you are precisely old, Miss Ambrose," Lucy burst out. "It's just that I didn't . . ." Her voice trailed away, but she tried to recover. "I don't know what I meant."

I do, Cecilia thought. Don't worry, my dear. You're not the first, and probably not the last. She smiled at her charge to put her at ease, and returned to her book. Lucy settled down quietly and soon slept. Cecilia put the book down then and glanced out the window on the snowy day. She could see her reflection in the glass. Not for the first time, she wondered what other people thought when they looked at her.

She knew she was nice-looking, and that her figure was trim. In Egypt, where her foster parents had labored for many years—Papa studying ancient Coptic Christian texts, and Mama doing good in many venues—her appearance excited no interest. In England, she was an exotic, Egyptian-looking. Or as her dear foster brother liked to tease her, "Ceely the Gift of the Nile." Cecilia looked at Lucinda again and smiled. And heaven knows I am old, in the bargain, she thought, all of eight and twenty. I doubt Lucinda knows which is worst.

She knew that her foster brother would find this exchange amusing, and she resolved to write him that night, when they stopped. It was her turn to sigh, knowing that a letter to William would languish three months in the hold of an East India merchant vessel bound for Calcutta, where he labored as a missionary with his parents now, who had been forced to abandon Egypt when Napoleon decided to invade. She looked out the window at the bare branches, wishing that her dear ones were not all so far away, especially at Christmas.

She had been quite content at the thought of spending Christmas in Bath at the Select Academy. Miss Dupree was engaged to visit her family in London, and the other teachers had made similar arrangements. She had remained at the Academy last year, and found the solitude to her liking, except for Christmas Day. Except for that one day, when it was too quiet, it was the perfect time to catch up on reading, grade papers, take walks without students tagging along, and write letters. That one day she had stood at the window, wanting to graft herself onto families hurrying to dinner engagements or visiting relatives. But the feeling passed, and soon the pupils and teachers returned.

Lady Maria Falstoke, Marchioness of Falstoke, had written to Cecilia a month ago, asking if she could escort Lucinda home to Chase Hall, on the great plain of York. *I cannot depend upon my brother-in-law, Lord Trevor Chase, to escort her because that dear man is woefully ramshackle. Do help us out, Miss Ambrose,* she had written.

At the time, Cecilia saw no reason to decline the invitation, which came with instructions about securing a post chaise, and the list of which inns would be expecting them. Miss Dupree had raised her eyebrows over the choice of inns, commenting that Cecilia would be in the lap of luxury, something out of the ordinary for a teacher, even a good one at a choice school. "I doubt you will suffer from damp sheets or underdone beef," had been her comment.

No, she did not wish to visit in Yorkshire. Lucinda had not meant to be rude, but there it was. *I am* different here in England, Cecilia thought. I might make my hosts uncomfortable. As they traveled over good roads and under a cold but bright sky, Cecilia resolved to remain at Chase Hall only long enough to express her concerns to her pupil's mother, and catch a mail coach south. It was too much to consider that the marquis would furnish her with a post chaise for the return trip.

Always observant of her students, especially the more promising ones, Cecilia had watched Lucy mope her way through the fall term. Her pupil, a budding artist, completed the required sketches and watercolors, but without enthusiasm. As she gave the matter serious consideration, Cecilia thought that the bloom left the rose with the letter from home in which Janet announced her engagement to Sir Lysander Polk of the Northumberland Polks, a dour collection of thin-lipped landowners—according to Lucinda, who already had an artist's eye for caricature—who had somehow begotten a thoroughly charming son. Not only was Lysander charming; he was handsome in the extreme, and rich enough in the bargain to make Lord Falstoke, a careful parent, smile. Or so Lucy had declared, when she shared the letter with Cecilia.

The actualities were confirmed a short time later, when Lord and Lady Falstoke and the betrothed pair stopped at the Select Academy on their way to London's modistes, cobblers, and milliners. On acquaintance with Sir Lysander, who did prove to be charming and handsome, Cecilia began to see the difficulty. She watched how Lady Janet hung on his every word, and found herself unable to tear herself from his side during the entire evening. Cecilia could not overlook the fact that the more Janet clung, the quieter Lucinda became.

Cecilia looked down at her sleeping charge. It *is* a most trying age, my dear, she thought. Hopefully a visit home would prove the antidote. At least Cecilia could lay the matter before Lady Falstoke, and get help from that quarter.

They arrived at Falstoke in the middle of the next afternoon, and the view, even in December, did not disappoint. Cecilia listened with a smile on her face as Lucy, more excited as the miles passed, pointed out favorite places. Her smile deepened as Lucy took hold of her arm and leaned forward.

"Oh, Miss Ambrose, just around this bend!"

She knew that Hugo Chase, Marquis of Falstoke, was a

wealthy man, but the estate that met her eyes surprised her a little. Chase Hall was smaller than she would have imagined, but discreet, tasteful, and totally in harmony with the setting of trees, meadow, and stream. She could see a small lake in the near distance.

"Oh, Lucinda!" she exclaimed.

"I love coming home," her pupil said softly.

They traveled the tree-lined lane to the circle drive and wide front steps, Lucy on the edge of the seat. When they came to a stop, Lucy remained where she was. "This is strange," she murmured. "No one is here to meet us." She frowned. "Usually the servants are lined up and Mama and Papa are standing on the steps." She took Cecilia's hand. "Can something be wrong?"

"Oh, surely not," Cecilia replied. "We would have heard." But we've been on the road, she added silently to herself. "Let us go inside." She patted Lucy's hand. "My dear, it is Christmastime and everyone is busy!" She saw the door open. "There, now. Uh, is that your butler? He is somewhat casual, is he not?"

Lucy looked up, her eyes even wider. "Something has happened! It is my uncle Trevor."

The man came down the steps as Lucy came up, and caught her in his arms. Cecilia was relieved to see the smile on his face; surely that did not signal bad news. It was a nice smile, she decided, even if the man behind it was as casually dressed as an out of work road mender. She couldn't really tell his age. She assumed that Lord Falstoke was in his middling forties. This uncle of Lucy's had to be a younger brother. How curious then, for his hair was already gray. She smiled to herself. And had not seen a comb or brush yet that day, even though it was late afternoon.

He was a tall man who, despite his disheveled appearance, managed to look quite graceful, even as he hugged his niece, then kissed the top of her head. No, graceful was not the precise word, she decided. He is dignified. I doubt anyone ever argues with him. I know I would not.

She left the post chaise herself, content to stand on the lowest step quite unnoticed, as a young boy hurtled out of the open door and into his sister's arms. The three of them—niece, nephew, and uncle—stood on the steps with their arms around one another. She came closer, feeling almost shy, and Lucy remembered her manners. "Miss Ambrose, I am sorry! Allow me . . . this is my uncle Trevor Chase, Papa's only brother. Uncle, this is my teacher, Miss Cecilia Ambrose."

Cecilia didn't see how he did it, not with children on both sides of him, but he managed an elegant bow. You are well trained enough, she thought as she curtsied back, even if you do look like a refugee from Bedlam. "Delighted to meet you," she said.

"I doubt it," he replied, and there was no mistaking the good humor in his wonderful voice. "You are probably wondering what lunatic asylum I escaped from."

It was not the comment she expected, and certainly not the appraisal she was used to: one glance, and then another, when the person did not think she was looking. Cecilia could see nothing but goodwill on his face, rather than suspicion.

"My uncle is a barrister," the young boy said. He tugged on the man's sleeve. "I shall go find Janet," he said, and went into the house.

"You are . . . you are a barrister?" she asked. The name was familiar to her. Was he a father of a student in her advanced watercolor class? No, that was not it. It will come to me, she thought.

"Miss Ambrose, he is the best barrister in the City," Lucinda assured her. She leaned against him, and Cecilia could tell that in the short space of a few minutes, all of Miss Dupree's deportment lessons had flown away on little wings. "Papa says he likes to right wrongs, and that is why he almost never comes here. There are more wrongs in London, apparently."

The man laughed. "You're too polite, dear Lucy," he

replied, and gave his niece a squeeze before he released her. "He refers to me as the patron saint of lost causes." He gestured toward Cecilia. "Come indoors, Miss Ambrose. You're looking a little chilly."

The foyer was as beautiful as she had thought it would be, soft color on the walls, delicate plasterwork above, and intricate parquetry underfoot. "What a wonderful place," she said.

"It is, indeed," Lord Trevor agreed. "I know there are many country seats larger than this one, but none more lovely, to my way of thinking." He rubbed his hands and looked around. "I love to come home, now and then."

"Where is Mama?" Lucy asked as a footman silently approached and divested her of her traveling cloak.

"Lucy! Thank God you have come! This family is beset with Trying Events!"

Well, I suppose I can safely say that others in this family besides Lucy tend to speak in capital letters, Cecilia thought as she allowed Lord Trevor to help in the removal of her cloak. Lucy ran to her sister Janet, who stood with her arms outstretched dramatically.

"I do believe the most trying event is Janet's propensity to be Yorkshire's premier actress of melodrama and melancholy," Lord Trevor murmured to her as he handed her cloak to the footman. "I have only been here three days myself, and already I want to strangle her."

She looked at him in surprise, then put her lips together so she would not laugh.

Lord Trevor only grinned at her, which made the matter worse. "Such forbearance, Miss Ambrose," he said. "You have my permission to laugh! If you can withstand this, then you must be the lady who teaches deportment at Miss Dupree's Whatchamacallit."

"Far from it," she replied. "I teach drawing and the pianoforte."

He took her arm through his and walked her down the hall toward the two young ladies. "My dear Janet, wouldn't this be a good time to tell your sister what is going on, before she thinks that pirates from the Barbary Coast have abducted your parents?"

"Lucy would never think such a thing!" Janet declared, looking at him earnestly. "I doubt there have ever been any pirates in Yorkshire."

Lord Trevor only sighed. Forcing down her laughter, Cecilia spoke up in what she hoped were her best educator's tones. "Lady Janet, perhaps you can tell us where your parents are? Your sister is concerned."

Janet looked at her, a tragic expression on her lovely face. "Oh, Miss . . . Miss Ambrose, is it? My parents have bravely gone into a charnel house of pestilence and disease."

Lord Trevor glowered at his older niece. "Cut line, Janet," he said. He put his arm around Lucy. "Amelia's brood came down with the measles three days ago, and your parents have gone to York to help. I expect them home tomorrow. Amelia is the oldest of my nieces," he explained to Cecilia over his shoulder. "It's just the dratted measles."

"Only this afternoon I wrote to my dear Lysander, who will drop everything to hurry to this beleaguered household and give us the benefit of his wisdom," Janet said.

"Janet, we can depend upon Uncle Trevor to look out for us," Lucy said shyly.

"Uncle Trevor is far too busy to worry about us, Lucy," her sister replied, dismissing her sister with a wave of her handkerchief. "And didn't he say over breakfast this morning that he must return to London immediately after our parents are restored to us? Depend upon it; Lysander will hurry to my side, and all will be well." She nodded to Cecilia. "Come, Lucinda. I have much to tell you about my dear Lysander."

"But shouldn't I show Miss Ambrose to her room?" Lucy asked.

"That is what servants are for, Lucy. Come along."

After a backward glance at Cecilia, Lucinda trailed upstairs after her sister. Cecilia's face burned with the snub. Lord Trevor regarded her with sympathy.

"What do you say, Miss Ambrose? Should we wait until Lysander arrives, tie him up with Janet, and throw them both in the river? It's too late to drown them at birth. Ah, that is better," he said when she laughed. "Do excuse my niece's manners. If I ever fall in love—and the prospect seems remote—I promise not to be so rude." He indicated the sitting room, with its open door and fire crackling in the grate. "Come sit down, and let me take a moment to reassure you that we are not all denatured, drooling simpletons."

She needed no proof of that, but was happy to accompany him into the sitting room. He saw that she was seated close to the fire, a hassock under her feet, and then spoke to the footman.

"Tea or coffee, Miss Ambrose?" he asked. "I know coffee isn't ordinarily served in the afternoon, but I am partial to it, and don't have a second's patience with what I should and should not do."

"Coffee, if you please," she answered, amused out of her embarrassment. She removed her gloves, and fluffed her hair, trapped too long by her bonnet.

The footman left, and Lord Trevor stood by the fireplace. She regarded him with some interest, because she remembered now who he was. Miss Dupree, considered a radical by some, subscribed to two London newspapers, even going so far as to encourage her employees to read them. The other female teachers seldom ventured beyond the first page. The Select Academy's two male instructors read the papers during the day while they drank tea between classes. When class was over, and if the downstairs maid hadn't made her circuit, Cecilia gathered up the papers from the commons room. She took them to her room to pore over in the evening hours, after she had finished grading papers, and when it was not her turn to be on duty in the sitting room when the young ladies were allowed visitors.

She knew next to nothing of the British criminal trial system, but could not resist reading about the cases that even Mrs. Dupree, for all her radical views, must have considered sordid and sensational. No matter; Cecilia read the papers, and here was a barrister well known to her from criminal trials, written up in the florid style of the London dailies.

I should say nothing, she told herself as she sat with her hands folded politely, her ankles together. He will think I am vulgar. Besides, I am leaving as soon as I can.

He cleared his throat and she looked up.

"Miss Ambrose, I am sorry for this disorder in which you find us."

He *is* self-conscious about this, she thought. I think he even wishes he had combed his hair. Look how he is running his fingers through it. She smiled. I suppose even brilliant barristers sometimes are caught up short. Well, join the human race, sir.

"Oh, please don't apologize, Lord Trevor," she said. She hesitated, then gave herself a mental shrug. This is a man I do admire, she thought. What can it hurt if I say something? I will be gone tomorrow. "Lord Trevor, I . . . I sometimes read in the newspaper of your legal work."

"What?"

She winced inwardly. How could one man invest so much weight in a single word? Was this part of his training? Oh, Lord, I am glad I will never, ever have to face this man in the docket, she thought. Or over a breakfast table.

She opened her eyes wider, wondering at the origin of that impish thought. She reminded herself that she was a teacher, and dedicated to the edification of her pupils. Breakfast table, indeed! She dared to glance at him, and saw, to her temporary relief at least, he had not turned from the fireplace, where he warmed his hands.

"I beg your pardon, Miss Ambrose," he was saying, "I must have misheard. Do forgive me. Did you say that you *read the newspaper*?"

"I do," she replied simply. She discovered that she could no more lie to this man than sprout wings and fly across the

plain of York. In for a penny, she thought grimly. "And . . .
and I am a great admirer of your work."

It must have been the wrong thing to say, she decided.
Why on earth did I admit that I read the paper? she asked
herself in misery as he slowly turned around from his hand
warming. As he raised his eyebrows, she wished she could
vanish without a trace and suddenly materialize in her Bath
sitting room, grading papers and waiting for the dinner bell.
"Well, I am," she said.

He smiled at her. "Why, thank you, Miss Ambrose." He
seated himself beside her. "Do you pass on what you learn
to your students?"

She listened hard for any sarcasm in his voice, but she
could detect none. She also did not see any disparagement
or condescension in his face, which gave her heart. "No, I
don't pass it on," she said quietly, then took a deep breath.
"I only wish that I could." She sat a little straighter then,
suddenly feeling herself very much the child of crusading
evangelists. "I believe you should receive great credit for
what you do, rather than derision, Lord Trevor. Didn't I read
only last week that you had been denied a position of Master of the Bench at Lincoln's Inn?"

"You did, indeed," he replied. "Sometimes I imagine that
the Benchers wish I had been called from another Inn." He
shrugged. "Even my brother Hugo calls this my 'deranged
hobby.' "

The maid came in with coffee, which Cecilia poured.
"You are going back to London tomorrow?" she asked.

"I am, as soon as Hugo and Maria arrive. Lowly Magistrate's Court does not sit during the holiday, but I have depositions to take." He took a sip and then sat back. "I know
my solicitor could do that, but he wanted to spend the week
with his family in Kent. I am, as you might suppose, a soft
touch for a bare pleading."

"I am delighted to have met you, Lord Trevor," she told
him.

The housekeeper stood at the door to the sitting room.

Lord Trevor rose, cup in hand, and indicated that Cecilia follow her. "She'll show you to your room. We keep country hours here, so we will eat in an hour." He winked at the housekeeper, who blushed, but made no attempt to hide the smile in her eyes. "As you can also imagine, there's no need to dress up!"

Smiling now, the housekeeper led her upstairs. "He's a great one, is Lord Trevor," she said to Cecilia. "We only wish he came around more often."

"I suppose he is quite busy in London," Cecilia said.

"Indeed he is," the woman replied, "even though I sometimes wonder at the low company he keeps." She stopped then, remembering her position. "Miss Ambrose, your pupil is across the hall. You'll hear the bell for dinner."

Cecilia decided before dinner that it would be easy to make her excuses the next day when Lord and Lady Falstoke returned, and take the mail coach back to Bath. She would express her concerns about Lucy to the marchioness before she left.

To her consternation, David looked as glum as his sister when he came into the dining room with Lord Trevor, who carried a letter. The man seated himself and looked at his nieces. "I received a post not twenty minutes ago from your parents," he said.

"They're not coming home tomorrow," David said. He looked down at his plate.

"Why ever not?" Janet asked, indignant. "Don't they know we need them? I mean, really, they took Chambliss with them, and Cook!"

"Chambliss is our butler," Lucy whispered to Cecilia.

"It seems that your older sister needs them more," Lord Trevor replied, his voice firm. "Do have a little compassion, Janet. They have promised to be here for Christmas. I'll be staying until they return."

Janet turned stricken eyes upon her uncle. "But they are to host Lysander!"

"Perhaps the earth will continue to orbit the sun if he has

to postpone his arrival for a few days," Lord Trevor remarked dryly. "David, eat your soup."

They ate in silence, Lord Trevor obviously reviewing in
his mind how this news would change his own plans. Cecilia
glanced at Lucy, who whispered, "I will hardly have any
time to be with her, before we must return to Bath."

"Then the time will be all the more precious, when it
comes, my dear," Cecilia said, thinking of her dear ones in
India.

David began to cry. Head down, he tried to choke back
his tears, but they flowed anyway. Lord Trevor looked at
him in dismay, then at Cecilia. As sorry as she felt for the little boy, she almost smiled at the desperation on the barrister's face. You can argue cases for the lowliest in the
dockets, she thought, but your nephew's tears are another
matter. She rose from the table. I have absolutely nothing to
lose here, she thought. No one should be crying at Christmastime.

She walked over to David's chair and knelt at his side.
"This is difficult, isn't it?" she asked him quietly. "I know
your mama wishes she were here, too."

"She's only twenty miles away!" Lord Trevor exclaimed,
exasperated.

"It's a long way, when you're only—are you six, my
dear?" she asked the little boy, who had stopped crying to
listen to her. She handed him her napkin.

"Seven," he mumbled into the cloth. "I am small for my
age."

"You know, perhaps we could go belowstairs and ask the
cook for . . ."

"Mama never coddles him like that," Janet said.

"I would," Cecilia answered. She looked at Lord Trevor,
who was watching her with a smile of appreciation. "Do you
mind, sir?"

"I don't mind at all," he replied. "Miss Ambrose, do as
you see fit."

Cecilia took David downstairs. The second cook beamed

at the boy, and suggested a bowl of the rabbit fricassee left from luncheon. In another minute, he was eating. Cecilia sat beside him, and Cook placed a bowl of stew before her, too. "If you don't mind leftovers," he said in apology. "I know Lord Trevor don't mind, but there are them above stairs who are a little too high in the instep these days."

"Janet makes us eat in the dining room," David said when he stopped to wipe his mouth. "We always eat in the breakfast room when Mama is here." He glared at the ceiling. "*She* thinks it is not grand enough."

"I think Janet is going through a trying time," Cecilia said, attempting to keep her face serious.

He shook his head. "Grown-ups do not have trying times."

They do, she thought. "Perhaps now and then."

She sat there, content in her surroundings, as David finished the stew. He pushed away the bowl when the cook brought in a tray of gingersnaps with a flourish, and remembered his manners to offer her one.

"Any left for me?"

You're a quiet man, Cecilia thought as she looked over to see Lord Trevor standing beside his nephew. David made room for his uncle on the bench. He passed the cookies, even as the cook set a glass of milk in front of Lord Trevor. He dipped a cookie in the milk and ate it, then looked at her. "Try it, Miss Ambrose. Anyone who reads newspapers can't mind dipping gingersnaps."

"Will I never be able to live that down?" she said as she dipped a gingersnap.

He touched David's shoulder. "It is safe to go above stairs now. Your sisters have retired to their room, where Janet, I fear, will continue to brag about darling Lysander."

"Oh, dear," Cecilia murmured. "I have to speak to Lady Falstoke about that."

"Then you must remain here through the week," Lord Trevor told her.

"I couldn't possibly do that," she replied as he gestured

for her to proceed them up the stairs. "I will write her a letter from Bath."

The three of them walked down the hall together, uncle and nephew hand in hand. They paused at the foot of the stairs. "David and I will say good night here," Lord Trevor told her. "I brought my files with me from Lincoln's Inn, and he is helping arrange my 1808 cases alphabetically."

"But it is 1810," she reminded him. "Nearly 1811."

"I'm behind." He ran his long fingers through his hair, a gesture she was coming to recognize. "Not all of us were kissed by the fairy of efficiency at birth, madam!"

She laughed, enjoying that visual picture. He smiled at her, then spoke to David, who went on down the hall.

"I can't get you to change your mind?" he asked, keeping his voice down. "You can see from my ham handling of David at the dinner table that I need help." He hesitated. "I seldom stay here until Christmas. Well, I never do."

"I am certain you will manage until your brother and sister-in-law return." Cecilia curtsied to him. "Thank you, Lord Trevor, for your hospitality. If you can arrange for a gig to take me tomorrow to the mail coach stop, I will be on my way to Bath."

He bowed. "Stubborn woman," he scolded. "What is the big attraction in Bath?"

There is no big attraction in Bath, she thought. "I . . . It's where I live."

He took her hand. "That is almost as illogical as some of the courtroom arguments I must endure! Good night, Miss Ambrose. We will see you on your way to Bath tomorrow, since you are determined to abandon us."

"You are as dramatic as your nieces," she chided him.

"I know," he said cheerfully. "Ain't it a shame?"

She wasn't certain what woke her, hours later. Her first inclination was to roll over and go back to sleep. All was quiet. She sat up and allowed her eyes to focus on the gloom around her. Nothing. She debated whether to get up and look

in the hall, but decided against it. That would mean searching for her robe, which she hadn't bothered to unpack, considering the brevity of her visit.

Then she heard it: someone pounding up the stairs and
banging on a door down the hall. She leaped out of bed, ran
to her door, and opened it at the same time she smelled
smoke. Her hand to her throat now, she stepped into the hall.
She thought she recognized the footman, even though he
was wearing his nightshirt. "My lord! My lord!" he yelled as
he banged on the door.

The door opened, and Lord Trevor stepped barefoot into
the hall. "Fire, my lord," the footman said, breathless from
dashing up the stairs. "The central chimney!"

Cecilia hurried back into her room, grabbed her traveling
case, and threw it out the window. She snatched her cloak,
stepped into her shoes, and turned around to see Lord Trevor
right behind her. He grabbed her arm and pulled her into the
hall. "Stay here," he ordered. "You don't know this manor."

Smoke wafted up the stairs like her vision of the last
plague of Egypt. She pulled a corner of her cloak across her
face to cover her nose, and watched Lord Trevor go in the
bedchambers and awaken his nieces and nephew.

He pulled David out first, and thrust him at her. She
locked her arms tight around the sleepy child. "We'll wait
right here for your uncle," she whispered into his hair.

Lucinda came next, her eyes wide with fear, and Janet
followed, wailing about her clothes. "Shut up, Janet," her
uncle ordered. "Take Lucy's hand and hold mine."

With his free hand he grabbed Cecilia around the waist
and started down the stairs. David coughed and tried to pull
away, but she clutched his hand. She put her other arm
around Lord Trevor and turned her face into his nightshirt so
she could breathe. No one said anything as they groped
down the stairs and across the foyer. In another blessed moment the footman, who must have been in front of them in
the smoky darkness, flung open the front door. They hurried
down the steps into the cold.

Still he did not release her. She kept her face tight against his chest, shivering from fright. If anything, he tightened his grip on her until his fingers were digging into the flesh of her waist. He must have realized then what he was doing, because he opened his hand, even though he did not let go of her.

She forced herself to remain calm, if not for herself, then for the children, and perhaps for Lord Trevor, who surely had more to do now than hold her so tight on the front lawn. She released her grip on his waist then, and stepped back slightly, so he had no choice but to let go.

Before he did, he leaned forward and kissed the top of her head. Because he offered no explanation for his curious act, and no apology, she decided that emergencies did strange things to people who were otherwise rational.

"Keep everyone here, Cecilia. No one goes back for anything." He turned and hurried up the steps again.

What about you? she wanted to call after him as he disappeared inside. She gathered his nieces and nephew around her. "We'll be fine, my dears," she told them, reaching out her arms to embrace them all. They stood together and watched the manor. Although smoke seeped from the front door, she saw no flames.

They endured several more minutes of discomfort, then Lord Trevor and the household staff came around the building from the back. The footman, more dignified with trousers now, carried the grip she had thrown out the window. Lord Trevor had also taken the time to find his own pants and shoes, although he still wore his nightshirt. To her amusement, the housekeeper was fully dressed. *I'll wager you would rather have burned to a crisp before leaving your room in a state of semi-dress,* she thought.

Lord Trevor hurried to her, the housekeeper and footman following. "Mrs. Grey will escort you and the children to the dower house for the night. It's in that little copse."

"Can you save our home, Uncle?" Janet asked, clutching his arm.

He kissed her cheek. "I rather think so. The servants are inside the kitchen now, where the fire appears to have originated. We'll know more in the morning, when it's light." He looked over Janet's shoulder at Cecilia. "If you can keep things organized, I'll be forever in your debt."

They followed Mrs. Grey to the dower house, which she hadn't even noticed yesterday when they arrived at Chase Hall. All the furniture was shrouded in holland covers, which made David cling even tighter to her. He relaxed a little when the footman flung away the covers, and then dumped coal in the grates and started fires.

She decided that the dower house gave new meaning to the word cozy. A trip upstairs revealed only two bedchambers, one with a small dressing room. Since it was so late, Cecilia directed Mrs. Grey to pull out blankets. "I think proper sheets and coverlets can wait for morning," she explained as she handed each girl a blanket. "You girls take the chamber with the dressing room, and I will put David in the other one. Come, Davy," she said, resting her hand on his shoulder, "I think that you and your uncle will have to share."

"He snores."

Cecilia laughed. "Then you will have to get to sleep before he does, won't you?"

Below stairs, Mrs. Grey had already made room for herself. "I'll send the footman to the manor for food, and you'll have a good breakfast in the morning," she assured Cecilia. "Where are you planning to sleep, Miss Ambrose?"

She took the blanket Mrs. Grey held out. "I will wait up for Lord Trevor in the sitting room. Perhaps tomorrow we can find a cot for the dressing room." She looked around, already anticipating a busy day of cleaning ahead. If Janet keeps busy, she won't have time to complain, Cecilia thought. If Lucinda keeps busy with her sister, they might even remember all those things they have in common. If Davy keeps busy, he won't have so much time to miss his mother.

She wrapped the blanket around her shoulders, savoring the heavy warmth. She thought at first that she might sit up on the sofa, but surely it wouldn't hurt to lie down just until Lord Trevor returned. She closed her eyes.

When she woke, the room was full of light. Lord Trevor sat in the chair across from her. She sat up quickly, then tugged the blanket down around her bare feet.

"I thought about covering them, but reckoned that would wake you." He coughed. "Lord, no wonder chimney sweeps seldom live past fifteen," he said when he finished coughing into his handkerchief that was already quite black.

"Let me get you something to drink," she told him, acutely aware that she was still in her nightgown, her favorite flannel monstrosity that was thin from washing.

"Mrs. Grey is bringing in coffee, and probably her latest harangue about the way I take care of myself." He sighed, then gave her a rueful look. "Lord spare us from lifelong retainers, Miss Ambrose! They must be worse than nagging wives."

She laughed, and pulled the blanket around her shoulders. *If ever a man looked exhausted,* she thought, *it is you.* He was filthy, too, his nightshirt gray with grime, and his hair black. Bloodshot eyes looked back at her. When he smiled, his teeth were a contrast in his face.

He held up his hand. "No harangue from you, Miss Ambrose, if you please."

"I wouldn't dream of it," she replied serenely. "I don't know you well enough to nag you." She paused and thought a moment. "And even if I did know you better, I do not think I would scold."

"Then you are rare, indeed."

She shook her head. "Just practical, sir! Don't we all pursue our own course, no matter what people who care about us say?"

She could tell that her words startled him; they startled her. "I mean . . ." she began, then stopped. "No, that was exactly what I meant. Anyone who does what you do in London's courts doesn't need advice from a teacher."

He sat back then, his legs out in front of him, in that familiar posture of men who feel entirely at home. "Miss Ambrose, you are wise, as well as clean," he teased.

"And you, sir, are dirty," she pointed out. "Mrs. Grey can arrange a bath for you."

She wrapped her blanket around her and started for the door. As she passed his chair, he put out his hand and took hold of hers. "That I will appreciate, Miss A. Do one thing more for me, please."

He did not release her hand, and she felt no inclination to remind him. His touch was warm and dry, and standing there in the parlor, she realized that she was still shivering inside from last night. "And that would be . . ."

"Reconsider your resolve to leave us on the morning coach, Miss A," he said, and gave her hand a squeeze before he released it. "I need help."

"Indeed you do, my lord," she replied quietly. She left him, spoke to the housekeeper, then returned to the parlor.

She thought he might be asleep, but he remained as she had left him, leaning his chin on his hand, his eyes half closed. He had tried to dab some of the soot from his eyes, because the area under them was smudged. Without comment, she took his handkerchief from him and wiped his face carefully. He watched her the whole time, but for some unaccountable reason, she did not feel shy.

When she finished, she sat down again. "How bad is the damage to the house?"

"Bad enough, I think," he said with a grimace. "When the Rumford was installed, the place where the pipe runs into the chimney must have settled. Ashes have been gathering behind it for some time now, I would imagine. It's not really something a sweep would have noticed." He shook his head. "That portion of the house is three hundred years old, so I can not involve the builder in any litigation."

She smiled at him. "I'm glad you can joke about it, Lord

Trevor. It didn't seem so funny last night, standing on the lawn."

"No, it wasn't." His face grew serious. "Miss Ambrose, I'm a little embarrassed to ask you, but I hope I did not leave bruises on your waist."

"You did," she replied, feeling warmth on her own face. "I put it down to your determination to get me down the stairs in a strange house."

He sat back. "This isn't shaping up to be much of a Christmas, is it?"

It seemed a strange remark, one that required a light reply. "No, indeed," she said. "I mean, you were planning to spend it in the City, weren't you, going over legal briefs, or . . ."

"Depositions, my dear, depositions," he corrected. "And now we have cranky children on our hands, and a broken house."

How quickly he seemed to have included her in the family. "You needn't try to appeal to my better nature," she teased. "I will stay for the duration, bruises or not. Only give me my orders and tell me what you want done here today."

"That is more like it!" he said. He stood up and stretched. "Let Mrs. Grey be your guide. I am certain there is enough cleaning here to keep the children busy. If they complain, remind them that the servants are involved at the hall."

"Very well." Cecilia stood next to him, noting that she came up only to his shoulder. "Perhaps you could take David with you to York, Lord Trevor," she suggested. "He so misses his mother, and he told me that he has already had the measles."

Lord Trevor shook his head. "I dare not, Miss Ambrose. What I did not tell anyone last night was that the letter was from their mother, and not my brother Hugo, who is ill from the measles himself. I am riding to York most specifically to see how he does."

"Oh, my!" Cecilia exclaimed. "Is his life in danger?"

Lord Trevor shrugged. "That is the principal reason I'm

leaving here as soon as possible, and without the encumbrance of a little boy, who would only be anxious."

"I promise to keep everyone quite busy here," she assured him.

"Excellent!" He stretched again, and then placed his hand briefly upon her shoulder. "Don't allow any of the children near the manor, either, if you please," he said, his voice quite serious. "I do not trust the timbers in that old place yet, not without an engineer to check it for soundness. The servants will bring over whatever clothing and books are needed." He wrinkled his nose. "And it will all smell of smoke."

He stopped in the doorway, and put his hand to his forehead. "Hell's bells, Miss Ambrose! Do excuse that. . . . I don't see how we can possibly have that annual dinner and dance on Christmas Eve."

"A dinner!" she exclaimed.

"It is the neighborhood's crowning event, which I have managed to avoid for years." He rubbed his eye. "My sister-in-law used to trot out all the local beauties and try to convince them that I was a worthy catch." He shuddered elaborately, to her amusement. "Maybe that is why I have never stayed for Christmas. No, the dinner must be cancelled. I will retrieve the guest list from the manor, and you can assign the imperious Janet the task of written apology to all concerned." He started for the door.

"Or I can go get the list while you bathe."

"No!"

His vehemence startled her. Before she should assure him that she didn't mind a return to the manor, he stood in front of the parlor door, as though to bar her way. "Miss Ambrose, I'd really rather no one from this house went to the manor. The soot is a trial, and the smoke quite clogs the throat."

"Very well, then," she agreed, gratified not a little by his concern. "I'm hardly a shrinking violet, my lord," she murmured.

He smiled at her, and she could have laughed at the effect of very white teeth in a black face. "Well, then, you may get

your list, once you have bathed," she said, acutely aware
that she had no business telling the second son of a marquis
what to do.

"What a nag you are, Miss Ambrose," he told her. He
turned toward the hall. "I will wash and then get the list. If
that does not meet with your whole approval, let me know
now."

She laughed, quite at ease again. "And comb your hair,
too! My father used to tell me that if you can't be a good example, you can always be a bad one." Lord, what am I saying? she asked herself.

Lord Trevor seemed to think it completely normal. He
nodded to her, and winked. In another moment she heard
him whistling on the stairs.

She was finishing her eggs and toast in the breakfast
room when Lord Trevor came into the room. He lofted the
guest list at her, and it glided to her plate. He then leaned
against the sideboard with the bacon platter in his hand and
ate from it.

"You have rag manners," she scolded, "or is this a typi-
cal breakfast in the City?"

"No, indeed," he assured her. He finished the bacon, and
looked at the baked eggs, then back at her. She raised her
eyebrows and handed him a plate. "Breakfast is usually a
sausage roll from a vendor's stall in front of Old Bailey." He
put two eggs on his plate and sat beside her. "*This* is Elysian
Fields, Miss Ambrose. I should visit my dear brother more
often. Not only is the food free, it is well cooked and must
be eaten sitting down."

He finished his eggs, then tipped back in his chair and
reached for a piece of toast from the sideboard. "Do I dare
wipe up this plate with toast?" he asked.

"Would it matter what I said?" she countered, amused.
He was the antithesis of everything that Miss Dupree at-
tempted to teach her select females, and quite the last man
on earth for any lady of quality. Why that should be a con-

cern for her, she had no clue. The idea came unbidden out of some little closet in her mind. "Do you really care?"

"Nope." He wiped up the plate. "I did ask, though," he said, before finishing the toast. "I probably ought to get a proper cook in my house, and maybe even a butler," he said, as though he spoke more to himself.

She thought he was going to leave then, but he turned slightly in his chair to face her. "Since we have already decided that I have no manners, would you mind my comment, Miss Ambrose, that you really don't look English?"

Her face felt warm again. When the embarrassment passed, she decided that she did not mind his question. "People usually just stare, my lord," she told him. "Politely, of course. My parents went to Egypt to study old documents, and do good. Perhaps you have heard of philanthropists like them. They found me on the steps of Alexandria's oldest archive. They could only assume that whoever left me there had seen them coming and going." She smiled. "They suspect that an erring Englishwoman from Alexandria's foreign community became too involved with an Egyptian of unexalted parentage."

"How diverting to be found, and at a dusty old archive," he said, without even batting an eye. "Much more interesting than the usual garden patch, or 'tucked up under mama's heart' entrance."

Is there *anything* you won't say? she thought in delight. "It's better. There was a note pinned to my rather expensive blanket, declaring I was a half-English love child."

He threw back his head and laughed. "That certainly trumps being a duty!"

"Yes, certainly," she agreed, trying not to laugh. "My foster mother named me Cecilia because she is a romantic doing *homage* to the patron saint of music." She looked at him, waiting for him to draw back a little or change the subject. To her delight, he did neither.

"Which means, as far as I can tell, that you will always look better in bright colors than nine-tenths of the population, and you probably will never burn in the sun, and should curly hair be in vogue, you are in the vanguard of fashion." He stood up. "Miss Cecilia Ambrose, you are quite the most exotic guest ever to visit this boring old manor. Do whip my nieces and nephew in line, and render a thorough report this evening! Good day to you, kind lady. Thank you for rescuing me from utter boredom this Christmas."

He left the room as quickly as he had entered it. For the tiniest minute, it seemed as though he had sucked all the air out with him. She was still smiling when she heard the front door close behind him. My lord, you are the exotic, she thought, not me. She took a final sip of her tea. I think it is time I woke the sleeping darlings in this lovely little house and put them all to work.

She got off to a rocky start. Lady Janet had no intention of turning a hand to dust or sweep the floors after the footman removed the elegant carpets to beat out the dust. "Lysander would be aghast," she declared. "I shan't, and you can't compel me."

Lucy gasped at her sister's rudeness. "I *always* do what Miss Ambrose says."

"You're supposed to," her sister sniffed. "You're still in school." She glared at Cecilia. "I have a grievance about this, and I will speak to my uncle when he returns. I will remind him that I Have Come Out."

"From under a rock," David muttered. He looked at Cecilia. "I do not know why my Uncle Trevor did not let me accompany him."

"Nor I," replied Lady Janet with a sniff. "Then we would be rid of a nasty little brother who would try a saint. I am going to write to Lysander this instant! I know my darling will rescue me from this . . . .this . . ."

"Your home?" Cecilia asked quietly. "Very well. Do write to him. Lucinda and I will dust, and then we will make beds." She noted the triumphant look that Janet gave her younger sister. "Lady Janet, when you have posted your letter to your fiancé, your uncle specifically asked me to have you write to your family's guests and tell them the Christmas dinner is canceled."

"No party?" Janet shrieked, her voice reaching the upper registers.

You could use a week or two at Miss Dupree's, Cecilia thought as she tried not to wince. "Not unless you think there is room for one hundred in the front parlor here, Lady Janet. Just give them the reason why, and offer your parents' apologies," she replied. "Your uncle has also gone to York, not only to see your parents and sister, but to procure workmen enough to put this place to rights again. Apparently there was considerable smoke damage, and the floor downstairs suffered."

Lady Janet's offended silence almost made the air hum. Cecilia touched Davy on the shoulder. "If you could help Lucinda and me, I'm certain we could ask the footman to fetch your uncle's briefs from the manor, and you could continue alphabetizing them."

"I can do that." Davy looked at his older sister, who had devoted all her attention to the still life over the sideboard. He glared at her rigid back, shrugged, and gestured to his other sister. "C'mon, Lucinda. I'll wager that I can dust the bookroom before you're halfway through the first bedchamber!"

So it went. Lord Trevor returned after dinner, when the fragrance of roasted meat and gravy had settled in the rooms like a benevolent spirit. They had finished eating before he began. Her voice firm, Cecilia told them to wait in the sitting room and allow him to eat in peace before they pounced on him. She held her breath, but Lady Janet only gave her a withering look before flouncing into the sitting room.

When the children were seated, Cecilia excused herself and went to the breakfast room, where Lord Trevor, leaning his hand on his chin, was finishing the last of the rice pudding. He looked up and smiled when she sat down.

"Was it the mutiny on the *Bounty,* Captain Bligh?" he teased.

"Very nearly," she replied. "Lady Janet wrote what I must imagine was an impassioned letter, begging for release, then condescended to write letters of apology to the guests. We tossed bread and water into the room. At least she did not have to gnaw her leg out of a trap to escape."

Lord Trevor laughed. "God help you, Miss Ambrose! Whenever I am tempted to marry and breed, I only have to think of Janet, and temptation recedes. Was Lucinda biddable?"

"Very much so, although she remains ill-used because her sister barely acknowledges her. Davy alphabetized your 1808 cases, and I started him on 1809."

"You are excellent," he said. He drained his teacup and stood up. "Let me brave the sitting room now, and listen to my ill-used, much-abused relatives."

She held out a hand to stop him. "Lord Trevor, how is your brother?"

Lord Trevor frowned. "He is better, but really can't leave before Christmas, no matter how I pleaded and groveled!" He leaned toward her. "He wants you to continue whatever it is you're doing, and not abandon his children to my ramshackle care."

She opened her eyes wider at that artless declaration. "Surely neither he nor Lady Falstoke have any qualms about you."

"They have many," he assured her. He bowed slightly, and indicated that she precede him through the door. "Miss Ambrose, whether you realize it or not, we are an odd pair. You were found on the steps of an archive—still quite romantical, to my way of thinking—and I am the black sheep."

He nudged her forward with a laugh. "When the little darlings in the sitting room have spilled out all their umbrage and ill-usage and flounced off to bed, I will fill you in on my dark career." He took her by the arm in the hall. "But you have already agreed to help me, and I know you would never go back on your word and abandon this household, however sorely you are tried, eh?"

If she had thought to bring along her sketchbook, Cecilia would have had three studies in contrast in the sitting room: Janet looked like a storm was about to break over her head. Lucinda picked at a loose thread in her dress and seemed to swell with questions. Davy, on the other hand, smiled at his uncle.

When Trevor entered the room and sat himself by the fire, they all began at once, Janet springing up to proclaim her ill-usage; Lucinda worried about her parents and whether Christmas would come with them so far removed; and Davy eager to tell his uncle that 1808 was safely filed. Lord Trevor held up his hand. "One moment, my dears," he said, and there was enough edge in his voice to encourage Janet to resume her seat. He looked at his eldest niece. "I am certain that your first concern is for your older sister and her family in York. All are much improved. I knew you wanted to know that." He turned to his nephew, and held out his hand to him. Davy did not hesitate to sit on his lap. Trevor ruffled his hair and kissed his cheek. "That is from your mother! She misses you."

Oh, you do have the touch, Cecilia thought as Davy relaxed against his uncle. "And I hear that you have finished my 1808 cases and started on 1809." Trevor put his arms around his nephew. "Do you think your mama would let me take you back to the City with me and become my secretary?"

"She would miss me," Davy said solemnly. "P'rhaps in a year or two."

"I shall look forward to it." Trevor smiled at Lucinda. "I hear that you have been helping all day to make this little place presentable. My thanks, Lucy."

Lucinda blushed and smiled at Cecilia. "Miss Ambrose says I will someday be able to command an entire household." She looked at her teacher, and her eyes were shy. "A duke's, even."

Janet laughed, but there was no humor in it. "Possibly when pigs fly, Lucinda," she snapped. "Uncle, I . . ."

"What you should do is apologize to your sister," Trevor said. "Your statement was somewhat graceless."

Lucinda was on her feet then, her face even redder, her eyes filled with tears. "I . . . I think I will go to bed now, Uncle Trevor. It's been a long day. Davy?" He followed her from the room. With a look at Lord Trevor, Cecilia rose quietly and joined them in the hall. She closed the door behind her, but not quick enough to escape Janet's words.

"I hope you do not expect us to take orders from that foreign woman, Uncle. That is outside of enough, and not to be tolerated. *Who* on earth is *she*?"

Cecilia closed the door as quietly as she could, her face hot. It's not the first insult, she reminded herself, and surely won't be the last. She turned to the children, who looked at her with stricken expressions, and put her finger to her lips. "Let's just go upstairs, my dears," she told them. "I do believe your uncle has his hands full now."

Even through the closed door, they could hear Janet's voice rising. Cecilia hurried up the stairs to escape the sound of it, with the children right behind. At the top of the stairs, Davy took her hand. "Miss Ambrose, I don't feel that way," he told her, his voice as earnest as his expression.

She hugged him. "I know you don't, my dear. Your sister is just upset with this turn of events. I am certain she did not mean what she said."

"You're too kind, Miss Ambrose," Lucinda said.

I'm nothing of the sort, Cecilia thought later after she closed the door to her pupil's room, after helping her into a nightgown, and listening to her prayers for her older sister's family and her parents, marooned in York with the measles.

"No, I am not kind, Lucy dear," she said softly. "I am fearful." She thought she had learned years ago to disregard the sidelong glances and the boorish questions, because to take offense at each one would be a fruitless venture. As much as she loved England now, after a lifetime spent in Egypt, it took little personal persuasion to keep her at Madame Dupree's safe haven. She doubted that she ever went beyond a three-block radius in Bath. I have made myself a prisoner, she thought, and the idea startled her so much that she could only stand there and wonder at her own cowardice.

Reluctant to go downstairs again, she knocked softly on the door of the room that Davy was sharing with his uncle. Better to be in there, she thought, than to have to run into Lady Janet and her spite on the stairs. Davy lay quietly as she had left him, reading in bed, his knees propped up to hold the book. She looked closer, and smiled. He was also fast asleep. She carefully took the book from him, marked the place, and set it on the bedside table. She watched him a moment, enjoying the way his face relaxed in slumber.

I would like to have a boy like you someday, she thought, and the very idea surprised her, because she had never considered it before. I wonder why ever not, she asked herself, then knew the answer before any further reflection. Even though her foster parents had endowed her with a respectable dowry, she had no expectations, not in a country whose people did not particularly relish the exotics among them.

To keep her thoughts at bay, she went around the room quickly, folding Davy's clothes that had been brought over from the manor and placing them in the bureau. He shared the room with his uncle, whose own clothes were jumbled on top of the bureau. Several legal-sized briefs rested precariously on his clothes, along with a pair of spectacles. She wondered if he even had a tailor, and decided that he did not, considering that his public appearances probably found him in a curled peruke and a black robe, which could easily hide a multitude of fashion sins.

She heard light feet on the stairs, and remained where she was until they receded down the short hall to Lucinda's room. The door slammed, and Davy sighed and turned onto his side. She left the room, but it occurred to her that she did not know where to go. She had arranged to sleep on a cot in the little dressing room, but wild horses could not drag her in there now. To go downstairs would mean having to face further embarrassment from Lord Trevor. She knew he would be well meaning, but that would only add to the humiliation. *Perhaps I can go below stairs,* she thought, then reconsidered. All the servants' rooms in this small dower house were probably full, too, considering that things were a mess at the manor. She also reckoned that a descent below stairs would only confirm Lady Janet's opinion of her.

Cecilia sat on the stairs and leaned against the banister, wishing herself away from the turmoil, uncertain what to do. Probably Lord Trevor would understand now if she wanted to leave in the morning, even if she had promised she would stay. *It was safe in Bath.* She shook her head, uneasy with the truthfulness of it.

"Is this seat taken?"

She looked up in surprise, shy again, but amused in spite of herself. "No. There are plenty of steps. You need only choose."

Lord Trevor climbed the stairs and sat on the step below her. He yawned, then rested his back against the banister. She didn't want him to say anything, because she didn't want his pity, but she was too timid to begin the conversation. When, after a lengthy silence, he did speak, he surprised her.

"Miss Ambrose, I wish you had slapped my wretched niece silly, instead of just closed the door on her. You have oceans more forbearance than I will ever possess."

"I doubt that, sir," she said, and chose her own words carefully, since he was doing the same. "I've learned that protestation is rarely effective."

"Not the first time, eh?" he asked, his voice casual.

"And probably not the last." She rose to go—where she did not know—but Lord Trevor took her hand and kept her where she was. "I . . . I do hope you were not too harsh with her."

He released his hold on her. "Just stay put a while, Miss Ambrose, if you will," he told her. "I was all ready to haul her over my knee and give her a smack." He chuckled. "That probably would have earned me a chapter in the tome she is undoubtedly going to write to her precious Lysander in the morning."

"But you didn't."

"No, indeed. I merely employed that tactic I learned years ago from watching some of the other barristers who plead in court, and looked her up and down until her knees knocked. Then I told her I was ashamed of her." He leaned his elbow on the tread above and looked at her. "And I am, Miss Ambrose. Believe me, I am."

The look that he gave her was so contrite that she felt tears behind her eyelids. *I had better make light of this,* she thought. *I'm sure he wants me to assure him that it is all right, and that I didn't mind.* She forced herself to look him in the eye. Even in the gloom of the stairwell, she could tell that nothing of the sort was on his mind. She had never seen a more honest gaze.

"I won't deny that it hurt, Lord Trevor," she replied, her voice quiet, "but do you know, I've been sitting here and thinking that it's been pretty easy the last few holidays to hide myself in Bath. And . . . and I really have nothing to hide, do I?"

There. She had told a near stranger something that she could not even write to her mother, when that dear woman had written many times from India to ask her how she really did, on her own and without the protection of her distinguished missionary family.

Again he surprised her. He took her hand and held it. "Nothing to hide at all, my dear Miss Ambrose. Would it surprise you that I have been doing that very thing? I have been confining myself to the area of my rooms near Lincoln's Inn and Old Bailey for nearly eleven years. We are more alike than my silly niece would credit."

Her bewilderment must have shown on her face, because he stood up and pulled her up, too. "If you're not too tired, or too irritated at the ignorance and ill-will in one little dower house, I believe I want to explain myself. My dear, do you care for sherry?"

"If it's good sherry."

"The best that smugglers can find! I'd forgotten how excellent my brother's wine cellar is. Do join me in the sitting room, Miss Ambrose."

She didn't really have a choice, because he never released her hand. Mystified rather than embarrassed now, she followed him into the sitting room. He let go of her hand to pull another chair close to the fireplace, and indicated that she sit. She did, with a sigh. The fire was just warm enough, and the pillow he had placed behind her back just the right touch. He poured her a glass of sherry from the table between them, handed it to her, then sat in the other chair and propped his feet on the fender.

"I told you I am the black sheep, didn't I?"

She had to laugh. "And I am, well, a little colorful, too."

He joined in her laughter, not the least self-conscious, which warmed her heart. He surprised her by quickly leaning forward to touch her cheek. "Your skin is the most amazing shade of olive. Ah, is that the Egyptian in you? How fine! And brown eyes that are probably the envy of nations." He chuckled. "I don't mean to sound like a rakehell, Miss A." He looked at the far wall. "I suppose I am used to speaking my mind."

"I suppose that's your privilege," she said.

He took a sip of sherry. "I do say what I please. I doubt anyone in the *ton* thinks I am a gentleman."

"You're the brother of a marquis," she reminded her. "Surely that counts for . . ."

"It counts for nothing," he interrupted, finishing her

thought. "I am not playing the game I was born to play, Miss Ambrose, and some take offense."

She sat up straight and turned to face him impulsively. "How can you say that? I have been reading of the good you have done!"

"You are too kind, my dear." He poured another drink. "When I was in York today, I spoke to the warden at the Abbey. You're from a crusading family, yourself, aren't you?"

She nodded. "Papa and Mama lived in Egypt for nearly twenty years. I am not their only 'extra child,' as Papa puts it."

"The warden was sufficiently impressed when I mentioned that a member of the Ambrose family was visiting the Marquis of Falstoke."

Cecilia smiled and swirled the sherry in her glass. "And now they are doing good in India, and plumbing the depths of Sanskrit." She looked up, pleased to see Lord Trevor smiling at her, for no particular reason that she could discern. At least he does not look so tired, she thought. "We came to England in 1798, when I was sixteen. I went four years to Miss Dupree's Select Academy, and now I teach drawing and pianoforte."

"You weren't tempted to go to India with them?"

"No, I was not," she said. He was still smiling at her, and she decided he was a most attractive man, even with his untidy hair and rumpled clothing. "I like it right here, even with . . . with its occasional difficulties." She set down the wineglass. "And that is all I am going to say now. It is your turn to tell me why someone of your rank and quality thinks he is a black sheep."

"It's a sordid tale," he warned her.

"I doubt that. Slide the hassock over, please. Thank you."

He made himself comfortable, too. "Miss Ambrose, the fun of being a younger son cannot be underrated. I did a double first at Oxford, contemplated taking Holy Orders, considered buying a pair of colors, and even thought I would travel to the Caribbean and invest in sugar cane and slaves."

She relaxed, completely at ease. "That sounds sufficiently energetic."

"I didn't have to *do* anything. Some younger sons must scramble about, I suppose, but our father was a wealthy man, and our mother equally endowed. She willed me her fortune. I am better provided for than most small countries."

"My congratulations," she murmured. "You know, so far this is not sordid. I have confiscated more daring stories from my students late at night, when they were supposed to be studying."

"Let me begin the dread tale of my downfall from polite society before you fall asleep and start to snore," he told her.

"You're the one who snores, according to Davy," she reminded him.

"And you must be a sore trial to the decorum of Miss Deprave's Select Academy," he teased.

"Dupree," she said, trying not to laugh.

"If you insist," he teased, then settled back. "I suppose I was running the usual course for second sons, engaging in one silly spree after another. It changed one evening at White's, while I was listening to my friends argue heatedly for an hour about whether to wear white or red roses in their lapels. It was an epiphany, Miss Ambrose."

"I don't suppose there are too many epiphanies in White's," she said.

"That may have been the first! I decided the very next morning, after my head cleared, to toddle over to Lincoln's Inn and see about the law. My friends were aghast, and concerned for my sanity, but do you know, Miss A, it suited me right down to the ground. I sat for law through several years, ate my required number of dinners at the Inn, and was called to the Bar."

"My congratulations. I would say that makes you stodgy rather than sordid."

He smiled at her, real appreciation in his eyes. "Miss Ambrose, you are a witty lady with a sharp tongue! Should I pity poor Janet if she actually tries your kindness beyond belief and you give her what she deserves?"

She was serious then. "She is young, and doesn't know what she says."

"Spoken like the daughter of the well churched!" He leaned across the table and touched her arm. "Here comes the sordid part, Miss A." And then his face was more serious than hers. "I went to Old Bailey one cold morning to shift some toff's heir from a cell where he'd languished—the three D's, m'dear: drunk, disorderly, and disturbing the peace. It was a matter of fifteen minutes, a plea to the magistrate, and a whopping fine for Papa to pay. Just fifteen minutes." He stood up, went to the fireplace, and stared into the flames. "There was a little boy in the docket ahead of my client. I could have bumped him and gone ahead. I had done it before, and no magistrate ever objected."

Cecilia slid her glass aside and tucked her legs under her. Have you ever told anyone this before? she wanted to ask. Something in his tone suggested that he had not, and she wondered why he was speaking to her. Of course, Mrs. Dupree always did say that people liked to confide in her. "It's your special gift, dearie," her employer had told her on more than one occasion.

"There he stood, not more than seven years old, I think, with only rags to cover him, and it was a frosty morning. It was all he could do to hold himself upright, so frightened was he."

She must have made some sound, because Lord Trevor looked at her. He sat down on the hassock. "Did he . . . was he represented?" she asked.

He nodded, his face a study in contempt. "They all are. We call ourselves a law-abiding nation, Miss A, don't we? His rep was one of the second year boys at Gray's Inn, getting a practice in. Getting a practice in! My God!"

Impulsively she leaned forward and touched his arm. He took her hand and held it. Something in her heart told her not to pull away. "He had copped two loaves of bread and, of all things, a pomegranate." Lord Trevor passed his free hand in front of his eyes. "The magistrate boomed at him, 'Why the pomegranate, you miscreant?'" He put her hand to his cheek. "The boy said, 'Because it's Christmas, your worship.'"

Cecilia felt the tears start in her eyes. She patted his cheek, and he released her hand, an apologetic look in his eyes. "Miss A, you'll think I'm the most forward rake who ever walked the planet. I don't know what I was thinking."

"*I* am thinking that you need to talk to people now and then," she told him.

He tried to smile, and failed. "His sentence was transportation to Van Diemen's Land. Some call it Tasmania. It is an entire island devoted to criminals, south of Australia. Poor little tyke fainted on the spot, and everyone in the courtroom laughed, my client loudest of all."

"You didn't laugh."

"No. All I saw was a little boy soiling his pants from fear, with not an advocate in the world, not a mother or father in sight, sentenced to a living death." He looked at her, and she saw the tears on his face. "And this is English justice," he concluded quietly.

She could think of nothing to say, beyond the fact that she knew it was better to be silent than to let some inanity tumble out of her face, after his narrative. She glanced at him, and his own gaze was unwavering upon her. She realized he was seeking permission from her to continue. "There must be more," she said finally. "Tell me."

He seemed to relax a little with the knowledge that she was not too repulsed to hear the rest. "Is it warm in here?" he asked, running his finger around his frayed collar.

"Yes, and isn't that delightful? I never can get really *warm* in this country!" she countered. "Don't stall me, sir. You have my entire attention."

He continued. "I could not get that child out of my mind.

In the afternoon I went back to Old Bailey, found the magistrate—he was so bored—and went to Newgate."

Cecilia shivered. Lord Trevor nodded. "You're right to feel a little frisson, Miss A. It's a terrible place." He grimaced. "I know it must be obvious to you that I am no Brummel. Nowadays, when I know I'm going to Newgate, I wear my Newgate clothes. I keep them in a room off the scullery at my house because I cannot get the smell out." He sighed. "Well, that was blunt, eh? I found Jimmy Daw—that was his name—in a cell with a score of older criminals. I gave him an old coat of mine."

Lord Trevor hung his head down. Cecilia had an almost overwhelming urge to touch his hair. She kept her hands clenched in her lap.

"My God, Miss A, he thanked me and wished me a happy Christmas!"

"Oh, dear," she breathed. She got up then and walked to the window and back again, because she knew she did not wish to hear the rest of his story. He stood, too, his lips tight together. He went to the fireplace again and rested his arm on the mantel.

"You know where this is going, don't you?" he asked, surprised.

She nodded. "I have lived a little in the world, my lord. I'm also no child."

"The magistrate met me in my chambers the next morning—it was Christmas Day—to tell me that those murderers, cutpurses, and thieves had tortured and killed Jimmy for the coat that I left for him, in my naïveté."

She could tell by looking at his eyes that the event might have happened yesterday. "That is hard, indeed, sir," she murmured, and sat down again, mainly because her legs would not hold her. She took a deep breath, and another, until her head did not feel so detached. "I did not know about Jimmy," she said softly, "but I told you that I have read about your work—or some of it—in the papers. I know you have made amends."

"With a vengeance, Miss A, with a vengeance," he assured her. "That frivolous fop I bailed out the day before had the distinction of being my last client among the titled and wealthy. I am a children's advocate now. When they come in the docket, I represent as many as I can. Yes, some are transported—I cannot stop the workings of justice—but they are *not* incarcerated with men old enough to do them evil, and they go to Australia, instead of Van Diemen's Land. It is but a small improvement, but the best I can do."

"How did . . . how did you manage that?"

He smiled for the first time in a long while. "Like all good barristers, I know the value of blackmail, Miss A! Let us just say that I lawyered away a juicy bit of scandal for our dear Prinny, and he owed me massively. God knows he has no interest in anyone's welfare but his own, but even he has a small bit of influence."

It was her turn to relax a little, relieved that his tone was lighter. She could not imagine the conditions under which he labored, and she had the oddest wish to hold him close and comfort him as a mother would a child. "Lord Trevor, I think what you are doing is noble. Why do you say that you are the family's black sheep?"

He sat down again and took another sip of his sherry, then looked at her over the rim of the glass. "It is your turn to be naïve. What I do, and where and how I do it, has cut me off completely from my peers. It is as though I wear my Newgate clothes everywhere. No one extends invitations to me, and I am the answer to no maiden's prayer."

"And people of your class are a little embarrassed to be seen with you, and you don't really have a niche," she said, understanding him perfectly, because she understood herself. "That life has made you bold and outspoken, and it has made me shy."

She looked at him with perfect understanding, and he smiled back. "We are both black sheep, Miss Ambrose," he said.

"How odd." Another thought occurred to her. "Why are you here?"

To answer her, he reached in his vest pocket and pulled out a folded sheet. "You may not be aware that my niece Lucinda has been writing to me."

"She did mention you in sketching class once," Cecilia said, and her comprehension grew. She put her hand to her mouth. "Oh! She said you worked with children, and several of the other pupils started to laugh! Their parents must have . . ."

"I told you I am a hiss and a byword in some circles. I sometimes keep stray children at my house until I can find situations for them." He hesitated.

"Go on," she told him. "I doubt there is anything you can say now that would surprise me."

"There might be," he replied. "Well! Some of my peers think I am a sodomite. These things are whispered about. Who knows what parents tell their children."

"Really, Lord Trevor," she said. "It *is* warm in here."

He crossed the room, and threw up the window sash. "I assure you I do *not* practice buggery, Miss A! What I do have are enlightened friends who are willing to take these children to agricultural settings and employ them gainfully."

"Bravo, sir," she said softly.

"I do it for Jimmy Daw." He tapped the letter. "Lucinda tells me how unhappy she is, and damn it, I've been neglecting my own family."

"She is sad and uncomfortable to see her sister growing away from her," Cecilia agreed. "I had wanted to talk to Lady Falstoke about that very thing. I suppose that is why I came."

He folded the letter and put it back in his waistcoat. "I came here with the intention of giving them a prosy lecture about gratitude, well larded with examples of children who have so much less than they do." He rubbed his hands together. "Thank God for a fire in the chimney! Now we are thrown together in close quarters to get reacquainted. Do you think there is silver to polish below stairs?"

She laughed. "If there is not, you will find it!" She grew serious again. "There is more to this than a prosy lecture, isn't there? Lord Trevor, when did Jimmy Daw . . ."

"Eleven years ago on Christmas Eve," he answered. "Miss Ambrose, for all that time I have thrown myself into my work, and ignored my own relations." He shook his head. "I see them so seldom."

She went to the window and closed it, now that the room was cooler, or at least she was not feeling so embarrassed by this singular man's blunt plain speaking. "I must own to a little sympathy for them, Lord Trevor. Here they are, stuck in close quarters with two people that they don't know well. It is nearly Christmas, and their parents are away."

He winked at her. "Should we go easy on the little blokes?"

"Lord Trevor, *where* do you get your language?" she said in exasperation.

"From the streets, ma'am," he told her, not a bit ruffled. "I feel as though I have been living on them for the past eleven years."

"That may be something that must change, sir," she replied.

He laughed and opened the window again. "Too warm for me, Miss Ambrose! You are an educator *and* a manager? Did one of your ancestors use a lash on those poor Israelites in Egypt?"

"Stuff and nonsense!" She went to the door. "And now I am going to bed." She stopped, and she frowned. "Except that . . ." Be a little braver, she ordered herself, if you think to be fit company this week for a man ten times braver than you. "I have no intention of sleeping on that servant's cot in the girls' chamber, not after the snippy way Lady Janet treated me! She already thinks of me as a servant, and I have no intention of encouraging that tendency. Is the sofa in the book room comfortable, sir?"

"I don't know. Seems as though we ought to do better for you than a couch in the office, Miss A," he told her as he joined her at the door.

"Are all dower houses this small?"

"I rather doubt it. Some of my ancestors must have been vastly frugal! What say you brave the sofa tonight, and we'll see if we can find you a closet under the stairs, or a secret room behind some paneling off the kitchen where the Chase family used to hide Royalists."

He tagged along while she went downstairs to the linen closet and selected a sheet and blanket. He found a pillow on a shelf. "You could sleep in here," he told her. "You're small enough to crawl onto that lower shelf."

She laughed out loud, then held out her hand to him. "I am going downstairs now. What plans do you have, if Sir Lysander whisks Janet away from this?"

He was still holding her hand. He released it, and handed her the pillow. "I happen to know Lysander's parents." They left the linen closet. "He is an only child, and my stars, Miss A, they are careful with him." He looked toward the ceiling. "Do you happen to know if she mentioned measles in her letter?"

"You can be certain I was not allowed to look at the letter." They started for the stairs. "Besides, the contagion is in York, and not here."

He only smiled. "Did I mention they are careful parents? Good night, m'dear."

The sofa in the book room realized her worst fears, but Cecilia was so tired that she slept anyway. When she finally woke, it was to a bright morning. She sat up, stretched, then went to the window. Lord Trevor had spent his time well in York, she decided. A veritable army of house menders had turned into the family property and were heading in carts toward the manor.

Someone knocked. She put her robe on over her nightgown and opened the door upon Lord Trevor. "Good morning, sir," she told him.

"It is, isn't it?" He grinned at her. "Miss A, what a picture you are!"

Her hands went to her hair. "I can never do anything with it in the morning. You are a beast to mention it."

He stepped back as if she had stabbed him. "Miss A! I was going to tell you how much I like short, curly hair! No lady wears it these days, and more's the pity." He winked at her. "Is it hard to drag a comb through such a superabundance of curls?"

"A perfect purgatory," she assured him. "I used a comb with very wide teeth." She felt her face go red. Mrs. Dupree would be shocked at this conversation. "Enough about my toilette, sir! What are your plans?"

"I am off to the manor to get the renovation started. Mrs. Grey will accompany me. She has set breakfast, and left one servant, should you need to send a message."

"And did she locate a plethora of silver begging for polish?"

"Indeed she did! There is more than enough to keep my relatives in cozy proximity with each other."

"If they choose to be so," she reminded him. "Sir Lysander . . ."

He put a finger to her lips. "Miss A, trust me there." He took his hand away, and she watched in unholy glee as his face reddened. "Sorry! And Janet is to apologize."

"Only if she means it," Cecilia said softly.

"She will," he told her, then leaned closer. "I am not her favorite uncle, at the moment, however." He straightened up. "I'll be back as soon as I can. Do carry on."

He left, and she suffered another moment of indecision before straightening her back and mounting the stairs to the room where the girls slept. They were awake and sitting up when she came in the room and pulled back the draperies. She took a deep breath, not wanting to look at Lady Janet and see the scorn in her eyes.

"Good morning, ladies," she said, her voice quiet but firm. "Your uncle has gone to the manor to direct the work there, and breakfast is ready." She took another deep breath. "Lady Janet, there are letters to finish. Lady Lucinda, you and your brother may wish to begin polishing some silver below stairs. Excuse me please while I dress."

It took all the dignity she could muster to retreat to the dressing room, throw on her clothes, and then pull that comb through her recalcitrant curls. When she came into the chamber again, Lucinda and Janet were making the bed. She almost smiled. The pupils at Mrs. Dupree's all did their own tidying, but Janet was obviously not acquainted with such hard service. Her eyes downcast, her lips tight together, she thumped her pillow down and yanked up the coverlet on her side of the bed. Lucy took a look at her sister and scurried into the dressing room. Cecilia stood by the door, not ready to face Janet, either. Her hand was on the knob when the young lady spoke.

"I am sorry, Miss Ambrose."

She turned around, wishing that her stomach did not churn at the words that sounded as if they were pulled from Janet's throat with tongs. "I know your uncle Trevor meant well, Lady Janet, but I know I am a stranger to you, and perhaps someone you are not accustomed to seeing."

"That doesn't mean I should be rude," Janet said, her voice quiet. "It seems like there is so much to think of right now, so many plans to make . . ." She looked up then, and her expression was shy, almost tentative. "Lucy tells me you are a wonderful artist."

"She is the one with great talent," Cecilia replied, happy to turn the compliment. She returned Janet's glance. "I hope Lord Trevor was not too hard on you."

Janet turned to the bed and smoothed out a nonexistent wrinkle. She shook her head. "I know I will feel better when Lysander arrives."

Well, that is hopeful, Cecilia thought as she went to the next room, woke Davy, then went to the breakfast room. By the time the children came into the room, chose their food, and sat down, her equilibrium had righted itself. Janet said nothing, but Lucinda, after several glances at her sister, began a conversation.

It was interrupted by the housekeeper, who brought a letter on a silver platter. Janet's eyes lighted up. She took it, cast a triumphant glance at the other diners, excused herself, and left the room, her head up.

"I hope Sir Lysander swoops down and carries her away," Davy said.

"Do you not call him just Lysander?" Cecilia asked, curious. "He is going to be your brother in February, is he not?"

Davy rolled his eyes, and Lucinda giggled. "Miss Ambrose, we have been informed that he is *Sir* Lysander to us," Lucinda said. She sighed then. "I hope she stays, Davy."

"Then you are probably the only one at the table with that wish!" her brother retorted. He blushed, and looked at his plate. "I don't mean to embarrass you, Miss Ambrose."

"You don't," she said, and touched his arm. "In fact, I think—"

What she thought left her head before the words were out. A loud scream came from the sitting room, and then noisy tears bordering on the hysterical. Lucinda's eyes opened wide, and Davy lay back in his chair and lolled his head, as though all hope was gone.

"Oh, dear," Cecilia whispered. "I fear that Sir Lysander did not meet Lady Janet's expectations. She's your sister, and you know her well. Should we *do* anything?"

"I could prop a chair under the door, so she can't get in here," Davy suggested helpfully.

"David, you know that is *not* what Miss Ambrose means!" Lucinda scolded. She looked at Cecilia. "Usually we make ourselves scarce when Janet is in full feather." She stood up. "Davy, I have a craving to go tramping over to the south orchard. There is holly there, and greenery that would look good on the mantelpiece. Would you like to join us,

Miss Ambrose?" She had to raise her voice to compete with the storm of tears from the sitting room across the hall, which was now accompanied by what sounded like someone drumming her feet on the floor.

"I think not," Cecilia said. She finished her now-cold tea. "Bundle up warm, children, and take the footman along. You might ask him to stop at the manor and inform your uncle."

Lucinda nodded. She opened the breakfast room door and peeked into the hall. "We don't really want to leave you here alone, Miss Ambrose."

"It is only just a temper tantrum, my dear," Cecilia said, using her most firm educator's voice. "I can manage." I think I can manage, she told herself as the children gave her doubtful glances, then scurried up the stairs to get their coats and mittens. She sat at the table until they left the dower house with the footman. The last person Janet wants to see is me, especially when we have just begun to be on speaking terms, she thought.

"Miss?"

Cecilia looked up to see the housekeeper in the doorway, holding a tray.

"Please come in, Mrs. Grey," she said, managing a half smile. "We seem to be in a storm of truly awesome dimensions."

Mrs. Grey frowned at the sitting-room door, then came to the table, where she set down the tray. "Between you and me, Miss Ambrose, I think that Sir Lysander is in for the surprise of his life, the first time she does *that* across the breakfast table!"

"Oh, my," Cecilia said faintly. "That will be a cold bath over baked eggs and bacon, will it not!"

Mrs. Grey smiled at her, in perfect agreement. "I am suggesting that you not go in there until she is a little quieter." She indicated the tray. "Lady Falstoke sometimes waves burnt feathers under her nose, and then puts cucumbers on her eyes to cut the swelling." She frowned. "What she really needs is a spoonful of cod-liver oil, and the admonition to act her age but . . ." She hesitated.

" . . . but Lady Falstoke is an indulgent mother," Cecilia continued. "I will give her a few minutes more, then go in there, Mrs. Grey, and be the perfect listener."

The look the housekeeper gave her was as doubtful as the one that Davy and Lucinda left the room with. "I could summon her uncle, except . . ."

" . . . this is a woman's work," Cecilia said. "Perhaps a little sympathy is in order."

"Can you do that? She has been less than polite to you." Mrs. Grey's face was beet red.

"She just doesn't know me," she said, and felt only the slightest twinge of conscience, considering how quick she had been ready to bolt from the place as recently as last night.

Her quietly spoken words seemed to satisfy Mrs. Grey, who nodded and left the room, but not without a backward glance of concern and sympathy as eloquent as speech. She considered Lord Trevor's words of last night, and the kind way he looked at her. If he can manage eleven years of what must be the worst work in the world, she could surely coddle one spoiled niece into a better humor.

She waited until the raging tears had degenerated into sobs and hiccups, and then silence, before she entered the sitting room. Janet had thrown herself facedown on the sofa. A broken vase against the wall, with succession-house flowers crumbled and twisted around it, offered further testimony of the girl's rage. Janet is one of those people who needs an audience, Cecilia thought. Well, here I am. She set the tray on a small table just out of Janet's reach, and sat down, holding herself very still.

After several minutes, Janet opened her swollen eyes and regarded Cecilia with real suspicion. Cecilia gritted her teeth and smiled back, hoping for a good mix of sympathy and comfort.

"I want my mother," Janet said finally. She sat up and

blew her nose vigorously on a handkerchief already water-logged. "I want her now!"

"I'm certain you do," Cecilia replied. "A young lady needs her mother at a time like this." She held her breath, hoping it was the right thing to say.

"But she is not here!" Janet burst out, and began to sob again. "Was there ever a more wretched person than I!"

I think an hour of horror stories in your uncle's company might suggest to you that perhaps one or two people have suffered just a smidgeon, Cecilia thought. She sat still a moment longer, and then her heart spoke to her head. She got up from her chair, and sat down next to Janet, not knowing what she would do, but calm in the knowledge that the girl was in real agony. After another hesitation, she touched Janet's arm. "I know I am only a poor substitute, but I will listen to you, my lady," she said.

Janet turned her head slowly. The suspicion in her eyes began to fade. Suddenly she looked very young, and quite disappointed. She put a trembling hand to her mouth. "Oh, Miss Ambrose, he doesn't love me anymore!" she whispered.

With a sigh more of relief than empathy, Cecilia put her arm around the girl. "My, but this is a dilemma!" she exclaimed. She gestured toward the letter crumpled in Janet's hand. "He said *that* in your letter?"

"He might as well have said it!" Janet said with a sob. She smoothed open the message and handed it to Cecilia. "Read it!"

Cecilia took the letter and read of Sir Lysander's regrets, and his fear of contracting any dread diseases.

Janet had been looking at the letter, too. "Miss Ambrose, I wrote most specifically that the measles were confined to my sister's house in York. He seems to think that he will come here and . . . and die!"

She could not argue with Janet's conclusion. The letter was a recitation of its writer's fear of contagion, putrid sore throat, consumption, and other maladies both foreign and domestic. "Look here," she said, pointing. "He writes here that he will fly to your side, the moment all danger is past."

"He should fly here now! At once!"

Lord Trevor Chase would, Cecilia thought suddenly. If the woman he loved was ill, or in distress, he would leap up from the breakfast table and fork the nearest horse in his rush to be by her side. Nothing would stop him. She sat back, as amazed at her thoughts as she was certain of them. But he was a rare man, she decided. This knowledge that had come to her unbidden warmed her. She tightened her grip on Janet. "My dear, didn't your uncle tell me that Sir Lysander is an only child?"

Janet nodded. She stared sorrowfully at the letter.

"I think we can safely conclude that his parents are overly concerned, and that is the source of this letter." She scanned the letter quickly, hoping that the timid Sir Lysander would not fail her. She sighed with relief; he did not. "And see here, my dear, how he has signed the letter!"

"'You have my devoted, eternal love,'" Janet read. She sniffed. "But not including measles, Miss Ambrose."

"No, not including measles," she echoed. "Surely we can allow him one small fault, Lady Janet, don't you think?"

Lady Janet thought. "Well, perhaps." She raised her handkerchief, and looked at it with faint disgust.

Cecilia pulled her own handkerchief out of her sleeve. "Here, my dear. This one is quite dry."

Janet took it gratefully and blew her nose. "You don't ever cry, Miss Ambrose?"

It was the smallest of jokes, but Cecilia felt the weight of the world melting from her own shoulders. "I wouldn't dare, Lady Janet!" she declared with a laugh. "Only think how that would ruin my credit at Mrs. Dupree's Select Academy." She touched Janet's shoulder. "This can be our secret." She stood up. "I recommend that you recline here again. Mrs. Grey has brought over a cucumber from the succession house. A couple of these slices on your eyes will quite remove all the swelling."

Janet did as she said. Cecilia tucked a light throw around her, then applied the cucumbers. "I would give the cucumber about fifteen minutes. Perhaps then you might finish the rest of those letters."

"I will do that," Janet agreed. The cucumber slices covered her eyes, but she pointed to the letter. "Do you think I should reply to Lysander's sorry letter, Miss Ambrose? I could tell him what I think and make him squirm."

"You could, I suppose, but wouldn't it be more noble of you to assure him that you understand, and look forward to seeing him in a week or so?" Janet's mulish expression, obvious even with the cucumbers, suggested to Cecilia that the milk of human kindness wasn't precisely flowing through Janet's veins yet. "I think it is what your dear mother would do," Cecilia continued, appealing to that higher power.

"I suppose you are right," Janet said reluctantly, after lengthy consideration. "But I will write him *only* after I have finished all the other letters!"

"That will show him!" Cecilia said, grateful that the cucumbers hid her smile from Janet's eyes. "My dear, Christmas can be such a trying time for some people."

"I should say. I do not know when I have suffered more."

Cecilia regarded Janet, who had settled herself quite comfortably into the sofa, cucumber slices and all. My credit seems to be on the rise, she thought. I wonder . . . "Lady Janet, perhaps you could help me with something that perplexes me."

The young lady raised one cucumber. "Perhaps. By the time I finish writing lists for wedding plans, I am usually quite fatigued at close of day."

No wonder Lord Trevor remains put off by the topic of reproduction, Cecilia thought. Even on this side of her better nature, Lady Janet is enough to make anyone think twice about producing children. "It is a small thing, truly it is," she said. "Your younger sister seems to have taken the nonsensical notion into her head that you are too busy with wedding plans to even remember that you are sisters."

"Impossible!" Janet declared.

"I agree, Lady Janet, but she is at that trying age of twelve, and feels that you haven't time for her."

"Of course I . . . .well, there may be some truth to that," Janet said. "H'mm."

She was silent then, and it occurred to Cecilia that this was probably more introspection than Janet had ever waded in before. "Something to think about, Lady Janet," she said.

She was in the book room, folding her blanket and wondering where to stash it, when Lady Janet came in. She smiled to see that the cucumbers had done their duty. "Ready to tackle the letters again, my lady?" she asked.

Janet shook her head, then looked at Cecilia shyly. "Not now. I think I will go find Lucinda and David. Did they mention where they were headed?"

"Your sister said something about the south orchard."

"Oh, yes! There is wonderful holly near the fence." She left the room as quickly as she had come into it.

"Someone needs to do these letters," Cecilia told herself when the house was quiet. She sat down at the desk and looked at the last one Janet had written. She picked up the pen to continue, then set it down, with no more desire to do the job than Lady Janet, evidently. She decided to go below stairs, and see if Lord Trevor had carried out his threat to find silver to polish.

She laughed out loud when she entered the servants' dining room to see Lord Trevor, an apron around his waist, sleeves rolled up, rubbing polish on an epergne that was breathtaking in its ugliness. He looked up and grinned at her. "Did ye ever see such a monstrosity?" He looked around her. "And where are my nieces and nephew? Isn't this supposed to be the time I have ordained for my prosy talk on gratitude and sibling affection?" He put down the cloth, and leaned across the table toward her. "Or is this the time when you scold me roundly for abandoning you to the lions upstairs?"

"I should," she told him as she found an apron on a hook

and put it around her middle. "Now don't bamboozle me. Did you leave me to face Lady Janet alone when that letter came from her dearly beloved?"

"I cannot lie," he began.

"Of course you can," she said, interrupting him. "You are a barrister, after all."

He slapped his forehead. "I suppose I deserved that."

"You did," she agreed, picking up a cloth. "For a man who fearlessly stalks the halls of Old Bailey, defending London's most vulnerable, you're remarkably cowardly."

"Guilty as charged, mum," he replied cheerfully. "I could never have soothed those ruffled feathers, but it appears that you did." He turned serious then. "And did my graceless niece apologize, too?"

"She is not so graceless, sir!" Cecilia chided. "Some people are more tried and sorely vexed by holidays and coming events than others. We did conclude that Sir Lysander is still the best of men, even though he dares not brave epidemics. We have also resolved to make some amends to Lucinda." She dipped the knife she had been polishing into the water bath. "I, sir, have freed you from the necessity of a prosy lecture! May I return to Bath?"

"No. You promised to stay," he reminded her, and handed her a spoon.

"I'm not needed now," she pointed out, even as she began to polish it. "Hopefully, Lord and Lady Falstoke will be here at Christmas, which will make the dower house decidedly crowded, unless the repairs at the manor can be finished by then. You will have ample time to get to know your nieces and nephew better, and do you know, I think they might not be as ungrateful as you seem to think."

He nodded, and concentrated on the epergne again. She watched his face, and wondered why he seemed to become more serious. Isn't family good cheer what you want? she asked herself.

It was a question she asked herself all that afternoon as she watched him grow quieter and more withdrawn. When the children came back—snow-covered, shivering, but cheerful—from gathering greenery, she watched uneasily how he had to force himself to smile at them. All through dinner, while Davy outlined his plans for the holly, and his sister planned an expedition to the kitchen in the morning to make Christmas sweets, he sat silent, staring at nothing in particular.

He is a man of action, she decided, and unaccustomed to the slower pace of events in country living. He must chafe to return to London. She stared down at her own dinner as though it writhed, then gave herself a mental shake. That couldn't be it. Hadn't he told her earlier that both King's Bench and Common Pleas were not in session? He had also declared that was true of Magistrate's Court, where most of his clients ended. Why could he not relax and enjoy the season, especially since he had come so far, and met with pleasant results so easily? Even after she told him before dinner that Janet had seemed genuinely contrite and willing to listen, he hadn't received the news with any enthusiasm. It was as though he was gearing himself up for a larger struggle. She wished she knew what it was.

Once the children were in bed, she wanted to ask him, but she knew she would never work up the nerve. Instead, she went into the sitting room to read. He joined her eventually, carrying a letter. He sat down and read through the closely written page again. "Maria writes to say that my brother is much better now, and will be home on Christmas Day," he told her.

"And your niece Amelia's brood?"

"Maria says they are all scratching and complaining, which certainly trumps the fever and vacant stare," he told her. He sat back in the chair and stared into the flames.

Now or never, she thought. "Lord Trevor, is there something the matter?"

He looked up quickly from his contemplation of the flames. "No, of course not." He smiled, but the smile didn't even approach his eyes. "Thanks to your help, I think my nieces and nephew will be charting a more even course."

Chilled by the bleakness on his face, she tried to make light of the moment: anything to see the same animation in his face that had been there when she arrived only a few days ago, or even just that morning. "We can really thank Sir Lysander and his fastidious parents."

"Oh? What? Oh, yes, I'm certain you are right," he said.

She might as well not have been in the room at all. His mind was miles away, oceans distant. "Well, I think it is time for me to go strangle four or five chickens," she said softly. "And then I will rob the mail coach in my shimmy."

"Ah, yes," he said, all affability. "Good night, Miss Ambrose."

She was a long time getting to sleep that night.

The next day, Christmas Eve, was the same. She woke, feeling decidedly unrested, and sat up on her cot in the dressing room, where the girls had cajoled her to return. Certainly it was better than the book room, and the reasons for avoiding the dressing room seemed to have vanished. Quietly she went into the girls' chamber and looked out the window. Although it was nearly eight o'clock, the sky was only beginning to lighten. The workers from York, who were saying at an inn in the village, were starting to arrive, their wagons and gigs lit with lanterns.

I wonder how much work is left to do there, she thought. If the marquis and marchioness are to return tomorrow, then they must be in a pelter to finish. She stood at the window until her bare feet were cold, then turned toward the dressing room. She moved as quietly as she could, but Janet sat up. "Good morning, Miss Ambrose," she said as she yawned. "Do you want to help Lucinda and me in the kitchen? Mrs. Grey has said we may make however many Christmas treats we want. Think what a welcome that will be for my parents."

Cecilia sat down on the bed beside her, and Janet obligingly shifted her legs. "You'll be glad to see them, won't you, my dear?" Cecilia asked.

"Oh, yes!" Janet touched her arm. "I can only wish they had been here for all of the season, but Amelia needed them." She sighed. "This is my last Christmas at Chase Hall, you know."

Cecilia smiled. "You'll be returning with a husband this time next year."

Janet drew up her legs and rested her chin on her knees. When Lucinda moved, she smoothed the coverlet over her sister's back. "Oh, I know that," she whispered, "but it is never the same, is it?"

"No, it is not," Cecilia agreed. "When my parents return from India, I wonder how we all will have changed."

"Does it make you sad, even a little?"

Cecilia was not certain she had ever considered the matter in that light. "I suppose it does, Lady Janet," she replied after a moment's thought. "Perhaps this is a lesson to us both: not to dwell in the past and wish for those times again, but to move on and change."

"It's a sobering consideration," Janet said. "Do you ever wish you could do something over?"

"Not really. I like to look ahead." She stood up. "My goodness, you have so much to look forward to!"

"Yes, indeed," Janet said, and Cecilia could hear the amusement in her voice. "Shortbread, drop cakes, and wafers below stairs!"

They smiled at each other with perfect understanding. "Lady Janet, you are going to make Sir Lysander a happy man," she said, keeping her voice low.

"I intend to," Janet replied, "even if he is not as brave as I would like. I love him." She said it softly, with so much tenderness that Cecilia almost felt her breath leave her body. Unable to meet Janet's eyes, because her own were filling with tears, she looked at Lucinda, sleeping so peacefully beside her sister. You are all so fine, she thought. Lord Trevor has no need of a prosy scold; nothing is broken here, not really. He was so wrong.

"Lady Janet," she began carefully, not even sure what she wanted to ask. "Do you . . . has Lord Trevor ever kept Christmas here with you?"

Janet thought a moment, a frown on her face. "Not that I recall. No. Never. I wonder what it is that he does?"

"I wish I knew."

Breakfast was a quiet affair. Lord Trevor ate quickly and retreated to the book room, saying something about reviewing his cases. David had to ask him twice if he could join him and continue alphabetizing the files. They left the room together. Lucinda and Janet hurried below stairs, and Cecilia found herself staring out the window toward the manor. She had tried to ask Mrs. Grey casually how the work was going, but the housekeeper just looked away and changed the subject. She had tried again after breakfast, with the same response. She found herself growing more uneasy as the morning passed, and she didn't really know why.

"Miss Ambrose?"

Startled out of her disquietude, she turned around to see Davy standing there. "Davy! Are you thinking it would be good to go below stairs and check on your sisters' progress? It already smells wonderful, doesn't it?"

To her surprise, he shook his head. To her amazement, he came closer and rested his head against her waist. In a moment she was on her knees before him, her arms tight around him. "My dear, you're missing your mother, aren't you? She'll be here tomorrow."

Davy burrowed as close to her as he could, and she tightened her grip. "Davy, what is it?"

She pulled him away a little so she could see his face, took a deep breath, then pulled him close again. "What's wrong?" she whispered in his ear, trying to sound firm without frightening him.

"It's my uncle," he said finally, the words almost forced out between his tight lips. "I'm afraid."

Cecilia sank down to the floor and pulled him onto her lap. "Oh, Davy, tell me," she ordered, fighting against her own rising tide of panic.

Davy shivered. "Miss Ambrose, he just sits and stares at the case files! I . . . I tried to talk to him, but he doesn't seem to hear me! It's as though there is a wall . . ." His voice trailed away.

Cecilia ran her hands over his arms, and rubbed his back as he clung to her. "Tell me, my dear," she urged.

He turned his face into her breast, and his words were muffled. "He told me not to look into the files, and I didn't, until this morning." He looked up at her, his eyes huge in his face. "Miss Ambrose, I have never read such things before!" He started to cry.

She held him close, murmuring nonsensicals, humming to him, until his tears subsided. "My dear, you don't know what he does, do you?"

Davy shook his head. "No, but I think it really bothers him."

"I think you are right, Davy." She put her hands on each side of his face and looked into his eyes. "Can you get your coat and mittens?"

He nodded, a question in his eyes.

"We're going outside to get some fresh air." She stood up, keeping Davy close. "Perhaps we can figure out what to do with all that holly you collected yesterday."

The coats were in a closet off the front entrance. She helped Davy with his muffler and made sure his shoes were well buckled, then got into her coat. Mrs. Grey and the cook were below stairs with the girls. She could hear laughter from the kitchen now and then. She tiptoed down the hall to the book room and pressed her ear against the door panel. Nothing.

They left through a side door out of sight of the book-room windows. She did not have a long stride herself, but she had to remind herself to slow down anyway, so Davy could keep up.

"We're not supposed to go to the manor," he reminded her as they hurried along. "Uncle Trevor is afraid we will be hurt while the repairs are going on." He stopped on the path. "He might be angry, Miss Ambrose!"

"I don't know what he will be, Davy, but I want to see the renovations." If a judge and jury had demanded to know why she was so determined, she could not have told them. Some alarm was clanging in her brain. She did not understand it, but she was not about to ignore it one more minute.

On Davy's advice, they approached the manor from the garden terrace. There was only a skiff of snow on the flower beds, which had been cleaned, raked, and prepared for a long Yorkshire winter. All was tidy and organized.

Her parents had done extensive renovations once on their Egyptian villa. She remembered the disorder, the dust, the smell of paint, the sound of saw and hammer. When she opened the door off the terrace and stepped inside with Davy, there was none of that confusion. Nothing. The house was completely silent. Nothing was out of place. She sniffed the air. Only the faintest smell of smoke remained; she couldn't be sure it wasn't just the ordinary smell of a household heated with coal.

Davy stared around him, and took her hand again. "There's nothing wrong."

"No, there isn't," she said, keeping her voice calm, especially when she saw the question in his eyes. "Where are the workers?"

They walked down the hall, holding tight to each other, until they came to the door that led belowstairs. Cecilia took a deep breath and opened it. As soon as she did, they heard voices, the soft slap of cards, and some laughter. She took a firmer grip on the boy's hand, and they walked down the stairs together.

The workers sitting around the table in the servants' hall looked up when she came into the room. The oldest man— he must have been the foreman—smiled at her. "G'day, miss!" he called, the voice of good cheer. "Are you from that dower house?"

She smiled back, even though she wanted to turn and run. "Yes, indeed. I am a teacher for one of the young ladies, and this is David Chase, Viscount Goodhue."

The men put down their cards and got to their feet.

"Is my uncle Trevor playing a joke on us?" Davy asked her.

"Let's ask these men," she said. "Sir, have you been repairing any damage at all?"

The foreman shrugged. "After Lord Trevor sent all the servants off on holiday, we opened up the windows and aired out the place. Watts, over there—perk up, Watts!—cleaned out the pipe behind the Rumford and seated it again, but that's all the place really needed." He scratched his head. "His lordship's a good man, he is. Said he just wanted us to stay here all week, and get paid regular wages."

"Did he . . . did he tell you why, precisely?" Cecilia asked.

"I don't usually ask questions like that of the gentry, miss, but he did say something about wanting to keep everyone close together."

He said as much to me, she thought, hoping that his young relatives would discover each other again, if they were in close quarters. "I can understand that," she said.

"Yes, mum, that's what he said," the foreman told her. "This is our last day on the job." He laughed and poked the cardplayer sitting next to him. "Guess we'll have to earn an honest wage next week again!"

The men laughed. The man called Watts spoke up shyly. "'E's made it a happy Christmas for all of us, miss. You, too, I hope."

"Oh, yes," Cecilia said, wishing she were a better actress. "Lord Trevor is a regular eccentric who likes a good quiz! Good day to you all, and happy Christmas."

They were both quiet on the walk back to the dower

house, until Davy finally stopped. "Why would he want us to keep close together?"

"He told me that first night, after you were all in bed, that he was worried that you were all growing apart, and were ungrateful for what you had," she explained. "He had a notion that if you were all together, he could give you what he called a 'prosy lecture' about gratitude." She took his hand, and set him in motion again. "Davy, the people he works with—his clients—are young, and have so little. He helps them all he can, but . . ." But I don't quite understand this, she thought to herself. He does so much good! *Why* is he so unhappy?

The dower house was still silent when they came inside, but the odors from the kitchen were not to be ignored. Without waiting to stamp off the snow upstairs, she and Davy went down to the kitchen, where his sisters were rolling dough on the marble slab. She watched them a moment, their heads together, laughing. Nothing wrong here, she thought. She looked at Davy, who was reaching for a buttery shortbread.

She noticed that Mrs. Grey was watching her, and she took the housekeeper aside. "Mrs. Grey, there's nothing going on at the manor. Do you know why Lord Trevor is doing this?"

"You weren't to know," the woman declared.

The room was quiet, and she knew the children were listening. The frown was back on Davy's face, and his sisters just looked mystified. "Uncle Trevor's been fooling us," Davy said. "There's nothing wrong with our home."

It took a moment to sink in, then Lady Janet sat down suddenly. "We . . . we could have had the Christmas entertainment? And Lysander could have come?"

"I think so, Lady Janet," Cecilia said. "He said he wanted everyone here in close quarters so you could all appreciate each other again." She reached out and touched Lucinda's arm. "But I don't think there ever really was a problem."

She smiled at Janet. "Well, maybe a word or two in the right ear was necessary, but that was a small thing."

"I know I'm glad to be here now," Lucinda said. She put her arm around her sister, then tightened her grip as her face grew serious. "I told Uncle Trevor that very thing this morning, but I'm not sure he heard me."

"I did the same thing in the book room," Davy said. "Told him I missed Mama, but it was all right. He didn't seem to be paying attention."

Davy looked at Cecilia, his eyes filled with sudden knowledge. "Miss Ambrose, he was trying to *fix* us, wasn't he? We're fine, so why isn't he happy?"

It was as though his question were a match struck in a dark room. Cecilia sucked in her breath and sat down on the bench, because her legs felt suddenly like pudding. She pulled Davy close to her. "Oh, my dear, I think he is trying to fix himself."

She knew they would not understand. She also knew she would have to tell them. "Mrs. Grey, would you please leave us and shut the door?"

The housekeeper put her hands on her hips. "I don't take orders from houseguests," she said.

Janet leaped to her feet. "Then you'll take them from me! Do as Miss Ambrose says, and . . . and not a word to my uncle!"

Bravo, Janet, Cecilia thought, feeling warmer. When the door closed with a decisive click, she motioned the children closer. "Do you know what your uncle really does? No? I didn't think so." She touched Davy's face. "You have some idea."

He shuddered. "Those files . . ."

"Your uncle is an advocate for children facing sentencing, deportation, and death."

Janet nodded, and pulled Lucinda closer to her. "We do know a little of that, but not much." She sighed. "I own it has embarrassed me, at times, but I am also proud of him." She looked at her sister. "I think we all are."

"And rightly so, my dear," Cecilia said. "It is hard, ugly work, among those who have no hope." She took a deep breath. "Let me tell you about Jimmy Daw."

She tried to keep the emotion from her voice, but there were tears on her cheeks when she finished. Janet sobbed openly, and Lucinda had turned her face into her sister's sleeve.

Davy spoke first. "Uncle Trevor didn't mean any harm to come to Jimmy Daw."

"Oh, no, no," Cecilia murmured. "He thought he was doing something kind."

"Is Jimmy Daw why he works so hard now?" Lucinda asked, her voice muffled in her sister's dress.

"I am certain of it," she said, with all the conviction of her heart.

"Then why isn't he *happy*?" Davy asked, through his tears. "He does so much good!"

Cecilia stood up, because the question demanded action from her. "Davy, I fear he has never been able to forgive himself for Jimmy's death, in spite of the enormous good he has done since." She perched on the edge of the table and looked at the three upturned faces, each so serious and full of questions. "He probably works hard all year, works constantly, so he can fall asleep and never dream. He probably has no time for anything except his desperate children."

"Father does say that when he and Mama go to London, they can never find a minute of time with Uncle Trevor," Janet said.

"Does he come here for Christmas?"

"Hardly ever," Lucinda replied. She stopped; her eyes grew wider. "He might stay a day or two, but he is always gone well before Christmas Eve. You said Jimmy died on Christmas Eve."

"He did." Cecilia got up again, too restless to sit. "I don't know what your uncle usually does on Christmas Eve, but somehow he must punish himself." She started to stride about the room again, then stopped. "I doubt he was plan-

ning to stay, in spite about what he said of his 'prosy lecture,' that he could have delivered and left."

"He was forced to, wasn't he?" Janet said slowly. "When
Mama and Papa went to be with Amelia, he had no choice!"

"No, he didn't," Cecilia replied. "I think he used the excuse of the fire to keep everyone close. My dears, I think he
wants to change now—if not, he would have bolted as soon
as I got here—but I think he is afraid to be alone. And that
is really why we are crammed so close here." She sat down
again, dumbfounded at the burden that one good man could
force upon himself.

They were all silent for a long moment. Janet looked at
her finally, and Cecilia saw all the pride in her eyes, as well
as the fear. "I love my uncle," she said, her voice low but intense. "There is not a better man anywhere, even if people
of our rank make fun of him." She smiled, but there was no
humor in it. "Even Lysander thinks him a fool for—oh, how
did he put it?—'wallowing in scummy waters with the
dregs.' My uncle is no fool." Her eyes filled with tears
again. "Miss Ambrose, how can we help him?"

She mulled over the question, and then spoke carefully.
"I think first that he would be furious if he knew I had told
you all this."

"Why did he tell you?" Davy asked.

It was a question she had been asking herself for several
days now. She shook her head, and started to say something,
when Janet interrupted.

"Because he is in love with Miss Ambrose, you silly
nod," she told her brother, her voice as matter-of-fact as
though she asked the time of day.

Cecilia stared at her in amazement. "How on earth . . ."

Janet shrugged, and then looked at Lucinda, as if seeking
confirmation. "We both notice how his eyes follow you
around the room, and the way he smiles when he looks at
you." She grew serious, but there was still that lurking smile
that made her so attractive. "Trust me, Miss Ambrose, I am
an expert on these matters."

Cecilia laughed, in spite of herself. "My goodness."

"Do you mind the idea?" Lucinda asked, doubt perfectly visible in her eyes.

Did she mind? Cecilia sat down again and considered the matter, putting it to that scrutiny she usually reserved for scholarship. Did she mind being thought well of by a man whose exploits had been known to her for some time, and whom she had admired for several years, without even knowing him? Her face grew warm as she thought of his grip on her waist as they left the smoky manor in the middle of the night. "He doesn't even know me," she protested weakly.

"As to that, Miss Ambrose, I have been writing him about you," Lucinda said.

"You have *what*?" she asked in amazement.

Her pupil shrugged. "He wanted to know if there was anyone interesting in my school, and I told him about you." She hesitated. "I even painted him a little picture."

"Of me?" she asked quietly. Me with my olive skin and slanted eyes, she thought.

"Of you, my most interesting teacher ever," was Lucinda's equally dignified reply. "He's no ordinary man."

And I am certainly no ordinary English woman, she thought. She reached across the table, took Lucinda's hand, and squeezed it briefly. "You are the most wonderful children."

Janet laughed. "No, we're not! We probably are as selfish and ungrateful as Uncle Trevor imagines. But do you know, we aim to be better." She grew serious and asked again, "How can we help our uncle?"

"Leave him to me," Cecilia said. "I know he does not want you to know about Jimmy Daw, or he would have told you long before now, Janet. How can I get time alone with him?"

Davy was on his feet then. "Lucinda, do you remember how fun it was last Christmas to spend it in the stable?"

"What?" Cecilia asked. "You probably needn't be *that* drastic!"

"You know, Miss Ambrose," Janet said. "There is that legend that on the night of Christ's birth, the animals start to speak." She nudged her brother. "What did Davy do last year but insist that he be allowed to spend the night in the stable! Mama was shocked, but Papa enjoyed the whole thing." She looked at her younger brother and sister. "We will be in the stable. The footman can light a good fire, and we have plenty of blankets."

The other children nodded, and Cecilia could almost touch the relief in the room. Precious ones, she thought, you will do anything to help your uncle, won't you? No, you most certainly do not require fixing. "Very well," she said. "Janet . . ." She stopped. "Oh, I should be calling you Lady Janet."

"I don't think that matters . . . Cecilia," the young woman replied. "I will make arrangements with Mrs. Grey, and we will go to the stables after dinner." She looked at her siblings. "Cecilia, we love him. We hope you can help him because I do believe you love him, too."

They were all quiet that afternoon, soberly putting Christmas treats and cakes into boxes for delivery to other great houses in the neighborhood on Boxing Day, arranging holly on mantelpieces, and getting ready for their parents' return on Christmas. After an hour's fruitless attempt to read in the sitting room, Cecilia went for a walk instead. How sterile the landscape was, with everything shut tight for a long winter. Little snow had fallen yet, but as she started back toward the dower house, it began, small flakes at first and then larger ones. Soon the late afternoon sky was filled with miniature jewels, set to transform the land and send it to sleep under a blanket of white. She stood in the modest driveway of the dower house and watched the workers leave the manor for the final time. Some of them called happy Christmas to her. She looked at the house again, wondering why it was that the most joyous season of the year should cause such pain in some. With a start, she realized that her preoccupation with Lord Trevor and his personal nightmare had quite driven out her own longing for her family in far-off India. "Tonight, I hope I remember all the wonderful things you taught me," she said out loud. "Especially that God is good and Christmas is more than sweets and gifts."

Before dinner, she went to the book room, squared her shoulders, and knocked on the door. When Lord Trevor did not answer, she opened the door.

He sat probably as he had sat all day, staring at his case files, which Davy had alphabetized and chronologized. Everything was tidy, except for his disordered mind. When she had been standing in the doorway for some time, he looked at her as though for one brief moment he did not recognize her. She thought she saw relief in his eyes, or maybe she only hoped she did.

"Dinner is ready, Lord Trevor," she said quietly. "We hope you will join us."

He shook his head, then deliberately turned around in his chair to face the window. She closed the door, chilled right down to the marrow in her bones.

Dinner was quiet, eaten quickly with small talk that trailed off into long pauses. A letter had come that afternoon from York with the good news that the marquis and marchioness would arrive at Chase Hall in time for dinner tomorrow. "I wish they were here right now," Davy said finally, making no attempt to disguise his fear.

"They'll be here tomorrow," she soothed. "Davy, I promise to take very good care of your uncle."

Her words seemed to reassure them all, and she could only applaud her acting ability, a talent she had not been aware of before this night. After a sweet course that no one ate, Janet rose from the table and calmly invited her younger brother and sister to follow her. Cecilia followed them into the hall, and waited there until they returned from their rooms bundled against the cold.

Janet looked almost cheerful. She tucked her arm through

Lucinda's and reached for Davy. "Do you know, this is my last Christmas to be a child," she said to Cecilia. "I will be married in February, and this part of my life will be over." She looked at her siblings. "Lucinda, you will marry someday, and even you, Davy!" He made a face at her, and she laughed softly. "I am lucky, Miss Ambrose, and I *did* need reminding."

"We all do, now and then," Cecilia replied. She opened the door, and kissed each of them as they passed through. "If you get cold, come back inside, of course, but do leave me alone in the book room with your uncle."

"Take good care of him," Lucinda begged.

"I will," she said. "I promise you."

Easier said than done. When the house was quiet, she found a shawl, wrapped it tight around her for courage, and went to the book room. She knocked. When he did not answer, she let herself into the room.

He sat at the desk still. This time there was only one file in front of him. He looked at her and his eyes were dark and troubled. "What are you doing here?" he asked, his voice harsh.

"The children wanted to spend Christmas in the stable," she said. "It's a silly thing."

"I remember when they did that, years ago," he said. "I remember . . ." Then he looked at the file before him, and he was silent.

Her heart in her throat, she came into the room and around the desk to stand beside him. "Is that Jimmy Daw's file?" she asked.

He put his hand over the name, as though to protect it. She wanted to touch him, to put her arms around his shoulders and press her cheek against his, all the while murmuring something in his ear that he might interpret as comfort. Instead, she moved to the front of the desk again and pulled up a chair.

"He died eleven years ago this night, didn't he?" She kept her voice normal, conversational.

Lord Trevor narrowed his eyes and glared at her. "You know he did. I told you."

"What is it you do on Christmas Eve to remember him?" There.

Silence. "Shouldn't you be in bed, Miss Ambrose?" he asked finally, in a most dismissive tone.

She smiled and leaned forward. "No. It's Christmas Eve, and the children are busy. I think I will just stay here with you, and see what you do to remember Jimmy Daw, because that's what you do, isn't it? You probably plan this all year."

More silence.

"Do you go to church? Read from the Bible? Work on someone else's charts? Visit old friends in the City? Have dinner out with your fellow barristers? Sing Christmas carols? Squeeze in another good work or two?" She stopped, hating the sound of her own rising voice and its relentless questions. She looked him straight in the eye. "Or do you just sit at your desk hating yourself?"

He leaped to his feet, fire in his eyes, and slammed the file onto the table like a truncheon. "I don't need this!"

She looked away, frightened, but held herself completely still in the chair. It was then that she noticed the row of bottles against the wall. My God, she thought, my God. With courage she knew she did not possess, she stood in front of him until they were practically toe to toe. "Or do you try to drink yourself to death, because you failed one little boy?"

He raised his hand and she steadied herself, because she knew it was going to hurt, considering his size and the look in his eyes. Almost without thinking, she grabbed him around the waist and pulled him close to her in a fierce grip. She closed her eyes and waited for him to send her flying across the room. She tightened her grip on the ties on his waistcoat. All right, she thought, you'll have to pry me off to hurt me.

To her unspeakable relief, the file dropped to the floor and his arms went around her. She released her grip and began to run her hands along his back instead. "Trevor, it's going to be all right. Really it is," she murmured.

He began to sob then as he rested his chin on her hair. "I line up a row of bottles and drink my way through Christmas Eve, Christmas, and Boxing Day, Cecilia," he said, when he could speak. "I almost died last Christmas, but damn me if one of the other barristers at the Inn didn't come knocking on Christmas afternoon. I woke up with a surgeon's finger down my throat!" He leaned against her until his weight almost toppled her. "Please stop me! I don't want to die!"

Holding him so close that she could feel his waistcoat buttons against her breast, she understood the enormity of his guilt, as irrational as it seemed to her logical mind. She moved him toward the sofa and sat down. He released her only to sink down beside her and lay his head in her lap. She twitched her shawl off her shoulders, spread it over him, and rested her hand on his hair—did he never comb it, ever?— as he cried. Sitting back, she felt his exhaustion and remorse seeping into her very skin. As he cried and agonized, she had the tiniest inkling of the Gethsemane that her dear foster father spoke of from the pulpit, upon occasion. "Bless your heart," she whispered, "you're atoning for the sins of the world. My dear, no mortal can do that! What's more, it's been done, and you don't have to."

"That's your theology," he managed to gasp, before agony engulfed him again.

"And I am utterly convinced of it, dear sir," she said. Cecilia pushed on his shoulder until he was forced to raise himself and look at her. She kissed his forehead. "Even someone as young as Davy understands that we celebrate Christmas because Christ gave us *hope*! Dear man, you're dragging around chains that He took care of long ago." She kissed him again, even though his face was wet and slimy now. "I really think it's time you stopped."

"But Jimmy's dead!"

It was a lament for the ages, and she felt suddenly as old

and tired as he, as though he had communicated the matter into her in a way that was almost intimate. She considered it, and understood her own faith, perhaps for the first time. "Yes, Jimmy Daw is dead," she whispered finally as he lowered himself back to her lap, his arm around her this time. "And you have done more to honor his memory than any other human being. Every child you save is a testimony to your goodness, and a memorial to Jimmy Daw. I know it is. I believe it."

He didn't say anything, but he had stopped crying. She knew he was listening this time. She cleared her throat, and wiped her own eyes with a hand that shook. "May I tell you how we are going to celebrate Christmas Eve next year? We are going to remember all the children you have *saved*. We are going to thank Kind Providence that you have the health and wealth to do this desperately hard work."

"We are?" he asked, his voice no more than a whisper.

"We are," she replied firmly. "You are not going to do it alone ever again."

What am I saying? she asked herself, waiting for the utter foolishness of her declaration to overtake her. When nothing of the kind happened, she bowed her head over his, then rested her cheek against his hair. "You're a good man, Trevor Chase. I even think I love you."

"Cecilia," was all he said, and she smiled, thinking how tired he must be. She could feel his whole body relaxing. After a long time of silence, she moved her legs, and he sat up.

"I believe I will go to bed now," she told him. She stood up and looked at the row of bottles, waiting there still. "Or should I stay?"

He shook his head, and reached for a handkerchief. He blew his nose vigorously. "If you want to open that window and drop them out, I think that would be a wise thing. Old habits, you know."

She knew. She opened the window and did as he said. The first bottle didn't break, but the others did as they landed on each other. She leaned out, then pulled back quickly from the fumes rising over the rosebed. She gathered up her shawl and went to the door. "Good night, and happy Christmas, Trevor," she said, and blew him a kiss.

The house was so quiet. She pulled herself up the stairs, practically hand over hand, and went into the girls' room. The bed looked far more inviting than her own little cot. Since they were in the stable, she shucked off her clothing down to her shimmy and crawled in.

She was nearly asleep when Lord Trevor opened the door, came to the bed, and stood there. "I threw the file on the fire," he said, his voice sounding as uncertain as a small child's.

"Good," she told him, and after only the slightest hesitation, pulled back the blankets.

"Are you certain?" he asked.

"Never more so."

"I don't want to be alone tonight," he told her as he took off his shoes, then started on his waistcoat. "I'm so tired."

"I know you are, but I have to know one more thing. I think you know what it is."

He sat down on the bed, and rested his head in his hands. "I do. I was going to go back to my chambers this year, lock the door, and keep drinking until . . ." He stopped, unable to speak.

Cecilia sat up and leaned her head against his back. "My God, Trevor, my God," she whispered. "What . . . what changed your mind?"

"Well, I had to stay here with the children when Hugo and Maria bolted, but even then . . ." He turned around and put his arm around her. "Then you came, and I had second thoughts. I didn't plan on falling in love."

"Just like that?"

"Just like that. Are you as skeptical as I am?"

"Probably. But, the bottles in the book room tonight?"

"I don't know if I would have drunk any of them, considering how matters had changed. I suppose I'll never know," he told her as she put her arms around him. "I think I was counting on you to stop me. Thank you from the bottom of my heart, Cecilia."

He lay down beside her and gathered her close. With a sigh, she threw her arm over his chest and rested her head in that nice spot below his collarbone. His hand was warm against her back. Her feet were cold and he flinched a little when she put them on his legs, but then he kissed her neck, and fell asleep.

He was gone in the morning. Cecilia reached out a tentative hand; his side of the bed was still a little warm. She got up and dressed quickly, then hurried downstairs. She heard laughter from the breakfast room, his laughter. She opened the door.

"Lucy, you are telling me that your graceless scamp of a little brother actually stood over by the horses and began to *talk*?" asked Lord Trevor. The picture of relaxation, he slouched negligently in his chair, with his arm along the back of Lucinda's chair.

Janet giggled. "He scared Lucy so bad that she jumped up and stepped in the water bucket the footman had left by the lantern!"

"Did not!"

"Oh, we both saw it!"

Lord Trevor held up both hands. "I've never met more disgraceful children," he scolded, but anyone with even the slightest hearing could have picked out the amusement in his voice. "It's never too late for my prosy lecture. Good morning, Miss Ambrose, how do you do?"

I know my face is red, she thought. "I do well," she replied. "Happy Christmas to you all."

Lord Trevor pushed out a chair with his foot. "Have a seat, my dear Miss Ambrose. I've told my long-suffering relatives all about my silliness next door at the manor. They have agreed that a week in the dower house was not too unpleasant." He smiled at them all. "And now they will move their belongings back, with some help from Mrs. Grey and the footman."

"Mama is coming home today," Davy said.

"I received a letter from Lysander only a few minutes ago," Janet said, holding out a piece of paper. She smiled at Cecilia. "He promises to come as soon as all contagion is gone."

Cecilia poured a cup of tea and sat down, just as the children rose and left the room. Davy even looked back and winked. "Scamp," she murmured under her breath, trying to concentrate on the tea before her, and not on Lord Trevor, who had decided to put his arm on her chair now. In another moment his hand rested on her shoulder, and then his fingers outlined her ear.

"You're making this tea hard to drink," she commented.

"It isn't very good tea, anyway," he told her as he took the cup from her hand and pushed it away. He cleared his throat. "Cecilia—Miss Ambrose—it has certainly come to my attention that I . . . er . . . uh . . . may have compromised you last night."

I love him, she thought, looking at him in his rumpled clothes, with his hair in need of cutting. I wonder why he does not stand closer to his razor, she thought. His eyes were tired, to be sure, but the hopeless look that had been increasing hour by hour on Christmas Eve was gone. She turned in her chair to face him.

"I would say that you certainly did compromise me. How loud you snore! What do you intend to do about it?"

"What, my snoring?"

She laughed and leaned toward him. He put his hand around her neck, drew her closer, and kissed her forehead.

"I suppose I must make you an offer now, eh?" he asked, the grin not gone from his face.

"I would like that," she told him. "We'll be an odd couple, don't you think?"

"Most certainly. I'm positive there will be doors that will never open to either of us," he replied, without the blink of an eye. "People of my sort will wonder if I have taken leave of my senses to marry Cleopatra herself, and those evangelizing, missionary friends of your parents will assume that you have taken pity on a man desperate for redemption." He kissed her again, his lips lingering this time. "Oh, my goodness. Cecilia, I will be bringing home scum, riffraff, and strays."

"Of course. I'm going to insist that you close your chambers at the Inn and move me into a house on a quiet street where the neighbors are kind and don't mind children," she said, reaching for him this time and rubbing her cheek against his. She felt the tears on his face.

"Miss Deprave is going to be awfully upset when you give your notice," he warned.

She giggled. "Your brother and sister-in-law will probably have a fit when you tell them this afternoon."

He laughed and pulled her onto his lap. "There you are wrong. They'll be so relieved to find a lady in my life that they won't even squeak!"

She tightened her arm around his neck as the fears returned momentarily. "I hope they are not disappointed."

"No one will be disappointed about this except Miss Deprave. Trust me, Cecilia."

"Trust a barrister?" she teased, putting her hands on both sides of his face and kissing him.

"Yes, indeed." His expression was serious then. "Trust me. I trusted you when I told you about Jimmy that second night." He took her hand. "I looked at your lovely face, and some intuition told me I could *say* something finally." He shook his head.

She knew she did not know him well yet, but she could tell he wanted to say something more. "What is it?" she prodded him. "I hardly think, at this point, that there is anything you might be embarrassed to tell me."

He looked at the closed door, then pulled her onto his lap. She sighed and felt completely at home there.

"Before I left London, I made a wish on a star. Is that beyond absurd?"

Resting there with her head against his chest and listening to the regular beating of his heart, she considered the matter. "Teachers are interested in results, dear sir, not absurdities. Did it come true?"

"Oh, my, in spades."

She went to kiss his cheek, but he turned his head and she found his lips instead. "Then I would say your wish came true," she murmured, once she could speak again.

He smiled. "I'm a skeptic still, but I like it."

"I like it, too," she admitted.

"D'ye think you'll still like it thirty or forty years from now?" he asked.

"Only if you're with me." She kissed him again. "Promise?"

"Promise."

About the Authors

Sandra Heath is the ever-popular author of numerous Regencies, historical romances, novellas, and short stories. Among other honors, she has won the *Romantic Times* Reviewers' Choice Awards for Best Regency Author and Best Regency Romance. She lives in Gloucester, England, and can be contacted at sandraheath@blueyonder.co.uk.

Emma Jensen has won numerous awards, including two RITAs and the *Romantic Times* Reviewers' Choice Award. She grew up in San Francisco and is a graduate of the University of Pennsylvania, with degrees in nineteenth-century literature, sociology, and public policy.

Carla Kelly has written more than a dozen novels and won two RITAs for Best Regency. She lives in Valley City, North Dakota, where she does historical research for the North Dakota State Historical Society, writes for various publications, edits the *Confluence News*, and works for the National Park Service on the North Dakota–Montana border.

Edith Layton has enthralled readers and critics with books that capture the spirit of historically distant places and peoples. For her work, she has received a Lifetime Achievement Award from *Romantic Times*, and excellent reviews, awards, and commendations from *Library Journal*, Romance Readers Anonymous, and Romance Writers of America. She lives on Long Island, where she devotes time as a volunteer for the North Shore Animal League. Edith loves hearing from readers and can be reached at www.edithlayton.com.

Barbara Metzger is the author of more than three dozen historical romances, most of them set in Regency-era England. She has won numerous awards, including the RITA, the National Readers' Choice Award, and two Career Achievement Awards from *Romantic Times*. She lives on the Long Island shore. When Barbara is not writing, she reads, paints, gardens, and volunteers at the local library. Her Web site is www.barbarametzger.com.